'A wonderfully creepy tale. Leda is a triumph'
Vanessa Lafaye, author of *Summertime*

Essie Fox divides her time between Windsor and Bow in the East End of London. Her debut novel, *The Somnambulist*, was selected for the Channel 4 Book Club and was shortlisted in the New Writer of the Year category of the 2012 National Book Awards. She is the author of The Virtual Victorian: www.virtualvictorian.blogspot.com. Find out more about Essie at www.essiefox.com or by following her on Twitter @essiefox

Also by Essie Fox

The Somnambulist
Elijah's Mermaid
The Goddess and the Thief

The
Last Days
of
Leda Grey

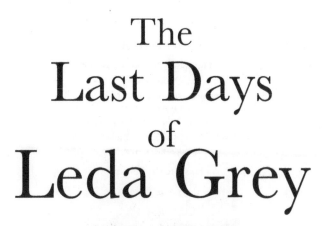

Essie Fox

An Orion paperback

First published in Great Britain in 2016
by Orion Books
This paperback edition published in 2017
by Orion Books,
an imprint of The Orion Publishing Group Ltd
Carmelite House, 50 Victoria Embankment
London EC4Y ODZ

An Hachette UK Company

1 3 5 7 9 10 8 6 4 2

A CIP catalogue record for this book is
available from the British Library.

ISBN 978 1 4091 4627 8

Typeset at The Spartan Press Ltd,
Lymington, Hants

Printed and bound in Great Britain by
Clays Ltd, St Ives plc

MIX
Paper from
responsible sources
FSC® C104740

www.orionbooks.co.uk

My thanks to Wendy Wallace
For friendship, grace, and wisdom

'Yea, all things live forever, though at times they sleep and are forgotten.'

From the novel *She*, by H Rider Haggard

A Note on the Chapter Titles

Each chapter heading is a quote from
William Shakespeare's *Macbeth*

Title Page Photograph

The image used on the title page is that of Theda Bara –
a star of early silent film who once played Cleopatra

Press Cutting ~ The Brightland Argos ~
Tuesday, August 17th, 1976

MYSTERY OF HUMAN REMAINS
DISCOVERED AT WHITE CLIFF HOUSE

Unidentified human remains have been found at a house near Cuckham Sands. Formerly used in Edwardian times as a base for creating silent films, a purpose-built studio in the grounds was completely destroyed when a fire broke out on the night of the discovery.

Initial pathology reports suggest that the body parts are male, most probably in middle age. However, officials are yet to establish why and when the death occurred.

A second body found that night has been named as Leda Grey, an elderly woman who is said to have lived at the house for sixty years.

The police are still waiting to interview a man in his late twenties who was also present at the scene. He is currently recovering from fire-related injuries at the Brightland General hospital.

THE DEAD ARE BUT AS PICTURES

The slightest thing can take me back to that early August afternoon. It's almost like running a film in reverse, until the frame is frozen and ready to set in play again. And it would have been in colour, but I always remember in monochrome. The scorched white glare of skies above. Black shadows in the cobbled Lanes. How I bought a postcard from a rack that showed the pier lit up at night in faded loops of silver. How I stared at bleached geraniums that drooped in baskets either side of the open doors to the Bath Arms bar – and something yet more mournful in the silhouettes that I could see through the gloomy dinge inside that pub. Two lovers rocking back and forth, locked in a sort of languid dance while a tinny radio blared out the hypnotic chords of skank guitars. The Eagles. 'Hotel California'.

At least I could have sworn it was. Time and memory confused. The warm air. The sweet smell of colitas …

I had no weed, but reached instead for the pack of Woodbines always kept in the back pocket of my jeans. The brand my mother always smoked, and I liked the rough cheap taste of them. I liked the smell of sulphur in the moments when I lit one up, when a match was scraped across the strip of sandpaper that edged the box.

Sucking deep on the acrid nicotine I felt it prickle through my scalp, through the fug of last night's hangover, as I wandered further on into the warren of the Brightland Lanes where the radio's fading melody was replaced by the sudden high-pitched bark of a small black terrier running past.

Turning to watch it disappear into the shimmering of haze where the passage opened up again onto the wider promenade,

I must have spun around too fast, feeling dizzy and dropping my cigarette as I stumbled against a window front.

Beneath a lowered awning, the glass was darkly shadowed, almost obsidian opaque. But my vision soon acclimatised to see the items on display. All the watered-down dregs of the hippy age, and the staples of Brightland's tourist trade in a faded pack of tarot cards, a crystal ball, some small brass bells, and the crackle-glazed porcelain head of a man, adorned with spidery black scrawls of *Caution. Despair. Ambition. Love. Hope. Destruction. Misery.*

The warnings were all there to see.

Less ubiquitous were the postcards of Hollywood legends from the past. Charlie Chaplin. Greta Garbo. Douglas Fairbanks in one of his swashbuckling roles. Valentino, holding a cigarette, with much of his face seductively obscured by trailing wisps of smoke. And then there was Bette Davis, always a favourite with my mum who'd sit for hours and hours on end before our television set, with the front room curtains closed to keep the light and outside world away while she lost herself in old film noirs like *Dangerous*, or *A Stolen Life*.

On a whim, I decided to go inside and buy that photograph of Bette – though I almost stopped when my palm was pressed on the mullioned panes of the shop's front door. Five fingers reaching out for mine. A lean brown arm extending from the white of a cotton T-shirt. The golden glint of stubble below two sharply angled cheeks. A pair of staring anxious eyes beneath fair curls turned dark with sweat.

I hardly recognised myself. So much gaunter than the glam-rock boy whose photograph and byline were displayed on the 'Hip and Happening' page of London's *City* magazine. My mornings spent in Fleet Street with the clatter and bash of typewriters, writing reviews on rising stars promoted on the London scene. Longer lazy afternoons with all the other boozed-up hacks who lushed in antiquated bars, until the evenings spent at gigs, or films, or parties after shows – before it all began again, when

I dragged myself from the crumpled beds of faceless, nameless strangers. Fucked into oblivion.

Oblivion. The perfect word. When had it all stopped being fun, leaving me lonely, restless, bored? And the odd electric charge I'd felt all through that summer's endless heat. Like insects buzzing through my veins.

It was with me then, a thrumming itch, vibrating to the jangling of the bell that rang above my head when I made my way into the shop – and seemingly stepped back in time, to see an imposing mahogany counter, and on top of that an old brass till, its gleaming sides embossed with shapes of flowers, leaves and curling scrolls. Next to the till, a small black dog was sitting on a wooden plinth, and if not for the grey around its snout it struck me as identical to the one that I'd just seen outside. Except that this was motionless. A silver crown upon its head.

I've never liked stuffed animals. Averting my gaze I looked instead at racks crammed full of vintage clothes, all giving off a musty smell. Something like roses, but dank as well, like washing that hadn't quite been dried and had then gone mildewed with the damp. My nose began to tickle. I couldn't stop a violent sneeze, which must have alerted the shopkeeper. I heard some creaks from overhead. The slow but steady beat of feet descending on some nearby stairs, and then a beaded curtain's hush...

He looked like an ancient game show host. A pinstriped suit with wide lapels that in another day and age could well have been considered sharp. Something Cagney might have worn in 1930s gangster films, when he'd pull a gun, or flick a knife. But this suit was too baggy. The cuffs were frayed. There were greasy stains across the front. And its owner fared no better. Whatever his hair had been before, all that now remained of it were a few white strands grown long on top in a Bobby Charlton comb-over, although this bobby-dazzler failed to hide the sores that marred his scalp. Slack jowls drooped round a pair of lips, so red I couldn't help but think he must be wearing lipstick. Above, two pale and rheumy eyes were large and almost childlike, magnified behind the rims of a pair of black-framed spectacles – though the old man's gaze grew keener as his steepled fingers lifted, the tips of them then burrowed in the flesh that sagged beneath his chin.

His voice was surprisingly youthful, being mellifluous and deep, just the slightest cracking quality when he asked, 'Can I be of assistance? Is there anything particular…'

'There's a picture, in the window front. I wondered if…'

Every thought of Bette was swept aside when I saw some other photographs hung on the wall behind his head. Turn of the century perhaps, all with a slightly faded charm.

A fierce-looking woman with both arms raised as if to show the draping sleeves of a medieval-looking gown; the fabric lustrous, shimmering in peacock shades of blues and greens. But the other prints were monochrome. A smiling woman, head inclined, her eyes and nose quite hidden by the roses stuck around the brim of the hat that she was wearing. At her side there was a little girl who couldn't be much more than six. Eyes glittering like jewels of jet as they filled a narrow elfin face. Coiling black ringlets that fell to her shoulders, on top of which she wore what might have been the very same garland of flowers now hooked on a corner of the frame, where the once fresh blooms had dried to brown, like scraps of creased-up tissue paper.

There was the girl in another frame, alone, and some years older, and something different on her head. Something more elaborate in those twists of metal leaves – and snakes? The skin around her eyes was smudged. Was she tired, or was that make-up? When sunlight dazzled on the glass it gave her the look of a living skull. It was such an odd illusion, and it lasted no more than a moment or so but I felt a prickling jolt of fear; a sense that if I stepped too close that girl might reach out through the frame and try to drag me into it.

I shook my head and closed my eyes, and when I looked back up again the natural features were restored, so perfect and alluring that before I knew it I'd enquired, 'How much do you

6

want for that … that girl, with the snakes around her head? Who is she? Do you know her name?'

'Ah …' The old man gave a sigh. A reek of sour beery breath, and a smile that quite unnerved me. The way the scarlet of his lips bled into wrinkled fissures, and the deeper grooves that etched two lines from his nose down to the chin below. Like the hinges on mouths of ventriloquist's dummies.

Once, when I was very young, my mum – what was she thinking of? – had let me stay up late to watch a horror film called *Dead of Night*. A collection of different ghost stories, with the last about a ventriloquist who believed his dummy was possessed by the spirit of a murderer, with all the other characters convinced the man had gone insane. Until the end, and the horrible twist, when—

Recalling the dummy's wide round eyes and the awful malevolence of its smile brought every childhood terror back, starting with genuine alarm when I heard the banshee wails of gulls that gathered in the Lane outside, and through that din the old man's voice:

'Well, I don't often have the pleasure of a handsome young man inside my shop … and I hope you won't mind me saying this, but you have quite a shine about you. Such a lovely golden light it is! I've only seen it once before. A coincidence for those of us who might be prone to, well … what shall we call it? To superstitious tendencies?'

He paused. When he started up again it was almost like a riddle. 'The light of attraction between lost souls. Do *you* also see between the veils? I sense a shared affinity.'

I was wondering if I should leave, presuming the man was drunk, or mad. Or worse, about to make a pass, like the mincing queens in West End bars, who always seemed to think that if they smiled and winked and bought me drinks then I might well be up for it.

Was it me? Misleading signals?

A relief to see his trembling hand had not been raised to touch my arm, but to point on past and indicate a painted sign propped on a shelf, where a large black eye had been designed in a mystical Egyptian style, and arched above were words that read:

PROFESSOR MYSTERIO
PALM READING, TAROT CARDS,
MYSTICAL COMMUNE
Ask and you shall receive advice

His voice was remorseful, reedier, when explaining, 'Mysterio was me. A trade I used to ply before the medicines I have to take blocked off those natural instincts. I'm an epileptic, you see, and the doctors say another fit would finish me entirely. So they dose me up with all these drugs to suppress "excitement" in the brain.'

My answer may have been too curt. 'I don't believe that psychic stuff.'

'Ah yes.' His gaze was doleful. 'You may well have a point. Most any fraud can read the "signs". The movements and the random words that hint at our most inner thoughts. Those things we never dare to tell. But perhaps it's only fair to say…' the coarse white hair above one eye had skewed to twist his furrowed brow, 'I think I still see more than most, even if my mind is slowing up… whether that's due to the medicines or this cursed blight of aging. The cruellest thief of all is Time.'

'I'm sorry,' I said, and really was, though I found it hard to understand why the sadness in the old man's voice should affect me quite so deeply.

'Oh, the years have been kind in many ways. Too generous, you might well say. I'm one of the last Victorians. Born in the 1880s! And I know you young folk think we're prudes, all frills around piano legs… what was it that John Lennon said? I heard him just the other day when he was on the radio. About getting old and missing it?'

He gave a sudden snorting laugh, after which he cleared his throat of phlegm and carried on more breathlessly. 'Well, we didn't miss so very much. The good old days are aptly named! What wonders we achieved back then. I'm crippled with arthritis now, but once I had a gift for art, creating all the backdrops for my father's photography studio. And later, sets for moving films.'

His eyes grew brighter, dreamier. 'If you could see the magic that we captured on those silent screens.' His head was shaking sadly. 'All gone, all gone. And now...'

Was she gone as well? I found my eyes drawn back to the girl with intense black eyes, who might be dead and in her grave. But her picture was vibrantly alive. Such a sexy, vampish air she had. Why, add a safety pin or two and that face could pass as easily for a singer I'd met the other night at a gig in a shabby East End pub.

The place had been packed to the ceilings, with the sweat from hot bodies condensing there and dripping on our heads like rain, dribbling through the purple spikes she'd fashioned from her short black hair. Her cat-like eyes blinked back the sting while jet-black lips had mouthed some words I didn't have a hope to hear. But I'd followed the liquorice sway of hips beneath her leather bondage gear to find her alone on a fire escape where she'd snatched the fag out of my mouth, taking a long slow draw on that before telling me about her band, and how Malcolm McLaren had fixed a gig at the 100 Club on Oxford Street. I'd said I'd like to be there, hoping to impress her more by offering to write it up in the pages of the magazine. But she'd only looked contemptuous. 'You work for *City* magazine? That pile of capitalist crap! If it's hip, then it's *not* happening.'

I hadn't tried to disagree. Why would I? Every word was true.

The femme fatale in sepia had eyes far less accusing, and a chance to look more closely came when the old man turned his back on me, shuffling towards her and grunting with the effort as he raised his arms to clutch the frame. Setting it down on the countertop, he used the cloth of his jacket sleeve to lovingly dust across the glass. When that was done his eyes met mine.

He smiled and said, 'Now, first things first. I think we should be introduced.'

'I'm Ed... Ed Peters,' I answered while offering to shake his hand, though that formal gesture was ignored as he turned his head away again, looking back at the beaded curtain through which he had at first emerged, the strands of which were rattling and parting slightly in a breeze.

A long dark passageway behind. A narrow run of wooden stairs. Beyond, another spacious room where a dome of glass in the ceiling space was covered with moss and sea gull shit. Any sun that could still penetrate created the eeriest atmosphere, like a bubble underneath the sea. And in that murky shimmering I saw a dark-red velvet chaise. Some painted backdrops on the walls. A stylised Brightland Pavilion. A jungle scene with ancient ruins – and then the curtain fell again, and my gaze returned to the black-eyed girl, asking more urgently than I'd intended, 'Won't you tell me about her... who she was?'

'Not who she *was*, Mr Peters.' The answer was slow and serious. 'It's more a case of who she *is*... still very much alive today.' He stopped, as if to let that news sink in before continuing. 'That is, if you call it living. The way she hides herself away like a doomed princess in a fairy tale. I used to visit, every month, as regular as clockwork. But my health, and these drugs I have to take, they mean I can no longer drive. Even if I could, the cliff-side road has grown too perilous. They've closed it off. The path's still there, but I'd never manage such a trek.' He was breathing very heavily, as if simply the thought of the exercise had been enough to wind him. 'I should write, but I doubt the post gets through. I wish she had a telephone. There's no such thing at White Cliff House. No electricity. No water mains. Not that it seems to bother her. She is a fly in amber. In stasis. In inertia.'

'Has she always lived that way?' I asked, still staring at the photograph.

'Oh no. She once lived here with me, when we managed our father's photography shop... before we met with Charles Beauvois and became involved with all his films.'

I felt excitement stirring. I asked, 'Was she an actress, then? I see she has that glamour.'

Seeming in better spirits now, the old man nodded earnestly while reaching beneath the countertop and pulling out a large square book that made a very solid thump when he dropped it down between the dog and the frame that held his sister's face.

'I saved this book of cuttings from a skip only the other week!' He made the proud announcement while he drew the marbled cover back. Inside, his swollen fingers fumbled, lifting flimsy tissue sheets, revealing prints that he then claimed to be a record of some films made in the Brightland area. All stills from work created there in the years before the First World War.

Listening with interest, I leaned a little closer, seeing men with elaborate facial hair, wearing bowler hats or flat tweed caps as they stood in roads, or fields, or woods with cameras perched on tripod stands. Cameras very much like those displayed on the shelves around us. Big wooden boxes with long metal lenses, like toilet rolls stuck on the front of them.

In one of the pictures – a close-up shot – a kitten was cradled in a lap, being fed some milk from a metal spoon. In another, a buxom woman wore nothing but a corset, giving the viewer a saucy smile while standing in front of an old tin bath. Was this some historical striptease? A quaintly pornographic film?

As each new page was turned my curiosity grew deeper, and I asked with some passion, 'These are genuine stills from early films ... all made right here in Brightland?'

'Here, or the near vicinity, and most some years before our own involvement in the industry. There was Friese-Greene, and Darling. Esmé Collings, and James Williamson. Each one of them a pioneer. Why, one of my earliest memories is of my parents taking me to St Ann's Well Gardens up in Hove, where G. A. Smith once showed his films ... with a fortune teller in the grounds. Even a hermit in a cave. I'm sure there are some photographs of that somewhere inside this book.'

'Why don't we know of this today? I'd always assumed the silent films first started in America.'

'America, and Europe too. But, it's safe enough to say that those who worked right here in Brightland were involved at the very dawn of things... although it's almost more than I can bear to think of, all the treasures lost. The celluloid is fragile, you see. Not so unlike our mortal flesh... melting, crumbling to dust.'

Questions tumbled through my mind. *How many of these people might still be alive in the present day? How many films had been preserved?* I asked, 'Do you think there's any chance that I could meet your sister too? I'm a journalist, and I really think there might be quite a story here.'

Again, the old man raised a brow. 'A story more intriguing than you'd ever dare imagine. My sister keeps many secrets. Many skeletons in her closets, and...' A frown of confusion filled his face as if not knowing whether he should stop or carry on with this – until his eyes fixed hard on mine. 'Those ghosts may rise to harm us all.'

Us all? Did he mean himself and his sister, or was he including me as well? I pushed such nonsense from my mind, asking as my fingers stroked around the picture's chipped gilt frame, 'How old was she, in this photograph?'

'Our father took this picture. Quite the David Bailey of his time. She was always his favourite subject... at least, after our mother died. And I know she might look older here, but I think she would have been fourteen. About the time when Charles Beauvois first showed his face here in the town. His first appearance. Not his last.'

He paused. His body stiffened. All at once he looked exhausted, as if his whole physique had shrunk within the creases of his suit. 'Ah well, what's done is done. Too late for us to change things now. And Charles Beauvois is surely dead. He was older than us by quite some years when he disappeared from White Cliff House... leaving misery behind.'

That stare. So terribly intense as he struggled to keep his dignity, to control the emotions clearly felt when beneath the weight of crepey lids his eyes grew blurred and watery. When he blinked a single drop splashed down across a photo in the book. The photo with the kitten. The spoon which now appeared to spill the milk contained within its bowl.

A magical illusion, and hard to drag my gaze away, while the old man carried on to say, 'If you have a genuine interest – and yes, I do believe you do – then I'll sell you my sister's photograph, and I'll let you have this book as well. Shall we say the sum of twenty pounds? Would that be agreeable?'

It was an extortionate price to pray, but before I'd even answered he was wrapping the frame in newspaper, and muttering beneath his breath, 'This may well be a can of worms you'll wish you never opened up. Are you sure you want to take these things?'

What a strange exchange of goods it was. What could he be afraid of? For myself, I would have paid much more, such a rush of excitement in my blood as I reached for the wallet in my jeans from which I pulled two ten-pound notes.

While placing them down on the countertop my fingers brushed against his hand, and I felt the heat of swollen joints, and the oddest sense of pity when, in any other circumstance, I'd probably have been repulsed. Not to mention losing patience during the small eternity before the cash was in the till, after which he picked a biro up to scrawl some details underneath the words emblazoned at the top of a flimsy sheet of paper:

THEO WILLIAMS ESQUIRE.
STAGE AND FILM MEMORABILIA

Barely giving that a second glance I stuffed it in my wallet. With the package held beneath one arm I made my way towards the door, where my eyes were almost dazzled by the shock of light on the other side, while behind I heard the old man call:

'Oh, Mr Peters, before you go … I don't think you asked my sister's name. Her name is Leda. Leda Grey. You'll see it, on the sales receipt. And if you do decide to go and find her up at White Cliff House, will you tell her Theo sent you?

'Will you tell her Theo thinks it's time to tell the truth ... to show her light?'

SET ME UP IN HOPE

Leda. Leda. Leda Grey. Chanting the name inside my head I walked back through the bustling Lanes, and then along the seafront road until I found the small hotel I'd booked into the night before.

Converted from a private home in the grandest of Regency crescents, it had wide stone steps and a pillared porch; though best not look too carefully at the crusting rust on ironwork or the paint that peeled from rotting wood when, back inside my room again, I forced the creaking window frames that opened to a balcony.

I was hoping to draw a breeze inside to cool the stifling atmosphere. The room was as hot as an oven. My head throbbed. I felt too shaky as I stripped off all my sweat-damp clothes and headed to the bathroom.

No shower. Just a chipped white bath in a room with little natural light, where a stark fluorescent strip light hummed and flickered wildly overhead as I turned the big brass tap marked cold, then lowered myself into the tub and closed my eyes against a sign fixed on the wall above it.

WE ASK OUR GUESTS TO PLEASE REFRAIN FROM BATHING DURING THE WATER DROUGHT.

I didn't linger. Did that count? After hauling myself back out again, I stood on the cracked and clammy tiles where puddles formed around my feet. I pressed a flannel to my chin, where I'd nicked myself with a razor blade. I watched the water drain away, gurgling in the plughole as it swirled with trails of ribboned red – when I slumped down to my knees and heaved.

A vivid flashback to a day when I'd still been a boy at school. The middle of my O levels. I'd written an essay on *Macbeth*, quoting lines I'd learned by heart; those words repeating in my mind when I came back home that afternoon to find my mother in the bath.

The multitudinous seas incarnadine, Making the green one red.

She'd slashed her wrists with a kitchen knife. On the floor, an upturned bottle of whisky had spilled across her dressing gown. A pale blue quilted thing it was, that used to give off sparking shocks whenever Mum brushed past me. The lapels had little orange spots. Stains from dribbled cups of tea, though the cups I made most mornings to leave by her bed when I went to school would still be there when I returned. Stone cold, with a skim of grey on top.

Next to the cups, a photograph. A place and a date inked on the back. About nine months before my birth. She never said who'd taken it, but they must have made her happy. Eyes laughing underneath a hat with *Kiss me Quick* across the front. Standing on a pebbled beach, her skirts hitched high above her thighs, waves washing round her feet like lace.

I'd taken her back to that beach last night, carrying a plastic bag with the urn I'd lugged around for years, wherever I'd happened to make my home. Ten years had passed, but finally I'd found my way to Brightland, where I'd flung her ashes in the sea, and then collapsed beneath the pier. With my legs splayed wide across the sand I'd been pouring whisky in my mouth until I'd thrown the bottle down, hearing the smash and then the hush of waves that claimed the broken glass. And over that I'd screamed the words my mother sometimes used to sing, when she played her old scratched records on the gramophone in our front room, closing her eyes and dancing while Frank Sinatra softly crooned: *Can't you see I'm no good without you? . . . How can I go on, dear, without you?*

In the bathroom, on my feet again, I wrapped a towel around my waist and told myself to get a grip.

Christ, did I need a cigarette. Heading back to the bedroom

to find one, I lit it up while staring out across the open balcony, where a swarm of scarlet ladybirds were crawling on the parapet. Beyond, the Crescent's scorched brown lawns sloped down towards the promenade, where the glisten of a dying sun shone red on all the towers and domes that loomed above the Brightland Pier.

Squinting my eyes against that glare, I turned to face the room again, seeing through the curling haze of smoke blown through my parting lips the sort of shabby dark antiques that no one wanted any more. But I liked their faded glory. And I liked the cracks in the plasterwork that lapped around the ceiling, and the way the geometric design of the vinyl paper on the walls had peeled away above the bed to reveal what had been there before. A faded green background with riots of roses. Roundels formed from stems and leaves.

Those patterns made me think about the crown on the head of Leda Grey. The package with her photograph was where I'd left it, on the bed. Soon I'd torn the wrappings off, drawing out the picture frame to prop against the bedside lamp, from where the dark-eyed girl could watch as I stubbed out the fag in an ashtray, then lifted up the scrapbook.

Opening its covers, I felt excitement rise again. This was *really* happening. I saw features in the broadsheets. Perhaps a documentary. And at the very heart of it was the lure the old man had hooked me with. The mystery about a girl who'd acted in some silent films before becoming a recluse for more than half a century.

I'd booked the hotel for a week. Time to visit the Brightland library. The museum. The local newspaper. Even without a telephone for listings in directories, there couldn't be that many White Cliff Houses in the area. Tomorrow was a Sunday, but I'd still make a start of sorts. Drive around the coastline. Get to know the area.

For then I was content to spend the evening with the scrapbook, sitting with my back against the greasy satin headboard as I turned the pages randomly – until pausing at a yellowed ad with illustrations of some films enthusiastically described as *productions with magical trick effects to astound and confound the audience, with moving images surpassing pre-existing stage events. The grandest of illusions will become as nothing when compared.*

Every still did look 'miraculous', more so as the light inside the room was dusted in a veil of grey, through which a stuttering white glow leached through the open bathroom door. It flickered on the images of men who'd had their heads cut off, those heads then juggled round like balls. It added yet more atmosphere to the sequence of eerie photographs where the portrait of a woman seemed to come alive within her frame, climbing out from that to creep across a darkened room towards the chair in which a man was sleeping, seemingly quite unaware of ...

The images blurred, refocused, blurred. My eyes grew heavier and closed, though I was vaguely still aware of the sound of footsteps in the room, like someone pacing round the bed, and now and then between those thuds the squeaking of a loosened board. Some scratching sounds. Some whimpering. Was that the growling of a dog? And then the dream – of Leda Grey. A lucid vision of her face as it hovered above me on the bed. Her lips so close that I could swear I felt her breath upon my own. But, rather than seeing two dark eyes, in my dream her lids were firmly closed, and due to the thick black greasepaint that had been smudged around them, it seemed once more as if she stared through the mask of a cadaver; that illusion more dramatic still when I lifted a hand to stroke her cheek and then lurched back in horror when my fingertips touched cold hard bone, when I heard a sudden hissing noise and saw a snake come slithering through the empty socket of her skull.

I woke with a shout, lashing out, knocking Leda's photograph from the table to the floor below, where the crashing tinkle of the glass brought me fully back to life – lurching up then falling back against the pillows with a groan, pressing a hand against the heart that was beating too fast, too erratically, where the hair that grew across my chest was running wet with sweat again. This time it was the sweat of fear.

Had I really been scared of a photograph? As the nightmare faded from my eyes I knew that was ridiculous. Even so, I felt much happier after switching on the bedside lamp which threw a far more even glow than the bathroom's jerky shimmering as I swung my legs down from the bed and set about the task of picking up those shards of broken glass.

When they were in the litter bin I held the fractured picture frame and saw the photograph inside was scratched, one of the corners torn – which was why I decided to keep it safe inside the pages of the book.

Call it fate. Call it serendipity, or had Theo Williams always known what I would find inside it? Because, right there, at the very back, and glued against the cover page, there was a sort of envelope, in the pocket of which someone had placed a selection of directors' cards. One of those cards was printed with the black-inked etching of a man. He wore a top hat, a flowing cape. He had both arms raised in the air, and bursting from his fingertips, along with a shower of tiny stars, were the letters embossed to form the words:

Charles Beauvois ~ Cinematographer
White Cliff House
Cuckham Sands ~ Sussex ~ England

THIS CASTLE HATH A PLEASANT SEAT

Cuckham Sands was five miles from Brightland, but I found it easily enough with a map from the hotel's receptionist. Parking on the roadside verge just opposite a village pub, I listened to the tick-tick-tick of the engine's cooling metal, and over that the weary tones of a radio station's weatherman. *Today, more soaring temperatures. One hundred degrees at least.*

I groaned, turned off the radio, and wound the Mini's windows up, getting out while dragging on the straps of a battered rucksack. All the tools of my trade were stored inside. Reporters' notebooks. Pencils. Pens. A camera, and microcassette machine. But, before I could think to use them for interviewing Leda Grey, I needed more directions, thinking to find them in the pub – only to discover that the old oak door beneath a rustic overhang of yellow thatch was locked, and not a sign of life behind its latticed windows.

Through steam that rose above the melting tarmac further down the road I saw some more thatched dwellings, and further on, towards the beach, a woman walked a large black dog. But long before I'd gone so far I found a leaning wooden post which showed the name of *White Cliff House*. It was next to one of those kissing gates. The turnstiles of another age. No option but to walk through that, with the wider access for a car having been blocked off by metal bars, and a local authority poster that warned of *Danger. Do Not Drive. Cliff Erosion. Falling Rocks.*

The steeply rising gravel path was hedged by clumps of brambles, eventually opening to show the sea spread wide below, glittering a jewel-like green within a cove of white cliff walls – though the beauty of that tranquil scene was tempered by the blasts of wind that whipped my hair into my eyes, and soon became so forceful that I had to keep my distance from the precipice and rocks below. The exertion made me breathless, unused to that much exercise. But unlike Theo Williams I was still young and fit enough, and in less than half an hour or so the track had levelled out again to lead me to a second gate.

Pushing against its unlocked catch I wandered down another track, heading away from the coastal path and through a dappled avenue where the branches of trees on either side had gradually become entwined. Beneath that shade, with cooler air, I soon picked up my stride again, avoiding any potholes by walking on the sloping banks, where my feet and spirits all but bounced on mats of mossy undergrowth – until the lane turned one last time, and White Cliff House came into view.

Surrounded by more conifers, all that remained of garden lawns were now a yellowed wilderness bisected by a weedy path that led towards what I assumed to be a Georgian dwelling. Built of mellowed rusty brick, the frontage had a large stone porch, but drawing nearer I could see that much of the back was older. A timbered construction that must date from several centuries before. A distinctive lack of symmetry, both in the walls and sagging slopes of many sharply gabled roofs, punctuated here and there by tall and twisting chimney stacks. Almost every visible surface had been swathed to some extent in green, though the closer I got to the house itself the less romantic that appeared. More the strangling parasite that such an ivy really was, with any windows not obscured revealing broken panes of glass, or barricaded from within by closed-up wooden shutters.

Already starting to suspect that the house had been abandoned, I stood beneath the shadowed porch and tugged a hanging metal chain. No sound of any bell inside, only the knocking of my hand as I pressed one ear against the splintered green where paint was flaking; so rough it might have grazed my skin without new stubble growing there.

'Damn!' I swore, stroking my chin. The place I'd cut myself last night. It would be a shame if Leda Grey opened the door, then slammed it shut when she saw a shabby sweating tramp. But nothing to do to change that now, so I knocked again, then crouched to lift the flap of a large brass letter box, to see a dimly lit square hall in which I could make out a chair, a table on some lion legs, an enormous mirror on one wall; and then some darker rectangles where inner doors were leading off.

Which door might lead to Leda Grey? Holding my mouth against the gap I called her name, then listened, but not a murmur could be heard in the secret depths of that old house. Only a stillness at its heart. A sweetly sour odour.

Standing again, the flap dropped back, and flinching at the metal's clang I knew that no one living there could possibly have failed to hear, unless they happened to be deaf; as older people sometimes were.

It might be best to leave a note. I wondered about a business card, but decided to keep things personal, taking a pen from the rucksack and scribbling on the postcard still in the pocket of my jeans. The one I'd bought the day before. The one that showed the Brightland Pier.

My name is Ed Peters. I came to White Cliff House today in the hope of meeting Leda Grey, after hearing of her work in film from her brother in his Brightland shop. I will try again this afternoon.

I pushed that through the letter box, then left the shelter of the porch, thinking I'd head back down the cliff to find the village pub again. But first, I'd try and take a glance around the house's gardens.

Striding off through stems of grass that grew so long they brushed my thighs, I passed the bleached and brittle struts of a long-discarded deckchair. The fraying strings of a hammock still hung between two conifers. Higher, in the branches, were the shreds of a tattered large white sheet, perhaps blown from a washing line and now forever fluttering, like ghosts among the evergreens.

Nearer to the house's walls, despite the summer's lack of rain some creamy roses clung to life, stems curled through all the ivy leaves and drooping with the weight of blooms. But most had shrivelled when in bud, turned brown and tightly mummified.

More roses tangled round a broken length of iron guttering that hung beneath a leaded bay and must have leaked for many years, rotting the wood of a window frame. Where bricks and mortar had collapsed they'd left a gaping hole behind, its edges furred with fungus. When I touched them with a fingertip some spores rose up and made me sneeze – that sound then echoed by the cries of gulls that wheeled in the skies that, in the last few hours, had turned from blue to a blinding white.

Those cries were other-worldly and I know it sounds ridiculous but I felt the gulls were warning me. A warning that I then ignored, grabbing at some woody stems to hoist myself onto the window's ledge, where I prayed the stone would hold my weight as I peered in through the broken wall.

The room I saw was very large, and most of it obscured in gloom due to the shutters being closed. But if I tipped my head one way a shaft of sunshine shone there. Filled with dancing motes of dust, it might have been a beam of light projected through a cinema, though no moving pictures on that screen. Everything that I could see was heavy, solid, stationary. A sewing machine on an iron stand. A piano placed against one wall with fancy brackets on the front for holding candles while you played. Books draped in nets of spiders' webs. Books everywhere I chanced to look, arranged on shelves around the walls, or piled in stacks upon the floor. More of them arranged between two vases on a mantelpiece where a carriage clock stood centre stage.

The hands were set at ten to twelve. Had it stopped, or was that the actual time? I didn't wear a wristwatch. For some reason they'd never worked on me, either running too fast, or slowing down until, eventually, they froze. But time was the very last thing on my mind when I saw something else in that shadowed room. Something that made me gasp out loud when the spotlight fell across the face of a woman sleeping in a chair.

Was she asleep? Or was she dead? Her eyes were closed. One

flaccid cheek was pressed against a cushion. But there – yes, there – the slightest rise and falling of the woollen rug that had been laid across her breast to show that she *was* breathing, and seemingly quite unaware of anyone observing her; or the fact that I then did something without a shred of decency.

Using one hand to reach behind and burrow in my rucksack, I grabbed for the camera kept there, looping the strap around my neck, then holding the lens to the damaged wall. There was always a film loaded up inside. It only needed a flick of a finger to set the flash, to light the shot, and *click*, I had my picture. But when trying to wind the camera on, to take a second photograph, a breeze got up around the house. The conifers were rustling. The broken gutter gave a creak. Long strands of trailing green blew out and lashed around my head and neck. More clouds of dust rose from the wall, and squinting past that reddish scrim I noticed that the light that shone so clearly through the hole before was now a fractured flickering. Black. White. Black. White. Such a mesmerising odd effect, till something else distracted me.

Surely the sleeping woman heard? And yet she didn't give the slightest twitch to show that she had been disturbed by those staccato beats that filled the shadows of the room. Rationally, I knew that noise was nothing but the ivy's tap-tap-tapping on the window panes. But how did that explain the shifting patterns on the mantelpiece, where the clock appeared to come to life, hands jerking, edging round the face, though instead of moving forwards, this time was running backwards. Slowly, steadily at first, then gradually speeding up into a whirling blur of black, while the vision seemed to suck me in towards its spinning gravity until, as quickly as it came, the breeze died down, the tapping stopped, and the clock hands juddered to a halt, exactly where they'd been before. At precisely ten minutes to twelve.

That also marked the moment when I lost my balance on the ledge, falling backwards through the air to hit the solid ground below. God knows how the camera wasn't smashed, and, for myself, perhaps a bruise. But not much more; not with the rucksack cushioning the impact. Only some criss-cross lines of red where thorns had scratched my hands and arms, though I hardly even noticed them – only how odd it seemed to be that the air was suddenly so still. No movement in the trees or leaves that draped about the house's walls. Only the dancing of a bee as it buzzed around one perfect rose.

With a pounding head and sore, parched throat I reached the Cuckham pub again. This time the door was open, leading me into the murk of timbered walls and ceilings built so low that I could barely stand without my head brushing against the hops hung up to dry there. The air smelled pungently of malt, as did the pint of beer I drank, its coolness like a balm to soothe my thirst – and also fraying nerves.

I didn't mind my thorn-scratched arms. The streaks of blood would soon wash off. Already they were healing. But the backwards clock, that rattled me, picking at the scabs of what I thought I'd seen inside the house. I *knew* that I'd imagined it. The tapping of stems against brick walls. The way the movement of the leaves created odd illusions in a room so densely shadowed. The fact that I'd had too much sun, was probably delirious.

Hungry too. I needed food, far more than I did alcohol. God knows what I'd be seeing if I wasn't even sober. But when some sandwiches arrived I really didn't fancy them. The crusts were dry and curling, slimed with greasy yellow trails where butter oozed across the plate.

The barmaid looked embarrassed. She was offering apologies. 'I'm sorry. I can take them back. The kitchen fridge is on the blink. This heat … affecting everything.'

I glanced her way, eyes dazzled by the silver hoops hung in her ears. The gleaming blueness of her eyes. The white-blonde hair cut in a bob, a bit like Debbie Harry's style. On any other day, I might have flirted, tried to ask her out. The way she grinned, so naturally, relaxed and easy in her skin. The skin that swelled quite unconstrained beneath her flimsy cotton vest.

I couldn't help but smile back, thinking of Hammer Horror

films, when the buxom Transylvanian wench is pouring frothing yards of ale in the courtyard of a country inn, with the unsuspecting Englishman about to head towards his fate in the castle of Count Dracula.

In the more prosaic everyday this girl's attention soon moved on to several other customers, though in between their raucous laughs and calls for glasses to be filled, I bought two cans of lemonade. Reserves to keep inside my bag for the journey up the cliff again.

Meanwhile, I wandered off into an empty snug to drink in peace. In there, the ceiling's low black beams and narrow latticed windows obscured more of the day outside to give a quiet solitude through which my mind returned again to what I'd seen at White Cliff House. Not the illusion of the clock – no, I wouldn't think of that – but the woman sleeping in the chair, her face more vivid in my mind than any in that village pub.

The glowing whiteness of her skin, like finely crumpled paper. The tangles of the long grey hair that fell across her shoulders. I hadn't seen her eyes, and yet much like her brother in the shop she'd exuded something ancient, but also such a childlike air. And it wasn't just the way the sunlight glinted on her passive face – that radiance of her repose – that made me wonder how she must have shone when she had still been young; when the aged and faded Leda Grey had once possessed the dark allure of the girl in the sepia photograph.

FAIR AND NOBLE HOSTESS

Leda Grey was calling out to me from the shadows of the house's porch. 'Oh, there you are, Mr Peters! You did come back, just as you said ... although when I first saw you, walking out of the garden lane like that, I thought you were my brother. It must have been your long fair curls. I often forget how old he is ... and very almost bald these days. Not the beautiful boy I used to know. But now that you are closer, I see the eyes ... quite different! Theo's are blue, whereas yours are brown.' She paused. Hands fluttered to her mouth. 'Oh dear, what must you think of me? I should calm myself, speak sensibly when a visitor is at my door. It's so rare, you see. So very ...'

The breathless welcome ended with a sagging of her features, brow knitted into lines of doubt when she took a few steps back and asked, 'You're not a bailiff playing tricks? It's a waste of time. You've had it all. There's nothing of any value left to stuff inside that bag of yours.'

'No! I don't want anything. Only to come and talk to you.' I spoke while walking forward, soon standing just outside the porch from where I saw that Leda Grey bore very little likeness to the man in the Brightland Lanes before. His sister was more finely made. Despite great age she had a grace. Head high, and standing quite erect, whereas he'd been stooped and shuffling, altogether more shambolic.

'I'm a journalist,' I carried on. 'I met your brother in his shop and heard about your work in films. He sold me an old photograph. You, in a crown of leaves and snakes. Won't you tell me more about it? Why you wore that costume? I'll pay you for an interview. More if it gets published. Your brother ... he suggested I should come and hear your story. He said' – I hoped I had it right – 'He said he thought that it was time for you to show the world your light.'

Her features widened in distress. She raised a hand to touch her brow. 'He gave you that old photograph? My brother spoke about my light? He must have had a reason… so perhaps the time *has* come then. Theo would never say such things unless he'd placed his trust in you. And if he has… then so must I.'

The warmth returned. It seemed that we were back to where we'd started off. 'Have you travelled very far, young man?'

I told her I'd driven from Brightland, and then walked up the cliff-side track. I mentioned the name of my hotel, to which she said, 'How curious. My brother and I were born and raised in that very part of town. I'm sure Theo once mentioned that our house was now a small hotel. I wonder if…' She shook her head. 'Oh well, we had to let it go. The debts we had. The cost of staff. But we kept those rooms above the shop, where Theo still lives to this very day. The name and the trade may have changed with the years, but there he is, still in the Lanes. And…' she gave the saddest smile, 'here I am in White Cliff House.'

She turned, glanced back towards the door, before her eyes met mine again. 'Would you like to come inside? I'm afraid a draught got up before. The door slammed shut behind me. But it isn't locked, just slightly stiff. If you could help to push, and then…'

She moved aside, allowing me into the porch while going on, 'My very own Ali Babi, come to Open Sesame… for which I must give some reward. You do look rather hot. Perhaps you'd like a drink of water? I only have what's in the well and it can be rather cloudy, especially in summer months. But it's never done me any harm.'

'Thanks, but I'm OK, Miss Grey. Or, is it Mrs?' I enquired, looking into two dark eyes that really hadn't changed so much from those in the photographs I'd seen. The lids were slack and hooded now, with the bruising blue of bags below and fanning lines spread out each side, but the brown of her irises were filled with such a glinting clarity through which her bell-like voice rang out, 'Oh please, just call me Leda. I suppose if you wanted to be correct then my name would be Miss Williams. But there really isn't any need.'

'Then, I'll stick with Leda. But why Grey, when your brother is Williams? Was Grey a stage name that you used?'

'That's something rather personal. Perhaps I'll tell you later.'

And that was where we left it, when the solid weight of the big front door gave way without the slightest creak and opened to the entrance hall – where the very first thing I noticed was my card, still lying on the floor.

Stooping down to pick it up and place it on the table top, I wondered if she'd seen it, if she'd read the message after all. But she must have done. She knew my name. She'd been outside, expecting me.

Almost as if she'd sensed my doubt, while following behind she said, 'When you posted the card through the letter box the bang of the metal woke me. I'd been in the very deepest sleep. Such a struggle to open up my eyes. And the dreams I had, calling me back. But, enough of my imaginings ... I do so like this picture. To see the Brightland pier again. It makes me think about the time when Theo and I made postcards too ... when I'd pose for all the photographs he took and then had printed up to sell to the ragtag and bobtails in Brightland on their holidays.'

She seemed to be in another world, lost in her own reflection in the mirror on the hallway wall, which allowed me time to take another good long look at Leda Grey. The shape of her slightly curving spine. How slender her frame appeared to be beneath the loose black dress she wore. A style that was almost fashionable, for those who liked the boho look, with sleeves concealing arms and wrists, though the hands below were swollen, wrinkled, roped with purple veins. Not as gnarled with arthritis as those of her brother, but still there was no hiding the fact that these were an old woman's hands. The same with what was visible above the neckline of her gown where, rising from her small slack breasts, white flesh was creased like muslin. But such a beauty still remained in the handsome bones of Leda's face – even though she seemed to disagree when looking back at me to say, 'What an ugly old woman I have become, and yet to sense you watching me, it comforts me in the strangest way. It makes me feel I'm still alive. Not quite yet numbering the dead.

'Will you tell me... tell me honestly.' She was staring at the glass again. 'What do you see in that mirror? It's just that when I look for you, standing there behind me, you are quite clear. Quite solid. Whereas I... I seem too shadowy. Oddly insubstantial.'

Stepping a little nearer I guessed what the problem was at once, blinking against a daze of light and saying, 'Well, from this angle, I also look a little blurred... with the dust that's covering the glass. The way the sun is slanting in.'

'Oh, yes!' Her lips twitched nervously before she gave another smile, revealing what were stained with brown but otherwise quite perfect teeth. I sensed she was embarrassed, when she turned to look my way, and said, 'I hardly ever see the dust. I really need some spectacles. Theo brought me some of his. The sort that help to magnify. I used them for my reading, but I can't think where I've put them now. This house is such a muddle.'

Her eyes looked clear and keen enough when darting round the hall just then, out through the door, beyond the porch where the sun was such a scorching blaze that my arms had burned a lobster red while walking up the cliff again; the fine fair hairs bleached almost white. But not the scratches on my hands. I hoped she wouldn't see those marks. I didn't want to tell her I'd been spying through the broken wall. Had seen her sleeping in the dark.

'Do you ever go out... in the sun?' I asked. And yes, I was trying to flatter her, when I said, 'Your skin... it's clichéd, but it really is like porcelain.' In fact, it looked translucent, so fine that at her temples I could see the veins, a throbbing mauve.

She laughed. 'I'm that not vain, young man, and this mirror is not *that* blurry! But it's true, I rarely go outside. Sometimes, at night, I like to walk. Along the cliff, or—'

'But,' I interrupted, 'how do you manage to exist? What do you do about buying food?'

'My brother brings me what I need... whenever he can... when visiting. I've been growing vegetables for years in a kitchen garden at the back. And the family, at the farm nearby... we have an understanding. A grace and favour arrangement. They put wood in the outhouse for the stove, and to burn for fires in the winter months. Sometimes they leave me food as well. Butter. Cheese. Fresh milk, and eggs. Not so much of it these days. Not since the ownership has changed. But the pantry shelves are filled with tins. Enough of them to last for years.'

'So you live entirely alone?'

Leda didn't answer, only glanced back through the door again and asked, 'Do you hear that rumbling? Is it thunder... or an engine? Do you think it's Theo's motorbike?'

Theo? On a motorbike? That was something I would like to see! But all I heard was screeching gulls; a breeze that swayed the trees again; perhaps the rush of distant waves – through which I hoped that Leda Grey hadn't grown too old and senile for a rational conversation. Meanwhile, I started to explain how her brother had said he couldn't drive because of his new medicines. How he simply wasn't fit enough for walking up the cliff-side track. Not now that it had been closed off.

'Ah! I might have guessed as much.' She gasped. A hand clutched to her breast. The sort of gesture you'd expect from a diva on an opera stage. 'Did my brother send you here today to say he won't be coming back? Is this to be the end of it?'

The end of what?

I tried to reassure her. 'I don't think he's quite as bad as that. He was still working in the shop.'

She didn't seem to hear at first, then laughed, 'Oh, Theo and that shop! It used to drive me mad, you know, the way he rummaged round this house. Like a magpie he was, always searching for things to take away and sell there. Not that the bailiffs left that much. But, poor Theo... always worrying about taxes and bills and expenses... always saying that I sit up here and have no idea how hard it can be to exist in the outside world today. I suppose it's true.' She frowned. 'I try my best to understand.

And now, I'd gladly pay the tax of all my brother's pilfering...
if only he'd come back again.'

She stopped to take a trembling breath. 'I suppose, it did
seem strange to me...how different he was, last time he came.
He barely spoke a word to me, and when he did his voice was
slurred. Did you notice that, when you met him?' Alert, enquiring eyes met mine. 'Was Theo still dragging that leg of his?
I'm not stupid. I told him, I know the signs. I saw it in our
father's stroke. But he simply shrugged it off and blamed his
poor arthritic bones again. Dear Theo. Always the fragile one.'

'His voice seemed clear enough to me. He may have limped
a little bit, but...' I wasn't sure what else to say, suddenly suggesting, 'You know, if you'd like to visit him, then maybe I could
help you. There must be a way to drive to town, to get a car up
here, and...'

'No!' She rose to her full height, eyes on a level with my own,
and filled with such a blazing zeal. 'There's only the path that
runs on past the fields behind Winstanley's farm. And Theo
always comes to me. I have to stay. I have to guard.'

Guard what? I felt confused, hearing the anguish in her voice,
wondering why she'd want to stay in this wreck of a collapsing
house. All that I could think to say was, 'I've upset you. I should
go away. Maybe come back another time, when—'

'No! Don't go! At least, not yet.' She paused, another breath,
and then, 'Mr Peters, please forgive me. I'm a lonely old woman
with no idea of how to behave in company. But, I'd like you stay,
and if you do I'll do my best to tell you all you wish to know
about my life...the one I lived as Leda Grey.'

'Did you have a life as someone else?' I hadn't meant to tease
her. I didn't expect her stark reply.

'I did. I'm sure you've done the same. I'm sure the man you
are today must be entirely different to the boy you were at, say,
sixteen?'

'I was sixteen when my mother died.'

I surprised myself with that blunt response, never having
mentioned it to anyone I'd met before.

'I'm sorry.' Leda's hands were clasped, her fingers twisting nervously. 'And now I have upset you. But your father. Is he still alive?'

Just who was interviewing who? Again, I answered honestly. 'I never knew my father. My mother and I, we lived alone. It was hard. She always felt ashamed. Not being married... having me. I don't think she had a happy life.'

'But I'm sure *you* made her happy.'

I thought of when I'd been a child – those nights when I would sometimes wake to see the street light shining through my flimsy bedroom curtains, and then across my mother's face as she knelt on the rug beside my bed. Her breath would be rank with wine and fags. I'd try to turn my head away while she stroked her fingers through my hair, and cooed, 'Did I ever tell you, Ed, how I came to meet your father... that holiday in Brightland? How we slept under the pier that night and—'

Mum! I'd push her hand away, growing hot with the embarrassment at this talk of a father I'd never met, knowing that tomorrow night I'd hear about another man. Perhaps the handsome gypsy who'd worked the rides on Brightland pier...

One year, when I was five or six, I'd thrown up all my candy floss while spinning on the waltzers when the fair was on in Hammersmith, desperately searching for myself in the features of the swarthy men collecting all the sixpences.

I'd had less hope of finding the American GI she said she'd danced with in Trafalgar Square, one night at the end of World War II, before he'd sailed back home again to another wife and family. But then, when I was old enough to do the maths on *that* affair, working forward nine months from a night in May in the year of 1945, it was clear she'd made the whole thing up. No normal human pregnancy could last the three years that she'd claimed.

How stupid did she think I was? My mother lived in a fantasy world. The only certainty in life was that she didn't have a clue as to who her child's father was. And that was how I'd liked it. Just her. Just me. All on our own...

I heard the laboured breathing of the living woman at my side, her eyes expressing sympathy, and the slightest catching in her voice when she raised one hand as if about to touch her fingers to my cheek. 'These old skins all slough off in time. Eventually we start anew, even when we think our hearts might break... abandoned by the ones we've loved.'

I had no thoughts of leaving then, only followed when she beckoned me, walking past the staircase where a newel post had split in two, protruding with sharp spikes of wood – as if someone had taken an axe to it.

That was somewhat unnerving, as was the musty smell of rot that mingled through the floral scent that drifted up in Leda's wake. Was it rose? I think it must have been, though looking at her trailing hems was somewhat less alluring, with the cloth collecting dust and crumbs as she led the way through double doors, into the room I'd seen before when spying through the broken wall.

The sun had moved on round the house. Now the light that trickled in was a great deal fainter than before. But enough to see when Leda Grey motioned to the mantelpiece where, beside the silent static clock, I saw the tall brass candlestick she must have been alluding to when she asked, 'Could you light that candle, please? I'm afraid that here in White Cliff House we have no electricity... and no more oil for any lamps.'

We?

After lighting the wick of the candle with a match from my own pocket, the room around was gleaming gold, illuminating zigzag cracks that riddled through the ceiling, all the corners where long spiders' webs were dangling down to reach the floor, all the juddering flowers, leaves and birds on a William Morris wallpaper. The very same design I'd seen at a Chelsea party recently. But there the paper had been new. A modern reproduction. Here, the walls were stained with years of mould and penetrating damp. The paper fell away in folds.

I noticed the basket in the hearth, overflowing with ash and half-charred wood. It could have been like that for months, or had a fire burned recently? Leda Grey appeared to be immune to the oppressive summer heat. When I'd seen her before, when she'd been asleep, she'd been covered in the blanket now heaped on the floor beside her chair – the chair which, on closer inspection, was covered in a green brocade, the very same fabric being used on a sofa standing opposite. In between them both a Turkish rug, and through its weave a worn white stripe that led my eye towards the doors. How many times over how many years had this woman walked to make that groove?

All at once I was aware again of a stale and fetid atmosphere, so bad I felt impelled to ask, 'Would you mind if I drew some shutters back?'

'I'm afraid that won't be possible. They've all been nailed to the window frames ... ever since that time the coastguard came and said that I should leave the house. It was after the Germans dropped the bomb, when it took half the cliff away with it. He insisted on sealing the lower floors in case the enemy got in. He told me that I had to leave. But I refused. I didn't care. I liked to see the bombs go off. I'd walk along the cliff and watch the flares go up like fireworks. Some near, and some as far as France ...'

She paused, appeared to be confused. 'There were two wars.' She stopped again, and then began to wring her hands. 'Do you think we'll have a third one? Will the Germans try to come again?'

'More likely the Russians. They'll drop the bomb, and that will be the end of us.'

'The Russians? I did hear of the Bolsheviks. The fate of the Tsar and his family. Is it anything to do with that?'

'God, no! That's ancient history.' Didn't she watch the TV news? No. No electricity. What about a radio? Something using batteries? Surely her brother told her things? How could she live in the world today and not be aware of the Cold War?

'Don't you miss the sun?' I asked. 'I could try to force those nails out ... to get the shutters working.'

'I only need to close my eyes and remember this house as it used to be.' As if to demonstrate her point, she squeezed them shut and carried on. 'Imagine the windows opened up. The room all sparkling with light...which was the very reason why Beauvois first came to work here...when he built the studio for his films.'

She smiled, eyes opened wide again. 'I first saw it one Sunday afternoon, in the spring of 1913.'

'That's...' I made a swift calculation, 'sixty-three years ago.'

'Sixty-three years? Can it be that long?' While Leda's voice echoed my own, I shrugged off the straps of my rucksack, setting the bag down on the rug before rummaging about inside to find the cassette recorder, enquiring while I dragged that out, 'Would you tell me more about that time? Would you mind if I tape the things you say?'

'Tape?' She gave a puzzled look.

'With this.' I placed the machine on the sofa, tearing away the cellophane wrapped around a new cassette. With the reel inserted on the spools, my fingers poised to press 'record', the barest click before she asked, 'But what is it? What does it do?'

'It picks up anything we say. It saves the sounds on plastic tape.'

'Like songs recorded on the wax?'

'Like this...'

I pressed 'rewind', then 'play', and watched as Leda's face lit up when she heard her words repeated back. Such a mellow, musical voice she had. A mesmerising quality. To hear it you'd never guess her age. To see her then, her sheer delight, when she cried, 'Ah, this is wonderful! So clear. No crackling at all.'

She clapped her hands, and laughed out loud. 'But where on earth should I begin? Such a tumble of memories in my mind, like the tinkling beads of coloured glass that you find in a child's kaleidoscope. Which patterns are the prettiest? How to know which random arrangement of shapes might be the best with which to start?'

I thought of the business card I'd found. The magician whose hands had scattered stars. I said, 'Why don't you tell me how you came to meet Charles Beauvois?'

'Beauvois.' She sighed his name, her eyes then flicking to the left and right, stopping when they rested on an ornamental cabinet. 'My cabinet of curiosities. I think *that* is the place to start. A sort of game. A box of tricks. Why don't you open up the doors and see what you can find there?'

I went to stand before it and traced my fingers over all the painted scenes, still bright to see, where nymphs and satyrs danced in woods, with cupids in the clouds above, and at the corner of each door the figure of a snow-white swan. A shame about the mirrors, the glass of which was badly cracked and where my image – hers as well – was horribly distorted, those fractures making it appear as if a hundred Leda Greys were sitting in the room behind.

She said, 'I broke the mirrors, when I dragged the cupboard all the way down here from where I used to sleep.'

'You carried this downstairs, alone?' The cupboard surely weighed a ton.

'I had to. There was such a storm. I wouldn't be at all surprised if we don't get another soon. This awful, humid weather. The heat of a hundred summers! But, that night, it was winter. Very cold. I woke up drenched and shivering to find the ceiling had collapsed... rain dripping down across the bed. Since then I've often climbed the steps that lead me to the attic rooms, looking for gaps where the light comes in, patching them up with plastic bags. Theo brings them from the shops. They really are so useful. I stuff them in, then seal around the edges with some candle wax. It is surprising what will do, if only for a little while.'

She raised one brow and gave a shrug, a gesture that reminded me of Theo in his shop before. 'I saved all sorts of things that night. My clothes. Some paintings on the walls. More trips than I could think to count... and the cabinet put up quite a fight. All those hours of pushing and dragging, until I had the notion of setting a blanket under it, skating it down the run of stairs and cheering as I watched it go. But it crashed into the newel post, and most of the back was sheared away... though you'd never know when the doors are closed. Just a few small cracks and splinters. No harm to all my treasures.'

'Your treasures?'

'Props from Beauvois's films. The ones that meant the most to me.' How mournful Leda sounded then, before her features hardened. 'But why should I let you see them? What possible interest can you have in a dried-out husk of flesh like me?'

'I'm interested in knowing more, about your life, about your films.' Again I found myself confessing things I'd never voiced before. 'My mother... she was mad for films.'

Why was my mother haunting me, so clear to see inside my mind? A tall thin woman. Bleached blonde hair with an inch of black grown at the roots. Her varnished fingernails chipped red. Her face plastered in make-up on those days when she managed to leave the house for our trips to the Hammersmith Gaumont.

God, I felt nostalgic, recalling Sunday matinees, sitting in the balcony and chewing our way through whole boxes of toffees while laughing at the *Carry Ons* – until she'd give my arm a nudge, pointing out the actors who she'd met at parties in her youth, when she'd had a job in the typing pool at the nearby Ealing Studios. *Oh, look... there's Sid... and Jimmy. Jimmy always said that they should get me acting in the films as well. He always said I had the looks.*

On the bus rides home again, she'd sometimes look at me and cry. I remember the way her powder cracked, as if the real skin beneath was breaking up before my eyes. And I'd desperately wanted to hold her together, but didn't know what to do or say when she'd grab my hand in hers and ask, 'Do I look old, Ed? Do I look tired? Can you see these wrinkles when I smile?'

Returning to the present day I realised that Leda Grey was watching me intently, her head tipped slightly to one side when she smiled and wrinkles deepened, though her eyes still shone with such a light when she said, 'I was mad for the films as well. All of those dramatic worlds... so thrilling and exciting. Much more vivid than my real life. Or did I simply hide away from truths I couldn't bear to see?

'I wonder…' Eyes were narrowed. 'Can *you* bear to open up those doors and look inside my cabinet… to see what truths they might expose?'

I sensed some threat in Leda's words. I thought of her brother's warnings. About skeletons in her closets. About opening a can of worms.

I couldn't wait to look inside.

LOOK INTO THE SEEDS OF TIME

'Wait, Mr Peters... wait,' she cried. 'Here, we must let Fate decide. Open the doors just far enough to be able to push your hands inside. The very first thing they touch, bring out.'

I thought about those spooky tricks that people play at Hallowe'en – of a day when I was just a kid, a blindfold wrapped around my eyes, and someone grabbing at my hand and pushing a finger into what had been so vividly described as the gouged out eye of a rotting corpse. In my mind I knew it wasn't real, but I'd screamed enough to wake the dead when I felt the sticky sucking glue, when almost on the brink of tears I'd torn the blindfold from my eyes and saw nothing more sinister than the flesh of half an orange.

Now, in the darkness of White Cliff House, I felt relieved to find my fingers brushing something smooth and dry, while above, in the fractured mirror, Leda Grey strained forward in her chair – like a bookie at a racecourse when they're watching the favourite coming in, about to cross the line and win. A tense excitement, also dread, though the atmosphere did lighten when I turned to show her what I held, when she exhaled a trembling breath, and said, 'Ah... so you have the shell! That's good. The perfect place to start! Come and sit on the sofa over here. Put it down on the table, and let me see, and... Oh!'

Her hands were clasped against her mouth, only lowered when she spoke again. 'Those scratches! How did you get them? Theo had cuts just like that once. When the mirror broke, when...' She looked down at her lap, then back at me. 'Tell me, Mr Peters, when you met my brother in the shop was he... was he wearing women's clothes? I know he sometimes does that. I worry so on his behalf. The gossip. The scandal of it all.'

Her question caught me by surprise, recalling the old man's glossy mouth. Perhaps it had been lipstick. But she visibly relaxed again when I answered, 'No. He wore a suit.' And although I was keen to ask her more, I let the matter rest and said, 'So … what about this prop?'

'We used it in *The Mermaid*. The first film Beauvois made with me.'

Leda Grey reached out and stroked the ridging whorls of a large white sea shell, tracing the frill-edged underside, and then the cleft in which a living creature once existed. And it might have been the way her hand caressed the shell, so tenderly, but the shape, the colour, everything about its form looked sexual. The knobbled protrusion, a clitoris. The frill, the lips of a labia. The rosy tones a deeper red within the hollow curling void …

I was filled with a sense of self-disgust. Leda Grey was more than eighty. I forced myself to concentrate, and asked, 'Can't you tell me something more … about this film, *The Mermaid*? Tell me what inspired it.'

'Me.' Her chin was lifted, face all but shining with the pride. '*I* was the muse for Beauvois's films. Every fantasy he made. Sweet fairy tales. Dark mysteries. None of the slapstick comedy that was so popular back then. He was terribly serious, you see. Quite passionate about his art, and that was very much inspired by the French phantasmagorias.'

'I don't think I've ever heard of them.'

'Elaborate dramatic shows when audiences would be primed into states of high anxiety … feet tingling as they walked across electrified metallic plates when they entered auditoriums. Or being led through graveyards where invisible drums were heard to beat, with rattlings from the tombs around, or eerie twisting moans created by small glass harmonicas. Not that his films used childish tricks. But he did share the general aim. To have an audience believe themselves immersed in spirit worlds. And I … I was immersed in them from the moment he sent this shell to me. This beautiful exotic thing you chose from my cabinet today.

'Won't you put it against your ear, Mr Peters … hear what I

44

heard so long ago? Won't you try and imagine how I felt when I opened the box that Beauvois sent along to our shop in the Brightland Lanes ... how I held it tightly in my hands and stood beside the open door, watching other traders who were starting up their morning's work? All the creakings of the awnings, and bangings of the shutters. All the clangings of the kegs of beer being rolled over cobbles towards the pub's cellar. But that rowdy symphony of life simply faded away to nothingness when I heard the promise of the shell. The hushing suck and wash of waves that ebbed into my consciousness.

'Would you like to see that film?' she asked, suddenly rising from her chair. 'We only need set up a screen and get the lantern working. But, first ... before we sort that out, I should take you to see the studio. The place we always called the shed.'

We'd hardly left the house's porch and already my brow was wet with sweat, eyes narrowing against the glaring of a sun much lower in the sky. Lower, but still not quite set – and hadn't Leda said before that she only left the house at night?

Still, the sunlight suited her. She looked entirely serene with her hair falling loose at her shoulders, and glinting bright with silver lights as it lifted slightly in a breeze. More of a mediaeval queen than an aged recluse of the Sussex coast. And however old she might have been, her springing step was vigorous as her skirts swished through the unmown grass, before she disappeared from view when she turned one corner of the house.

Wondering at her energy, I was distracted for a while by the flapping of the ragged sheet suspended in the trees ahead, before I turned to follow in the trail of flattened grass she'd left. Or had my own feet trodden down that furrow hours earlier? It stopped exactly where I had, at the side of the damaged window where I'd peered through the missing bricks and taken Leda's photograph – for which I felt a stab of guilt. To think I'd spied so brazenly. But I told myself she'd never know, that I could throw that picture out and take some other, better ones. I still had the camera round my neck, its solid weight against my

45

breast. I'd ask if she would pose right then. That is, if I could find her.

I called her name, heard no reply, only the whisper of a breeze that played among the conifers. The shadows formed by all those trees appeared as solid as a wall. But not completely solid. There was a gap between them, that continuous line of tall straight trunks only being an illusion. A second stage of trees stepped back. The gap through which she must have passed to head on down a sloping track before it forked in two again.

At the end I had to make a choice. One way led to a stable block. At least I presumed that's what it was when I saw the wreck of a vintage car. More like a horse-drawn carriage than anything that's built today. A crank at the front to start it up. Brass lamps high on the bonnet top. Running boards on either side, and a roof of cracking leather. It must have been quite something once, but now the paint was rusted, the lamps a dirty tarnished black, and those wheels weren't going anywhere. Not with every spoke so clogged in choking stems of bindweed.

I glanced along the other path, towards the end of which I saw a statue on a pedestal. In places the plaster had fallen off to reveal an inner iron frame, but the shape was more or less intact. It could be a classical deity. A goddess in a sleeping spell, with the distant hushing of the sea providing the music by which she dreamed. And such a similarity to the features of my host as well, especially when Leda Grey had closed her eyes, inclined her head…

The woman made of flesh and blood I saw about ten yards ahead, standing in a field of grass, her back to me while staring at what loomed above the steep cliff edge.

An enormous structure made of glass. What a magical dramatic scene! A picture that I *had* to have, grabbing my camera to set the mechanics and pointing the lens at Leda Grey, whose long black dress, grey hair, pale face already looked as if she'd come to life from a monochrome photograph. As motionless as a photo too. It was only when I'd taken mine and was walking on towards her that she turned around and called to me through

46

the crystal shimmer of the air. 'What do you think about the shed ... where all the wonders were achieved?'

I lifted an arm to shield my eyes, seeing two brick 'houses' at each end, and in between the central frame of wood that formed a chequerboard. Glass squares were white with flashing light. The empty panes much darker.

'Where are the doors? Can we go inside?' Excitement quivered in my voice.

She raised an arm to draw a line. 'There they are. In front of us ... but you'll have to pull the creeper back. I used to cut it down myself, but it grows so fast, and these past years I haven't had the heart or strength. A long time since I've been here.'

I walked on and, once I'd reached the shed, began to drag at stubborn stems, gradually exposing the structure of some folding doors. No longer fixed to any frame, with only weeds supporting them, one of the doors fell inwards, collapsing with a cracking thud. The weight of its impact caused the corpse of a seagull on the floor nearby to shudder, as if it had come to life. But the bird must have been dead for years, bleached bones entirely exposed among the ragged feathers.

Taking a moment to catch my breath, I felt a tickling on my arms where some scratches made by thorns before had now been opened up again. Crawling through thin trails of blood were several tiny beetles that must have been dislodged when I was tearing at the ivy leaves. They made me feel queasy, having to stop to shake them off my head, my arms, even my legs, before I headed on into the cavern of the studio.

The interior was very still, despite the gaping areas left open to the elements. Hardly any breeze at all despite our nearness to the cliff. Only the constant rhythm of the gently crashing waves below. Only the beating of my feet as they crunched on shards of broken glass, and over slabs where weeds had seeded in the crumbling grout between.

This was a place where ghosts might walk, if I'd been inclined to believe in them. I certainly feared becoming one when I heard a sudden wrenching groan, looking up – and just in time

– before quickly leaping to one side with both arms raised above my head, to try and give protection when a single pane of glass slipped free from weathered timbers in the roof. It landed with a violent crash, and barely more than a foot away from where I cowered on the ground, hardly daring to breathe, heart banging, as I opened up my eyes again to see the spiked glass daggers that might well have sliced right through my flesh.

Warily, on hands and knees, I crawled on past and to a space where I felt I might be safer, where all of the ceiling glass was gone, with only splintered warping slats from which the paint-work peeled away in curling wormy ribbons.

Slowly, standing up again, I began to take more photographs. Some parts of the building were well preserved – those brick-built rooms at either end protected from the elements by roof slates perfectly intact. One held rows of metal racks with costumes hanging underneath, or folded on some shelves above. I saw dyed feathers. Long fur throws beside more mundane household things, such as porcelain teacups, tables, chairs. Exotic taxidermy too. A snake. A cobra poised to strike. A tiger. Three small crocodiles. Ferocious-looking reptiles with their jaws held wide and fangs exposed, as if lined up for some attack.

Nearby, a confusion of metal pipes were dangling from metal chains. One held a painted backdrop, and the colours may have faded but I still made out a starry sky, some desert pyramids below – and all created in a style resembling those canvases I'd glimpsed in Theo's Brightland shop.

The opposite brick alcove was protected by some sliding doors, and through an open gap in those I saw all sorts of building tools. Saws and hammers. Planks of wood. That must have been the workroom where the sets had been constructed – such as the central boarded stage now towering in front of me, though I wouldn't try to climb the ladder steps propped up against it. Only a fool would place his weight on wood so full of beetle holes.

Nothing but air and gleaming light between that stage and the vault above, where some of the crossing rafters were still draped with dusty curtains. Old cameras were set on tripods.

Metal tarnished. Lenses cracked. All seemingly beyond repair. Lengths of rubber wires appeared to lead to ancient arc lamps.

So there'd been *some* electricity? Perhaps a generator, from which the wiring must have run. And, was it fanciful of me to think those cables looked like snakes as they wound through yet more broken glass, across the rug where flowering weeds added vibrant reds and pinks to whatever colours had been lost in the washed-out pattern of the weave?

More natural flowers grew around some ornate plaster pillars, before which stood two chairs, or thrones still showing signs of golden paint. Near them, a thing that made me gasp. A sarcophagus. Egyptian style. As fine a looking artefact as anything that might be found in the British Museum in Bloomsbury. And the painted face on the coffin lid could be a Nefertiti, but it also resembled Leda Grey. Leda as she'd been when young.

I couldn't begin to describe it all. The old woman had been entirely right. There were wonders here. Exquisite things. Horrific things as well – such as the swan with its wings held wide, the feathered tips a filthy grey, and the barrel of its torso torn apart into a gaping hole where, in between the softer plumes, the inner stuffing of the beast had been replaced with twigs and leaves. Among the downy fluffings of more feathers scattered on the floor were the cracked blue shells where chicks had hatched from the nest of some much smaller bird.

However disturbing I might have found that cannibalistic imagery, it was all but forgotten when walking on, when I was able to make out what lay behind the wooden stage. There, an old black iron stove reminded me of ones I'd known in all the schoolrooms of my youth. Its venting funnel still rose up, though where it might have once run out, that was impossible to tell. Not with the back of the building gone, with two of the stove's small iron legs no longer settled on a floor, but hanging free, in nothingness, and at such a precarious angle that the slightest nudge might send the whole thing crashing to the sea below.

Was this where Leda's bomb went off? What other objects had been lost?

While wondering that I turned to see that she was now inside the shed, though only a foot or so away from the door that I had broken down. Framed beneath a parasol formed by the gloss of ivy leaves her face took on a greenish shade. She looked alien and luminous, and also full of sadness while she stared a while at the dead gull, before she raised her eyes to mine and called, 'There used to be yards of land between here and the edge of the precipice. In time' – she spread her arms out wide – 'all of this will fall away. Whatever the bomb did not destroy will be claimed by the sea and the rocks below, just like *The Mermaid* set before ... which does seem rather fitting.'

Her lips twitched in a bitter smile. 'But, not the tank. That still survives.' She pointed to a box of glass that I had failed to notice, being fooled by its translucence. But now, looking more carefully, I saw four corners bound in lead. I saw thick rinds of limescale, and the smearing brown of algae that spread across the dull glass walls. Inside, a sludge-green residue, no doubt replenished when it rained, though barely an inch or so just then to hold the needle bones of fish, the shells of crabs, black flies and ants who'd drowned inside the putrid slime.

Not a pretty sight at all, but Leda's face was beaming. 'Can you imagine how it looked when Beauvois filmed his scenes through glass ... with all the water poured inside? It was terribly expensive, but such a mystical effect, whether I swam about inside with my hair left loose and fanning out ... or acted on the other side, when it *looked* as if I'd been submerged in some elusive water world.

'Sometimes ...' Her voice was faltering. 'Sometimes I think I am still there. Still floating in the limbo land of every fantasy he made.'

THE INSTRUMENTS OF
DARKNESS TELL US TRUTHS

The Mermaid was shorter than I had expected. Less than five minutes from start to end, despite it taking more than an hour to erect the screen to view it. And what a gimcrack carry-on, me wobbling precariously while balanced on the sofa's end to fix a sheet to some picture hooks.

The cloth had been rolled and lay beneath the legs of the projector's box, both stored in one dark corner of Leda's cluttered sitting room. I'd looked for them, and then the films, while Leda rested in her chair – instructing me on how to open up the lantern's metal door, then to thread the end of celluloid through what she called the feed reel. From there, while I turned a handle, the film ran through a maze of rolls, that motion also charging up the dynamo that lit a bulb inside a cylinder of glass. A mirror then intensified the beam of brightly shining light through which the pictures came to life.

Too slow, or too fast, and the images flickered, the characters looked unnatural. Either lurching, mindless zombies, or jerky mannequins on speed. But with the right tension, a steady beat, their movements were as smooth as anything that you might see today – though the noise as the handle rattled round! I feared some nuts and bolts were loose, that the whole bloody thing would fall apart. Still, the mechanics seemed to hold, and not even such a racket spoiled the atmosphere in White Cliff House as the film's enchantment took its hold.

I can only really liken it to the European fantasies I'd seen on sixties' kids' TV. *The Singing Ringing Tree* was one, an ominous dark fairy tale where a wicked dwarf had cast a spell to change a prince into a bear; the beautiful princess he'd loved into a drab and ugly witch. The series of *Robinson Crusoe*, too, with hypnotic views of ocean waves that lapped on miles of ridged wet sand, with the opening scene of *The Mermaid* appearing very similar, as the solitary figure of a man walked on an empty beach.

He exuded such an energy. He looked entirely of today. Not his clothes. They certainly belonged to a certain time in history. It was more the way he carried himself, that nonchalance and confidence in a man of some maturity who knows exactly who he is; who believes the world will mould itself around the space where he exists. Strange though, how the air through which he walked appeared to ripple when he came much closer to the camera's lens, when every facial feature was distinct and clearly visible. The hair that blew about his head; some strands turned grey amongst the black. The manic quality in eyes as large and dark as Leda's were, but with threads of tiny broken veins riddled through the whites of them which made him look not only tired, but fierce, and not a little mad. Like a rock star flying high on drugs.

Before that face loomed up on screen Leda had remained quite still, a blank expression in her eyes. But she suddenly leaned forward, the frowning features of her face gilded by the lantern's glow when she murmured with such menace, 'There you are then, Charles Beauvois. You *dare* to come back here again!'

What did she mean by that? For a moment or two I was unnerved, until the question slipped my mind, when Charles Beauvois had disappeared and Leda's mermaid filled the screen, when I couldn't help from blurting out, 'My God ... how beautiful you were!'

She wore a wig of long white curls. A garland made of sea shells. But no mistaking Leda's face, and only the creases of the sheet that rippled through the beams of light to blemish what was perfect flesh. Even then, at my side in White Cliff House, when Leda was so very old, she possessed a fragile elegance that somehow made me feel in awe. But, the breathtaking glamour of her youth. She really was a goddess. Like Botticelli's Venus. In fact, each frame of *The Mermaid* film had the look of a classical painting. That, and the seductive feel of a dreamy art house movie – though the star who shone within its frames refused to acknowledge my compliment. She didn't speak another word until a second man appeared. A man much younger than Beauvois.

'That's Theo!' she said, very matter-of-fact, to which I gave my shocked response, 'That's your brother… from the shop?'

To think that crippled gnomic man could once have been so straight of back, so slight of build, with tousled curls to give a coyly boyish look; especially when viewed against the bearish bulk of Charles Beauvois. There was something almost ethereal in the way that Theo moved and looked. And the silver paleness of his eyes, not glittering like burning coals against the white of flesh around; like those of his sister and Charles Beauvois. Theo's eyes were barely visible in the contrast of the black and white, which made him look more like a ghost than a man of any substance.

How old would the brother and sister have been at the time when Beauvois made that film? The date scrawled on a label that was stuck to the side of the canister had been given as 1913. The same year that Leda mentioned for her first arrival at the house – that was when I'd managed to find the film, after she'd directed me to look in the drawers of a flat-topped desk that almost filled the window bay.

My heart had sunk when searching there, opening each drawer in turn and finding only rubbers, some bits of string, some dark green ink, a silver magnifying glass. There were boxes of ribbons, spares to use with the dinosaur of a typewriter placed on its leathered surface. And something lying next to that. A sheaf of papers neatly bound and knotted with a length of string – the knots that I would soon untie, although my only interest then was in the glints of metal I could see on the floor behind the desk, where several flat round tins were piled beside two stacks of magazines.

Seeing some of those papers gnawed to shreds, while lifting

the cans onto the desk, I asked, 'Leda, have you ever thought about keeping a cat here at the house? Something to kill the vermin? Have you thought of putting poison down?'

'Amy... she used to be our maid. She brought some kittens for me once... a litter from Winstanley's farm. But they soon ran off. They were barn cats, you see, and much too wild for me to tame. Always hissing or scratching if anyone so much as tried to stroke them. To be honest, I'd rather have the rats... though Rex was quick. He'd catch them. He'd shake and break their little necks.'

While blowing cobwebs off the cans, revealing labels underneath, I thought of the dog in Theo's shop. But before I'd had a chance to ask, Leda carried on to say, 'Rex was a dog we used to have. A present when I was a girl.' Her voice took on a wistful note. 'He didn't come here very much.'

By then I'd found *The Mermaid* film, with all my concentration used in trying to unscrew the tin, with the lid of it appearing to have been welded to the base. But finally, brute strength prevailed and I was looking down to see the contents of the canister, where an envelope was lying on the top of a glossy reel of film. Inside the envelope I found a paper, neatly folded. It opened up to show some words typed out and still quite legible, despite the smudges here and there where errors had been rubbed away, where creases in the page had worn. Not exactly what we'd call a script, after all this was a silent film, but meticulous directions around which actions were described.

THE MERMAID
DIRECTED BY CHARLES BEAUVOIS
STARRING CHARLES BEAUVOIS, LEDA GREY,
& THEO WILLIAMS

Waves are breaking on a shore. The scene then blurs to show the illustration of a mermaid who is floating in her grotto. Over this the Title Frames.

SCENE CHANGE. A man is walking on the beach. White cliffs are rising up behind. He is dressed in casual clothing as if he is on a holiday. He wears a straw boater on his head, which he then removes to mop his brow. The day is hot. He is thirsty and tired. He sits to rest upon some rocks where the incoming tide has formed a pool. Leaning forward and dipping his hand in the water, he fishes out a large white shell, peering inside to better look at something that has shocked him.

SCENE CHANGE. The screen is darkened. Through that black an enormous eye appears. It is that of the man who observes the shell.

SCENE CHANGE. We now see what that eye has viewed. A tiny, waving human arm, reaching from inside the shell. A miniature aquatic world. Octopus. Jellyfish. Starfish. Eels. Sea anemones. Et cetera.

SCENE CHANGE. A seaweed curtain parts to show a mermaid on the other side, waving her arms about her in a slow and undulating dance. As the camera draws much closer, she looks directly through the frame at whoever is observing her (the actor, the camera, the audience). Her look is a challenge. Why are they there? But then she smiles and extends a hand, as if in invitation. The smile says, Come, enter the shell. Come inside and share my world.

SCENE CHANGE. A close-up as two hands entwine while underneath the water. One is a woman's. One a man's.

SCENE CHANGE. By some magic the man has been reduced, no larger than the mermaid who now leads him on towards a throne formed from a giant clam shell. There, the two sit side by side as if an ocean king and queen. Meanwhile more ghostly mermaid forms dance through the waves around them.

SCENE CHANGE. The beach again. Another man is searching for his friend. He finds the rock pool where he sees the first man's hat, still floating there. He fishes it out and looks confused, before he carries it away, retracing his path along the sand.

SCENE CHANGE. The film ends with a close-up of the trails of footprints in the sand. The camera slowly pans away.

When the film had reached its final frame, when my aching wrist could stop its constant turning of the handle, Leda Grey looked up and asked, 'What did you think about the film? You can be as honest as you like. I don't want to hear false flattery.'

Wiping a hand across my brow, I was feeling slightly feverish, sweating very heavily from the heat of the projector's lamp while I told her that I'd been amazed at the cinematographer's vision, with the acting style so natural that it could have been a real-life scene – *if* creatures such a mermaids ever existed in the real world.

So many questions were in my mind. 'How did Beauvois film those sliding shots? Was the camera set on wheels? And the scenes filmed through the water tank. They really were remarkable. The double exposures. The ...'

I didn't go on to mention the simmering sexual tension between Leda Grey and Charles Beauvois, which made her brother's acting role no more than an irrelevance. And when Leda seemed to lapse into a dreamy sort of reverie, I left the projector on its stand to sit beside my tape machine, hoping it had carried on recording everything we'd said, and only then discovering the batteries completely drained.

I hadn't brought replacements. There wasn't usually a need, not with the cables that I had to plug into electrical sockets. But there were no sockets in that house, and I felt such a sense of sharp dismay – only for that to be eclipsed by the sudden stifled sob I heard.

I had no idea what to do or say, how to offer any comfort when I looked up to see that Leda's face was hidden in her hands. She stayed like that for quite some time, until she raised her head again, blinking back a veil of tears through which she gazed at me and said, 'I really didn't realise how much it would affect me … reliving all these memories from the time when we were happiest. When the future promised everything.'

Her face had turned as pale as death. Her breathing was too laboured. And something else I noticed then. Above black eyes that glittered in the candle's quaking yellow glow, the brows that grew above them looked as thick and dark as in her youth – when I would swear that earlier, before we'd come to view the film, they'd been quite sparse, as colourless as the hair that grew upon her head.

I needed to pay more attention. I needed to find some water too. To wash my sweating hands and face, to quench the raging thirst I felt. But before I could ask where the kitchen was, Leda began to speak again.

'You know … all the time, while we watched that film, I was thinking how docile the mermaid was. No more than a sexualised ideal. No part to play in the world of men.'

'I thought she held all the power,' I said. 'Tempting the man from the land of air, to join the mermaid's water world … though he looked pretty happy about his fate.'

'But what about the other man? Left alone on the beach, at the very end? Ah … there are truths in Beauvois's films, and I see them far more clearly now than I ever did when we were young. Or perhaps I only closed my eyes to the things I didn't want to see … never wanting the filming to reach its end, quite bereft when it was over … when I went back home to my Brightland bed and sobbed and sobbed for hours on end. You see, I knew *my* fate was sealed. It wasn't the mermaid who'd captured the man. It was Charles Beauvois who'd captured me. With every turn of the camera's crank, with each exposure of the lens, he'd drawn me in a little more. And now …' She slowly shook her head. 'I am still trapped, his prisoner. Just like the mermaid in her shell.'

'Should I go?' I asked, hearing the grief and sheer exhaustion in her voice. 'I must have been in the house for hours. Perhaps, if you'll agree, I could come back again tomorrow?'

'Tomorrow ... and tomorrow ... and tomorrow ...' She gave the bleakest, saddest smile. 'But yes, perhaps I need to sleep. The sweet oblivion of sleep. The death of each day's life ...'

Those echoes from the play, *Macbeth*. A desperate pleading in her voice when she said, 'Or you could stay a while. You're really more than welcome, and ...'

She cast her eyes around the room, fixing on the desk again. 'You asked to know about my past. Why not read my *Mirrors*? Years ago, I wrote them down. The memories I still recalled before they all began to blur and muddle up inside my head.'

Before I could answer she'd closed her eyes, chin resting on her sagging breast, and looking much as she had done when I'd first seen her through the wall. She gave a little shiver. Surely Leda wasn't cold? But, remembering the blanket beneath which she had slept before, I lifted that up from the floor and gently laid it on her lap.

After that, I really wasn't sure whether to stay or go away. What time was it now? Nine? Ten? Unconsciously, I raised my eyes to the hands of the clock on the mantelpiece. Still stopped at exactly ten to twelve, its cogs as silent as the dead.

At the broken wall, no light shone in and the void of black on the other side seemed to blur and spread before my eyes. I was much too hot. Too thirsty. Could I reach the pub before it closed – or drink the lemonade I'd bought when I'd been in there earlier?

My choice was made. I found a can, gulping tepid sweetness down and barely even noticing the rank metallic aftertaste when I reached across where Leda slept to lift the tall brass candlestick.

An inch or so of stub still burned to spread some light across the desk where, once I'd set it down, the flame grew long and danced erratically in a draught that gusted through the hole.

I liked that breeze. I liked the way its fingers ruffled through my hair when I'd settled in a leather chair before the big black typewriter. On one side of it were the canisters containing all of

Beauvois's films. On the other, the stack of papers, bound and knotted in some string.

Reaching into my jeans for my cigarettes, I placed the packet on the desk, then lit one in the candle's flame. A taste of ash and honey. A stinging prickle in my eyes. The veil of smoke through which I strained to see while fingers worked the string, as the sheets of yellowed papers were released and I began to read...

The Mirrors of Leda Grey

My brother visited today. He said it was September. He said it was 1948. But how can that be possible? Is it true that almost forty years have passed since I first came here?

And yet, the years are there to see whenever I look at Theo's face. The blue of his eyes is fading. His lovely golden curls are grey. And what does he think when he looks at me? My hair, once black, now streaked with white. The skin of my face so wrinkled. The skull beneath too prominent.

In that face I see my future, the bones remaining when I'm dead. And when that happens who will ever think of Leda Grey again? If they do, what will they say of her?

This is why I must write about the past, which is all I have to cling to as I sit in the gloom of White Cliff House. But still, sometimes, I close my eyes, and all this darkness disappears, and I see a gleaming prism, each facet with a diamond light, each light with its own tale to tell.

Look ~ here ~ this one, where the morning sun is streaming through the domed glass light in the roof of my father's studio. And here, the sound of my father's voice as he calls through a crack in his darkroom door . . .

'What do you think of this, Leda? I was reading just the other day that there are some primitive peoples who live in other parts of the world, who genuinely believe it true that a camera can steal a human soul.'

My father was developing that morning's set of photographs, for which he'd had me posing in one of those old costumes that he often hired from the Theatre Royal ~ which was something he did from time to time when creating his own 'artistic' works, instead of the everyday portraits, when the everyday customers paid to come and sit inside his studio.

I was standing behind the Chinese screen, set up as a sort of changing room, where I'd spent a good half hour or so in rubbing away the thick black paint that he had dabbed around my eyes. To give me a foreign exotic look. And what a struggle it had been to free the tangles of my hair from the crown that I'd been wearing! My head still ached from the weight of it, being made of twisted metal, and attached to that were leaves and snakes.

Oh, those snakes! I thought them hideous! Not that I minded the least little bit about dressing up in fancy clothes. I would happily do that all the time. When I think back to Beauvois's films ...

But when I saw that headdress, well, it took some degree of persuasion for Papa to convince me to put it on, his exasperation clear to see when he raised his hands and pushed them back through the thick grey mane above his brow, which, although he was over seventy (he'd been much older than Mama when they first met and fell in love), still held some darker streaks of black to show the glory of his youth.

'As black as the devil's, and three times as handsome. As black as yours is now, Leda.' That's what my mother used to say, when she stroked her fingers through my hair.

That's one of the things I remember. I only wish there could be more.

But, anyway, that darkness, what Papa called my 'gypsy looks', that's why he had imagined me in the guise of an Egyptian queen, when he held the crown for me to see, and I could only stare and ask, 'What on earth is it supposed to be?'

'It's very dramatic, don't you think? It was used in a play some years ago.'

'What play was that?'

'The Unlucky Mummy. Supposedly based on true events from back in the 1880s, when three Englishmen travelled to Egypt, where a terrible fate befell them all after one of the party paid thousands of pounds to possess the mummified remains of an ancient queen who had once served in the temple of Amen-Ra.'

Papa then told me how that man walked off into the desert night and was never seen alive again; and that event occurring soon after the priestess's sarcophagus had been delivered to his rooms. The second man was to lose an arm when a servant asked to clean his gun had accidentally fired it off. The third returned to England to find himself entirely ruined when the bank in which his wealth was held had catastrophically failed, after which he was reduced to selling matches on the streets to live.

And that was not the end of it! Some years later, the mummy had been acquired by the British Museum in London where the night guards started speaking of some strange and ghostly happenings, with objects flying round the room, with banging sounds and wailings rising up from beneath the coffin's lid. A journalist who came along to investigate the strange events was then tormented in his mind by a photograph he'd taken that showed the casket's painted face ~ a face normally quite serene ~ as having changed into a mask of such a Hellish countenance that he'd lost his wits and killed himself.

'Is the mummy still there, still on display, still in the British Museum? Does that picture still exist today, or has the evil been destroyed? And what do you think could have happened to the man who disappeared that night... who walked into the desert and was never seen alive again?'

My father had no answer when I questioned him about those things, but to think of them, it frightened me, as did the thought that I should pose as if this cursed queen.

'Papa!' I'm sure I stamped my feet while staring down in dis-belief at the basket where the crown still lay. 'Those are snakes! Real snakes! Stuffed snakes! Only a witch would think to place such a contraption on her head. What's more, some scales have fallen off. And the smell. Can't you smell it? Like rotting fish! How can you bear it? I feel sick!'

'Not a witch, Leda. An exotic queen.' My father gave a weary smile. Oh, such a lovely smile he had! Such warm expressive dark brown eyes, although it was embarrassing, the way some female customers might simper in the studio, or if we met them in the street when he would stop to tip his hat, and his voice so deep and musical; not strained as it was with me that day. 'Leda, you are too fanciful!

63

The smell really isn't as bad as that. Surely you can hold your breath? If I open the window, will that help? It's only for a little while, before my customers arrive. I really think this portrait could be something quite exceptional, if you'll simply agree to get on with it!'

His portraits were often exceptional. The attention he paid to detail. And when his magic had been worked on the photographs of me that day then the best would be mailed to London, to the Royal Photographic Society, whose theme for that year's summer show was 'The English and the Exotic'. What's more, Papa had promised me that if our picture won a prize then I should go along with him to the private view in Russell Square ~ though I hardly even dared to hope that such a day would ever come. To travel to London. To go to a party. To see, and to be seen in turn. My portrait hanging on the wall!

Ah, my foolish, foolish pride. But what was I thinking of before? Ah yes. London. The Society. My father had been a member for years, since he first took a shop in Kensington, where his talents were in such demand that once the 'divine' Ellen Terry spent hours in his studio, posing in a costume that she'd worn for the part of Lady Macbeth.

Macbeth. Another warning of a future I was yet to see. Back then, I only thought about that gown, how glorious it was. It had thousands of jewel beetle wings, and my father somehow made them gleam, achieving such a lustre in all the swimming greens and blues when he had tinted up the prints. A thousand times I'd stood and stared at a copy that he kept displayed behind the counter in our shop. A thousand times I'd wished that I could also pose in such a gown. To become a romantic Arthurian legend, not some demon gorgon casting spells.

But every objection was set aside and the crown of snakes set on my head for, apart from all my other hopes, I never could resist the lure ~ that frisson of electricity that buzzed in the air of the studio whenever I posed there for Papa. And then, to see those photographs, and the way they looked like paintings, and yet more real than paintings. The way my eyes were filled with light. The way I looked much older. More confident. More beautiful than I ever really was.

But not so very beautiful when the headdress was removed again. Those blackened smudges round my eyes, they made me look exhausted, as if I hadn't slept in months. And was it too contrary of me to stare into the mirror then and feel myself diminished, to see not a witch but a plain-faced girl, a girl so scrawny she was all but drowned in the summer dress she wore?

I used to call it my Happiness dress. My father brought it home for me from one of his London business trips. But with no idea about my size he'd had to guess, and guessed quite wrong. I feared I would never grow into it. But neither could I bear to wait; to hang that lovely white behind the darkness of my closet doors. So I wore it, regardless of the fit, and whatever I happened to be about, whether paddling in the rock pools, searching for starfish, shells and crabs, or racing on my bicycle, all the way from Black Rock to the Brightland pier. Little wonder that it soon became the shabbiest of specimens. No surprise that Mrs Cadwallader, the housekeeper Papa employed, would drag me to his side and ask, 'Mr Williams, do you think it right for this girl to roam the town alone, and always hopping off from school? Last week I caught her on the pier, holding her hat out and singing for pennies. Dancing she was, with her hems so high, that . . . well, you could almost see her drawers! What will it be next, I ask myself? A turn as a London Gaiety Girl?'

A Gaiety Girl? In London? I wasn't sure what that entailed but I thought it sounded wonderful. And Papa never minded if my dress was worn away to rags, only that I loved it so ~ and the way that I could drag it on, pulling it down across my head without ever having to undo the buttons, which saved a great deal of precious time when I needed to rush, as I had that day, when I'd snatched up yesterday's stockings and boots, and not even a thought to brush my hair. But then, it had been early, the house still draped in night-time gloom, and me still dozy, half asleep when Papa tapped my bedroom door. Because we were going to the Lanes. To catch the lovely rosy light of dawn inside his studio.

And there, but an hour later, while I saw a glow of red leak out through the crack in Papa's darkroom door ~ while I closed up the lid of the basket with all the vile stuffed snakes inside, and swore

65

I'd never ever put that crown upon my head again ~ I suddenly felt moved to ask, 'Papa... do people really think that a camera can steal a human soul? How strange that anyone believes such silly superstitious things.'

Another mirror shining now, but still that same blue summer's day when I'd left the shop to make my way back home along the prom- enade ~ and heard my brother call my name.

At first I couldn't see him. Only a man in a tall top hat, and some ladies walking at his side, and one of those ladies very nearly smacking me full in the face with her brolly. Twirling it round like a baton she was. I had to duck down to avoid it, and only when righting myself again did I catch the glint of sunlight as it caught in Theo's golden hair.

Whereas I was dark, just like Papa, Theo was all our mother's child. Not as glamorous as she had been, but he had a certain cupid charm. The honeypot around which all the local girls would come and buzz ~ for all the notice that he took! My brother might be in another world.

And what world was he in that morning, walking the dog along the front, when he should be heading for the shop, where Theo always helped Papa before heading off to study at the art school in the after- noons? And why was he tossing his cap in the air like a creature gone demented, running behind a horse and cab where a man was standing in the back? A man behind a camera. And there, on the side of the vehicle, was a poster with the words that read ~

Visit The Brightland Pier Theatre At Six O'clock Tomorrow Night Only 3d To View Yourself In The Finest Cinematographic Works

Directed By Monsieur Charles Beauvois
Sponsored By The Edison Film Company

Who was this Monsieur Charles Beauvois? I'd never heard the name before, though there was quite an industry in town when it came to the business of kinema. Papa was well acquainted with a few of the local directors, and we often went to see their shows at the Theatre Royal, or on the pier, even in the aquarium. There was always something on the bill to satisfy each one of us, with news reports, and travelogues, or what we called the 'actuals' ~ those scenes of normal daily life, when normal people swarmed in droves to see themselves appear on screen. It was like being caught in a time machine. It was like a living miracle. Oh, such an age of wonders!

But, for me, the greatest wonders were the films we knew as 'narratives', with proper actors playing parts in rip-roaring adventures, or comedies, with motorised cars and aeroplanes, or rockets that flew to the moon and back, with skeletons that came to life, or people so reduced in size they might be Lilliputians.

Papa would sometimes spoil things by telling Theo and myself how those effects had been achieved, and very often based upon the smoke-and-mirror tricks performed by stage magicians in their acts. Or else the methods first contrived by charlatan Victorians who cruelly tricked all those who thought their loved ones' souls could reappear as spirits in the photographs. It was double exposure, nothing more. He showed me how to do it once, when he stood me in front of a black velvet hanging, then re-exposed the film again while I was posing differently, when my previous image then appeared like a will-o'-the-wisp within the frame.

But, even knowing how it worked, so often I would see my 'ghost' and wish it could have been Mama's. How strange that in our times of grief, we try to see what isn't real, when the hopes and dreams we cling to are no more than scraps of fantasy.

As a child, I was desperate to believe in the moving fantasies on screens, and very often when in bed I'd dream of new scenarios in which the grown-up Leda Grey might one day have a starring role; though when I told my father he would answer in his sternest voice, 'We'll simply have to wait and see. Who knows what the future has to hold.'

'But, Papa,' I pleaded, many times, 'why don't you make some films yourself? Theo and I could act in them. What about that one we saw where a baby's kidnapped by a thief and the family dog then tracks it down. Didn't the director's wife and child appear in the starring roles? Wasn't that their own pet dog? I'm sure that we could train Rex up and—'

'My darling Leda, are you mad? I've never known a dog to be as disobedient as ours is. He won't even sit when he's told to! And Theo has no desire to act, though he does have other useful skills, but...' Papa was so very dour, 'these "movies" require a great deal of investment. Investment of money. Equipment. Time. Sadly, the shop is nowhere near as profitable as it used to be. Not since any amateur on the street can buy a box to take his snaps. Perhaps, when you are older, if our circumstances have improved. If so, my brave and lovely girl shall follow all her childhood dreams. If her heart hasn't set on something else.'

But my heart was not a fickle thing, and that day, when I stood on the promenade, while I read that poster on the cab ~ those words ~ oh, how they raised my hopes! To think that I might chance to see myself lit large upon a screen. Even so, when Charles Beauvois had turned his camera's eye on me I was overcome by a sense of nerves, such as I'd never known before. A terrible, terrible fear it was. I hardly knew what best to do to stop the trembling in my hands when I walked towards my brother's side, and then stooped down and lifted Rex, to hold him tightly to my breast, to feel that solid living warmth while I tried to calm myself again with thoughts of Papa's studio, where nothing existed but myself and the camera into which I stared ~ though perhaps I should have listened more to the drum of caution in my heart, because, that beat, it formed the words of Papa's recent prophecy.

A camera can steal a human soul.

My soul had been stolen. Or was it cursed? I only know, from that day on, my fate would be forever bound to the man who'd filmed the promenade. Who didn't even know my name.

My name ~ the name of Leda Grey ~ that was a gift my father gave. Our family name was Williams. But Grey, it fitted very well.

Before that time I see my life as only colourful and bright, like the scorching pinks and velvet reds of the roses that my mother picked from our Brunswick Crescent garden, some pinned around her big straw hat, the rest of them then woven as a birthday crown for me to wear while Papa took the photographs to mark my seventh birthday.

When I saw those pictures afterwards ~ Mama with roses on her hat ~ me with roses on my head ~ I cried, 'Papa, how can it be? Why have you made our pictures grey? Why didn't you paint our colours in, like you did with Ellen Terry's?'

'My dearest little Leda Grey.' Papa was kneeling at my side, holding me tightly in his arms, so tight that I can still recall the way his heart was thudding, and the leathery smell of his cologne, and the catch in his voice when he spoke again. 'My lovely Leda always shines. What colours can compare to that? I would only be gilding the lily flower.'

Ah, my darling father. Always thinking me a precious thing. But the day of my seventh birthday, that was also the day my mother died. And I feel such burning stabs of pain whenever I recall what happened after Papa's photographs. How I'd seen my brother's smiling face through the swirling glass of the shop's front door, and how, when the door was opened up, Theo held a ribbon out, and on the other end of that was a tiny ball of shaggy black.

How I'd squealed with delight, but the ribbon slipped right through my hand. The puppy scampered down the Lane with Theo giving chase behind, and me then running after him ~ not even looking left or right as we dashed our way across the road and reached the other side with neither coming to the slightest harm. But, my mother ~ I heard her screaming. A grinding of brakes, a man's loud shout. I felt the shock of rushing air when a stranger scooped me in his arms. I heard that stranger ask my name but I had no words to answer him. I couldn't speak a single word. I couldn't drag my eyes away from where my mother lay just then. The golden ring upon her hand. The diamonds all around that band sparkling with rainbow lights, while the light in Mama's pale blue eyes was dulling, dulling into grey.

That was the picture in my mind when I saw the portraits Papa made. And yes, I suppose that he was right. There was a shining quality, a glistening within my eyes as if with sorrow for Mama, which made it seem as if the past and future had been jumbled up. Because, while we'd been posing my mother had still been alive.

She'd been trying to distract me while I was squirming on the chaise, moaning about the roses being much too itchy on my head. She'd been searching about inside her bag to try and find my favourite book. The Tale of Samuel Whiskers. The one where Tom Kitten gets trapped in the attic and rolled around with pastry, when the rats plan to bake him in a pie.

'Roly-poly, roly: roly, poly, roly.' I chanted those words and laughed so much that my eyes were filling up with tears, and Mama sighed, 'Oh, Leda . . . enough of all this silliness! Your father has more clients soon. Please think of something serious, for two or three minutes at the most? And, if you can manage that, my sweet' ~ she was teasing me with promises ~ 'then Papa will be a happy man, and you will be a happy girl, because Theo is waiting just outside. And Theo has your birthday gift.'

'My birthday gift?' I couldn't wait. So I made the greatest effort to imagine something serious. I thought about the gull I'd seen, down on the beach the day before, when I'd been paddling in the waves, and Theo had been throwing stones, and one of the stones had hit the bird ~ and oh, I'd thought my heart would break when I saw it falling to the sand, and heard such lonely piercing cries from all its other friends above. But the dead one was too silent, and only the breeze upon the shore to ripple through its feathers. Feathers made of grey and white. Grey like the stones on which it lay. White like the frothing of the waves.

The lace of my mother's petticoats had turned from white to a wet dark red, as red as the flowers on her hat now crushed beneath a horse's hooves. The sweat on the horse's flanks had dripped to puddles made of frothing foam.

Many weeks have passed since I last wrote. Now, sitting at this desk again, I shiver in a bitter draught that blows through the damaged window frame. I should find some rags to stuff inside. But since they nailed the shutters up it gives me hope when I can't sleep, when I see the moonlight shafting through.

I hate the nights in White Cliff House, always filled with the scratching of the rats, or the distant hushing of the waves. In. Out. In. Out. Those waves seem to echo my every breath, ebbing and flowing with my thoughts. All my old woman remembering.

I remember when I was a child, in the months after my mother died when the darkness of the night-time house always seemed to be too empty, the air inside so thick with grief you could almost reach out with your fingers and touch it.

In my mind, my sorrow was a beast with an oily pelt of thick black hair, with bloodied fangs and tearing claws. Sometimes I'd wake to see it, only inches from my pillow, and then I'd have to leave my bed to creep along the passageway, my palms pressed tight against my ears because I couldn't bear to hear the sobbing from my brother's room.

Theo was twelve years old then, but he wept as if a baby, and the weight of that sadness, it cracked my heart as I tiptoed past his bedroom door, then made my way down unlit stairs, across the hall towards the room where a golden light was shining in ~ where the street lamp just outside the house would cast a gleam to guide my path. It would shine across the mirror where, and not so very long ago, I used to sit in daylight hours and play at mixing magic spells with Mama's powders, scents and creams. And there she'd be, behind me, to brush the knots out of my hair, 'A hundred times to make it shine.'

I wished and wished that she'd appear within that mirror's blackened glass. I looked for her in shadows that were draped around the big brass bed, from where her arms had once reached down to draw me into spooning flesh, when I'd snuggle underneath warm sheets, and close my eyes, and drift away. The smell of roses in my nose.

That room still smelled of roses, long long after she'd gone away. My father still slept in the same big bed. But I never heard or saw him cry. My father's grief was silent, spilling underneath the sheets and trickling towards me, where it pooled in shadows at his door. It kept me out. It screamed of shame. To think that I had been the cause...

Why do I think of my mother now? So many years have passed since then. I can hardly think it possible that somewhere in this ageing flesh a little girl once used to live. I try and imagine how it felt to bear the burden of such guilt, when my father would have been appalled if he'd known about my suffering. And yet, I think he must have known about my night-time wanderings. I think that's why he finally allowed the dog upstairs as well, when Rex ~ Papa had named him Rex, when he said the pup should wear a crown, the way we always spoiled him so ~ when Rex began to share our beds, snoring, twitching, whimpering in the fevers of his doggy dreams. And if I woke, and if the dog was not asleep on Theo's bed, then he would follow as I paced around my bed for hours on end, where I'd sometimes hear the faintest noise. A squeaking underneath the rug.

At first, I used to think it was a rat come down from the attic floor, wanting to steal the dog away ~ and how brave Rex was to growl and scratch, to try and dig the creature out. But there were no rats in our Brightland house, and when I looked beneath the rug I found only a loosened board where the nails had worked free from the wooden joists, and under that the space that soon became my secret hiding place. In which I kept my treasured things.

I started with a photograph. One from my seventh birthday. I stole it from the studio when I saw it drying on the line. There were so many more of them. Papa would never notice. So, while he was busy in the front, talking with a customer, I found a chair and stood on that, stretching with my fingertips until they clutched the precious print. And later, when we went back home, when I was in my room again, caged in by all the floral wreaths that circled round green-papered walls, I stared at Mama in her hat with all the lovely roses. Me, at her side, in the floral crown, with long black ringlets hanging down. Two heads. Two pairs of shining eyes.

Other things kept underneath my floor ~ I am trying to remember now. A bottle of Mama's perfume. One of her shawls. One of her shoes. Some stones and feathers from the beach. A little bird that Theo carved from a piece of driftwood that he'd found. The words 'I AM' scratched on one wing. 'SORRY' on the other one.

And then, there was the letter. The letter and the reel of film, though they arrived much later on.

I was a girl of fourteen years when a package was posted through the box of our shop down in the Brightland Lanes, which is where it stayed for several days, until I came to find it.

Inside there was a reel of film. A copy of Brightland Promenade, which Theo, Papa and myself had been to see the week before.

Oh, what a thrilling visit! Sitting in the darkness while the glow from the projector's lamp shone through the theatre on the pier. And Rex was there, on Theo's lap, because whatever Papa said, the dog was all grown up by then and sometimes even well behaved, especially when bribed with sweets. Theo and I were giggling at the way he dribbled, slathered, chewed, and how his tongue kept slurping out while sucking toffees from his teeth. But such high spirits were soon lost when Theo touched my arm and warned, 'Leda, you won't be too upset if they don't show our film tonight? It's just that the stage's menu card says nothing of the promenade.'

I felt such panic rise inside when I also read that menu card, where every feature mentioned was to be an actual of the town, with titles like A Cliff Top Walk, or A Visit to the Aquarium. But Theo was right. There was no sign of any Brightland Promenade.

Taking my brother's hand in mine, I squeezed it hard, and harder still as every moving film was played, and even though each one was short, two or three minutes at the most, for me they seemed to last an age. The lantern's rattle was too loud. The piano's notes were jangling. The sneezes, and the hacking coughs. The peanut shells that two old ladies crunched and cracked in seats behind. All that noise! My fraying nerves. I couldn't begin to enjoy the show ~ until the last film flickered up. The slightest judder of the frame, and then four curling corner scrolls around the fancy title script: A VIEW OF BRIGHTLAND PROMENADE!

Too soon we saw the words, THE END, and while my brother clapped and whooped I couldn't move a single inch. I was feeling quite delirious, shivering with excitement, thinking my heart might burst with pride when Papa smiled and gave a sigh, and then his murmur in my ear. 'Well, I may be biased, but whoever this Beauvois chap might be, he certainly does have a gift. The very best was saved till last. My daughter was magnificent!'

'Oh, Papa? Was I really?' It had all been over in a flash. I only wished the frames could roll right back and then run through again, for people in the seats around to look at me and realise that I had been the girl in white whose face filled up the final frames.

But would they know me anyway? They'd see a girl who'd spent all afternoon in brushing out her hair, a hundred times to make it shine, and nothing like the frizzy mess when she'd been on the promenade. They wouldn't see the waif and stray dressed in her shabby muslin dress for, very much to my dismay, Mrs C had gone and laundered it. It was dripping on the garden line, and I'd been forced to wear my green. The one she liked to see me in, always saying it suited my colouring. But what an irony it was that whereas my white was much too large, the green had shrunk when in the wash. The hem too short, the bodice tight... so tight that I could barely breathe when the final curtain fell again, when we sat there waiting patiently for the director to appear, to bow and give a little speech, as was the usual way of things. But no. There was no sign at all of the man who, just the day before, had stood behind his camera in the back of the open horse-drawn cab.

The theatre's lights blazed up to leave me standing in a giddy daze while we shuffled through the narrow aisle that led towards the exit doors, though before we left the foyer to walk back down the pier again, Papa approached the manager (that gentleman well known to him through shared professional ventures, with my father photographing acts for the hall's publicity and such), and said, after some other chat, 'If you happen to see Monsieur Beauvois won't you tell him I would be so pleased if he'd visit my studio in the Lanes... or if he'd like to come along and dine in Brunswick Crescent. I would also be obliged if you could ask if there might be a chance to purchase a copy of his film. The one of Brightland Promenade.'

That night I could not sleep a wink, so excited I was at the prospect of possibly meeting Charles Beauvois, should he happen to do as my father suggested and call at the shop, or else the house. I imagined the most elaborate dinner. Iced platters with lobsters, oysters, prawns. Roast mutton with capers and anchovies, or the chicken and pineapple brochettes that Mrs C could do so well. There'd be passion fruit sorbets and almond creams. There'd be jellies made from real champagne. And I would be wearing my Happiness, and I would tell Monsieur Beauvois of how one day I hoped to be an actress in the moving films.

But such a night was not to be. All the shivering and nerves I'd felt when in the theatre on the pier, that boded something more severe than simply my excitement.

The next day I fell ill with a fever. So did Theo, and Papa. A summer flu that caused our very bones to ache, our throats to burn, and our lungs to fill with choking phlegm. For days, the name of Charles Beauvois did not so much as cross my mind. I could barely think to lift my head from the sweat-drenched pillow underneath while I sipped at cups of hot beef tea that Mrs C insisted were 'a cure for every ailment that might be sent to test mankind ... soon to have you up and out again.'

There may have been something in her brew, because before the week was up my health was quite restored again, though I didn't fancy going out. The weather had turned much colder. Such bitter winds and squally storms, and with only Rex for company I was very pleased one afternoon when Theo left his bed at last to join me in the drawing room, when he found a deck of cards and asked to play a round of whist.

It wasn't a very successful game. He had to keep stopping to blow his nose. He kept complaining wheezily, 'I wish this bloody grippe would shift. I feel so fuddled in my head. Do you think you could close those curtains? The light's too bright. It hurts my eyes. Could you go downstairs ... ask Mrs C to bring us up a pot of char? And see if she's been to the pharmacy, to buy that linctus that I like?'

'What did your last slavey die of? Shall we call in Florence Nightingale, and...'

I didn't go on. He looked so strange. The way his eyes bored into mine. How the rheumy bloodshot blue of them seemed to stare, but not to see at all. Even Rex sensed something wrong, beginning to growl deep in his throat when Theo's head jerked back like that, with every playing card he'd held thrown up and flying through the air. It was like seeing someone possessed by a devil, his body shaking violently, and his eyes rolled back into his head. Thank goodness Mrs C was there to hear the thumping of his feet while she worked in the kitchen down below, her own then rushing up the stairs to find out what was going on.

Panting in the doorway, her puffs of grizzled bouffant hair were trembling as she shook her head, though she soon recovered her senses, shouting for me to stay and watch while she went off to find her coat, then ran to fetch the doctor. But what was I supposed to do, short of trying to silence little Rex, who now began to howl and whine, so plaintively, so desperately, the whole street must have heard him?

Papa certainly heard him, dragging himself from his sick bed, still fastening his dressing gown while rushing in to kneel down among the mess of playing cards, shaking Theo by the arms to try and wake him up again.

My brother now lay still and pale, but at least he looked to be at peace... not like Papa, his breaths so strained, his skin a waxy yellow hue, and the spittle running from his mouth as he tried to speak, but couldn't. The words all slurred and jumbled up.

I was panicking quite desperately when Mrs C came back again, and the doctor shortly after that – when he calmly opened up his bag to fill a syringe with something clear from a small glass vial that he'd uncorked. It could have been water for all I knew, but when it was stuck in Theo's arm my brother revived dramatically, after which Mrs C then gave a hand with leading him back to his bed ~ and there he slept for three whole days. And thankfully, despite the fact that the doctor had warned of side effects, of some possible damage to the brain after a lack of oxygen, when Theo woke he showed no sign of any ill effects at all. One morning he got up and dressed, came down to the *kitchen ravenous, demanding toast and scrambled eggs. Although, that was a little strange, when he'd always hated eggs before.*

And there were other changes too.

Much later on the doctor said he thought my brother's episodes all stemmed from that initial fit, when now and then Theo would slip into a sort of staring trance and speak about the coloured lights that he could see round people's heads. He said each shine was different, some dim and only inches wide, while others were great glowing hoops, sparking out like fireworks. He said he felt quite faint with joy to see the whirling halos round the heads of little children. But whenever he 'saw' such energies his own would be depleted. He would suffer from terrible headaches and stay in his room for days on end, no lamps or candles being lit, the curtains firmly drawn across. He said the darkness healed his soul.

My light? I didn't ask, not then ~ though he has told me of it since. At the time, my thoughts were only filled with worrying about Papa who never would be well again. The strain of the influenza combined with the shock of Theo's fit had caused a seizure of the brain.

The next few days seemed endless. No balm of night to heal my soul when I sat for hours by Papa's bed and held his hand and sometimes sang. When Mrs C came in by day she'd take my place and read to him from newspapers, or books he liked, or the Bible that she liked herself. When he slept she'd fish her knitting out, the needles click-click-clicking, almost sounding like a metronome, like the seconds counting down as ticking hands moved slowly round a clock. But counting down to what?

I soon found out ~ that night when Theo said that he felt well enough to take my place by Papa's side. I was so very weary, hardly able to drag my feet upstairs, lying down on my covers fully dressed, and already drifting into sleep when I heard my brother shout my name ~ when I rushed back down the stairs to stand beside my father's big brass bed, to stare into my father's face, where every twisted muscle that had been contorted by the stroke had suddenly relaxed again.

My father looked as dignified and handsome as he'd ever done. It was a lovely thing to see. But then it also broke my heart because I knew just what it meant. I'm sure that Theo did as well.

Staring up at me, he said, 'Leda, it is very strange, but I see a light around his head. It was brown before, but now it's blue. Like the blue of the sky. Like an azure sea. A blue with flecks of purest gold.'

Those words, I thought it must be shock, bringing on delusions. But now ~ I hope ~ I like to think my brother really has a gift, that Theo truly saw a sign to prove that Papa's soul lived on.

The next day the undertakers came and Theo stayed to deal with them while I took my father's keys and let myself into the shop again. I placed a notice in the door, saying the business had been closed due to a bereavement. I sat on the stool at the counter and worked through all the mail that had collected underneath the door, which included a letter that had come from the Royal Photographic Society, expressing disappointment that Papa had sent no work that year and had therefore missed the deadline for the annual exhibition.

I could hardly bear the thought of that. A terrible rage thrummed through my blood, screwing that letter in my hands and throwing it across the shop, thinking I'd worn that crown of snakes, and the photograph had never even left my father's studio. Worse still, it was the very last that he would ever take of me.

I wept, how long I do not know. But there was one glimpse of joy that day. One package that I opened up when I had dried my eyes again, it held a leather canister and, seeing that, I guessed at once what must have been contained inside, that the theatre manager had passed on Papa's words about the film that we had viewed the week before ~ though it felt more like a hundred years.

With shaking hands I opened up the envelope that was attached. I read a letter penned in green, with the signature of Charles Beauvois. And, what the film director wrote, those words, they meant the world to me. I still know every one by heart.

I regret being unable to accept your invitation. I should very much have liked to meet but am due to leave the town today, returning to America where I am currently employed at the Edison Manhattan Studios. It was on behalf of that company that I recently travelled to England to create my shorts of local

scenes, every one of which will now be shown on screens in
nickelodeons across the whole United States.

I understand that you expressed an interest in Brightland
Promenade. Please accept this copy of the film intended as a gift
for you, and also as a token of my admiration for the child who
appears towards the very end. I am told she is your daughter,
and I hope you do not think it somewhat indiscreet of me to
say that she has a unique presence when viewed through the
medium of film.

I shall not easily forget the star of Brightland Promenade.

But he had forgotten me. He'd gone! Gone, just like my father had.
Oh, what passion we feel when we are young. How black and
white the world can seem. But there, in the blacks and whites and
greys contained in Brightland Promenade there was a spell of hap-
piness that I could cherish secretly.

I took that film and letter home and hid them underneath my floor,
and so often, in the years to come, I'd open up that box again ~ though
just as well I did not think how flammable the celluloid, unspooling
the ribbon in my hands and wrapping its length around one wrist,
until I reached the very end and saw myself revealed again, but
looking different to the girl in the film seen on the theatre screen.

Now, I know the trick of it. Then, I had no notion how Beauvois
had used a razor blade to scratch away the celluloid, to leave some
parts entirely clear so that when the film came to be viewed ~ in my
case, through a candle's flame ~ all around my head there seemed to
be a living halo made of fire.

There were hundreds of tiny stars as well. They shimmered round
the entrance flags that flew above the promenade, around the towers
and the domes that loomed within the frame behind. And with that
halo, with those stars, Beauvois had made me magical.

Theo once made me sparkle too.

I'd reached the age of seventeen. My brother, he was twenty-two, and since the time of Papa's death had given up his art school place to carry on the portrait trade.

Business was slower than before, but he did his best to make it work, with new electric wires installed to light the shop and studio. He bought fresh drapes and furniture when the old ones looked too shabby underneath that brighter, vibrant glare. He painted brand-new backdrops. Ivy-clad ruins, or rural scenes with woodlands, streams and flowers. A sandy beach with bathing huts, with donkey rides, and Mr Punch. Very popular with the children.

But not quite popular enough ~ added to which my brother spent so many of his idle hours behind the doors of the Bath Arms pub, meeting with all those art school friends who'd now found jobs working backstage at the Brightland Theatre Royal.

Sometimes he came home tipsy. Sometimes, he simply disappeared, not showing his face for days on end, and I'd be forced to close the shop and send the customers away. And, yes, I know I should have made attempts to do the work myself, but I never felt that confident when handling the cameras. No matter how often Theo tried to give me lessons in the art, I simply didn't have the eye. Every picture I took lacked focus, came out too light, or else too dark. Not to mention all the chopped-off heads.

I could have chopped off Theo's head one night when he was rolling drunk, when my brother barged into my room, shaking my arm until I woke ~ when I shouted over Rex's barks, 'What are you doing, Theo? Leave me alone to get some sleep!'

'You have to listen, Leda . . .' His words were all a tumble. 'I've heard that there's a wardrobe sale, tomorrow at the Theatre Royal. They're clearing out old costumes, from all the Christmas panto-mimes . . . the sort of thing our customers could pose in for their photographs, and to hire out for parties too. I've had a look this

evening. There's racks and racks to choose from. Grecian priestesses. Fairy queens. Mermaids. Milkmaids. Valkyries. For the men there's crowns and ermine capes. Viking helmets stuck with horns ... or sporting caps and bats and balls. Something there for everyone.'

The lamplight from the hall outside was gleaming on my brother's curls. His apple cheeks were flushed and pink. He looked so sweetly earnest, and I couldn't help but laugh out loud when I saw what he was wearing then. A paste tiara on his head. A long fur stole around his neck ~ and already Princess Charming's eyes were closing as her head lolled back to rest against my pillow, when I kissed her nose and whispered, 'Sweet dreams, my dearest Theo. I think that's a wonderful idea. The best that you have ever had.'

He was still snoring at my side when Mrs C called up the stairs to wake us in the morning. Thank goodness she had not come up to bring a cup of tea for me, as she sometimes did, when in the mood. If she'd found us there, so compromised, would she believe our innocence? Still, we laughed about it later, when Theo's head was clear again, when we dragged those rattling costume racks from the theatre stores down through the Lanes. By the end of the day we'd even made a space for the customers to change. A cupboard in the passageway that led them to the studio, which we dressed with a chair and mirrored stand, with pots of cosmetics, brushes, combs, and several different coloured wigs.

I wore one of those wigs myself when I posed as Theo's mermaid. A tumbling mass of silver curls. On top a garland made of shells, with green silk ribbons hanging down to look like strands of seaweed. There were more shells and coloured beads sewn onto a corset of pink coutil which gave the most convincing look of naked flesh when caught on film, though very little was revealed. Only my shoulders and my arms, with anything below the waist quite hidden by my fish's tail ~ the cardboard prop I lay behind, with all its overlapping scales in lovely glistening greens and blues. Much like the colours Papa used for Ellen Terry's beetle wings.

Behind, an underwater scene was painted on a canvas drop. There was real sand that we'd arranged with pebbles, shells and starfish. We had models of crabs and lobsters too, that we'd bought from the local fishmonger, and several other kinds of fish that dangled down from metal wires, to look as if they swam around my head while I was posing.

Oh, the end result was glorious. A brightly coloured autochrome, with hundreds of those pictures being printed up as postcards which we sold from a stand outside the shop, to kiosks on the pier as well.

They sold so well that we were soon devising more scenarios. Me, in an old-fashioned bathing suit while I dipped bare toes into the sea. Me, being photographed from behind, my underwear invisible behind the spangled fairy wings that spread when both my arms were raised. And then, there was the night-time scene. Stars painted on a midnight drop. The model of a crescent moon on which I lay while swathed in net, and really very little else but the crown of stars upon my head. And dangling from the wires around, not fish that time but cardboard stars. Great puffs of cotton wool for clouds.

We sprinkled those cards with glitter dust. Sparkles were turning up for months in the pages of books, in the seams of clothes, even the pillows of our beds. But I didn't mind the mess at all. I loved the way those pictures turned me into something glamorous, and how that glamour stuck like glue, and how, although I wore my mourning black whenever in the shop, when I was left alone at home I started to explore the clothes inside my mother's wardrobe. All the lovely silks and furs and lace that I then took upstairs with me, to hold before the looking glass.

To see a different Leda Grey.

✦

Another year. A new idea, with Theo asking me one day, 'Should we think about a lodger?'

'You mean take in a stranger... to live in our Brunswick Crescent house?' I confess that I was somewhat shocked.

'An actor. Ivor Davies. You met him, just the other day. He came in with the manager. Some publicity shots for the latest play they're staging at the theatre.'

'Oh... you mean the Scottish play? There were several actors in that day. I'm not sure I remember him.'

'The one who's got the leading role.'

'Oh, yes! The rather handsome one.'

'Rather.' My brother smiled at me. 'Right now he's in rehearsals, but the show is opening quite soon, and as it happens Ivor doesn't like the digs he's living in. So, if the show is a success... if it runs for any decent time, we'd have good money coming in.'

'But, do we really need it? I know the winter months are slow, but...'

'All the traders are feeling the pinch right now. Some say it's old King Edward's death. Our happy times come to an end. But a house as large as ours is... well, it really is a drain, you know, with all the running costs to bear. And not forgetting Mrs C.'

'But what about the neighbours? What will they say if we rent out rooms?'

My brother sighed. 'Oh, sticks and stones. Won't you at least consider it?'

I can't imagine why we hadn't thought of letting any rooms before. It seemed our happy days were back, and with Ivor Davies promising to pay three months' rent in advance, instead of every penny earned then going straight back out on bills there might be spare for luxuries. And what a lovely thing it was to give our Mrs C a rise, with her wages never having changed since Papa had first hired her in, and *twenty years had passed since then. It also helped to soothe her doubts when Ivor took the basement rooms, for which he had exclusive use of the door in the house front area ~ which meant her own comings and goings were restricted to the garden gate, which she thought beneath her dignity, which may have explained the set of rules she pasted in the bottom hall, right next to Ivor's bedroom door. In capital letters, to be quite clear ~*

NO DIRTINESS.
NO DRUNKENNESS.
NO FEMALE VISITORS AT NIGHT.

'Are you sure he'll get the point?' I asked. 'You don't think you might have been too vague?'

'You'll thank me for this. And I'll thank you for a little less of the cheeky tongue.' Mrs C gave me a long hard look. 'You hear about such goings-on. The morals of these theatre folk. Unmarried men away from home are often not much better than ... well ... a pretty girl like you! You just make sure to lock your door when you go off to sleep at night. What if this friend of Theo's is too fond of the hanky-panky lark?'

Whatever Ivor's lark might be, Mrs C was soon his friend, chin-wagging over cups of tea during all those daytime hours when Theo and I were at the shop. Most evenings when we were at home Ivor was at the theatre, or spending time with other friends ~ though sometimes I might wake to hear him clanking down the basement steps. And once, the racket going on! I couldn't sleep and left my bed, looking through the window glass and down into the area where, gilded in the streetlamp's glow, Ivor was laughing and waving a bottle. And Ivor had no trousers on, only his flapping shirt-tails to conceal his naked legs beneath. As brazen as you like, he was, grabbing at some woman's waist. Perhaps another member of the Theatre Royal's acting cast! Not that I looked for all that long because I felt quite flushed and faint and had to turn my eyes away. To have seen those shocking goings-on. To have heard the laughter of his friends as they cheered at such debauchery, when he touched her, when she touched him…

But it was a different Ivor who shared our Sunday lunches, when Mrs C would cook for us before she headed off for church, and then went ~ well, who really knew? We never were invited back to see where Mrs C might live, though she sometimes mentioned that she shared a home with an old widowed friend. Anyway, that's where she'd go while we remained to eat our roasted lunch around the kitchen table. Too much bother to set up the dining room, and so nice and toasty by the range, and warmer still when drinking all the sherry Ivor brought along. We had the very best of times, playing charades and games of cards, and twice Ivor invited us along to see the Scottish play.

Mrs C came with us too. We three sat in a private box and felt as grand as royalty. But the run was over much too soon, and Ivor said that he must leave to take another role elsewhere ~ which was when Theo and I made plans to mark our final Sunday lunch by putting on a show for him.

It was me who came up with the notion of performing a magician's trick, after sitting in my bed one night and flicking through the pages of a book Papa once gave to me. Three Hundred and One Things A Bright Girl Can Do ~ and every single page of it filled up with recipes and games, with scripts for plays, and also tricks, though I doubted the brightest girl in the world could have managed without some expertise or, in this case, with my brother's help. The miracle of his set design.

On the evening before our 'Cremated Alive! A Dramatic and Fiery Spectacular', I spent hours on my costume. It was one of the vestal virgin robes from the fancy dress racks in the shop, to which I'd added pins and chains found in our mother's jewellery box.

During these preparations my brother was in the drawing room, arranging the window's large box bay into a sort of a private stage, just as the book suggested. With the window's shutters being closed so as not to be seen from the street outside, he'd erected a wooden table that was customised with mirrors, along with the sack in which I'd hide when I ducked behind the furniture, with a bell that I would jangle, and the most convincing charred black skull that he'd made from papier mâché . . . just waiting there to be revealed when I vanished in a puff of smoke.

When we came to perform the thing itself, Rex ~ with the ringing of the bell and the sudden flaring of the flames ~ could only be subdued again when we put him in the garden, along with any scraps of meat left over from our leg of lamb. He'd barked, and Mrs C (who'd also stayed with us for lunch that day) had screamed, becoming very red, with a creaking of her corset bones when leaping from her seat to grab a vase of flowers on a stand, and about to fling its contents out to douse the conflagration, before Ivor had the common sense to make her sit back down again.

But how delighted I had been to think she'd really been convinced, even if that wild reaction might have been enhanced by Ivor's wine, whereas Theo and I had been reserved, only sipping a little over lunch to be sure of our wits while we performed. But to hear our audience applaud! And then, when Ivor said that if we did a turn at the Theatre Royal we'd be sure of a standing ovation ~ well, I'm sure his tongue was in his cheek, but still, I felt so happy. I felt not the least cremated. I felt as if I'd walked through fire and found a new me on the other side. I felt a humming in my blood, as exultant as I'd ever been when I'd dared to dream of a future life as an actress in the moving films.

My only sadness was that Papa wasn't there to see it, and I think that Ivor Davies must have sensed my melancholic air, coming near to touch my arm and giving it a gentle squeeze ~ which was also round about the time when Mrs C asked Theo if he'd see her down the basement stairs, to help her make a pot of tea: 'Or I'm likely to go and break my neck, with all this wine I've taken. I'll never be sober to walk back home. There's folks fall off the pier for less. Get drowned and never seen again.'

I should have gone upstairs to change, but settled on the sofa, folding my arms and shivering, for there'd been such a draught in the window bay ~ until the flash of burning heat when I noticed Ivor's eyes so firmly fixed upon the flimsy cloth that I had wound around my breasts. Dragging a shawl from the sofa back I tried to cover up with that, attempting to divert his thoughts by asking, 'Won't you tell me more... about this new play you'll be in?'

'A musical drama being staged at the Almeida in London. The name is Kismet, I believe.' The horsehair groaned and the springs all twanged as he sat beside me with a thump. 'Turkish for Fate or Destiny, and I heard today that we begin rehearsals tomorrow afternoon. So, it must be my sorry fate to leave you sooner than I'd hoped... to catch the early morning train.'

He shuffled a little closer, his wine breath soft and tickling against my cheek when whispering, 'I'm going to miss you, Leda.' And then, his sudden lunging move when, had I not swiftly turned away, I'm sure he would have kissed me. His lips brushed lightly on my neck. I heard him murmur in my ear, 'Oh, come now... just one kiss for luck, while the others aren't here to interfere. We don't want petty jealousies.'

'Ivor! No!' I pushed him off. No matter how much I liked him, and I did, I liked him very much, I didn't fancy him one jot. I might have slapped him then and there if not for the footsteps in the hall, with the tinkling china on the tray to announce the others back again; though I doubt they noticed anything. Not with Ivor leaping to his feet, and me still sitting there bemused when he turned to smile at Theo, an arm clapped round his shoulder while proclaiming with such bonhomie, 'I was telling Leda all about the next show I'll be working in. If that goes well my agent says there's a chance for a run on Broadway too. He thinks your photograph has helped. That one you printed up as cards to give to all my ardent fans' ~ Ivor paused and grinned at me ~ 'when they gather around the backstage door and pester me for kisses. He's been sending them out to everyone. And what with Marie Lloyd on board, not to mention the lovely Miss Gabrielle Ray... well, I've heard those theatres in New York pay as much as a thousand pounds a week.'

'A thousand pounds a week!' Mrs C's jaw dropped so wide, I swear if there'd been any flies around she would have swallowed them.

'The camera does love you,' I announced, remembering a photograph that Theo took of Ivor once. We'd already closed up the shop that night, when Ivor called by to say hello before making his way to the theatre, lounging on the studio chaise with his feet on the cushions like Lord Dick, and puffing away on a cigarette as if he thought he owned the place. Apart from which, it was dangerous to smoke in there at any time, with the film and all the chemicals. But Theo didn't seem to mind, and hard to be cross with Ivor when he was such pleasant company. Always a smile and a ready laugh.

And on that final Sunday, when Ivor stood with one arm resting on our marble mantelpiece, I saw that photograph again, only able to think that Mrs C ~ another of his ardent fans ~ had placed it by the mirror's frame.

Unless he'd put it there himself.

Unless it had been Theo?

Well, there it was, in pride of place, a rather dim and moody shot where Ivor's face was half concealed by the trail of smoke that drifted out from the cigarette that he had smoked. Amazingly skilful of Theo, to capture that mist of vapour, behind which Ivor's features seemed, not blurred, but somehow more defined than ever in reality. The planes of his bones looked sharper. Lips firmer, much more sensual. And his teeth, not large, but very good, were gleaming white against his skin which, in the light of real life, possessed a sort of olive hue ~ though I wondered at its natural tone, for he dabbed the greasepaint liberally, whether on or off the stage.

Ivor was very affected, you see. Very fussy about the way he looked, with his neat checked suits and slicked down hair, always scented with vanilla oil, though what appeared as gleaming black when captured in that photograph was actually a conker brown.

Oh, that smell of vanilla Ivor used ~ even now, when all these years have passed, I sometimes catch it on the air, drifting round at White Cliff House. But it's only the faintest memory, not at all the densely pungent pall that had surrounded him that day, when he moved away from the fireplace to perch on our piano stool and, despite it never being tuned ~ not since the time of Mama's death ~ was not the least bit daunted by the random twanging of its notes, bashing out the latest tunes to lead us in a singalong. When we clapped, when Ivor left the stool, he whisked Mrs C into his arms and twirled her *all around the room, before impersonating some comedians he'd come to know while working in the music halls.*

Finally, he gave a bow, collapsing down into a chair, long arms and legs sprawled everywhere, eyes closed, a smile upon his lips ~ until that smile was frozen when Theo suddenly enquired, 'You'd really go to America?'

'Of course!' Ivor's eyes were opened. 'Think of the opportunities. Better than any I'd have here.'

'I'd be happy to visit London,' I said. 'To see some of the theatres there. The electric palace cinemas. And then, of course, it's London where our parents used to live before they set up home in Brightland. I sometimes wonder if there might be relatives that we could find. Although, it's strange the way our parents never mentioned anyone. Papa would talk about his work, but ...'

'Good God, Leda!' Theo snapped. 'Are you living in a fairy tale? Any relatives our parents had, why should they give a damn for us?'

'Oh!' That left me speechless, shocked at my brother's brutal tone, wondering what he might know that I had not been privy to.

Meanwhile, Mrs C went on. 'Well, that won't stop us heading off to board the London train one day for a trip to Modern Babylon, and a visit to Ivor's latest show. Perhaps he'll demonstrate more of those comic skills we've seen today. Who'd ever think it possible, after seeing him playing that Macbeth.'

'Mrs C! You shouldn't use that name!' I quickly interrupted. 'You must only say the Scottish play!'

'Oh, Leda! Superstitious rot!' My brother spoke with such disdain. What had got into him that night?

Mrs C then had another shot at smoothing troubled waters. 'Bad luck is not contained in names ... though I feel our luck is running low to have dear Ivor leaving, when it seems he's only just arrived. He's certainly brightened up this place.' Smiling at Ivor, she went on, 'And now, this new play. Kismet? The name is very fitting, dear. I believe you're destined for great fame.'

Theo raised his brows and groaned ~ and me, I was simply staring off at some vague point in the carpet's weave, embarrassed to hear our Mrs C pandering like a love-struck girl, when Ivor must be half her age.

A great relief for everyone when Ivor finally announced, 'Well, however much it pains me, I think it's time to take my leave. I've promised to join some of the cast for a farewell drink at the Bath Arms. And Theo, didn't you mention having printed up more photographs? My agent's very keen for them. Could we collect them from the shop?'

Mrs C gave both a sternish look. 'Haven't you had sufficient fun? Surely on a Sunday night the public bars should all be closed? Still, whatever day it is, I'm more than ready for my bed. I'll stroll along to the end of the road with you two gents for company.'

Ivor got up from his chair and said, while looking pointedly at me, 'Shall we all take a breath of evening air?'

'I'm hardly dressed for walking out.'

'Oh, I don't know.' He took my hand and pulled me to my feet again, and I must have been quite tipsy for the room to whirl around like that, for the blazing fire to make the air so hot and, oh, so fuggy. I could hardly even catch a breath when he twined his fingers through my own and said, 'So this is au revoir. Until we come to meet again.'

As it happened I tried to meet him again before that night was even done. After falling asleep on the sofa, I woke with a much clearer head and saw a glint of silver shining under the piano stool. It was Ivor's cigarette case. And yes, I could have posted it straight through the basement letter box, but I felt a little lonely. I felt a little sad to think I wouldn't see him any more.

Dressed once again in my plain black clothes, I walked along the promenade, though even for a Sunday night the town was strangely empty. No sounds of any clopping hooves to echo through the misty air. Just the suck and the pull of ocean waves, and a sort of rustling rattling as stones were shifting on the beach. I stopped to listen for a while. Those sounds were otherworldly. They could have come from any time ~ unlike the riot that I heard when turning off into the Lanes where the Bath Arms pub still glowed with light. But not one face I recognised when I pressed my nose against the glass; then chided myself for doing so when one of the drinkers looked my way, and then came stumbling out to try and grab my arm ~ to drag me in.

I suppose it was no wonder. I hadn't thought to wash my face, which I'd painted up so garishly in preparation for our show. But, I shook him off and scurried on, so glad to reach the shop's front step and find the door had not been locked ~ which meant that Ivor and Theo were surely still inside. Though it was odd to see no light, and what a prickling chill I felt to hear those low and muffled groans as I headed past the counter, then on along the passageway that led me to the studio, when every rational thought I had was screaming silently to warn that what I saw could not be real.

And yet, I surely saw a ghost. My mother, just as she had looked on the day of my seventh birthday. And such a sweetly poignant thing, if only for a little time, to see her lovely face again, to hear the whispering of silk as her pose was slightly shifted, when one of her slender bare white arms rose limply from the chaise's back.

Thinking she was beckoning, I took a step, and then one more, inhaling lovely scents of rose. A tang of some vanilla oil. And then the sourer odours of fresh vomit, and the rust of blood, through which I heard another moan and realised that 'she' was 'he' ~ that Theo was lying on the chaise, and Theo had gone and dressed himself in one of our fancy dress affairs.

How like our mother he had looked with his buttery mop of golden curls. How languid and elegant he was, even in that drunken state, surrounded by the beer bottles that leaked through all the shards of glass around the broken mirror. The glass that must have caused the criss-cross cuts upon my brother's hands.

It was with a very heavy heart that I turned away from where he slept and went to find a brush and pan to clear the broken glass away. And then, unsure what else to do, I squeezed myself onto the chaise, wrapping myself in Theo's skirts to keep away the night-time chill, which is where I fell asleep for hours, only waking when I felt the weight of my brother's head upon my breast, where he lay quite still while I stroked his curls and listened to his sobbing words. 'I'm sorry, Leda. I'm sorry. But why ... why did you come here?'

'I found Ivor's cigarette case. I thought he might be needing it.'

'He didn't stay here very long. He took those photographs, and then went off to party with his friends.'

With those words my brother pulled away, and I didn't know whether to laugh or cry to see him stand before me, so shambolic and so farcical, and yet also how glorious when he lifted his arms in the air like that, when the folds of silk in the garment's sleeves billowed out like the wings of a butterfly. But his voice, that was not beautiful, only cracked with drink and bitterness, when he said, 'So, now you know the truth.'

'What truth?' I didn't want to hear. Ice-cold fingers gripped my heart, squeezing, squeezing till it ached. I also felt impelled to ask, 'What if I hadn't been alone? What if someone else had come with me, to see you dressed in such a way. And the blood, Theo! The broken glass!'

'I smashed the mirror.'

'Yes . . . but why?'

'Because I hate to see myself. Because I was angry. Because I'm trapped . . . unable to ever leave this shop, or this town where I'm a prisoner.'

How naive I was back then. How foolish and innocent my thoughts, when I said, 'But you're not a prisoner. If you hate the shop so much then we can hire another photographer. Someone to do the portrait work. I can still work at the counter, and you can go back to study art. Perhaps you'll find some theatre work. You have such a talent for design, such an eye for . . .'

'You cannot have the least idea of what I want, or what I need.'

His aggressive tone was shocking. A relief when he finally turned away, when the hems that dragged behind him caused those bits of glass I hadn't cleared to tinkle as he walked on them; until he reached the darkroom door, when he glanced back round at me again and spoke in far more level tones. 'Who cares about this studio, now that our father's dead and gone? Why should we be trapped here? Didn't he and our mother run away from lives they didn't want?'

'Then go!' I said, more frightened now, sensing a tilting of my world. 'Go and find the life you want to lead.'

He hung his head and looked ashamed. 'If only I could do that. If only I'd never discovered the nightmare of this business.'

'What do you mean? You must tell me!'

'Not that long before he died, our father remortgaged the Crescent. A loan that was to be secured against all profits from the shop. But, should there be no profits, then . . .' My brother waved an arm again, this time a gesture of contempt as he swept an arc around the room. 'All these renovations . . . they only increased that wretched loan, and now the debt has formed the noose that's tightening around my neck. We don't make enough money to cover the interest, never mind to pay another wage.'

My mind was awhirl. I couldn't think. Even worse than the tipsy spinning head I'd had when Ivor left last night. 'But couldn't we take more lodgers in? We could ask Mrs C to work fewer hours. I'll scrub floors if I have to, I'll . . .'

'You scrub floors! Our father's spoiled princess. You were never cut out for real life.'

'And what are you cut out for?' Suddenly rising from the chaise I slowly walked to Theo's side, where my hand reached out to touch the lace sewn at the bodice of his gown, when he raised his own to grab my wrist, and with such force I couldn't help but give a little yelp of pain, over which my brother shouted, 'What you're looking at right now . . . this is part of who I really am. You and I . . . are we so different? I know how you feel when you dress up. How you felt when you posed for the cards we made . . . and Papa's photographs before. That's when you really come to life. Something more than flesh and blood.'

Finally, dragging my hand away and stumbling a few steps back, I said, 'But why wear a woman's clothes?'

'Can my little sister be that blind? Can't she see how lonely I have been? How I miss our mother every day? How I sometimes try to bring her back?'

I felt a jolt of panic, crying out, 'But this won't bring her back!'

My grief at the loss of our parents' deaths now mingled with the desperate fear that I might lose my brother too, if Theo was the way I *thought; if Theo embraced the Greek concept of Love for which Oscar Wilde had suffered so, being vilified and locked away.*

Everything solid beneath my feet was falling away, like shifting sands. I hardly knew what words to say to offer any comfort, until the thought occurred to me. 'We'll sell the shop. We'll raise some funds to pay this loan, and then . . .'

And then . . .

Theo was ranting back at me with such a strenuous contempt. 'You think you know the answer! We can only thank the bank manager . . . the fondness he held for our father's name, for allowing this situation to continue as long as it has done. But the interest has compounded so. There is no option left to us but to sell the house and hope that that will satisfy those creditors who are now snapping at our heels.'

'Oh, Theo!' I couldn't believe it. 'Where shall we go and live instead?'

'I'm hoping we can keep the shop . . . then you and I can move in here and use the upstairs storage rooms. More cramped than what we've known before, but at least we won't be on the streets.'

'And what shall we do about Mrs C?'

Theo gave a dismal shrug that told me all there was to know, though I simply couldn't take it in, still trying to find solutions. 'I know you dismissed them earlier, but what about our grandparents? There could be cousins, uncles, aunts? Don't you think, if we could find them, then they might agree to offer help?'

My brother's tone had softened, taking both my hands in his. 'Papa was very old, Leda. His parents would be dead by now. Once, when I asked, he told me that he had no other siblings . . . so I don't think we would have much luck in tracking down his relatives.'

When it came to our mother's family, it was a little different. Theo told me about the documents he'd found when sorting Papa's desk some days after the funeral. They'd revealed the names and whereabouts of our mother's family, but when Theo wrote a letter he'd received an answer in return from the lawyers they'd instructed. In no uncertain terms they'd said that our grandparents had no intent of meeting with their grandchildren. When making further enquiries, Theo was finally informed of what had caused this attitude ~ with our mother being newly wed to an entirely different man when Papa, who was twice her age, had been hired to take her photograph. The two of them then fell in love, becoming quite a cause célèbre, which was why they moved to Brightland. But our mother had never been divorced, which made us illegitimate. As far as her parents were concerned, my brother and I did not exist.

It was now my turn for bitterness. 'How they must have despised our father, to also hate his children ... when their daughter's blood runs through our veins.'

Theo's reply was more subdued, but still that trembling in his voice. 'How could Papa be so reckless? The shame of this. We must never tell. The scandal would be terrible. And now, the ruin of his debt.'

'He'd always seemed so young and well. He must have thought he'd pay it off.'

'He didn't think! He couldn't have. If you only knew the half of it!'

'But ...' I broke in, more hopefully, 'the bank manager, won't he agree to extend the loan a few more years?'

'For what? By what small miracle shall we make our fortunes in this shop when the custom dwindles by the week?'

Theo shook his head and turned away to enter the darkroom's shadows. He closed the door behind him and I saw the dim red glow of light seep out through any gaps around. I heard the splash of water while he ran the taps to wash himself. And then, my brother re-emerged, dressed in his normal clothes again. His shirt, his trousers, waistcoat, tie. Any trace of blood and vomit all scrubbed clean away from face and hands. The hands that clutched the dress he'd worn, the silk screwed up as if mere rags before he flung it down to lie across the mound of broken glass.

We didn't have the time to go back home before we opened up. And what an irony it was that, while I felt like the living dead, my brother managed to appear as fresh as a daisy all day long. The cuts on his hands weren't very deep. If the customers asked about the scabs, he blithely mentioned having tripped, having thrown out his hands to prevent his fall when he'd crashed into the mirror's glass.

I suppose it was a truth of sorts.

How glad I was when the evening came, when we locked the

shop and walked back home, for as long as we could call it home. On the way we passed the Bath Arms pub, but no one mentioned Ivor's name. Not even when we found his keys pushed through our front door letter box.

For a while we both just stood there, staring down at their gleam on the hallway tiles, which was when I suddenly recalled the silver cigarette case. Pulling it from my pocket, I held it out, while muttering, 'I never got the chance to give this back to Ivor after all.'

Without a word, Theo reached out and took the case away from me. He stepped across the keys and then began to walk on up the stairs, where a ray of sunshine slanted in through a window on the landing, in which my brother stood quite still while turning back and saying, 'I'm sorry, Leda ... for last night.'

Theo looked like an angel then, his face caught in that shaft of gold, so pure and clean among the swirling glisten of the motes of dust. I had the strangest notion that if he should take another step he'd melt away into that haze. He'd disappear for evermore.

But then my brother broke the spell. His eyes took on a vacant stare. He spoke in low and droning tones. 'I see our destinies will change. A man returning from the past will influence our future lives.'

'Do you mean Ivor? Will Ivor come back?' I was terribly unnerved just then, touching a hand to my collarbone to feel the flutter of a vein. And then a pounding in my head when, still in that robotic voice, he said, 'Not Ivor Davies.'

I thought he was pretending. I felt too tired for games like that, a surge of anger rising up, and almost tempted to applaud as he stood there on his little stage. But, this riddle, this latest trick of his, I couldn't begin to comprehend, still trying to work the puzzle out when I heard the slam of his bedroom door. The click as the key inside was turned.

Back in my own room once again I looked into the mirror's glass and saw my eyes, all shadowed. My hair a tangled mass of knots. The rouge now streaked across clown cheeks. What must the customers have thought?

I felt sick with exhaustion and lack of food, with the misery of *having learned the full extent of all our debts. I looked about my bedroom walls, at the coiling flowers on the green, and I feared those shapes imprisoned me.*

The next morning I got up at dawn and made a bonfire out the back where I burned every stitch of my mourning clothes, though Mrs C was shocked when she arrived to see what I had done. She said I should have given them to one of the local charities; that she knew some people who would sell their teeth for stuff as fine as that. But destroying those garments pleased me. It symbolised an ending, although I sometimes wonder now if it was much too cruel of me ~ how I took to wearing my mother's clothes, reworking them as something new, not minding any cobbled seams or knotted threads below the hems as I copied all the latest styles from the fashion magazines I bought, then flaunted myself around the town as if I was her living ghost.

But, you see, if Theo's claim was true, if any stranger from the past might come to change our future lives, there was one thing I knew for sure. I'd make myself so bright and gay, he couldn't miss me if he tried.

How Fate can turn on little things. Some people call that Kismet.

My fate now leads me to a day when the mirror's light is darkening. Not that it seemed that way at all, only filled with light and happiness when I first spoke with Charles Beauvois ... when I was drawn into his sphere like a moth which flutters round a flame.

I wonder why they use that term? If a moth flies too close to a candle's flame its wings catch fire. They burn away. A fatal attraction, that's for sure.

I was nineteen. He was forty-two, which didn't seem that strange to me. Not after my parents' age difference. I felt myself quite old and grown, my childhood days all left behind, with this also around about the time we'd sold the Crescent house and were living in rooms above the shop.

Mrs C had found employment with another local family. But we did our best to stay in touch, and on this one occasion had invited her to join us for a tea at the aquarium. We always loved to go there, though Theo says it's different now. He says they've demolished the clock tower, along with the statues cast in bronze that used to show the seasons. He says that they hold tea parties with tables full of chimpanzees, with jellies and cakes thrown everywhere while people stand and gawp at them. How strange that always sounds to me. Since when have monkeys lived at sea?

Ah well, it was quite different on that April Sunday afternoon when I wore my very finest dress. A plain white muslin modelled on the Happiness I used to love, except that this was more ornate, with pearls seeded into the sash, with scalloped lace to edge around the neck and hems of tulip skirts. The sort of shape you didn't need to wear a corset underneath, so unconstrained that if the fancy took I might have run through town ~ if not for Theo's trudging steps.

My brother was terribly slow that day. He'd been nebuchadnez-zared the night before. He was moaning about a headache, for which I had no sympathy, only hoping that it wouldn't lead to another of those episodes that Theo could be prone to. When he talked about his coloured lights, or made strange sorts of prophecies.

At least my hat amused him. A brim that stretched a foot each side. Such a riot of flowers and feathers, it had taken a good three nights for me to stitch them round the ribbon band. And yet it was entirely thanks to that ridiculous affair that Charles Beauvois discovered me ~ though I think he would have tracked me down. In another place. Another time.

We finally arrived and went upstairs to the Winter Garden rooms. Mrs C, who was already there, had saved a table by the stage, very near to the musicians as they played their violins before a wall of rocks and fancy ferns, with water trickling down between to splash into a little pool. It really was enchanting, until a haughty gentleman sitting very close behind gave my shoulder quite a nudge, with complaints that I obscured the stage, and demanding that I shift my seat or place my hat down on the ground. Such tuts of irritation, and mutterings beneath his breath about vulgar exhibitionists, and the way young women carry on, and 'God help us if they get the vote. These bloody hats are bad enough ... they'll be dressing up in khaki next. They'll be going off to fight the wars!'

Why, I'd half a mind to turn around and give that tiresome old buffer a slapping. I'd give him a war if he wanted one! But, not wanting to spoil the afternoon, I decided to go and calm myself, mumbling to Mrs C about needing to use the ladies' room, then making my way back down the stairs towards the marble entrance hall.

Now, let me think. What happened next? I must make sure I get it right, to set the scene just as it was.

A group of people queuing for tickets. The distant strains of violins as musicians continued to play above ~ over which my footsteps tapped a beat as they clicked across the hard stone floor, then dawdled at the kiosk shelves to spend a little while in browsing through the gifts on sale there. I liked the wooden boxes. The tops and sides all stuck with shells. I pulled a postcard from the rack and smiled with pride to see myself the mermaid on the front of it.

Ah, pride. It comes before a fall. And my time to fall was very near, even though I was oblivious when I walked beneath the marble arch with its sculptures of Neptune and water nymphs, when I entered the dark exhibit aisle where, bathed in different coloured lights that beamed through all water tanks, eventually I found my way to the one that held the manatees. Those creatures had intrigued ever since Papa once told me tales of sailors who'd spent months at sea, who might then glimpse a manatee and think they'd seen a mermaid.

Such lumpen docile creatures! Were the sailors mad, or drunk on rum?

I chuckled to myself while climbing up the run of wide stone steps to view their tank more closely, from where one manatee looked out and seemed to wave its fins at me, then played a game of hide and seek, swimming back and forth between some swaying drapes of ferny weed.

Waiting for it to re-emerge, I fell into a kind of a trance, seeing myself reflected back in the inky blue of rippling light, surrounded by anemones, and the darting silver flash of fish. And, thinking I was quite alone, I raised my arms up in the air, slowly waving them about just as the manatee had done ~ which was when I heard a cough. A cough from someone close behind, who I had failed to see at all because of the hat upon my head, which really was so very large I think a whole army of tourists could have gathered in the aisle to watch, and still I wouldn't notice them.

Perhaps it was romantic, but romance with a touch of the music hall farce, for realising I must look like some demented octopus, I whirled around in embarrassment, and one of my heels caught in my hems to send me flying me down the steps ~ straight into the arms of Charles Beauvois. Not that I knew that it was him. Not then. Not with my cheek pressed to his chest, hearing the beating of his heart, and breathing in what seemed to me an intoxicating fragrance of sweat, and salt, and something else. Something hot and fiercely animal.

It excited me. It frightened me, to be in such proximity to a man I'd never met before, before I came to my senses and forced myself to pull away. But even when the stranger's hands had fallen to his sides again I felt as if I was still held. Held by the eyes that fused with mine, so dark, intense, and curious.

Stepping back a little more, I saw a man in his middle years, and of considerable physique. Not fat. Not overweight at all, but he had the solid musculature that would certainly make him seem that way whenever my brother was at his side. Theo was very slender then, his fairness something almost fey, whereas Beauvois had my gypsy looks. Hair black as night apart from strands of silver at his temples, and where the hair receded above a high broad forehead. Heavy brows above his eyes. A large straight nose, and full red lips, sensually smiling from beneath the line of a clipped moustache.

How perfectly groomed that facial hair compared to the rest upon his head, which was long and rather tangled. His clothes looked creased. They felt quite damp. And then, that smell of salt again, and before I could think to stop myself the words were rushing from my mouth, 'You're wet, and you smell a bit fishy. Did you fall into one of the water tanks?'

He glanced down at himself and laughed. A deep resounding chuckle that echoed round us in the aisle. 'My appearance... I must apologise! I was walking along the beach today when I managed to slip on a piece of weed, ending up on my back in a rock pool. As you can see I'm quite unharmed. Only my dignity was lost. Oh... and my hat! That was blown off. By now it might well be in France.'

I also laughed, but nervously, altogether too aware of how boldly this man was staring. I was wondering where he might be from, hearing the slightest twanging of American accent in his voice, and then, when he'd stopped talking, fearing I'd be swallowed up in the chasm of silence expanding around us ~ which was when I almost lost control, wanting to feel his warmth again, wanting to press my lips to his, instead of which I stammered, 'I... I have to thank you... for catching me.'

'And unlike myself, you kept your hat!'

I couldn't help but smile back, telling him that hat had caused more trouble than he realised, after which I dragged my eyes away and back towards the entrance hall, from where a sudden shaft of light illuminated people who now walked the aisle towards us ~ and also shone on something lying on the ground between our feet.

Something the stranger must have dropped when I'd fallen forward in his arms.

It was a postcard, and perhaps the very one that I had held while standing at the kiosk rack, though surely no one else would see that siren's wig of silver curls and link her with my raven self. But he had done, and after stooping down to pick it up again, his tone was much more serious. 'It is you, isn't it?' he said, eyes meeting mine directly. 'The profile . . . unmistakable! I knew it the moment I saw you . . . out there in the reception hall. What a strange coincidence it is.'

'A coincidence? I don't understand.'

'My name is Charles Beauvois . . . and I know it was some years ago, but I filmed you once, on the promenade. I hope your father was happy with the actual that I arranged to be delivered afterwards.'

I was doubly shocked when he spoke those words. I could hardly begin to take it in. At first, to hear my father's name, but even more to realise that this was Monsieur Charles Beauvois, that somehow he'd remembered me. That morning on the promenade.

'My father . . . I'm afraid he's dead.' But with no wish to speak of that I continued much more tartly. 'You don't sound very French to me. Not for someone who calls himself Monsieur.'

He explained that his father had been French. A banker based in Paris. But his mother was English, and when she'd died, when he was only three years old, his father sent him to the care of various English boarding schools, with his holidays then being spent with an elderly unmarried aunt who lived not far from Cuckham Sands. Having developed a passion for photography in her old age, that aunt had passed her expertise onto the nephew she'd adored; their mutual interest then evolved into his work in moving films. When she had died and Beauvois then inherited her money, he'd travelled to America where he took up an apprenticeship with the Edison Company in New York. But now, some twenty years had passed, and he had ambitions of his own, for which he had decided to return and live in England.

All this was delivered in moments, after which he never spoke another word about his aunt again, or the father who'd abandoned him. He'd claimed the name, but nothing else, and I never thought to press him, so taken up with other things. With our love affair. With the films we made.

The films. The films obsessed him, and I know he was delighted when I told him how entranced I'd been by that copy of Brightland Promenade. But I didn't say I cherished it, how still some nights when left alone I would unreel the film again to stare at the ghost of the girl I'd been through the light of a lamp, or candle flame. I didn't tell him that Papa had never seen that version. And neither had my brother. Not so far as I had been aware, although I sometimes wondered. When Theo spoke about his lights.

No. Those things I kept close to my heart, only trying to keep my voice quite calm when I said, 'What you did was wonderful. It was inspired. It was like art . . . to make that halo round my head.'

His unrelenting stare again, when he seemed to see into my soul, and said, 'I was inspired by you. And today you've worked your charms again. I wonder . . . would you act for me? At least audition for some scenes?'

That took the wind out of my sails. 'What . . . now? In the aquarium? Isn't it too dark to film?'

He grinned. 'You'd light the darkness up. Though it's true, when I filmed here before, when I made the Brightland actuals, we had strings of electric light bulbs hung up in the aisles . . . around the water tanks. But I have no interest any more in making documentary films. These past twelve months I've overseen the building of a studio to rival that of Méliès'.'

My chest felt constricted, my head growing dizzy with all the possibilities. I feared I might well faint away. I gushed, 'Oh, I adore his films! He creates such worlds. Such fantasies.'

He didn't answer for a while, but turned the postcard in his hands, and while still looking down at that he said he'd make a fantasy the likes of which George Méliès could only ever dream about.

It was shocking, to hear such arrogance. If anyone else had said such things ~ but I did so want to believe him, and perhaps I was too eager, much too 'fast' to be respectable, but if Charles Beauvois had told the truth when he mentioned making films with me, then I must leave him in no doubt of exactly where I could be found ~ explaining *that my brother had made my portrait for the mermaid card, with most of the set still on display in Williams' Studio in the Lanes, where he would most welcome if he'd like to come and take a look.*

Such audacity! I blushed with shame. I had to turn my face away. When the other visitors drew near I walked back down the aisle again without so much as a goodbye, though I did glance round to see that Charles Beauvois still stood there, watching me, almost as if he'd been transformed into another marble god. But his mouth was soft, not made of stone, and how contagious was his smile! I couldn't help but laugh out loud when I lifted an arm to wave at him, and only then to realise he hadn't even asked my name. So, I called, 'My name is Leda Grey. L –E –D –A – G –R – E –Y.'

I didn't care who might have heard, or who might stare with open mouths when I all but raced my way upstairs and back into the Winter Rooms. The music was done, but I didn't mind, only pleased to find that rude old man had gone when I sat down again. I hardly even noticed that the tea was cold inside my cup. But then, everything else around me was so warm and bright and beautiful. The golden sun on fronds of ferns, each tiny coiled spring of green soon to unfurl and spread its seed into the splashing waterfall. And the sound of that water, its trickling plash was the sweetest music to my ears. The music of the mermaids.

While lost in that my eyes dropped down to see the ugly tags of bitten skin around my fingernails. It was not a day to be ugly. I pushed them under the tablecloth and lifted my gaze to my brother's face, which still looked green about the gills, and not the slightest hint that he might ask me why I'd been so long.

But Mrs C was curious. I think she saw a change in me. She placed her hand upon my arm, pressing down as if to stop me floating up like a balloon. She said my cheeks looked red and flushed. She feared I must be falling ill when I failed to eat a single crumb of the cakes she'd piled upon my plate. But, where before I'd scoff them down, my appetite had disappeared. My only hunger was desire, as if some dormant thing inside had woken and been stirred to life. And how it gnawed, and ached, and burned when I lay beneath my sheets that night and dreamed that I might fall again into the arms of Charles Beauvois.

I suppose it was an illness, the fretting of my nerves next day, when I spent each waking moment either preening in the looking glass, or staring at the shop's front door while hoping he might walk on through.

In the end, the postman did arrive, delivering a large brown box, and underneath the knots of string securing all the packaging I found the mermaid postcard, and on the back was Beauvois's note . . .

To the divine Miss Leda Grey,

Please accept this token of my deepest admiration. I would hope to offer so much more, and with that in mind would you agree to meet with me this Sunday?

It will be our third encounter. Three is a good number. I believe it is a magic one. I believe that Leda Grey will bring much more than magic to my life.

Will you invite your brother too? Not only as a chaperon. Having seen this example of his work I would like to discuss the prospect of employing him at White Cliff House. I have need of artists with such flair, not to mention those who understand the workings of the cameras.

Please do write and say you'll come. Shall we say at 6 o'clock? The house is not that hard to find. Above the cliff at Cuckham Sands. There is a signpost in the road.

Divine. Beauvois called me divine. That thrilled me more than I can say. And Theo was delighted too, quite sure that this must be the man of whom he had once prophesised. The man returning from the past, who'd come to change our future lives. And not a moment of that future life did Theo mean to waste.

He headed straight down to the Bath Arms bar to enquire about a horse and trap for us to hire on Sunday, returning up the Lane again while wheeling a contraption that he said a friend had sold to him. A motorised bicycle it was. So many metal pipes and grilles it might have dropped from outer space; an illusion only heightened by the goggles Theo had to wear to save his eyes from dust and grit when sitting in the driving seat. But he didn't have a set for me, supposing I could close my eyes while clutching on for dearest life in the carriage bolted to the back.

Sheer madness to think of getting in. Then again, short of knocking or drugging me senseless, short of locking me up in my bedroom and tying my arms to the bedposts, there was nothing in this world to stop me travelling to White Cliff House ~ even if in the process of doing so I ended up looking as if I had been dragged through a hedge and back again. And that's because I almost had!

All those hours I'd wasted in front of the mirror, with item after item of clothing discarded to the floor below, until, at last, I smiled to see the reflection looking back at me, when I fancied myself to be just the spit of the actress and singer, Miss Gabrielle Ray ~ whose name Ivor had mentioned once, before he'd left our Brightland house, whose face was one of many more staring back from the posters and magazine cuttings I'd pasted all across the walls of my bedroom up above the shop.

My personal Gabriellic look was achieved with rouged lips and blackened eyes, and by wearing my mother's kimono. A riot of red and oranges, and a little frayed at the edges too, but I did so love the embroidery. All those vibrantly coloured chrysanthemum flowers. Not to mention the lingering smell of rose that still exuded from the weave.

I felt myself Bohemian. I was sure Beauvois would be impressed. But my hair! Despite sleeping in rags, it was not at all the gleaming twist of curls that I had hoped for. More like the bristles of a broom. I had to pin it up instead, winding a chiffon scarf around. And, when that was done I simply hoped no one would look at me that day and think of The Mikado. That song about the little maids.

We left Rex inside, on the window shelf. By then a venerable old man when it came to counting canine years, he would often stay in there all the day, watching people strolling past. Not so much as a whine or whimper when we waved goodbye and locked the door, when Theo started up the bike, which gave off such a growling thrum that all the window frames around were rattling like tambourines. But, being a Sunday afternoon, no traders were there to make complaints or to watch us wobble down the Lane ~ though when Theo steered onto the main King's Road I wished we'd wobble back again, suddenly thinking about Mama and panicking quite horribly while gripping at the basket's sides. I was all but blinded by the dust thrown up by other wheels and hooves when I caught a blast of the engine's heat, and then a whiff of paraffin leaking from the fuel tank. I really did become convinced that the whole caboodle would explode. But I gritted my teeth, and ducked my head, like an ostrich hiding in the sand to miss all dangers passing by, and sooner than expected we were driving through the country lanes ~ and how exhilarating then, to see the hedges blurring by, before we had to slow again, chugging along as the engine coughed and rattled up a cliff-side track. But that was really just as well. Any faster and we might have died, when the wheels went skidding on some stones and Theo lost all control of the steering, screaming for me to bail out ~ after which there was only the rush of wind, and that awful clanging in our ears as the bike crashed down to rocks below.

Lying on a scrubby verge, I was somewhat dazed and shaken, but luckily, no broken bones, and bruises, well, they would soon fade. Theo was in a far worse state, with his jacket and his trousers torn, and that swelling egg upon his brow. It really looked quite comical, with his bulging goggled eyes beneath. I couldn't help but laugh out loud, becoming quite hysterical with the fright and the joy all mixed in one, before dragging myself to my feet again and walking to the precipice where the wind caught my kimono sleeves and made them flap and snap about, so much that I could hardly hear when Theo called, 'For God's sake, Leda! Come away! Don't you know how dangerous it is?'

I turned, and he was at my side, dragging the goggles from his face before flinging them over the edge as well. He wouldn't need them any more. And then he started hugging me, as if he'd never let me go. When he did, he lifted up a hand to smooth the tangles from my hair. He pulled a handkerchief out of his pocket and dabbed away the smuts of ash and grass stains smeared across my cheeks. And then without another word he took my hand in one of his and we walked the rest of the way on foot, and only a little blistered when we finally came to a wooden gate with the name of White Cliff House on front.

I stood before that gate and froze, hardly able to give an answer when my brother looked at me and sighed, 'Don't tell me you're shy... when we've come this far.'

'But whatever must I look like?'

'Like a lovely windblown geisha girl. All this fresh air has done you good. Your cheeks are pink, and your eyes are...'

'Sore! I should have been wearing goggles too!'

I didn't dare to rub them, not with all the kohl I'd used. All the blacking on my lashes too. But clearly my sight had not been harmed, because that was when I saw Beauvois, appearing through the shadows in an avenue of conifers. And when he smiled, and when he waved, that sign was all it took for me to walk towards my destiny.

'I feared you weren't coming,' he called to us, barely shaking Theo's hand and not a single comment on my brother's state of disarray. He simply carried on to say, 'But here you are, and just in time for me to show you both the shed... before the light has faded.'

'The shed?' I asked, while wondering if we were there to look at spades.

'It's what I call the studio. The builders say just one more week, and then it shall be ours to use.'

Ours. Wasn't that a lovely word! I was all but walking on the air as we turned from the lane to a narrow path. Some way ahead it widened out into a swathe of meadow grass, across which Beauvois pointed, and my heart was pounding in my breast when seeing such a vision there. I had to squint against the flashing red of what then looked like fire, where the glare of the setting evening sun reflected back on panes of glass. And the view exposed through the back of it, where the grass sloped down some twenty yards to join a path along the cliff, then further still to where the sea and sky appeared to melt away in shifting veils of turquoise mists.

My mouth was open wide in awe when Beauvois turned around to say, 'The light here is remarkable. It sparkles off the water. The perfect clarity for films.'

'Can we go inside the studio? Can we take a look around?' Theo's excitement was clear to hear, and he was surely as disappointed as me when our host said it would not be safe. But soon the construction would be complete, and then we'd also see the wealth of props he'd bought and stored there, having scoured the local newspapers to learn of sales at large estates; bidding for antique furniture, for rugs and drapes and ornaments with which to dress the set designs.

I must confess it made me sad to think about those auctions, to be so blithe and cavalier about possessions being sold to stave off fears of bankruptcy. So much of that was going on, as my brother and I knew all too well. But, we must not dwell upon the past, not when this man was offering an altogether brighter life ~ into which I walked quite blindly, following in Beauvois's wake when he led us back towards his house, and then into a dining room. Not that I really noticed where we sat, or what we ate that night, whether the wine was red or white, or the face of the maid who served it. Only that Charles Beauvois was there. Only rapt to listen when he talked of all the films he planned to make.

'I mean to create a series of bold dramatic narratives, each film uniquely of itself, but also with a common theme. I want you to be my star, Leda. I want you to be my mermaid. To look exactly as you did when Theo made his postcard.

'And Theo,' he turned to my brother, 'I want you to help me with the sets. I see it all so vividly in my imagination. But thoughts alone are not enough. I need someone with expertise. Someone who has the talent to transform dreams to realities.'

'Reality can be expensive.' My brother was being cautious, and almost sounding like Papa when he'd once tried to curb my hopes. 'One thing to make a painted drop for a portrait, or a theatre stage. But, a film, to be convincing, needs sets in three dimensions. And that requires carpenters, materials, and wages paid, and ...'

Beauvois interrupted. 'Naturally, there will be funds. More than enough to pay you well, and any other employees. I'm already in correspondence with the Edison Company in New York. And if they fail to bite my hook there are other English companies already looking to invest. The films are where the future lies. But the thing I need to know right now is whether you'll be joining me . . . if you'll enter the world of White Cliff House and help create my fantasies?'

I didn't need persuading. I'd already entered a different world. I really didn't want to leave when Beauvois said he'd use his car to drive us both back home again. And what an experience that was, better than any chugging bike as we sped along the cliff-side track, where I fancied myself an Arabian Queen who flew on a magic carpet ride, transported on a path of stars while seeing the silver mirrored light of the moon in the black of waves below.

I wasn't the least bit frightened. I'd already cheated death that day. I knew my life was somehow charmed.

A spell of immortality conjured up by Charles Beauvois.

WHAT SEEMED CORPOREAL
MELTED AS BREATH INTO
THE WIND

Leda's words were swimming on the page. I was finding it hard to stay awake. The hands of the mantel clock still told the time as being ten to twelve. But my instinct said much later. The early hours. The dead of night. A pungent silence in that room where the candle flame was soon to die, smoking long and throwing such strange shadows all around me.

Glancing at the clock again, fearing what my mind might try to conjure in those looming shapes, my fingers raised to douse the wick, then felt its burn and shouted '*Fuck!*' – and feared I'd woken Leda up. But she didn't seem to hear a thing. Still sleeping, I was sure of that. Breaths deep and very regular.

My own began to echo them as I slumped back in the leather chair while contemplating what I'd read. What Leda called her *Mirrors*.

I'd been moved when she wrote of the loss of her parents, by what she and Theo had endured. But what was haunting me the most was the time she'd met with Charles Beauvois, when she'd been in the aquarium, when the physical attraction she'd described was almost tangible. Perhaps that's why I fell asleep and dreamed that I'd been there as well – standing in that darkened aisle and seeing my reflection in the glassy sheen of a water tank. Except those eyes were never mine. Those eyes belonged to Charles Beauvois. The same bold gaze I'd seen look out from the screen during the *The Mermaid* film.

I felt him in my body too. That shivery, clammy sensation you get when wearing clothes too cold or damp. But what was that discomfort when Leda was in front of me dancing through the waving weeds – when an unknown voice rang in my mind, its tenor deep and clearly heard. *She is an ocean flower. Shall I pluck, or shall I let her stay?*

I felt the stranger's mind then, as he willed her to turn and look at him. As if she heard, she did just that. But it wasn't the face I expected to see. This Leda was much younger. The features beneath the fancy hat were those of the girl in the crown of snakes. And while gazing at her bruised black eyes, the 'other' voice was whispering: *It's her! The girl on the promenade. The face that's haunted me for years.*

Leda then removed her hat and lifted her eyes to meet with mine, and I saw the mermaid from the film, so dreamily seductive beneath her curling silver wig. Every fibre in my being burned with the need to hold her in my arms, to touch her skin, to kiss her lips and—

And then, the focus changed again and I seemed to be above her, looking down on yet another face. This time the aged woman who lived alone in White Cliff House, whose smiling lips were parting, growing wider and yet wider until they formed a pleading 'o', with that tragic look of mute despair subsumed into a void of black, through which I heard her screaming. A sound so loud, so full of rage. I had to wake, to get away...

In fact, I thought I *was* awake, opening my eyes to see the older woman's features twisted in a mask of hate, through which she hissed, 'You *dare* come back... to come back here to White Cliff House... after all that you have done to me?'

That echo of some words she'd said while *The Mermaid* film played earlier. But I couldn't reply. I was paralysed, unable to protect myself when one of her hands was lifted, when I saw the lines of jagged scars in the loose, scaled flesh above her wrists. And below, in bony fingers, the spear of broken glass they held. It could have been one of the shards I'd seen while visiting the filming shed, and she held it like a weapon, and – I was so sure of this – she meant to stab that blade in me.

I thought she had. Another flash, which could have been the dagger's plunge, and then the trickling warmth I felt as blood leaked out across my breast, which was when I started crying out for Leda to stop, to go away – which was when I *really* did wake up.

Blinking against a shaft of sunlight leaking through the damaged wall, I realised that must have caused the heat I felt upon my chest. Daring to look up again, I saw its brightness fracturing around the face of Leda Grey. It was not the kindest halo. Every wrinkle she had was magnified, with the drooping bags beneath her eyes weighed down yet more by gravity, when she arched her body over mine and called my name so plaintively.

'Mr Peters ... please! You must wake up. I think you've had a nightmare.'

I dragged myself up in the creaking chair and saw her memoirs on the desk. Next to them my cigarettes. My fingers itched to grab one, to put a fag into my mouth. Something comforting, habitual. Something to try and calm my nerves.

Meanwhile, she gave a rueful smile and asked, 'You've read my *Mirrors* then?'

'Not all of them. I got as far as ... as the day you came to White Cliff House.'

My voice was slow. Thoughts slower. I was rubbing my eyes, still feeling trapped inside the horrors of the dream. Which Leda was the real one? The screaming, leering harpy, or this calmer, sweet old woman whose voice was low and measured when she said, 'Perhaps you'll read the rest of them a little later on ... that is, if you have the time to stay.'

I asked what time it was just then, surprised when Leda answered, 'From the way the light is shining in, I'd say it's early afternoon. That's when I often wake now. I sleep longer during daylight hours than ever in the darker ones ... although last night I had more rest than I have done for many months, only stirring back to life again when I heard you calling out my name.'

'I'm sorry. I had the strangest dreams.'

How could I tell her what I'd seen? Such a horrible vision of Leda Grey, and so intent on killing me.

She answered with a heavy sigh. 'In a way I almost envy you. I hardly ever dream now. I wish I did. Only that way can that this old flesh feel young again.'

At that, she turned her back on me, her movements as supple as a girl's when she walked towards the cabinet that held the props for Beauvois's films. From there, she turned to offer me that lovely radiant smile she had, which lifted all the sagging flesh and made it seem as if no time had passed since I'd been standing there to find the shell the day before.

She said, 'Would you mind so very much if we changed the rules for the game today … if I choose the next object instead of you? You see I think we need to view the films in the order they were made. *The Mermaid* was first, but now you need to see how she came to find her legs. Come over. Come and look inside!'

I did as she asked, though it took a while. My legs were stiff and cramping after sitting in the chair for hours. But then, just like a little child who's standing in a sweet shop, I felt the sluggishness dissolve while peering through the cupboard doors.

What treat might be brought out today? It was impossible to tell. The interior was very dim. There was no candle lit outside. But when she stepped aside the light that shafted through the broken wall then glistened on the dark green glass of what looked like a bottle of medicine from an old Victorian pharmacy. Quite small, and formed of six flat sides, each panel deeply fluted. And, at the top, above the neck, a stop to keep the contents in.

'This is what I choose today. Won't you bring it to the table?' Her voice was soft, but urging, and I felt the lightest brush of air against the skin of one bare arm, as soft as the flutter of butterfly wings when Leda turned to walk away, her long dress whispering behind as it trailed across the worn out rug – which almost made it seem as if she'd floated to her fireside chair; as if this Leda needed neither tail nor legs to cross that space.

'What is it?' I asked, while holding the bottle up towards the light, to read the label on the front. *The Elixir of Dreaming Delights*.

'It's opium,' she answered.

'Opium?' I was intrigued. The bottle looked to be half full, so that when I gave a gentle shake some liquid swirled about inside. 'Did … do you ever take this stuff?'

I was trying to imagine Leda Grey in the role of an Alice in Wonderland, indulging in 'Drink Me, Eat Me' games,

'I did try it, once or twice. But I never really liked it. The acting … that was my release. These potions might give confidence, some solace in our darker hours, but in the end we're all alone. Alone with our thoughts. Our consciences. With the knowledge of everything we've done.'

She paused, and looked into my eyes. 'Beauvois called it his St Peter's. A few drops to sleep as if the dead, to enter the gates of Heaven, and all delights on offer there … or else to find himself condemned to every misery in hell.'

She gave another rueful smile. 'It all depended on his mood. He could be as changeable as the wind. He had such depths. Such passions. To be with him could feel as if you were clinging onto the tail of a comet, blazing through the midnight skies. It could also feel like being plunged into the deepest, blackest sea. No light to ever shine again.'

During these confessions my fingers twisted at the cork. When I felt it slip from the funnel's mouth I held it to my nose and sniffed. Something sweet, with a note of cinnamon. It reminded me of the cough medicine Mum used to buy when I was small, which I'd sometimes drink when I was well; creeping through the bathroom door and locking it behind me, clambering onto the loo seat to open the cupboard on the wall, then slugging down a hefty gulp from the bottle of sticky viscous brown. I'd loved the tingle in my throat, how it numbed the real world away. And now, as a man, in White Cliff House, I tipped this bottle upside down and felt its contents splash against the tip of the finger held across – hoping that Leda hadn't seen when I licked the wetness from my skin.

Hardly a moment had gone by before I felt as if I'd been propelled into a dream again, seeing the face of Charles Beauvois floating there before my eyes, at the same time swallowing against a flood of saliva in my mouth. I seemed to be responding to some urgent physical craving coursing madly through my veins, during which I tried to keep a grasp on who and what and where I was, suddenly impelled to ask, 'Did Beauvois often use this drug?'

'Yes, he used it every night. Though I didn't realise at first. We were not so intimate, you see. Not when we made *The Mermaid*. Then, I was still travelling up here from Brightland every day. Our relationship … it only changed when the second film was finished. The film of *The Dreamer's Delirium*, for which this bottle was a prop.'

She frowned at me with some concern. 'You seem to be distracted, Ed. Are you thirsty? It's so hot again … and I'm sure you must be hungry. If you go on out to the corridor, turn left, then down to the very end, you can't fail to find the kitchen. Plenty of water in the tap, and I think there's still some bread and fruit. Do help yourself to anything. Young men can have such appetites.'

Such appetites?

Had she noticed my reaction to that single drop of Beauvois's drug? But yes, she was right. My throat was dry, tickling and sore with thirst, and thinking hers must be the same I asked, 'Can I bring you anything?'

'Nothing for me,' she answered. 'But I'd like to sit alone a while. These memories, I find they are—'

She broke off. I couldn't fail to hear the note of sadness in her voice. Was I right to stay at White Cliff House when these memories distressed her? Wouldn't I be better off going back to my hotel, to try and get some decent rest before I visited again?

But the bottle – the film it signified. How could I go without seeing that? So I followed her instructions, walking down the passageway, at the end of which were three stone steps descending to another door. A smaller one off to the right.

A loo. Just what I needed. I pissed into the stained white bowl, then tugged down on the long brass chain suspended from the tank above. It gave a clunking, hollow sound. No water there for any flush.

Fearing for the kitchen tap I closed the toilet door behind, about to walk on through the next when I heard the faintest scratching, and then a high pitched droning – though both those sounds had faded by the time my fingers curled around the knob to push my way inside.

The room was large and orderly; at least it seemed that way at first. Rows of cream china upon a pine dresser. The dull grey gleam of colanders hung next to pans and wooden spoons. An old black range in a chimney breast with an iron kettle on the top, but – thank God – no fire lit there to give the heat to boil it up, or to air the folded sheets and clothes that draped across a drying rack.

Perhaps, with Leda's eyes so bad, she hadn't noticed all the dust smeared across the window panes, so thick the blazing sun outside could only spread a muted light to expose what lay upon the floor beneath a big pine table, where a debris of crumbs was scattered in the shadows of the old stone flags – and where my eyes then caught a streak of grey as a mouse ran through them.

It disappeared beneath a door that opened to pantry. Boxes of rumpled plastic bags. Others full of candles. Shelf upon shelf piled high with tins, their peeling vintage labels showing fruits and meats and vegetables. Potatoes and onions hung in nets, all sprouting roots and fungus, only fit to be thrown on a compost heap. At least some bottles of red wine looked tempting and were probably a great deal better for their age, though not what lay beneath them. The bags of flour, rice and oats with contents spilling everywhere, providing quite a feast for ants, or else the other mice I turned to see there on the table top.

One nibbled at a loaf of bread. Another, apples in a bowl. But some of those fruits appeared untouched, smooth flesh a glowing russet red. And while fancying a bite myself, already savouring the taste of tart-sweet juice upon my tongue, a strange thing happened in that room.

The air around me juddered, rippling as I'd seen it do while

I was watching Leda's film. All those scenes shown through the water tank, or the close-up view of Charles Beauvois when he'd been walking on the beach. And then a sudden rolling jerk, like standing on a ship while being tossed and rocked about by waves – which was when I stumbled forward, clinging onto the edge of the table where, before my very eyes, the loaf of bread turned green with mould. The apples were decaying too, each one a shrinking flaccid brown and giving off a cloying smell as the syrups of fermentation juice were dribbling into the bowl. I gagged at the thick rank sweetness while watching tiny grubs emerge to wriggle through that putrid ooze, with some of those maggots already mutating into whining adult flies that buzzed in circles round my head.

Swatting an arm against them, I held my breath against the stink and snatched a sheet from the airing rack, wrapping the rotting food in that, then stumbling towards a sink where I raised one hand to work the latch of the window set above it.

Grunting with the effort, at last I flung the bundle out into the garden's tangled growth, wincing to hear the smash of china breaking on the baked hard ground. The more organic soft wet thud as decomposing fruits rolled out. And then, inhaling fresher air, I stared at all the dead black flies that lay across the window sill. The straggling black of brittle legs. The torsos lit with rain-bow lights of iridescent greens and blues.

How had they died so quickly? Every single one of them?

In death there can be beauty.

I was hearing words in my head again. Some new hallucination brought on by Leda's opiate? I'd barely licked a drop of it, but I knew that dehydration also led to strange delusions. So, perhaps I'd imagined the food was fresh when that was what I'd hoped to see. After all, in such humidity what food would not go on to rot? What vermin would not breed and thrive?

At least I could try and quench my thirst. Fixed on a board above the sink there *was* a copper water tap, though the crusts of limescale round its spout didn't fill me with the highest hopes. Neither did the banging pipes – before a gush of water spluttered out into the sink below, and what first ran a dirty red was soon as clear as crystal, inviting me to duck my head, to open up my mouth and taste the sweetness splashing into it.

When satisfied, I stood and held my wrists beneath the cooling flow, seeing again the fading red where thorns had scratched against the skin. But they didn't cause me any pain, and the porcelain coolness of the sink where my shirt had ridden upwards to expose the belly underneath, was not at all unpleasant.

I'm not sure how long I rested there, listening to the water's rush while images of Leda as the mermaid swam inside my mind – until I heard the sound of someone singing in another room. A piano being played as well. And I knew every word from my childhood, from when my mother used to sing: *Oh! You beautiful doll, You great big beautiful doll! Let me put my arms around you, I could never live without you...*

The music stopped and never reached the part I'd always liked the best. *Squeeze me dear, I don't care! Hug me just as if you were a grizzly bear.* Still, my mind raced on to form those words, thinking of the way Mum always used to grab my hands in hers, to swing me round and round the room, and the dizzy spinning breathless laughs when I'd plead and beg for her to stop when I'd only ever wanted more. More singing. More swinging. More beautiful boying...

Odd that Leda Grey had such a high and reedy singing voice, when she spoke with deeper husky tones. While pondering that I saw a glass left on the wooden drainer, rinsing off a layer of dust, then filling it with water. Something to offer my musical host, who was surely in need of a cooling drink, whatever she'd said to the contrary.

After stopping the tap I observed the glass in which some grit was swirling round. Like the ashes scattered at the pier. Through that liquid prism, I saw the room anew again. Walls warping, bending round me, distorted through a fish-eye lens – though I knew that was only a natural effect caused by the curvature of glass. Nothing to do with any drug.

As the kitchen door slammed shut behind, I paused and took

a long deep breath. Wherever my mother's remains might be, I'd said goodbye. I'd made my peace. Only the living mattered now.

Back in the shadowed sitting room, I placed the glass of water down on the table next to Leda's shell, and the bottle of elixir. Meanwhile, she smiled up at me and asked, 'Shall we watch the second film? The one called *The Dreamer's Delirium*.'

'Great title. It sounds psychedelic.' I tried to force a cheerful tone, but clearly that confused her. Perhaps a word she did not know.

'Psychedelic?' she frowned, then carried on. 'Beauvois based this narrative on visions that he'd had one night when he fell asleep in this very room ... having drunk from this very bottle.'

Again, that twitching in my hand as my fingers longed to wrap around the ribbings in the dark green glass – instead of which I focused on the stationary wheels of the memo tape.

I wished I'd brought more batteries. It could have recorded Leda's song, or picked up sounds that I then made as I loosened the projector's catch, releasing the previous reel of film, and then, when that was reinterred inside its metal canister, the thud of my feet as I crossed the rug, returning to the window desk to find the label that was marked with the name of Leda's second film.

This time the lid unscrewed at once to reveal the sleek black reel inside. There was also another envelope and, just as I'd done with *The Mermaid* before, I opened that and scanned the words unfolding in my shaking hands, before heading back to the lantern's stand where I set the film in place to screen. And finally, I gripped the crank, turning that until the film revealed what Beauvois had described:

THE DREAMER'S DELIRIUM

Story and Direction by Charles Beauvois

Camera by Charles Beauvois and Theo Williams

Set Design by Charles Beauvois and Theo Williams

Starring Leda Grey as The Vampire & Charles Beauvois as The Collector

With Amy Philips as The Maid

The above credits to be created in an hallucinatory style, as if viewed when under the influence of alcohol of opiates. The same with the frame of words below.

'A wealthy art collector has purchased a marble statue created centuries before. It is called the Pale Lady, and legend claims that any man who owns it meets a tragic end...'

SCENE ONE – The camera pans over a drawing room. Shutters are closed at the windows. The walls are full of shelves of books, with many more stacked on the floor and piled on furniture around. The remains of a fire is smouldering in the basket of a large stone hearth. On the mantelpiece above it, a candle has been lit. Distorted shadows fill the room and fall across the open door, at the side of which there has been placed the semi-classical statue of a woman standing on a plinth.

SCENE TWO – Being unable to sleep one night, dressed only in his dressing gown, The Collector enters the drawing room. He pauses to look at the statue, caressing one of the marble arms, then reaches up to touch one cheek before he walks towards the hearth, where he looks at the face of a carriage clock.

SCENE THREE – A close-up view of the clock hands. The time is ten minutes to midnight. NB: Any musical accompaniment should be the sound of a tapping drum to denote the sense of tension as every moment passes by.

SCENE FOUR – The Collector lifts the candlestick and carries that towards a couch where he sets it on a table and uses its light to read a book. Also on the table is a bottle of wine, an empty glass, a large white shell, and a bowl filled with fresh apples. The Collector sighs as he sits down, picking a fruit, and about to eat when he changes his mind and returns the fruit back to its place in the bowl again. He seems about to lift the wine, but instead reaches a hand into the pocket of his dressing gown. He withdraws a bottle of medicine.

SCENE FIVE – Close-up of the bottle label: THE ELIXIR OF DREAMING DELIGHTS.

SCENE SIX – The Collector drinks from the bottle and then lies back upon the couch. For a little while he reads the book, but the drug very swiftly takes effect. He closes his eyes and falls asleep. The camera blurs and pulls away.

SCENE SEVEN – A close-up of the sculpture which now appears to come to life. White marble turns to milk-white flesh. White hair turns black, as do the brows and eyes carved in the face below. Those eyes are glittering and bright with light thrown from the candle's flame. With the hint of a smile upon her lips, the woman steps down from her pedestal and walks towards the sleeping man.

SCENE EIGHT – She removes the book still in his hands, and the camera then moves close enough to show the title on the front: THE SPELL TO WAKE THE VAMPYRE.

SCENE NINE – Another wider shot to show the woman turning pages, immersed in what she reads there.

SCENE TEN – Looking shocked, she drops the book. She walks to a mirror above the hearth and stares at her reflection through the glimmer of the light behind.

SCENE ELEVEN – Her face is seen in close-up, as if reflected in the glass. We see confusion, also dread, as if a long lost memory is now returning to her mind.

SCENE TWELVE – The sleeping man is stirring and seems about to wake when she then turns and walks towards him. She arches her body over his, her lips about to kiss his mouth. During this action the screen will blur.

SCENE THIRTEEN – It is morning. The room is filled with light as the curtains are opened by a maid. She is holding a feather duster, cleaning the marble statue which is standing on its plinth again. Then, as if she's heard some sound, the maid spins round and notices her master lying on the couch. She leaves the room in great distress.

SCENE FOURTEEN – A close-up of the sculpture's face, where everything is marble white, except for the lips. A wet dark red.

SCENE FIFTEEN – A close-up of the lifeless man with a bloody gash upon his throat. The camera shot then pulls away, exposing the table and the bowl where the apples have all rotted, alive with crawling maggots.

END

The effect of night-time darkness had been utterly convincing, though Leda said they'd filmed by day, with the mood of night being achieved by colour washes on the film, those greens and blues as filmy as the scarves that stage magicians use. She said the candle 'sparkled' due to scratches on the celluloid. (Not the first time Beauvois used that trick.) And when the story reached its end, when those large white letters filled the screen, they'd then been drenched in vibrant reds to look as if they dripped with blood.

It was chillingly effective, and almost more than I could do to keep the handle turning when cold marble turned to human flesh, when I realised that what I'd viewed while walking down towards the shed was the very statue that they'd used to make this film, *Delirium*.

But when I saw the rotting fruit, creating such a mirror of my vision in the kitchen, the shock was such that I could hardly concentrate at all when Leda started telling me about the days and days of camera work that Beauvois had then speeded up for a few brief seconds on the screen.

'Very clever, don't you think?' She looked at me intently. 'Though what he could never reproduce was the stink that all those maggots made. But I think you need to know these things ... to put them in your article ... to understand how Beauvois hoped to convey a sense of corruption far deeper than the physical. The frailty of our mortal state. How sex and life and death are all to be found in the kiss of the vampire.'

'Not as much fun as *The Mermaid*, then?' I endeavoured to make light of things, to conceal the confusion in my mind.

Leda frowned while looking down at the hands clasped tightly in her lap, and said, 'No, I suppose not. The innocence and prettiness of that first film was not to last.'

'But what a femme fatale you made. Those scenes when the statue comes to life.'

Her movements had been sensual, almost an erotic dance. Her costume, which was little more than a winding of some sheer white cloth, had allowed her thighs to be exposed, the swell of her belly, her high round breasts. And not a touch of innocence when she'd changed from stone to living flesh, oozing sex and mystery.

Even when the film was done, the sense of encroaching dread remained. I could have sworn I saw a trail of scarlet mist drift through the screen to stain the shadows of the room, and on that mist I'm sure I caught the hot metallic smell of blood.

I knew it was impossible. I needed to breathe some fresher air, to return to my hotel and sleep – explaining to Leda how tired I felt, how I needed to wash and change my clothes. Get back to some normality.

'Oh, so soon?' She looked dismayed. 'But, before you go,' she pressed me, 'you must tell me what you thought about the maid who appeared at the very end ... who found The Collector lying dead?

I'd almost forgotten about her. Like Theo in the film before she'd seemed a mere accessory, of no real relevance at all.

'That was Amy,' Leda carried on. 'The maid employed here at the house. She'd been desperate to have a part on film, though not so pleased when it was done ... at the way that Beauvois tricked her.

'He'd directed her to enter the room, to open the curtains and dust down the statue, then shake the dreamer from his sleep. But he'd failed to say a thing about the gash she'd see upon his throat. He wanted a true reaction, you see, and the way you saw her on the screen ... all that waving of arms and hysteria ... every moment of that was genuine.

'Beauvois, he offered no remorse, was only delighted when the scene had gone exactly as he'd planned. I suppose he tried to make amends when Amy had recovered, inviting her into the dining room when he wore her cap and apron, grovelling and curtsying while he served her tea from a silver tray. But, I sensed no sincerity in that act and, as I know to my own cost, that wasn't to be the only time when Beauvois would deceive his cast.' Leda sadly shook her head. 'He had no guilt about such things. For him, the art was everything. The art was his reality ... no matter how uncomfortable.'

'That's interesting,' I answered. 'Alfred Hitchcock ... he was another director who liked to play games with his casts. The magazine I work for published a feature on him once. Things that happened on the set of a film he made called *Psycho*, when he had some replica dummies made to simulate a murdered corpse, then hid those dolls around the set for the actors to find by accident. He pretended it was all a joke, saying he'd only wanted to know which model was most frightening ... though his leading actress wasn't pleased to find one in her dressing room, or to hear how Hitchcock laughed it off, insisting that the trauma had drawn out her best performance.'

'How cruel,' she bluntly answered.

'He was a genius of suspense. His earliest films were silent too. Dark and twisted thrillers, obsessed with sex and murder.'

'*L'amour et la mort.*' She sighed. For a moment she was lost in thought, eyes narrowed in a haggard face. But when her gaze met mine again, there was only a warm affection.

'Amy.' Her voice was wistful. 'I believe it means beloved in French ... I really was so fond of her. That tongue she had! The jokes she told. The filthy songs she learned from all her friends who lived at Cuckham Sands. I met them too ... eventually. The music hall gang we called them. Some were hired as extras when we came to make another film. The one we called *The Cursed Queen*. Not Amy though. She wouldn't act in any more of Beauvois's films. Which,' Leda's face grew sterner, 'made Amy cleverer than me.

'But she still helped with the costumes, sitting here for hours on end at the sewing machine that Beauvois bought. There it is, over there by that dressmaker's dummy, though much too rusted up these days. This house grows damp in the winter months. Everything spoils eventually. Anyway ...' She closed her eyes a while. 'I missed her when she went away to marry Joe Winstanley. He and his father used to farm the land adjoining White Cliff House. Joe helped us in the gardens too. Cutting lawns and pruning trees. Odd jobs down at the filming shed ... Ah, well, their love was not to last. The First World War made sure of that.'

Leda stopped, her lips clamped shut, and when no other words came out, I said, 'Maybe I'll look her up? Ask her for an interview?'

She answered abruptly. 'Amy's dead!' And then, the flicker of a smile. 'But it's strange, you know. These past few weeks I sometimes wake and I could swear she's in the house with me again. I hear that song she liked to sing when I was dressing for the films.'

Leda's head was tilting. She closed her eyes and softly croaked, 'Oh, you beautiful doll ... you great big beautiful doll.'

'You were singing that earlier,' I said. 'You were playing the piano, when I was in the kitchen, but ...' *But you sounded completely different.*

'The piano?' Leda looked puzzled, staring across the room to where the lid of the instrument was closed and furred in an even coat of dust. It didn't appear to have been disturbed. 'Unless... unless,' she carried on, 'unless I grow forgetful. It worries me...' her voice was tense, 'the way my mind can be confused.'

When I looked back into her eyes I saw a fierce intelligence. Also a vulnerability. I tried to reassure her, tried to fool myself as well. 'It's me. I must be hearing things. I'm exhausted... really need some sleep.'

But surely I *had* heard that song. If I hadn't, what was going on? I felt such a pressure in my head. My vision was distorting as it had in the kitchen earlier, only now it was Leda's sitting room where walls were refracting and warping around me. Nothing solid any more.

I looked at the old woman, and I wondered if she saw the same – at which point my eyes became transfixed by the vivid colour of her mouth, where a dark red blush now tinged the lips which, before, had been so pale they'd almost been invisible.

I pressed a hand to my temples, where I felt a sudden throbbing ache, and heard the words that Leda spoke: 'My brother was prone to headaches too, when he was still a younger man. Sometimes he'd have to go and lie in bed for hours, for days on end. But then...' She looked more thoughtful, upper teeth biting down on her bottom lip – which was when I realised that pressure must have been what made them red. Of course! That must have been the cause.

'With Theo,' Leda carried on, 'I think it was mostly in his mind, the effect of the stresses he'd had to bear... sometimes leading on to fits. But, with you, do you think that it could be the atmosphere inside this house? So humid and oppressive. I'd never normally suggest... but if your head is all that bad, why not take the St Peter's before you sleep? A drop or two won't harm you. Whenever Beauvois used it – before it all grew out of hand – he was like a new man in the morning. Such energy. Such new ideas.'

'Thank you! But...' I wanted it. Such a struggle to deny the urge, ever since I'd tasted that one drop. But had the opium been so strong that it could still affect me now, with that sense of dislocation? The things I'd seen. The things I'd heard?

It must be the heat, just as Leda said. A storm was surely on its way. I could almost feel the static charge. The smell of ozone in the air. Add to that the lack of food. The mesmerising atmosphere created by the films I'd seen...

The films. My mind was clear enough to calculate and ask her, 'Would you let me take the films away, to try and get some copies made? The films are what people will want to see, whatever I write about your past.'

'Oh yes. I'll let you have them. But only when we've seen them all... when my story finds its end. For now' – she glanced towards the desk – 'I'd rather keep them here with me. Something to lure you back again. But I'll let you take my *Mirrors.* You said you hadn't finished them, and as I told you earlier my mind can sometimes be confused. Better you know *that* Leda Grey than the one who sits before you now.'

I gathered up those papers and placed them in my rucksack, the bottle of elixir too. My cigarettes, I stashed them back into the pocket of my jeans, then said goodbye to Leda Grey and promised that I would return. Tomorrow. Early afternoon.

The front door closed. A solid thud. I all but ran along the path and on into the tunnel formed of densely shadowed conifers, towards the glinting light that shone from the cliff-side path at the other end.

There, the air was fresher, but it didn't help to clear my head. My temples were pounding. My bones felt 'old'. My throat was dry and very sore by the time I'd reached the village road where, had the pub been open, I would have gone to buy a beer. But it wasn't. Every room was dark. So I headed straight towards the car, rolling every window down to cool the stagnant atmosphere.

The ignition turned, the engine thrummed and came to grating life again. Wheels skidded over gravel. Several little stones threw up and tapped against the windscreen, pattering like drops of rain.

If only it would rain again. If it did, I would happily stop the car, get out and strip off all my clothes and dance stark naked in the road. Instead of which I drove too fast, hands gripping tightly on the wheel as I tried my best to focus on the bouncing shafts of yellow light thrown forwards by the headlamps – and all the while still wondering if I'd really seen those wisps of red come floating through the linen screen and into Leda's sitting room.

Lost inside those memories, rather than turning in the road and heading back to Brightland, I drove straight on through Cuckham Sands and stopped beside the seafront wall. A wall so wide that you could set a deckchair on the top of it, sitting there while looking down at waves that lapped the beach below, or rocks that clustered underneath the sheer expanse of rising cliff.

Where was Beauvois's studio? In daylight, any panes of glass would dazzle and reflect the sun. At night, the only light I saw was the faintest radiance that shone from the face of the hanging moon above, that's when the moon was not concealed by drifts of clouds that scudded past.

I struck a match and lit a fag, turned on the dashboard mirror lamp, then reached into my bag again and pulled out Leda's memories. It didn't take me very long to find the page where I'd left off, hearing her voice so vividly, as if I was still at her side. Still mired in the webs of White Cliff House.

This mirror is a crystal. A bead of dew on a spider's web. In that, the trembling features of the girl who lay in her Brightland bed and could not sleep for thinking of the heat of Charles Beauvois's embrace in the aisle of a dark aquarium. She also thought about the way his hand had gently held her own when acting as the mermaid's love. And when they made Delirium, the way his fingers gripped her chin to turn her face this way or that, as if she was his mannequin, when beneath the coolly pliant flesh her blood was simmering with lust. The passion that reached its boiling point late one summer evening when we'd finished filming our last scene.

Beauvois, Theo and myself had been walking back to White Cliff House. I remember the way our shadows merged, like some strange three-headed monster when it fell across the meadow grass, while my brother was suggesting that we go for a drink at the Cuckham pub ~ though that came as a surprise to me, when Theo only ever wished to rush straight back to Brightland, to all those other friends of his who gathered in the Bath Arms bar. He'd never so much as contemplate staying the night at White Cliff House. Not even when we started work at dawn and carried on till dusk.

I used to think it must have been because of his moral concern for me. My name. My reputation. Especially when, now and then, the carpenters he'd hired in to help with building all the sets might hang around to see me act. And, now and then, I'd see them smirk. And once, I heard one muttering, 'That Leda Grey... more like Leda Godiva. Shameless it is, how she goes on. What else takes place when we're not here?'

But nothing went on. Nothing at all. Not until that night when Theo said, 'Come on, Leda, you dull old bun strangler. You liked to have a drink before... all those Sundays spent with Ivor. Hurry up and get your glad rags on. The gang won't wait for ever.'

'Ivor? Who's Ivor?' Beauvois asked. 'And what's this gang you're on about?'

Theo answered him in part. 'The friends I've made from Cuckham Sands. Didn't Amy tell you? It's the village summer party. There'll be a hog roast on the beach. A play up on the seafront wall. A cricket match, and...'

'And beer?' I smiled wryly, knowing my brother's weakness, and suddenly remembering how Amy might have mentioned something of this party earlier, though I'd hardly heard a word she'd said, being too engrossed right then in posing on the pedestal, trying my best to keep the stance that I had made the day before ~ at that moment when the marble woman turns into a living one. The transition must be seamless for the double exposures in the film. But all that concentration left my muscles feeling stiff and sore, which was why I wasn't in the mood for heading down to Cuckham Sands.

'Well, I don't think I'll be coming. This greasepaint all needs washing off and that takes hours... and longer now, with Amy gone off partying.'

'Why bother to wash?' my brother teased. 'Just tighten your kimono belt. You always look divine in that. There'll be plenty of chance to get cleaned up when we all go swimming in the sea.'

'Swimming... with people I've never met? Without a bathing dress to wear?'

'Don't be such a spoilsport!' Theo's elbow nudged my arm. 'I always thought my sister brave, and you might as well get used to other people seeing you undressed, when The Mermaid and Delirium are finally on public view. But seriously, Leda, you should come and meet these friends I've made. Some singers from the London halls who travel down here most weekends... and very keen to take a part in any future films we make.'

Beauvois broke in. A warning tone. 'I shouldn't go raising any hopes. There'll be nothing new made here till spring. Not with Delirium still in hand. All the special effects I must complete.'

But then his voice grew softer, more thoughtful when he smiled back. 'Still, you might have something. These people could be useful. I should come to the pub and say hello. And then, if you decide to stay I don't mind walking back up here and driving Leda home again.'

I stood in the porch and watched them go. When they reached the end of the garden path Beauvois turned to wave at me. But all too soon he'd disappeared in the tunnel of the conifers.

I was glad to miss that cliff-side walk. I felt horribly sticky, much too hot, hardly able to face the prospect of carrying the old tin bath upstairs into the bedroom where, normally, I'd bathe and change back into all my normal clothes ~ when Amy was there for the donkey work.

Oh, what I would have given then for the luxury of our Brightland house, with the sink and the bath in a tiled room. No such delights above the shop, and none up here at White Cliff House. But with only me in the house just then, what harm would it do to fill the bath and wash beside the kitchen range, although, when I threw off my robe and climbed into the steaming tub I only wished I had some ice to cool the water down again; to hold against my sweating brow.

Soaping myself with the lump of carbolic I'd found beside the kitchen sink, my skin turned pink as slicks of grease slid off and stained the water white. Sinking further down in that I fell into a reverie, becoming Cleopatra as she bathed her flesh in asses' milk, before I sighed to realise that if I didn't soon get out I'd be as wrinkled as a prune.

One moment more I gave myself to lie there while I listened to the constant dripping of the tap; that sound then being echoed by a patter on the window glass, as rain began to fall outside.

The rain! How cooling that would be. I dragged myself out of the tub, leaving a trail of puddles as I wandered through the kitchen door, and then on past a wooden gate to a part of the garden that was walled. Once, someone had tended it, but now it was a wilderness. Old fruit trees trained to spread their branches out on wires across brick walls were sagging with the weight of pears, of red-skinned apples, purple plums ~ though very few you'd wish to eat, most having fallen to the grass where birds and worms were feasting. But, luckily, no drunken wasps were buzzing round that sweetness. Wasps did not fly in the pouring rain, unlike myself, who laughed and danced, with my head held back, my eyes tight closed as water ran across them, tickling my lips, and...

Surely that bang was the kitchen door! I froze as if I'd turned to stone when I heard the cracking sound of twigs as feet were walking over them ~ which was when I span around and saw Beauvois, his clothes all soaking wet, his dark hair flattened on his head. And I, who did not wear a stitch, I really didn't mind at all when he stared at me so brazenly. After all, my brother told the truth. I'd posed in very little more while acting in the filming shed.

But this ~ this did feel different. For one thing, Theo wasn't there. My ever-present guardian. For another, I was magnetised, as if the rain between us had been made of tiny iron files. I couldn't move to run away, even had I wanted to when, without a single word, Beauvois walked towards me and wove his fingers through my own, then led me to the garden's end, where some honeysuckle stems had knitted tightly through the years to form a trailing canopy.

It wasn't the least bit damp to sit on the bench concealed within that growth, where Beauvois then removed his shirt and spread that down across the wood in case of any splinters. And there we perched, as if two birds, me thinking how ridiculous and decadent we must have looked. But he didn't share my laughter, the laughter to conceal my nerves. He only stared into my eyes while fingers traced the tiny drops of water running down my neck, and then my breasts ~ and, during that, my own hand raised to touch the hair that grew so thickly on his chest.

I had never seen Papa undressed, and Theo had skin as smooth as me, so this was something quite unknown. A man as hairy as a bear. I shivered, but I wasn't cold. I felt too hot and feverish. And it was a fever of a kind, just like the one I'd suffered when we'd met at the aquarium, and only later did I fear that in my madness I had given much too freely of myself. You see, he'd promised nothing back. He'd only asked me, 'Are you sure?'

'I've never been surer in my life!' I didn't have a moment's doubt.

'But, if people know about this? The things they might go on to say. You realise your life would change, and...' I had to strain to catch his words, when the weight of the rain intensified, such a hissing stream of pattering around the nest in which we hid.

'I can't marry you, Leda... if that's what you want. I already have a wife, still living in America. It's finished. I should have secured an annulment before I ever left the place. Perhaps, I could still do that now, but ...'

'Was she an actress too?' I asked. 'Did you work with her? Make films with her?' What pangs of jealousy I felt, though I told myself I had no right to be so angered by this news. Why, hadn't my very own mother once been married to another man, when she and Papa fell in love?

While sitting there in a fug of confusion, I heard him say, 'We could pretend. You could always wear a wedding ring, but ...' His tone became much colder. 'Please, don't ask about my past. My present and my future life is now with you, at White Cliff House. That's all you need to know about.'

Not the proposal of which I'd dreamed. But then, when I thought of my little bed in that dreary room above the shop, was that the life I wanted? What price was I prepared to pay to take on yet another role? To play the part of Beauvois's wife? To keep on acting in his films? To ensure that Theo would be paid to do the work he also loved? Neither one of us to be enslaved to the drudgery of our father's shop.

'I don't care if you're married!' I told him. 'I don't care what other people say. I'm not too young or too naive to know what I want ... what I've known for months.'

He answered with a strangled groan as his mouth touched mine. A long, long kiss. I was lost when he pulled away again, when he kneeled on the grass before me, his fingers fumbling to work the buttons of his trouser flies. And what a shocking sight it was to see his sex revealed like that. But shock is not the same as fear, and then, that rushing of my blood when he called me his garden Venus, and the note of wonder in his voice, which I do believe was genuine, when he said, 'I fell in love with you, that day in the aquarium.'

'Kiss me again!' How I rejoiced in the scratching of his stubbled cheek, and my thudding heart, and gasping breaths, when I felt as if I might well drown with the air so close and wet and hot, and the sweetest honeysuckle smell, and the constant hissing of the rain that dripped around us like a veil. How strangely magnified it seemed, *the snail that crawled upon a leaf, the mucous trail it left behind. The beads of water trembling on the silver threads of a spider's web.*

I didn't feel the least remorse. It was lovely. Lovely. Lovely. I wanted to do it all again and, oh, so happy when he groaned, 'Stay with me, Leda. Promise me . . . you'll always stay at White Cliff House.'

And I did stay with Charles Beauvois, for once we had begun this thing there really was no going back. I couldn't get enough of him. So many nights of lovemaking in all those lingering summer weeks, though I doubt that anyone was fooled when Beauvois hinted that we'd wed, and still no ring upon my hand. No, the only fool was me. Always the one for self-deceit, content to sit within this house's walls and never leave again ~ except when working in the shed.

And when we were there, with the glass above, with the blue of the sea and the sky around, I really thought that I might be the Venus that he said I was. He worshipped me. He adored me. But he wanted to possess me too, to mould me like a thing of clay. And that is not the same as love.

WE ARE YET BUT YOUNG IN DEED

I finished reading Leda's words. My thoughts were turning round and round. Had she really never left that house after losing her virginity, before – for whatever reason – Charles Beauvois had disappeared?

I needed to know the truth of it. He sounded too controlling, and yet she'd seemed to love the man, though with more than a hint in what she wrote that she'd willingly used that garden bench as the casting couch for the fame she'd sought, for those dreams she'd had to be a star. Her brother's happiness as well.

With the papers folded and returned to a pocket in my ruck-sack, I lit another cigarette, then left the car to stretch my legs, climbing up the few wide steps to stand on top of the granite wall, before descending down a longer run that led me to the beach.

There, I walked on shingle, and then across a stretch of sand where my breaths fell naturally in time with the roaring crash of waves ahead. In – Out – In – Out. Each time the fag smoke drifted off I felt a little emptier, as if some essence of myself had also drained away into the shifting black expanse of sea, where the rippling texture of the waves reminded me of creases in the sheet hung up at White Cliff House. The silver gleam of a full white moon reflected in their zigzag path provided the wavering line of light that led my eyes towards the cliffs. Up there, in her reclusive world, was Leda Grey still sleeping? Or was she awake and standing at a window in a higher room, looking down on this beach so far below? Could she see the silver sprays of foam that shone and then dissolved into a million frothing bubbles, melting into—

My thoughts were broken by the violent whooshing sound

of lightning as it speared into the seas ahead, the whole horizon gleaming in a branching forest made of gold. What would Charles Beauvois have made of that? A stunning vision so untamed, the like of which he'd never hope to replicate within his films. Or had he? There were more to see.

As the lightning died, as thunder boomed and rumbled, still some distance off, I saw a paler glimmering far out along the coastline. It could have been the Brightland Pier.

Mum. I groaned. Grief gripped my heart, an aching tightness in my throat. Was she still there, still on *that* beach? Could she hear if I shouted out her name?

For a moment I almost believed she had. But it wasn't her. It was someone else who called, 'Hey! Hey you, out there in the water… don't you know how fast the tide comes in? How dangerous this place can be? A man can get caught in those riptides… get sucked right under and be drowned before he knows what's happening."

I glanced back to see the silhouette of the woman who stood beneath the wall, as vague as a photo negative.

'Christ! I hadn't noticed.' My reply was muffled by the wind that rose in gusts from crashing waves. But I noticed then, with my legs grown stiff, glancing down to see how high the tide had risen round them, lapping just above my knees where the denim clung against the skin.

I began to fear she might be right. When I tried to move my feet were stuck, sinking into gluey sand. No timber groyne to grab for when falling back into the foam, so blinded by the stinging salt I couldn't even see the pair of hands that grabbed around one wrist, then dragged me to my feet again. All I could do was follow the slapping beat of flip-flopped feet, my trainers squelching in reply as we trudged across the slipping stones.

But, by the time we'd reached the wall the throbbing in my head had gone, as if the metal vice that had been twisting tightly there before had somehow had its catch released. Even my eyes were sharper, the stinging salt all blinked away, when my saviour stopped to look around and said, 'I know you, don't I ... from the pub? You were in the other day.'

'You were drinking there as well?' I asked. 'I'm sorry. I don't ...'

The moon broke through the clouds again, and by its light I saw her face. 'Oh ... you're the girl behind the bar. What are you doing here so late?'

'Would you believe me if I said I spend my nights walking this beach searching for waifs and strays to save?' She paused, and stood there grinning. 'I'm actually looking for my dog. I often walk her here at night when I've finished working at the pub. Great big black retriever. Wouldn't hurt a fly. But the lightning spooked her. She ran off. Still ...' she shrugged, 'it's over now. She'll be hunting round the rock pools. She'll be as happy as Larry, sniffing for any flotsam or jetsam that she can bring back home again. A bit like me, collecting you!'

'Are you going to take me home then?'

'I don't live very far away. You can get dried off there if you like.'

So that was that. We climbed more steps. At the top, a gravel path led past a row of little bungalows, though the one at which my new friend chose to stop was less conventional.

'My God,' I exclaimed when I recognised the distinctive shape of the narrow door with the words 'First Class' etched in the glass. 'Is this really what I think it is? You live in ...'

'Yes, I do! Welcome to Railway-Carriage-on-Sea, otherwise known as Bungalow Bay. Old rolling stock that got sold off by the London to Brightland Company. There used to be a whole lot more, before the Germans bombed them.'

'How on earth did anyone get them here?' I asked above the groaning swing of the picket gate through which she passed, walking onto a decked veranda where the wooden eaves above were strung with sparkling loops of fairy lights. And something whiter glowing through the window from the other side, where a TV set was flickering.

Lit by that phosphorescence, she could have been standing on a stage, with a luminous halo of bleached blonde hair to frame a red-lipped smiling face, when she said, 'Tilly, an old friend of my gran's, she left me this place when she passed away. She used to say they'd floated the carriages across the bay. She said fishermen once lived in them, until a London businessman was visiting the beach one day and saw the potential in buying up more pitches that he'd then sell on. Advertising seaside dreams in all the London newspapers.

'Some people paid enormous sums to live down here on Cuckham Sands. A lot of them were Tilly's friends. Other singers and actors she'd worked with. They used to call this Pantomime Row. And they really did give shows, you know. Mainly in the summer months when they'd meet with all the villagers and throw a party on the beach.'

She gave a half-cocked smile and said, 'I'd say you need a party too ... a bit of fun to cheer you up. Have you come down here on holiday? You look as if you need one.'

'You're not backwards in coming forwards then.' I was trying to keep my mind on everything this girl was telling me – thinking back to Leda's *Mirrors*, when she'd also mentioned parties being held down here on Cuckham beach.

'Well, ain't that just the truth!' She grinned, and then, 'I know, I should hold my tongue. Sometimes I just can't help myself. Comes in useful at the pub. At other times ... I go too far.'

She crouched down by the carriage door, reaching underneath a mangled mess of metal lying there.

'Was that a motorbike?' I asked, thinking of Leda Grey again, and the day when she and Theo crashed while driving up the cliff side track.

'Who knows. I found it by the rocks. There was a sort of sidecar too. Bits of old leather and basket weave. I made these from the engine pipes ...' She stood and tapped a key against some metal tubes hung from the porch, and while those hollow chimes rang out her hand reached out to touch my arm. She said, 'You're shivering. You're cold.'

'No, I'm fine,' I answered, not really feeling fine at all as I watched her open up the door, from where she grinned again, and said, 'Welcome to my humble abode. I'm Lucy Winstanley. Lucy, as in short for Lucinda. But I always think that seems too posh. Apparently, it means She Knows. I can't tell you how often I wish I did!'

She laughed again as we shook hands. She seemed so free. So happy. I wasn't lying when I said, 'Delighted to meet you, Lucy She Knows. My name is Edward Peters, but everybody calls me Ed. And, if I can remember...'

What was that thing Mum used to say? *You're my very own little protector. My knight in shining armour. That's what Edward means, you know.*

'I think my name means guardian.' I'd barely finished saying that when Lucy gave a sudden gasp, seeing the scratches on my arms and mistaking them for something else.

'You need a guardian of your own. Looks like you took a bashing when you fell into the sea back there. The salt in those cuts must hurt like hell. You'll really should come in and wash. Get out of those wet clothes as well. And then, maybe a good strong drink? Something to warm the cockles up.'

The carriage door stood open, held in place by a large grey stone that allowed the breeze to blow right in, on through to the back where a wooden extension provided extra living space. A galley kitchen. A bedroom. A bathroom where I'd stripped and stood inside the shallow plastic tub that doubled as a shower tray, while a feeble spray of water dribbled down to rinse me clean again.

Now, my clothes were dripping from a wire fixed above it, along with the ruined cigarettes, crushed in the pocket of my jeans. A shame, but I was more concerned with wondering what to wear just then, with none of Lucy's towels being large enough to wrap around. But a floral woman's dressing gown was hanging on the door peg, and Lucy didn't seem to mind when I draped myself in that instead.

'Wow! Get you!' She giggled when I re-emerged in her front room.

Looking down at the riot of pinks and reds, I said, 'If you have something else, then ...'

'No. It's the perfect camouflage!' She patted a hand against a mound of garish cushions on a couch. 'Looks better on you than it does on me. You need bones to wear a thing like that. You need angles and cheeks and narrow hips. Everything you've got in spades. A shave, and a bit of lipstick, and I bet you'd look just like a girl. As good as Tony Curtis did when he got damed up for that old film ... what was it?'

'*Some Like it Hot*! You know, this is quite comfortable. I might have been missing a trick or two.'

I liked the sensuality of the brush of silk against my skin. I felt at ease with Lucy too, as if I'd known the girl for years, so familiar when she touched the sleeve, and sighed, 'It's lovely, isn't it? The most glamorous thing I've ever owned. Fragile though ... the silk's so old. Falling apart at the seams a bit. And it's got some marks that won't come out. Red wine, I think. But I don't mind. I'd rather wear it than hide it away. Beautiful things *should* be displayed.'

I glanced around the carriage, which was certainly falling apart a bit, though it also had a vintage charm. More chintzy plump stuffed furniture, shelves and tables cluttered up with bits of driftwood, feathers, shells, and what appeared to be bleached bones. Some objects in their natural state while others had been joined or carved to form entirely different shapes. Elegant, but fetish-like, especially in that dim light, with the on-off flicker of the lights strung up around the porch outside – the way those lights were glistening on the artwork hanging on the walls. All impressions of the sea. All filled with subtle liquid tones.

'Who made these things? The paintings too.'

'They're mine,' Lucy explained. 'The pub job ... well, it pays the bills, but I'm starting to get some interest now from galleries in London. A lot of local gift shops. What about you? What do you do?'

'I'm a hack. I live in London. I work on *City* magazine.'

'Oh. I've seen it. Pretty flash.'

'I used to think so. Now…' I shrugged. 'I'm spending a few days off round here, contemplating the meaning of life… and stuff.'

I made no mention of the 'stuff' that was going on at White Cliff House, and turning my face from Lucy's gaze I became distracted by the glint of light across the aerial fixed above the TV set, the sort of metal antennae that you usually had to fiddle with for hours to make a signal work. But the picture here was perfect, even if the sound had been turned down – so low I couldn't hear a word that anyone was saying. But then, I didn't need to. Or rather, didn't want to.

The film was called *The Haunting*. Made in 1963. Directed by Robert Wise. It had Claire Bloom in a starring role, and I had seen it more than once. The first time, that had been the worst. I'd been thirteen. Mum was in bed. Drunk, I think. She often was.

I'd bought myself some fish and chips. I was eating them out of my lap, licking salty fingertips while steeped in the film's dark menace, both mesmerised and petrified when I saw a warping bedroom door begin to swell as if alive, the handle turning on its own, and then that awful banging noise – like a drum – like a monstrous beating heart. There was something sounding like a dog, snuffling, panting, just outside. There'd been a woman. Was it Nell? She'd been cowering under the covers, reaching out to grasp the hand of the woman in another bed. But when the noises stopped again, when Nell turned on the bedroom light, that was the chilling moment when she realised her friend had been asleep throughout the whole of it. Nell was staring at the shape made by her curling fingers, as if they were still being held by someone else, invisible – which was the moment when she'd wailed, 'Whose hand have I been holding?'

After I'd first seen that film I'd hardly slept a wink for months, always keeping my hands and feet and head well hidden by the covers. And now, seeing those scenes again, even after all these years, such a sense of uneasiness returned, not helped by the high persistent whine the TV set began to make.

'Do you mind if I turn it off?' I asked, turning around to see my host bending over a little cabinet, something kitsch from the 1950s.

'No, go ahead.' She was standing now, two long-stemmed glasses in her hands. 'I think it must be the weather, causing interference. But I wasn't really watching. Only put it on for company. How about a drink instead?'

I nodded while she carried on. 'Give me a few minutes more. I'll make it in the kitchen. I've been drinking this cocktail for weeks now. Packed to the brim with vitamins. Oh...' She bit down on her bottom lip. 'I hope I've got some grapefruit left. I bought a great big box of them.' She laughed. 'The latest wonder diet! But I only lasted for one day, and then had all the fruit to use... which was when I had the brainwave of putting them in the blender, then adding gin and vermouth, and... well, you're going to love it.'

I very much doubted that I would. But I didn't have the heart to say when Lucy came back in again and passed a glass into my hand, smiling when she made her toast, 'Down the hatch and forget the rest. That's what our Tilly used to say.'

As the swirling pink concoction bled its way through mounds of crushed white ice I felt a little hesitant. But then, refusal would be rude, and she was right, I liked the taste. Refreshingly cool and bittersweet as the liquid trickled down my throat. Somehow, it felt like coming home – and looking into pale blue eyes, I asked, 'How long have you lived here?'

'I was twenty. So that would be five years. I did go up to London. A place at the Camberwell art college... until my gran was taken ill and I came back home to care for her. My parents died when I was young, so she was like a mum to me. We lived on the farm she'd run for years, since her husband was killed in the First World War. But it seems he'd had a brother who'd gone off to make a life elsewhere, and due to something in the deeds the farm was left to him... not Gran. Still, he didn't interfere. Left her alone until the end. It's only since she died that he's moved back and made the place his own. So now, what used to be my home is—'

'I'm sorry,' I said when she broke off. 'I know how tricky it can be … to pick up the pieces and start again.'

I was thinking back to when Mum died, and how a few weeks after that the landlord came to visit, saying the rent was overdue, already in arrears for months. That night I reduced my entire life to what fitted in my rucksack. The very one I use today. I left my mother's clothes in her wardrobe, her make-up on the bathroom shelves. But I did take the urn with her ashes inside it, along with her packs of Quaalude pills. All the uppers and downers she'd practically lived on, which I then sold, using the cash to pay for hostel beds at night. When the pills ran out I slept on streets, surviving any way I could, sometimes only drinking milk from bottles left on doorsteps. But eventually I found some work in a café on the Gloucester Road, never being paid for washing up but eating for free after every shift, and sleeping on the kitchen floor – until another casual invited me to share a squat.

I found a new kind of family in that huge house in Kensington. Five floors full of artists, musicians and writers. Free art. Free food. Free booze. Free love. Sharing musky bed sheets in a different room most every night, though I never really got that close to any of the girls there. I knew how quickly things could change. Somehow, I always felt as if I was looking in from the outside, as if I was watching a film roll by, or reading a story in a book. A book with death on every page, in every breast and spreading thigh cocooned in black and purple walls – where the pungent aromas of dope and patchouli hung in a misty yellow pall over frauds with rich daddies pretending to slum it while wearing dark glasses and PVC jackets, or mangy old furs and strings of beads – who thought those disguises were all it took for the world to spin off in a different sphere.

Mine did, when I read a newspaper dropped in a local litter bin, seeing a competition for writers under twenty-one to submit a story for the prize of a job on *City* magazine.

I wrote about a London squat, and then I left that house for good, using my first pay cheque to secure the rent on a bedsit, since when I'd always lived alone. And that was how I liked it. Although, I wasn't quite so sure when seeing Lucy's smiling face...

Lucy was saying, 'My gran always told me there's little point in brooding on the things that can't be changed. We, the living, the ones who still survive, we're the only ones who matter. Unless you do the God thing. Unless you believe in a heaven where all the dead meet up again, singing Hallelujah! We are saved!'

'By that, I'd say you don't believe.'

I stared out through the carriage windows, beyond the white-washed wooden fence to the sloping shingled beach below. I couldn't see the water, only heard its constant shushing break. The rustle of the shifting stones. Those sounds were otherworldly. They could have come from any time. They soothed me, sounded like a prayer.

'Do you?' Lucy looked out as well, but she was staring at the skies. 'When you think of that Viking spaceship, heading all the way to Mars... who knows what they might find up there?'

'So long as it's not the *War of the Worlds*.'

'Who'd ever want to live on Mars? Don't they say that there's no water there? I love it here, down by the sea. It grounds me. Feels right... you know? I tried to make a go of it, those months I was in London, but I never really seemed to fit. Here, I can lose myself in work. I think it's the light. Have you noticed that? I try to catch it in my art. And I know the work doesn't suit this place where everything's so cluttered up, but the furniture was Tilly's, and I like to keep her things around. Other bits and bobs were Gran's... some stuff she kept from White Cliff House, before she left and married Joe. That kimono, the one that you're wearing now... that belonged to Leda Grey, the woman Gran once worked for. Cleaning, cooking in the house, helping with the costumes that they made for all the silent films. Even Tilly got involved. Here they all are. Come and see... in this old photo on the wall.'

At first I couldn't answer, staring down at what I wore. Leda Grey's kimono?

The air was buzzing round me, as thick as syrup, much too hot. I almost lost my balance when I went to stand at Lucy's side, leaning hard against her arm, and watching as her fingertip caressed the glass above a print.

I saw the front of White Cliff House. A black-and-white idyllic view of a summer picnic on the lawns, where the light that shone in smiling eyes contained no hint of knowledge of the carnage in the war to come. The guests reclined on blankets, between them glasses, cups and plates, and several bottles of champagne kept cool in silver buckets.

Lucy pointed out her grandmother, and I knew that face immediately from her part in *The Dreamer's Delirium*, though this Amy looked a lot more fun. A cheeky grin upon her face, and dressed, not in a uniform, but a starched white blouse with ruffs of lace around the neck and wrists of it. No one would dream she was a maid.

Beside her, and wearing a formal tweed jacket, with a waist-coat neatly buttoned, was Leda's brother Theo. How dapper, how golden he looked to be, with his loosely curling hair alight with sunlight slanting through the trees – though, once again, it was a shock to think that this young man could be the shuffling wreck who I had met in the dinge of his old Brightland shop.

Next to him, a face I didn't know from either of the films I'd seen. He looked to be mid-thirties, perhaps a little older. No jacket. Waistcoat hanging loose. Shirtsleeves rolled to his elbows, and a necktie casually flung back to drape across one shoulder. Despite that state of disarray, he exuded sophistication. The swarthily distinctive looks of a silent matinee film idol. A lot like Valentino in the print I'd seen in Theo's shop. If it *had* been Valentino. Not this man in Lucy's photograph?

Behind him, a middle-aged woman, her face all blurred due to the fact that she'd thrown it back while laughing. 'That's Tilly.' Lucy tapped the glass. 'Won't you look at the state of her! That feather boa round her neck. She dressed like that right till the end. Always larking about. Always acting up. And if she'd been on the sherry pot, there'd often be a singalong. All those songs with their rude double meanings. It was quite an education! More daring than anything you'd hear on that TV show, *The Good Old Days*. Oh, she and Gran did love that!'

Lucy's smile was wistful. 'I should really try and find out more about Tilly's music hall career. I wish you could have seen her. Not a tooth in her head, with her dyed red hair, and bright green shadow round her eyes. Awful, the way it used to smear. But it was wonderful as well. She never gave in to getting old. "Enjoy yourself, Lucy. You only live once." That was Tilly's mantra. They really don't make them like that these days. I doubt they even did back then. I mean look at that bosom ... that tiny waist. Imagine a corset worn that tight! She wasn't like *that* when I knew her though. More like the size of a house by then ... and never a stitch of underwear to – as she very often said – restrict the healthy flow of air, or to hinder the hands of gentlemen.

'Ugh.' Lucy's face contorted. 'When I think of those old fogies who used to come and visit her. I did love Tilly – very much – but I had to throw her mattress out. Had to buy myself a brand new bed. Could never rest on that in peace.'

'Who's this?' My finger lifted to indicate another man with a thick moustache above his lips, with bushy side burns like two brushes growing from his ears to chin. Add to that his flat tweed cap, and he had a real country look. Somehow too stiff and out of place among the general company.

'That's my granddad. Joe Winstanley. The only picture I have of him. He and Gran were courting then. They married quite soon afterwards. I think she was pregnant with my dad. But then Joe went away to France and never came back home again. It must have been so hard for Gran. I know she often missed her youth ... the time she spent at White Cliff House. Especially when they made the films.'

Lucy gave a wistful smile. 'I wish I could have seen those films. Gran said they were remarkable, and always starring Leda

Grey. Gran said she was so beautiful that everyone who met her always fell a little bit in love.'

'Me too,' I said, and then, 'I mean ... I'd like to see the films as well.'

Why did I lie, so shamelessly? Why didn't I tell Lucy that I'd spent two days with Leda Grey, and had already seen some of the films she made with Charles Beauvois?

Instead I let her carry on. 'Gran said the films are lost now. Well, that's what Leda told her ... those times when she went visiting. I was never allowed to tag along, and I don't know what went on up there, but whenever Gran came home again she always seemed to be upset.'

While Lucy spoke her fingers dropped from the left-hand edge of the photo frame to reveal the face of Leda Grey – when everyone else in the picture seemed to pale away before my eyes.

Her hair was a mass of thick black curls cascading from a ribbon that she'd tied around her forehead. She wore a choker at her neck made of darkly sparkling stones. Her gown – whatever the colour was – had a pattern of beadwork on the breast and silky flowing hems that draped across the curves of folded legs. But her arms were visible to see through the fine diaphanous fabric of which the upper dress was cut and, somehow, that tantalising glimpse of the flesh beneath the veil of gauze was even more alluring than the way she'd looked when naked; when the vampire sculpture came to life in the film of *The Dreamer's Delirium*.

'Shit!' I suddenly recalled the cans I'd stored inside my bag.

'What's wrong? What is it?' Lucy asked.

'My camera. My wallet ... everything! I left my car on the road unlocked when I went walking on the beach. What the hell was I even thinking of? The key in the ignition too.'

'Calm down. I'm sure it's safe. This place is as quiet as the grave at any time past ten o'clock, and most times earlier as well. But look, you can't go out like that. Tell me what make of car it is ... exactly where you left it.'

I was more relieved than I could say when Lucy reappeared

again with a look of triumph on her face. Cheeks flushed, sweat beaded on her lip, breasts heaving as she caught her breath and waved my car keys in the air, then dropped the rucksack on the floor and asked, 'Well, are you happy now?'

'Lucy, I'm delirious. Seriously, you're an angel. If you only knew what—'

'I'm no angel,' she broke in, flashing me a wicked smile, then asking in a gasping voice that only added to the heat already rushing in my veins, 'Would you like another drink or...' The slightest hesitation. 'I've got some dope, if you'd prefer? If that's your thing?'

'I think you know that that's my thing.' Already I could taste the weed.

'OK! Then make yourself at home. I'll go and see what I can find... soon as I've put some music on.'

The flapping percussion of record sleeves as Lucy sorted through a stack piled in one corner of the room, during which my mind repeated: *Make yourself at home.*

Hadn't Leda said the very same, so recently in White Cliff House?

I shook my head to clear the fug clouding through my thoughts again, closing gritty tired eyes while lying back across the couch, enjoying the cushions' soft embrace as I heard the click and humming scratch of a needle skidding on a disc, before it settled in its groove and the jumping chords were smooth again. The lullaby I'd swear I heard when standing in the Brightland Lanes, and the perfect music for that night, with the cool sea breezes, and far off lights, and my head growing heavy, my eyes grown dim, and a woman standing in a door, and a bell, and a candle, and pink champagne, and the voices that were warning me that this could be heaven, or...

I could hear. I could feel, but I couldn't move. A kind of sleep paralysis. It had happened before when I'd smoked bad weed, or too much weed, or weed I'd mixed with other things.

What *other* things went on last night?

Panicking, I tried to grasp at any fleeting memories. The bottle from my rucksack. The sticky sweetness of the drops. The dream. So real. Was it a dream?

Falling back, I hazily recalled a big four-poster bed. Tapestry curtains drawn around. I'd been cold, and I'd been shivering, my breaths like ice upon the air, like strands of lace unravelling. That lace then turned to foamy waves as the sea rose up around me, sucking me down, spitting me out into... could it have been a cave? I seemed to be lying on a slab, something hard and cold and damp, and I felt no pain, only rapture, when a woman loomed above me, when she arched her body over mine, when I saw the red smeared on her lips which parted when she whispered: *Stay. Won't you stay here with me? Won't you stay with me for ever?*

'Ugh!' I lurched up, then gasped with pain when my head hit one of the sofa's legs, lashing out with both my hands to push away the big black dog whose tongue was slobbering on mine; breath panting, hot, and meaty rank. Spitting, wiping at my mouth, I saw my sprawling naked legs, my cock still half erect above the weight of heavy, aching balls. But that state of arousal dwindled fast as consciousness returned again, hearing the tap of receding paws now mingled with the calls of gulls, and the hush of waves on nearby sand – which was when I remembered where I was.

Lucy. Her carriage by the sea.

Where was she? What had we done last night?

I found myself trapped behind walls of soft cushions, empty glasses, record sleeves – and the gleaming dark green bottle that lay across a red silk gown. I saw its cork was still in place, and the contents looked about the same as they'd been before in White Cliff House and, feeling some relief at that, I put it back inside my bag. That is, when I had found the bag, having used it as a pillow, which explained the cricking in my neck when I tried to turn too quickly, when a shadow shafted over me, thrown down from the open carriage door.

There was Lucy, framed before a wide expanse of clear blue

sky. In front, the big black dog again, nuzzling against her thigh, her fingers dropping down to rub the velvet sleekness of its ears. Over one of her arms, a basket. The yeasty scent of fresh-baked bread. My mouth already watering when Lucy looked at me and said, 'Hello! I see the dog came back. Hope she didn't wake you.'

'As a matter of fact…' I gave a yawn, eyeing the dog with a look of suspicion while I reached for Leda's kimono and pulled the garment on again. For a man so used to casual sex, I felt embarrassed at the thought of lying there stark naked while Lucy looked amused and asked, 'Fancy a coffee? I've got fresh milk. Otherwise there's orange juice. Some ham to put in sandwiches. We could walk around the bay a bit. Find somewhere safe enough to swim. So long as I'm back for work at six.'

'I… I don't know. What time is it now?'

'Nearly three in the afternoon. I tried to wake you up before. But all you did was moan and snore. I guess we did get pretty high.'

'What did… I mean. Did we …' I was wondering if we'd fucked last night. But how could I ask a thing like? I felt stupid, still a little drunk, hardly able to string a sentence together, and stammering like an idiot when I asked, 'Lucy, did … did we drink anything from that little green bottle? The one I had inside my bag? Are you sure you feel all right today?'

'I feel great!' Lucy was beaming back. 'Do you think it's absinthe? I dreamed about green fairies. Everything they say is true!'

'Did you really dream of fairies?'

She frowned, then answered with a laugh, 'No! Don't be an idiot! But I did have a great night's sleep. I was up at dawn… even washed your clothes. You couldn't wear them in that state, still covered in salt and seaweed. They're hanging outside, on the porch rail. Should be as dry as bone by now.'

She did look well, refreshed, all 'new', with her bleached white hair scraped back like that; her flip-flopped feet sugared in sand, and a down of the palest golden hairs on the brown of slender thighs that showed beneath the hems of cut-off jeans. When my

154

eyes lifted yet higher I saw the shape of Lucy's breasts, all too clearly visible beneath a flimsy cheesecloth top – so flimsy that the darker brown around her nipples could be seen – as brown as the freckles that were scattered all across her flushing cheeks.

I wanted to trace every one of those freckles. I wanted to lick away the sheen of moisture on her unlined brow, to kiss her lips, her lovely lips. If only they weren't painted red, just like the mouth in last night's dream. So like the lips of Leda Grey, when Leda played the vampire.

'Leda!' I said her name out loud, and then, 'I'm sorry, Lucy. I'd love to stay, I really would. But I have to go back to White Cliff House.'

'What?' Lucy was all surprise.

'I've been interviewing Leda Grey about the films she used to make. I'm hoping to write an article and—'

'And you didn't mention that last night ... that you knew anything about the films, when I showed you that old photograph and told you all about my gran? Is that why you befriended me, nosing around for gossip to write in your glossy magazine?'

'No! How could I have known that you had any connection with the place? You found me, down on the beach. Remember ... you collected me! And that photograph ... a coincidence. Nothing but a coincidence. Look, I really have to go. It's late. Leda's expecting me, and I don't want to let her down. She's old. She's very fragile. Can't we talk about this later on? I could come and meet you at the pub ... then drive you back here afterwards?'

Lucy spoke in neutral flattened tones. 'That old woman ... Leda Grey. I used to think she was a witch, the way she could upset my gran. She looks like a witch. I saw her once.'

'She's not a witch!' My voice was sharp.

'No. I don't believe she is.' Lucy's gaze was steady. 'When I was younger, just a kid, still living on the farm with Gran, I'd go off with my school friends and sometimes walk along the cliff ... the path that ran to White Cliff House. One summer, we all had a dare, to throw stones at the windows ... to knock on the door, and then to hide among the trees.'

'You thought that was amusing.' I felt my temper rising.

'You never did anything like that?'

'No.' I heard my mother's voice. *My Ed... always such a good boy.*

'Well, we did,' Lucy went on. 'Not that I'm not proud about it now. I felt pretty bad at the time as well. The way that Leda Grey would come and stand there in the porch and wail... and always screaming out a name. It sounded foreign. French, I think. I asked my gran before she died. She said it must have been Beauvois. Charles Beauvois...' She glanced back at the photograph where sunlight glinted on the glass, obscuring every smiling face. 'The man who took that picture, which is why he isn't there to see. The man who directed the silent films, before he went and disappeared.'

She paused. Her lips were parted, and I noticed how her two front teeth were also stained with lipstick, my eyes fixed on that colour when she said, 'To be honest, the tables turned. One night we went to have a look around the glass house on the cliff. Gran said it was the studio where all the silent films were made. But she warned me off from going there. Used to hint the place was haunted.'

She stopped again, eyes curious while asking, 'Have you seen it?'

I nodded. Lucy carried on. 'We were going to try and get inside. I don't know if it's the same these days, but then it was full of old cameras. All sorts of weird stuffed animals. It would have made the coolest den, but... well, I wasn't the only one who saw.'

'Saw what?'

'Lights. We saw lots of flickering lights flashing through the panes of glass, as if each window was a screen... as if someone there inside the shed was projecting a film back out through them. As if every pane was filled with ghosts.'

'Do you think it was Leda Grey down there, watching one of her old films?'

'Maybe. But, you know what it's like, when you're young and

scared... when it's turning dark, and you start to think all the rumours that you've heard are really true. And we had been drinking cider, and most of us were off our heads. But we never went up there again.'

Setting her basket on the couch, Lucy sat beside it, reaching down to take my hand where the scratches stung and made me wince. But, I don't think she noticed that, only gripped more tightly when she said, 'My gran's not here... she's dead now. But, you should follow her advice.

'You should stay away from White Cliff House. There's something not quite right there.'

AND I, THE MISTRESS
OF YOUR CHARMS

The big front door to White Cliff House was standing open wide again. I called from the porch and waited, on the verge of deciding to go away, to head back down to Cuckham Sands. To lie on a beach with Lucy. To swim with Lucy in the sea. To touch her flesh, and kiss her lips.

It could have been so different, if only I hadn't made the choice to enter Leda's twilight world.

After dropping my bag beside the stairs, I walked along the passageway, looking through the open doors to where, if it was possible, the room looked darker than before. Even though the sun was high, the skies still bright and blue outside, in there the faintest glimmering of gold shone through the broken wall.

But still, enough to make me pause, to see that everything had changed, if almost imperceptibly, with furniture, walls and skirting boards arranged at different angles, with the books and clock and vases standing on the marble mantelpiece about to totter off and fall into the grate below it. On the desk, even the typewriter had moved some inches to one side. The still unopened cans of films that had been neatly stacked before were now chaotically piled, as if defying gravity.

I lifted my hands to rub my eyes, thinking they must be full of dust. When I opened them the room appeared to fall back to its normal state again. Everything entirely 'straight', inviting me on through the doors to see that Leda was still sleeping in her chair beside the hearth; and looking much as she had done when I'd left the house the night before. Just the softest squeak of wheezing breaths that caused her breast to rise and fall.

I decided not to wake her. After all, what hurry was there?

Why not fetch the camera from my bag and take a look around the house?

Two other ground floor rooms were bare. Dark, with all the shutters closed, and the plaster ceilings sagging down, so low I feared they might collapse as my footsteps rang on boards below.

The same air of abandonment when I began to climb the stairs, with sprays of dust exploding from a patterned woollen runner. Boards were groaning in the hall where doors led off on either side to mirror those I'd found below; the first directly over that where Leda Grey was sleeping. No signs of any structural harm. But bare again. Just pale blue walls. Some darker patches here and there to show where picture frames had hung.

The next room was more interesting, if only for its vastness, spanning half of the house's frontage, and one side elevation. No shutters here to block the light, though the air was steeped in a strange green glow reflected back from ivy leaves that grew across the outer panes. Inside were drapes of red damask. That fabric also lined the walls. A sumptuous, sensual colour scheme to frame what looked identical to the bed seen in my dream last night.

Feeling more than a little anxious I slowly walked towards it, feet making hardly any sound as they crossed an oriental rug. Around that rug I noticed how the stained black boards were deeply scarred. Gouging marks that led my eyes right back towards the door again.

Something heavy had been dragged there. Perhaps the very cabinet I'd seen in the sitting room below. The one with the props for Beauvois's films, what Leda said she'd saved one night when the rain was pouring in on her.

Only then did I look up to see the void in the damaged ceiling, beneath which sheets and blankets still held rubbled chunks of plasterwork. Stepping a little nearer, I raised a hand to touch a drape drawn back against a bedpost, where the furring dust of many years had formed a bloom of silver. More veiled a marble washstand where I saw a cut-throat razor, a tortoiseshell comb, a small creased towel, a bar of soap, a china jug – and the matching bowl where small dark specks of hairs were scattered round the rim, as if, and very recently, someone had had a morning shave.

It was such an ordinary thing to see, but also the strongest sign I'd had in all my hours at White Cliff House that anyone but Leda Grey had actually lived there.

Had she and Beauvois shared this room?

I lifted my camera from the strap I'd looped around my neck again, framing shots I thought I'd call *Still life in a bedroom in White Cliff House*. Next, the lens was pointed towards a japanned table holding bottles of perfume, a silver brush, a necklace made of rubies. Were they the jewels that Leda wore for Lucy's picnic photograph?

Fixed to the table, an oval glass was marred with small black speckles. Its reflection didn't seem quite true, creating the sort of warping effect you find in funfair mirrors, seeing yourself as much too tall, too short, too thin – or, as I viewed myself just then while sitting on the dressing stool, a man proportioned perfectly, but with shoulders broader than my own. A high-domed brow, and a dense black beard, in place of my much paler growth of stubble from the past few days.

Could it be the watery emerald light creating that illusion? But how could it make my hair look black? The same with the brows above my eyes. Eyes where the whites were riddled red with tiny threads of broken veins.

That was the face of Charles Beauvois. The face I'd seen in *The Mermaid* film when his features almost filled the screen. And the rippling effect around, a sort of shudder on the air – that was happening again in the atmosphere inside the room. Through its heavy silence I heard a sudden clicking sound. Like the snapping of a camera lens. A rattling, grinding hum as well, exactly like the noise I'd made when I'd turned the handle round and round to work the old projector.

Oh God! I was ill. I was going mad. I shook my head and closed my eyes, hardly daring open them again, though when I did – such a relief – to see my own brown eyes reflected back inside the looking glass. But, my body looked too shadowy, like a double exposure on a print, and so translucent I could see the details of the room behind, until the air shook yet again and every colour bleached away, fading to the black and grey and white of Beauvois's silent films.

Through that, I watched the embers in the fire's grate start flickering, grey flames all leaping into life. The dark grey drapes around the bed, drawn back against the posts before, had now been closed about it. The gaping ceiling hole was gone. No dust or rubble anywhere.

It was then I sensed a presence. Someone standing near, in the window bay, and turning my head to look that way I saw that it was Leda. Leda as she'd been when young, and all but hidden by the heavy fabric of a curtain.

One of her hands touched the window's glass, on the other side of which there was no ivy growing any more. No summer sun to offer warmth. Only thick white swirls of winter mist. An icy chill was blowing in. I shivered. So did Leda; that vibration running through black hair that hung in tangles down her back, where the only thing to cover up the whiteness of her naked flesh was the woollen blanket held in place by the hand that clutched it to her breast.

There was a voice, but younger, sweeter and much flutier than the deeper throaty tones of Leda living in the present day – though I'm sure she didn't speak out loud. Those words, had they been Leda's thoughts?

'I hate these endless dull dark days. They muffle us in silence. I feel trapped . . . a stranger in this house where there's nothing I can call my own. Not Beauvois, who's not my husband. Not the bed on which we sleep at night. Not the rugs, or paintings on the walls.

I'm too lonely without the filming work. I feel naked without my characters. The mermaid. The lady made of stone . . . all sloughed away like the skins of snakes. Some days, I hardly know myself. I stare at my face in this window now, and see another Leda Grey. She looks ill. She looks exhausted, hunched and withered, hair turned grey, her eyes too dull and sunken. It's a horrible face. An old woman's face. It makes me feel frightened, even if it's nothing more than an illusion of the light, created by these crusts of ice that bloom across the window glass.

What was it Mama used to say? Jack Frost has been here in the night to paint his patterns on the panes? These patterns look like flowers and ferns. Like the ferns in the Brightland aquarium. But they'd been green and full of life. These are grey, and soon they'll melt, as elusive as the bridal wreath of roses I have never held. The same with the hoar frost on the lawns. The icing on my wedding cake.

Oh, I wish Beauvois would wake. He sleeps in later every morning. It must be the drops. All the wine he drinks. All the editing work down in the shed . . .

I heard her sigh, and then she turned, looking back towards the bed, her face as ethereal and pale as in the film, *Delirium.* Her voice a plaintive pleading when she called – and now, I'm sure, out loud – 'Soon it will be Christmas. I wish Theo would come and visit us. For all I know he could be dead. He was going to buy a new motorbike. What if he tried to drive up here and then went flying off the cliff? Who'd know if it crashed to the rocks below? What if no angel spread its wings to stop him falling to his death?'

'Angel wings?' Another voice. A deeper gruffer echoing. A rattling whoosh of metal rings as the drapes on the bed were drawn aside, and my nostrils filled, not with the stench of any mildewed rotting cloth, but the musky sweaty odours of the unwashed man who was then rising from the muddle of the sheets. Again, that shimmer on the air, as if his energy was such that the very atmosphere around was forced to split and break apart.

I couldn't drag my eyes away when his bulk was dragged to the mattress edge, where he groaned and then slumped forwards, arms dangling down between his legs. I saw the pelt of hair that grew so dense across his barrel chest. The way it tapered down to meet the bush, in which a flaccid prick began to twitch and harden, when this bear of a man looked back at me – or so I thought, until I realised it must be Leda – Leda who was standing even closer to the mirror now. The looking glass through which I saw this vision in the room behind.

He spoke again. The heavy tones of a man who wasn't quite awake. 'I think an angel could well be the theme for what we film next spring. I wonder how we'd make it work? You're Leda. Leda loved the swan. A swan has wings. Angels have wings…'

He yawned and stretched his arms up high, dragging the sheets behind him when he stood and strode across the room, thoughts coming faster, clearer now, translated into gushing words. 'So many possibilities! What could be more magical? A god transformed into a bird. You know the story, don't you?'

'Yes… I know it very well.' That was Leda, answering. 'When I was still a little girl, when my father was working at home in his study I'd often go and join him there, taking books down from the shelves and lying by the fireside, kicking my legs in the air behind while I lost myself in other worlds. More often than not I'd choose a book with tales about the old Greek gods… with the one that featured my own name, which is, I suppose, why I loved it so. But there were other reasons too. Reasons I didn't understand… when I looked at the illustration of a woman lying by a stream, and the big white swan between her legs… and the neck of the swan upon her breasts… and the beak of the swan against her lips.'

Her expression was knowing, tempting him. Not a hint of meekness in her eyes when her hands were lowered to her sides, shrugging off the blanket to expose her breasts and pubic hair while smiling, softly murmuring, 'You're my swan, Beauvois. You are my Zeus.'

Seeing the beauty of her flesh, I felt such pangs of jealousy when I saw him lift her in his arms, when he spoke through fast, excited breaths, 'Will this Leda spread her legs for me?'

Was I lost inside some lucid dream, or did I really see it? I can hardly put it into words. It was tender. It was intimate. It was also something animal. The way they fucked there on the floor, so driven and so desperate. That need of his to possess her. That look on her face when he plunged inside.

She loved Beauvois. I have no doubt – whatever happened afterwards. I can still see them on the bed, where they went to lie when they were done, their bodies gleaming, slick with sweat, with Leda propped on pillows, her legs crossed like a Buddha, staring down through half-closed eyes while Beauvois lay across the sheets. His head was resting in her lap. She trailed her fingers through his hair, pushing its dampness back to trace down to the nape of his bull-like neck, calling it soft and delicate, that place where the sun had never burned because he wore his hair so long.

I remember feeling certain that I could also feel her touch, like a feather brushing down my spine, and I could have wept when the vision died, when I heard the cries of gulls outside. Such eerie wailing voices.

I also heard another sound, like paper being scrunched and torn, ripped to shreds in someone's hands. Through that, the snapping beat of wings, some burbling coos, and then a small white feather floating in the air above me, slowly drifting round and round until it landed in my lap.

I looked at that and then glanced back into the silvered mirror. There, in the room exposed behind, the hole in the ceiling had returned. No flames burned in the empty grate. The dark grey walls were now dark red, glowing with a purple tinge when washed with light that filtered through the green of all the ivy leaves.

I felt so desperately alone, touching the feather's snow-white barbs, as soft as silk, as gossamer; until the mood was broken by the slamming of the bedroom door – followed by another loud vibrating thud that surely came from somewhere lower in the house.

Startled, leaping up in fright, my mind was filled with crazy thoughts. *The house doesn't like me being here.* That fear then swiftly followed by: *The house doesn't want to let me go.*

I was entirely convinced that the bedroom door had somehow locked, dropping the feather and rushing towards it, then laughing like a mad man when the knob was turned so easily and the door swung open once again without the least resistance. My exit route had not being blocked by anything more sinister than a draught of air blown up the stairs, and that no doubt had also caused the slamming of the hall's front door. From outside, I heard the rushing wind that whispered through the conifers, and I couldn't help but wonder just what secrets those old trees could tell. Because there *were* secrets at White Cliff House, the ghosts that tried to force themselves into my dreams and fantasies, slowly seeping through the walls, and—

Another sound to break my thoughts. I rushed back down the stairs and into Leda's sitting room again, where I fell to my knees beside her chair and stared into a passive face that showed no signs of any life.

But it had to be her who'd made that cry, who'd called my name so urgently.

I raised a hand to touch her cheek, and then abruptly pulled it back when the papery texture of her flesh felt as cold as marble. Even her eyes were dull and white, having rolled back up into her head; unblinking, blind, and much too still – until her lips were parted to release a fetid spicy smell on a breath that seemed to last an age, during which I feared the worst. *Is this it? Is this the end?*

My own breaths came as gasping moans, begging, 'No, Leda! Don't go like this. There's so much more we need to say. So many things to ask you.'

I was scanning the room in the desperate hope of finding something there to help. *Too dark. Too bloody dark to see.* Standing, almost stumbling on the rucking edge of the worn out rug, I rushed towards the window bay, taking the handle of one of the shutters and hearing the cracking groan of wood as nails wrenched free from rotting frames, as the orange rays of a setting sun fought through the ivy barricade to slant across the table where the shell from *The Mermaid* film still lay, along with the glass of water that I'd left for Leda yesterday.

She hadn't touched a drop of it.

Crouching at her side again, I lifted the glass and nudged its rim against the blue of cracking lips, almost mesmerised to see the way the light now emphasised the lines etched deeply on her face. It was a cruel comparison to the youth of the girl I'd seen upstairs. All those other perfect images preserved in the reels of Beauvois's films.

With those visions in my mind it was a while before I saw that the water in the glass was drained, that Leda's eyes had rolled back down. Two large dark orbs then stared at me while her hands were slowly lifted. Not the smooth soft hands that had caressed the naked flesh of Charles Beauvois, but rough and callused fingers where the nails were ridged and yellowed, or bitten down to bleeding quicks. And the bones of those hands, too prominent, looking as fragile as a bird's. But still with the strength to push away the glass I held against her mouth.

Setting it down on the table again, I asked, 'Are you sure ... you've had enough?'

'Enough!' She spoke in a feeble voice, and unless I'd just got used to it, the nauseating odour that had hovered thickly in the air had now entirely dissolved. But the squalor of the sitting room was suddenly too visible, with sunlight shining over what the shadows had concealed before.

The mounds of empty food tins dropped to the grate beside her chair. A grimy pair of spectacles. The food-smeared spoons and forks that lay amongst small mounds of rodent shit. The silver mucous trails of slugs that covered almost everything. Had they crawled in through the broken wall?

Leda seemed oblivious to any shock I might have felt on seeing that revolting mess. She was sitting up much straighter, sounding offended when she asked, 'Why have you taken the shutter down? What will I do if it rains again ... if someone tries to break inside?'

I tried to soothe her, saying, 'I don't think it's going to rain today. How about I spend tomorrow trying to find a glazier to come up here and fix the glass? Someone to mend the shutters too ... to get them working properly? Then you'll be dry and safe as well.'

'But, tonight?' Her voice was sharp with fear.

'I'll make sure that everything's secure. I saw some tools down in the shed. If not, I'll stay. I'll...'

I felt exasperated now. 'What's the point in locking the shutters up when you sit in here and fall asleep with the front door standing open wide ... when anyone could walk straight in, which is what I did this afternoon?'

A pause before she answered, her fingers twisting in her lap. 'It was open because I expected you ... though I feared you'd gone away for good.'

'But I told you ... I promised I'd be back.'

'You were late.' Her tone was petulant.

'I'm sorry. I was at Cuckham Sands, staying with a friend I'd met. Much nearer to here than Brightland, so no excuse for being late. Except...' I thought of the little green bottle. 'I think I must have drunk too much.'

What an understatement that had been. The things I'd seen, or dreamed I'd seen. But I didn't need describe them. Her butterfly mind had flown away and landed on a new idea.

'Ah! I know just where you mean. Tilly Davenport, a friend of mine ... a better one than I had known, she used to live at Cuckham Sands.'

Should I tell her that was where I'd been? Should I talk about the photograph I'd seen on Lucy's carriage wall? But again, no need. Leda went on, 'Tilly was an extra in the third and final film we made.'

I could hardly conceal the regret in my voice when I echoed her. 'The final film?'

Looking back at the pile of canisters, no longer the muddled tower that they'd seemed when I had first arrived, I was trying hard to concentrate. 'But there are ten ... eleven cans we haven't even opened yet.'

'Most of them empty ... of film anyway. Beauvois had a habit, one of his superstitions, that as soon as a project was in his mind he would store ideas in the very can that would later hold the finished film. Sometimes there would be photographs. I often

posed for him back then. Or pages torn from magazines. Whatever caught his fancy. But with each film taking so long, often
lasting many months, with the special effects and editing... well,
those empty cans kept piling up.'

'And the cabinet. The props inside?'

'Not so many of them.'

Leda sat back and closed her eyes while, silently, I pleaded:
No, don't sleep. Don't sleep again! I need to hear the rest of this.

'This last film...' I pressed, and then stopped short, seeing
Leda's eyes grow wide, and the way they seemed to stare ahead,
as if she gazed right through me, as if she saw something –
somebody – else there in the room behind.

I looked around in panic. I was fully expecting to see Beauvois.
I was speaking much too loudly in the hope of calming my own
nerves, as much as Leda's when I asked, 'Are you feeling ill? Do
you think that I should walk back down to Cuckham Sands...
to try and find a doctor?'

'No. There is no need for that.' With the slightest shaking of
her head she returned to a coherent state. 'No doctor can stop
the march of time. The fate in store for all of us.'

She smiled directly up at me with what, in the years that followed on, I would always remember as being the most beautiful
eyes I'd ever seen. Even in one so very old.

Yes, beautiful, but brimming with the sheen of sadness when
she said, 'When you've seen this final film I know you'll have
to leave me. You'll go, and you'll take these films away, and
you'll write about what we achieved. There has to have been
some point to...' she waved a hand about as if to indicate the
pit of filth in which she was then living, 'to these years of my
imprisonment. I can trust you to do that... can't I, Ed?'

'Of course!' Her pleading tore my heart. More silently I
answered, *Of course you can trust me. We're friends, aren't we, Leda?
If we'd been born in different times, who knows... we might have
been much more.*

I felt such abject misery, to be yearning for a woman's youth
which no longer existed in any form but the two dimensions of

her films – to realise I'd never once experienced a fraction of the passion that I'd seen play out in the visions in that upstairs room. And the thought of leaving her for good, of never returning to White Cliff House – I tried to put that from my mind when I stood in front of the cabinet with the doors held back to their full extent, when I felt excitement surge again as the light that filled the room behind then shone across the cupboard shelves.

Which of those props to choose today? Should it be the gem-encrusted knife, or the big white-feathered wing of what? A duck? Too small to be a swan. Or the little silver Buddha, sitting cross-legged, with slitted eyes. Or the book with a black leather cover, with the words *Malleus Maleficarum* printed in gold on the cracking spine. Witches – that was interesting.

So many possibilities.

Spoiled for choice, I turned to say, 'Can't you offer me a clue?'

'Look at the bottom shelf,' she said.

'You mean this wicker basket?'

'That's it. Can you hear them rustling? They're waking. You must lift the lid, and then you'll see just what I mean.'

Imagining rats or mice inside, I held the handles gingerly, then placed the basket by her chair, tipping back the lid to find more than one object stored inside.

The first was a large metal symbol, and one I vaguely recognised from history lessons back in school. The ancient Egyptian ankh sign. Something about the Breath of Life. And the shape, a bit like a Christian cross, with the topmost vertical bar of it being split in two to form a curve. A circle of eternity.

The second thing – the size of my fist – was an ornate beetle made of brass, with the base of its belly being fused onto a round flat metal plate. In the centre of the beetle's back, a bright blue stone was glittering. And, on each side, where wings stretched wide, some tiny azure gems were set.

'Do you like it?' Leda asked. 'The scarab, or the dung beetle, often buried with Egyptian dead to ensure they reached the afterlife … used as a weight above their hearts during the time of embalming, to prevent the organ crying out and confessing all its owner's sins.'

She gave an enigmatic smile. 'Is your heart heavier than the beetle's, Ed? Does it have any sins it needs to tell?'

I felt a prickling in my spine, though nothing so pleasant as upstairs when I'd thought of Leda's fingertips. I said, 'Don't we all have regrets?'

'Some more than others,' she answered, giving me a brief bleak smile, and reaching out a hand as if she was about to touch my face.

Only later did I realise that even though I'd touched her flesh, Leda never once touched mine. But still, I think it was enough to see the way her features were suffused with such affection, when she dropped her hand to let it settle back on the arm of the chair again, when she looked deeply in my eyes, and said, 'You are the dearest boy... to come and sit with me like this and hear my last confessions. But...' She brightened up again, so changeable, I could hardly tell where I was from one moment to the next – when a finger wagged chastisingly. 'You still haven't found the prop we need... what's underneath that velvet cloth. But, do be careful, won't you. It was about to fall apart the very first time I wore it. And many years have passed since then.'

I lifted up the velvet and saw what had been stored beneath. Something glorious, also hideous, with the faintest smell of rotting fish. Something that I had seen before, in the photograph of Leda Grey I'd taken from her brother's shop.

'Put the snakes back on my head, Ed.' She lowered her face as if in prayer, as if she was sitting on a throne. And when I'd crowned her queen again I took a few steps backwards – and saw Leda, the girl in the photograph with the blackened smudges round her eyes – and Leda, the lovely goddess who'd featured in the silent films – and Leda, the aged and sad recluse that both were destined to become.

I asked to take her photograph, moving around the room so as to try and find the perfect view while she sat there in her majesty and said, 'This picture that you take... it will be cruel, exposing me as a frail old woman. All alone. A Medusa from a horror tale. But then, in many ways this crown is as much a part of me as not.'

I asked, 'Why do you have it here? It's just that, in your *Mirrors*, when you wrote about the time you wore this for your father's photograph, it was pretty clear you'd hated it.'

She pondered my question for some time. 'I didn't write about the day when we found it again, when we brought it here. But I'll tell you now ... if you want to know. If you'll agree to take the risk, for I fear this crown of snakes is cursed. It has the power to enchant. But this is no sweet fairy tale. No happy endings in this house.'

A GENTLEMAN ON WHOM
I BUILT AN ABSOLUTE TRUST

I collected my rucksack from the hall, stashed the camera back inside, and found a pen and notepad, in readiness to write down every word that Leda Grey might say. And she, as if to draw suspense, to ratchet up the drama more, took a lingering deep breath, and then –

'I wanted to see my brother again. Since we'd finished *The Dreamer's Delirium* he hadn't come to White Cliff House.' She paused and very slowly blinked. 'Theo had put his heart and soul into the sets for that second film. Little left of him but skin and bone by the time September came around. I understood he had to rest. But still, he could have thought to send a postcard to me now and then. He could have replied to the notes I wrote. That silence of his, it made me fear that the way I lived offended him ... that my brother had grown ashamed of me, even though Beauvois had laughed and said if our love was to be a mortal sin then he would gladly burn in Hell ... that I should take no heed of any petty bourgeois prejudice.

'Beauvois ... he never understood how alone I felt, how spurned as well ... missing the bustle of the town where I'd always lived and worked before. How I'd died a thousand little deaths after writing a letter to Mrs C, inviting her to White Cliff House, only to receive one back to say that she would never think to step inside this house of sin. How her only consolation for the choices I had made in life was the fact that my father was in his grave, not here to witness my disgrace.

'Oh, if Mrs C had only known the truth of my father's own affairs! But if *she*, who'd surely cared for me, could think to write such hurtful things, what else was being said in town? What if my brother felt the same? I had to go and visit him.

'It was a bitter winter's day when Beauvois finally agreed and drove me into Brightland. Ice cracked like whips beneath the wheels as we edged along the cliff-side track for fear of skidding off the edge. I closed my eyes and clapped my hands, blowing hard on my fingers to keep them warm, trying to think myself into an altogether safer place; pretending to be a Russian queen in a troika speeding through the snow, with jangling bells upon the reins held safely in her driver's hands.

'We parked along the promenade, and although it wasn't even four the afternoon was darkening. The Christmas lights along the pier were glittering like diamonds, so many looping silver strings blown back and forth in blasts of wind thrown up from steely seas below. I shivered, even though I'd worn one of Beauvois's winter coats, and two of his knitted overslips pulled down across my tea gowns. It was how I often used to dress, with the draughts that blew about this house, or if I walked along the cliff when Beauvois worked inside the shed, when I only had to hold those fabrics up against my nose to smell the essence of the man I loved ... to know that soon the night would come.

'Oh, how brazen I was. How I craved his touch. His mouth on mine. His heaviness. The shameful, blissful things we did.'

She stopped and looked embarrassed, as if recalling where she was, and who she was addressing, before returning once again to talk about her Brightland trip.

'The wind was flapping underneath the shawl I'd wrapped around my head, with barely a gap through which to see ... which was partly for warmth, and partly to conceal my face from anyone who might have known me there before, who might now chance to look my way and scorn me as a Jezebel.

'But Beauvois knew no shame at all, linking his arm through mine as we wandered about the town that day ... and rather than heading for the Lanes, he guided me along Queen's Road where he stopped at Mr Swaysland's shop, saying he'd like to go inside ... to make some brief enquiries.

'I preferred to stand and wait outside the taxidermist's premises, not wanting to see the things inside. All the birds imprisoned in glass domes, never to sing or fly again. All those boxes filled with tiny skulls, or trays of moths and butterflies. All the weasels and otters, the foxes and rabbits that stared through vacant marble eyes.

'Stamping my feet against the chill, I looked instead at the window front, where behind the panes of glass some wicker cages hung from metal hooks. Each cage contained a living bird, and such a pretty pair in one, their white-ringed eyes alight with life, their feathers vibrant greens and reds ... as Christmassy in colour as the ivy wreaths and ribbons hung around so many entrance doors. And, perhaps, while he had been inside, Beauvois had chanced to glance back out and saw the longing in my eyes, and how I wished that I could take those birds with us to White Cliff House, because one of Mr Swaysland's staff – a pimply young man I recognised as having studied with Theo at the Brightland Art School years before – he lifted the cage down from its hook, then opened up the door to come and stand at the top of the entrance steps, from where he offered me the gift ... and leered with such malicious spite when he bent his body forwards, and muttered softly in my ear, "For the *mistress* of White Cliff House."'

'The mistress, he said. Not the wife. What could I think to answer? My mouth was set in a rictus smile until Beauvois emerged again, standing on the pavement with a bag of birdseed in his hands, and seemingly oblivious to any distress I might be in while reporting that Mr Swaysland had promised to do his very best to obtain a large stuffed swan in time for the enterprise we had in mind—'

'I saw a swan in the filming shed!' I interrupted Leda, also thinking back to what I'd heard when in the room upstairs. Perhaps a psychic echo? That tale of Leda and the Swan?

She answered, 'Yes. And afterwards, I realised that was the only reason why Beauvois agreed to drive me into town that day. Nothing to do with a shared concern as to where my brother might have been. Not that we ever used that swan. Not for making any film. Swans are protected by the crown. If such a bird is killed, or stuffed, well it could have caused problems with Beauvois' investors. With the distribution for the films. There could have been legal issues raised, and ... oh, what does it matter now?'

Her voice broke off. A little pause before she carried on again. 'I should have protected my own birds ... the living ones inside their cage. But all that I could think about was the man who'd called me "mistress", and was even more downhearted by the time we'd walked into the Lanes, when I knocked against the locked shop door and no one came to answer it.

'Luckily, I'd brought some keys, setting the cage down on the step while I fished them from my pocket, then heard the jangle of the bell as I opened the door and walked inside ... where the air was dark and very still. The sort of dank stale atmosphere that only settles when a room is undisturbed for weeks on end. And cold. As cold as the streets outside, so that when I called my brother's name, my breath formed ice clouds on the air.

'Theo gave no answer. There was only the sound of Beauvois's feet as they trudged behind me on the boards. The soft dull thuds as he dumped the cage and birdseed on the countertop. Meanwhile, I found the switch to bathe the room in the stark white glare of lights that Theo had installed in those first months after our father died ... through which Beauvois looked round the shop where he had never been before. Not in all the time we'd known him. Always picking us up from the promenade. Always dropping us in the self-same spot.

'He trailed a finger through some dust on the frame of an old photograph. Ellen Terry as Lady Macbeth. He browsed through all the hangers that still held the fancy costumes. He flicked through postcards on a rack. All those pretty fantasies, which made me feel nostalgic ... until the present drew me back, with the stench of ammonia in my nose, when I looked down to see some yellow marks that stained the wooden boards and started to explain that our old dog was prone to accidents, although I also thought it strange that Rex was nowhere to be seen. Even if Theo had gone out, the dog so rarely left the shop.

'I said I'd go and find a cloth with which to try and clean the mess, heading down the passageway that led me to the studio, where all at once I felt afraid of finding Theo lying there, drunk, or in some disarray. And would on earth would Beauvois think if…

'But he wasn't there, for which I was both disappointed and relieved. And I soon forgot about a cloth when I saw what he'd been working on… seeing a still from *The Mermaid* that Theo had enlarged, and to which he'd added colours, with our names and the title of the film, to make a poster just as fine as those we sometimes saw framed up outside the bioscopes in town.'

Leda smiled wistfully. 'You simply can't imagine how that lovely poster raised my hopes, suddenly believing that the dreams produced at White Cliff House might one day be realities. I think that Beauvois felt the same when he followed me through and I left him there to admire the work while I went upstairs, in case my brother was asleep… though I knew that was an empty hope. As empty and cold as Theo's bed.

'Where had he gone, without a word?

'I went into my own room next, as undisturbed as it had been when I'd left it all those months before. But then, it had been summer, with sunlight slanting through the glass. Now, the windowpanes were iced. The faces on my collage wall were stained with damp and peeling off. It is ironic, don't you think…' She paused and gave a bitter smile. 'How then, I couldn't contemplate leaving the splendour of this house to live in such a state again.'

Her laugh held little humour, ending when she seemed to drift back into those past memories, lifting a hand as if to mime the things that she had done that day.

'I tugged at cupboard doors and drawers, grabbing any winter clothes that I could take away with me. My mother's cashmere coat and hat, her long mink stole, her jewellery box. How foolish I'd been to leave that, to risk it being stolen. And there was something else as well. Another box of precious things. The one that used to lie beneath my bedroom boards in our old house. But, for some reason ... I don't know ... I left that underneath my bed. Already the bundle in my arms was so large it made it hard to see the stairs while walking down again ... when I placed everything on the counter top, right next to the cage which held the birds ... and then heard Beauvois call my name and rushed back to the studio to see that he was holding up that photograph my father made. The one where I wore the crown of snakes.'

Leda took a long deep breath, as if to control her emotions, during which she raised a hand to touch the snakes above her head, closing her eyes while going on.

'The years were spinning backwards. I could hear my father's words again, when he spoke of cameras stealing souls. I looked around that studio, and saw my eyes in all the other frames he'd hung around his walls ... which Theo never had removed. I saw my face reflected back in every single window pane. In the dressing mirror by the door. In the dome of glass in the ceiling vault. So many different Leda Greys. All circling me. Circling Beauvois ... but then his eyes no longer stared at any human features. His eyes were only focused on the basket lying near his feet, the lid already lifted up to show what had been hidden there. The cursed crown. The crown of snakes.

'He was smiling at me, triumphantly. He said, "Forget about the swan. This ..." he set the portrait down to lift the crown high in the air, his booming voice then ringing out as if he addressed the whole wide world, "this will inspire our next film. And you, my darling ... you will be my very own Egyptian queen."'

As Leda's voice rang round the room, imitating Charles Beauvois, I was staring down at the table where the ankh sign and the scarab lay beside the mermaid's shell. And while I looked at those, I said, 'So, the final film is Egyptian. I saw some sets down in the shed.'

'Yes. That was the general theme. But for all Beauvois's excitement after our trip to Brightland, I didn't really share it. I fretted over Theo so. I was taken with a dreadful cold. Christmas day, and then New Year went by before my health returned again. It was all that I could do to lie in bed while Beauvois sat with me and read aloud from text books he'd raided from the library. Anything and everything about his new obsession … much of which he then worked up into directions for the film, making a copy of the script and sending it to Theo … who happened to be in London, and—'

'Theo was in London? But how did you come to find that out?' I wondered if I'd missed something.

'Ah yes. I'm getting ahead of myself. Theo had been there all along, and Beauvois knew of his whereabouts. Perhaps not on the day when we'd gone to the shop to look for him, but certainly in the coming weeks … though the first I came to hear of it was towards the end of January.

'Beauvois was working in the shed when I heard the clang of the letter box. And knowing Amy wasn't there to gather up the post just then, not due until the afternoon, I came downstairs to find a pile of letters lying on the mat, and one of them addressed to me.

'In that letter my brother had written, asking me not to hold a grudge for his being away at Christmas time. Not only that, but he also said what a shame it had been that I'd refused to travel up to London to join him for the party that his friends had held on New Year's Eve … at which I had been sorely missed.

'But I'd known of no such party. And who could Theo's friends have been? Or had he had a change of heart and somehow sought to make amends with our mother's long-lost family?

'As it turned out, when reading on, I found it was the Cuckham gang. Those theatre people who he'd met, one of whom had held a soirée in a house in Kensington, which my brother then described as being so rowdy and so decadent that it made the one on Cuckham beach look like a vicar's tea party.

'I told myself I didn't care … that I wouldn't have wished to go along, preferring to stay in White Cliff House with my pile of soggy handkerchiefs, lungs wheezing, coughing day and night, nose running like a water tap. But, harder not to be disturbed when I realised that Beauvois must have opened post addressed to me. Not only that, he'd written back as if it was on my behalf... as proven when my brother then went on to say he hoped that I was now recovered from my chill... and how he had imagined me snuggled up beside Beauvois, just like the lovebirds in their cage. He said he'd soon be coming back to start the building of new sets. He said he had some sketches made, having gone to the British Museum where he'd viewed the very exhibits that Beauvois mentioned in his notes...'

Leda broke off and swallowed. 'It was the Unlucky Mummy, Ed! My brother said he planned to build a sarcophagus that looked the same. He said how helpful he had found the curator of the mummy rooms... that gentleman advising him on reference books, and costumes too.

'Oh, there was more. Some silly things regarding the trouble Theo had with sneaking Rex into his rooms. How the landlady was furious, complaining of fleas in the mattress, but who then became so fond of Rex that she liked to nurse him on her lap, and the dog was gaining a pound a day from all the biscuits that she would insist on popping in his mouth.

'Dear Rex. He was the sweetest dog, though I've missed him more these later years than I ever really did back then. But the thought of that nameless landlady holding *my* dog upon her lap. I was consumed with jealousy. It went beyond all common sense... when the real reason for my rage was the fact that Beauvois had concealed the truth of Theo's whereabouts.

'I reminded myself that I'd been ill, so ill that I'd allowed Beauvois to dose me with St Peter's, and it may have suppressed my cough at night, but it brought about the strangest dreams. Dreams that lingered through the days. So, perhaps Beauvois had told me about my brother's letters. Perhaps I'd known about them, and then I had forgotten. Or perhaps I was making excuses, just as I am doing now, not wanting to confront him with the anguish of my nagging doubts. Because that would have been to know that Beauvois was not quite the god that I had built him up to be.

'As for Theo, I was delighted to read that he would soon be home. Although, when I tried to picture him on that trip to the

British Museum, looking down to see the painted face of the Unlucky Mummy... that thought, it chilled me to the bone. And his mention of my lovebirds... whatever else they might have been, those birds were never lucky. Both died within a week of being brought to live at White Cliff House.

'I blamed myself. I cried for days. I should have covered up the cage when I carried them through the town that day. And then, in the car when we'd driven back. The wind so bitter on the cliff. They would not drink. They would not eat, no matter how patient Beauvois was, tempting them with seeds and nuts while I lay ill in bed and watched. And although the room was warm enough, their cage on a stand beside the fire, all they did was huddle on their perch... until the morning when I woke and went to look and found one dead. It was lying in the sawdust on the bottom of the cage. The other nestled at its side. It seemed too cruel to take it out... to leave its mate to grieve alone, but how could we let it rot there?

'I think the very worst of all was having to admit that I was glad to find the second dead. It had plucked out all its breast feathers. It was too pitiful to see. I felt it was a blessing when Beauvois took the cage away. I thought he'd buried those poor birds, and that would be an end of it.

'But it wasn't, Ed. It wasn't. He returned them both to Swaysland's shop, and some weeks after that he came back home with yet another cage, and through its bars I saw my lovebirds sitting on their perch again. I don't know what upset me most, seeing the poor things stuffed like that, or realising that Charles Beauvois knew so little of my mind that he could ever think that I would cherish such a morbid gift.'

LOOK LIKE TH' INNOCENT FLOWER, BUT BE THE SERPENT UNDER 'T

I had no idea what time it was. The light was fading rapidly, and Leda hadn't moved or said a word since speaking of her birds. I began to feel fidgety, thinking of Lucy in the pub. My promise to go and pick her up. But what about the final film?

As if she'd sensed my thoughts, Leda raised her eyes to mine. She said, 'You know, I think *The Cursed Queen* the finest film we made. But then, you'll see it for yourself... *now* that the light has dimmed again.'

That hint of irritation about the broken shutter? I ignored the gripe, and answered, '*The Cursed Queen*. You know, that sounds more like a modern horror film. Was it based on the story your father told?'

'Yes... which I then told to Charles Beauvois... how any man who dared to look upon the queen's sarcophagus would then be cursed for evermore.'

She closed her eyes and heaved a sigh. 'If only my brother hadn't gone to visit the British Museum. Ah well. What did we know? We took some aspects of her myth and then embellished them yet more, with much of our drama also based on a novel by H. Rider Haggard. The one called *She*.

'Have you ever read that novel, Ed? If you haven't...' she pointed towards a shelf, 'you'll find a copy over there. You may take it away if you want to. I shall never read that book again, though I often think about the part where the author wrote that his story was either the greatest mystery in the world, or else – and I think I have it right – "an idle fable, originating in a woman's disordered brain".'

'I've seen a film called *She*,' I said. 'It was made about ten years ago. It starred Ursula Andress. I remember exactly how she looked. Less about the movie's plot.'

'Really? There is another film? Well, it is a thrilling story, all about an ancient queen who ruled a tribe in Africa. She had the power of soothsaying, of reading men's minds, and healing wounds. She also claimed to have been born over two thousand years ago. And for all those years she'd mourned the death of the man who she once loved... and lost.'

Leda Grey broke off and frowned. 'Do you begin to see the significance? Should I go on, or end this now? It's up to you, whether you stay, or...'

Her threat was subtle, but potent. What was this change in Leda's face? This menacing expression? Part of me wanted to run away, fearing something dangerous. But how could I even think to go, when this story might be so much more than I had ever hoped for?

I said, 'I'll stay... if that's all right.'

'Very well.' She nodded gravely, while my mind conjured the final scene in the much more recent Hammer film, when the ancient queen bathes in a flame that promises eternal life – but she then begins to age and die, until nothing is left but ash and bone. And while recalling that, I asked, 'How did Beauvois manage to create the story's climax?'

'You mean the queen's destruction? Oh, by the use of make-up. We used theatrical putty and stuck it on with spirit gum. Though there was one time it set so hard the paint rags wouldn't strip it off. We had to warm it up again with the flame of a paraffin burner. My cheeks were sore and red for days! But they soon healed, and what remained on film was quite astonishing. All the wrinkles, and the drooping jowls. All the horror of the melting skin when the cursed queen became a crone while dancing through the sacred fire... until nothing was left but a charred black skull. Some dusty heaps of gritty ash.

'We used a real skeleton, bought from a London medical school. Terrible really, to burn those bones when they should have been decently interred. I always thought there had to be a punishment for such a crime.

'Ah well...' She smiled benignly. 'It wasn't all so ghoulish. We had such fun with *The Cursed Queen*. Beauvois hired other actors in... those people I mentioned from the Sands. He had some postcards printed up, and then delivered them by hand... setting out a date and time, along with the offer of a fee for anyone prepared to come and get dressed up in costume.

'Days he spent, filming them, walking around the shed and beach. We fixed them up in wigs and paint. There was barely a room not plundered when making all the costumes. The sheets we lifted from the beds... the curtains dragged from window frames... and the coloured beads we bought and threaded up to make the necklace capes. If you had been here at the time you might have been excused for thinking that you'd gone to sleep and woken up in Alexandria. And Theo's sets... so wonderful! Almost every surface had been draped in the most gorgeous tapestries. There were figures of Egyptian gods depicted on the canvas drops. Enormous pillars looked as if they really had been carved from stone... and that was only part of it. So many things my brother built to emulate the objects that he'd seen in the British Museum. But the most impressive ones of all were the dais with its double throne. And then, the queen's sarcophagus. You saw them, Ed. Still in the shed... though little else has been preserved.'

'Couldn't you try to have what's left removed to somewhere safer? There must be film museums who'd display ephemera like that.'

'Theo took what he wanted.' She glanced away and blinked, a blink that might be Sphinx-like, as if all time around had paused – only to be speeded up when Leda quickly turned her face, her dark eyes fused with mine again. 'No one would ever want those things, not if they knew the truth of them. Some things are best left undisturbed.'

What things? What else might Leda say? I was thinking of Lucy's photograph, that summer picnic on the lawns, when

I asked, 'The members of the cast... could you tell me their names? I'll write them down.'

'Have patience, Ed!' She smiled again. 'You'll see them when we play the film. You only have to set it up.'

I went to find it straight away, twisting off the canister lid to reveal more sheets of script inside. But I didn't even glance at them. All that I could think of was removing the previous reel of film from the grips of the projector lamp, then loading up this latest one. My fingers gripped the crank and turned. The whirring rattle recommenced. And there it was:

THE CURSED QUEEN
A DARK EGYPTIAN FANTASY

THERE HANGS A VAPOROUS
DROP PROFOUND

The title flared across the screen. White words on a jet black background. A border of palm trees, pyramids, crocodiles, camels, even fish. Much like the images you'd see on the walls of an Egyptian tomb.

The acting cast – my fingers froze around the wheel when I read the list of names displayed, and then looked down at Leda. 'So, for this, you had a new male lead. Not Beauvois, but Ivor Davies. Didn't he once rent a room when you still had your Brightland house? Wasn't he your lodger?'

At first she made no answer. As a breeze blew through the damaged wall, and also through the broken panes no longer blocked by shutters, that little draught was strong enough to cause the flimsy metal leaves of Leda's crown to flutter up and rattle round the coiling snakes – though why that sudden movement should have caused their beady eyes to glint with tiny sparks of flashing red?

I assumed they must have caught the light beamed out from the projector's lamp, just as it gleamed in Leda's eyes when she looked back at me, and said, 'Yes, the same Ivor Davies. He'd left Brightland to act on the London stage. He hadn't worked in film before, but how the camera loved him! Such a charisma on the screen. An exotic Latin quality.'

'Like Rudolph Valentino.' Again, I recalled the handsome face I'd seen in Theo's Brightland shop, and then in Lucy's photograph.

'Valentino?' Leda looked confused.

'Oh, I am forgetting. You wouldn't have seen that actor's films. They were made in the 1920s. He was one of the greatest matinee idols. A heart-throb of the silver screen, most famous for the roles he took as Arab sheiks in desert tents...though his films were rather risqué. I'm surprised they passed the censors.'

'Do you mean that Universal code?' She sounded nervous when she asked, 'Could that cause us any problems now. I mean, if you tried to show our films?'

'I wouldn't think so,' I assured. 'Not from what I've seen so far. Most anything tends to go these days. It's just that films that feature things like graphic sex or violence, or the ones so frightening that they might risk giving people nightmares... those are the ones they rate as X, which means that only adults are supposed to go and view them.'

'Beauvois's films still give me nightmares. Especially *The Cursed Queen*.' Again, she did that blinking thing, as if she was turning into stone, her voice coming low and robotic when she eventually went on. 'This film portrays the dark desires that exist in every human soul. A film of truths and secrets too.'

When Leda finished speaking, I felt a perceptible dropping off in the temperature around us. But my hands remained sticky, slick with sweat while cranking the projector's wheel – when the slackened ribbon of the film grew tense and whirred upon its wheels, and I saw a brand new frame appear, each corner with a palm tree, and set between those trees the words:

A Victorian historian and his friends are travelling in Egypt.

A mysterious trader arrives one night, to visit them in their hotel...

Where he offers them the chance to buy an ancient queen's sarcophagus.

Looking like stage curtains, a fretwork screen was drawn aside, revealing an exotic room with pillars shaped like palm trees, with Arabic rugs and wall hangings, and a bed draped with mosquito nets, beside which, on a table, there was some sort of shisha pipe. On the floor, in the middle of the room, an Egyptian sarcophagus was placed. Four men were standing around it. Three of them – the Englishmen – were ridiculously formal in their dress, each wearing Victorian evening suits with high white collars and bow ties. But the fourth one was a native. An older man, who wore a fez, with a grizzled beard upon his face, and the bulk of his body then concealed by a traditional Arab shift. He appeared to be haggling with the men, regarding the price of the artefact. But soon an agreement had been reached, with all of them then shaking hands across the ancient casket's lid, at which the Egyptian left the room, though he paused for a moment at the door, gesticulating with his arms as if to give a warning, before another frame of script:

'Beware the curse of the ancient Queen.

She has lived for many centuries, still potent to love, afflict and slay.

Seek her, and you shall find your doom.

Leda said, 'That was Beauvois. The old Egyptian trader. You might have seen him limping. At the start of the film he still relied on the aid of a stick to get about. There'd been an accident, you see. He'd had a fall, down in the shed, and his ankle had been badly sprained... which is why Ivor Davies was hired in.'

I nodded, but gave no reply, being too engrossed by then in staring at a close-up shot where the focus of the camera lens looked down on the sarcophagus, first lingering on the painted feet, then moving on along the box to show two neatly folded arms; two small white hands arranged so that the fingers looked like spreading wings. And, finally, what made me gasp, were the facial features painted there, where the black-rimmed eyes on the woman's face were so perfect a copy of Leda Grey's – just as I'd seen it in the shed. But here, so clear, not worn by age, and somehow more dramatic in the starkness of the monotones.

Next on the screen flashed up the face of the handsome young Historian, who, left alone in his hotel room, now stared down at the coffin too, eyes full of wonder and desire before he stooped to lift the lid. But he found no mummified remains. The coffin was quite empty – except for a mound of ashes, and a single scroll of paper which he then picked up and opened to show – in another close-up shot – rows of hieroglyphics, and what appeared to be a map.

How immersive and clever the film became, when, in the scenes that followed, a panoramic night-time view of desert sands appeared on screen, with stars above in dense black skies that spiralled downwards, showering across the tips of pyramids.

And then the scene was changed again. The Historian was on a horse, riding through a fissure in some rocks which opened up to show a run of marble palace steps; each base of which was guarded by the figure of a great stone sphinx. Every detail was rendered exquisitely, but I hardly even noticed them, so involved in the plot of the story as I watched the exhausted traveller referring to the map once more – then giving a nod as if he knew that here he'd found the place he sought.

Some natives were approaching, walking down the run of steps to greet the man with smiling bows, and then – a blurring of the screen – he was inside a temple room. His formal English suit had been removed and in its place he wore no more than a plain white linen shift. (One of Leda's sheets perhaps?) While lying on a narrow chaise he was attended by a group of women who were dancing round, or bringing goblets filled with wine, or fruits and breads on metal plates. But before too long his eye was drawn to a curtain which was fluttering, as if caught in the very gentlest breeze.

A close-up shot. A slim pale hand with fingers folded round the drape, until the camera pulled away to show the woman standing there – her face at first invisible due to the length of sheer white cloth that had been wound around her head. She might be a living mummy, until those windings fell away and the woman's beauty was revealed.

The Historian, much affected, clutched his breast dramatically, almost falling in a swoon when she then walked towards him, taking both his hands in hers and kissing him upon the lips before she disappeared again, gliding off behind the drape.

Meanwhile, as if still in a trance, the Historian made to follow her, with the very same curtain drawn aside to reveal two splendid golden thrones, with peacocks, ferns and flowers blooming in the alcoves all around, through which the painted night-time sky was once again quite visible, still full of gleaming floating stars – and under them the queen appeared.

She wore a different costume now. From the jewelled girdle at her waist there fell a skirt of sheerest silk. The bracelets coiled around her arms were crafted to appear like snakes. Around her breasts, the same motif, each serpent with a single eye in the form of a glittering gemstone to conceal the nipples underneath. But perhaps the most arresting thing about this sexualised ideal of an exotic femme female was the crown she wore upon her head. The very crown that Leda Grey was wearing while she watched the film.

Her hair was now a grizzled white as it hung below the leaves and snakes, and those snakes, however you looked at them, were definitely the worse for wear. But seeing her ghost upon the screen, that astonishing woman with jet black hair, the headdress looked magnificent as she smiled directly through the lens.

Was the smile for me, or Ivor? That intoxicating sultry glance as she gazed straight from the picture's frame, when she gave the slightest shrug of one shoulder and raised a sinuous waving arm, when the bracelets coiled around that arm appeared to look like living snakes?

She stopped beside a table on which a crystal ball was placed, identical in every way to the one that I had seen before in the window of the Brightland shop. The queen's two hands caressed that ball and when she drew them up again her fingers joined as if in prayer, while yet more words flashed on the screen:

'Two thousand times earth hath circled the sun . . .

During which I have waited for your return.'

The camera moved towards the orb, and then another close-up shot in which, within the crystal, a tableau from the past played out. There was the queen upon her throne, and at her side there was a man, both of them sitting motionless, their heads held proud beneath black wigs, their eyes defined with wings of kohl, their bodies wrapped in pure white gowns. And in one hand he held a spear, whereas she gripped a metal rod topped with the sacred ankh sign.

Back in the film's more present day, the Historian who'd watched this scene unfolding in the crystal ball was seen to gasp and stumble back, as if unable to believe the vision played before his eyes. Quite undaunted by his fear, the queen took one of his hands in hers, leading him through another door that opened up behind the thrones, where the two of them soon disappeared into a swirling black abyss – a blackness that then filled the screen, through which the words loomed up to say:

'Now, you shall share my eternity.'

The bemused Historian simply stared as the queen took hold of a flaming torch from a niche carved in the rough cave wall. By that light, she led him down some steps – down and down – and on and on – until they saw the distant gleam of another fire flickering, following that glow until they reached a cavern where great flames were leaping from the cracked stone ground.

Also in that cave there was a slab on which a mummy lay, and here the queen then knelt while she unwrapped the windings of his shroud, to reveal the face and body of the king in the crystal ball before; who was in every single way a twin of the Historian.

This king had been dead two thousand years but his flesh was perfectly preserved, except for the livid scar that could be seen beneath the large brass scarab beetle placed above his heart.

The living Historian raised his hands to tear the fabric of his shift and expose a birthmark on his breast that might have been identical. And, as he stared at that in shock, the camera focused on the queen, whose eyes were glazed with tears when she looked first at him, then at the flames, which flared a sudden vibrant red, changing from that to green, then blue, through which the words were rippling:

'For two thousand years, at every dawn, I have bathed
within the sacred flame.

Here, in the purest bluest fire is the gift I hoped
to share with you, before

I learned of your deceit – that you loved another
more than I – when

In raging jealousy I struck my dagger through your heart.

Since then, I have prayed here, every day,
in the hope that your soul will be reborn.

And here you are. And now our joy endures until the end of Time.'

The Historian was wary, edging away when the queen came near, laughing and throwing back her head to show her curving snake-like throat – before:

'I see you are afeared!'

But, this fire, it will not hurt your flesh.'

The Historian remained quite still and watched as the queen removed her robes, with only the crown upon her head as she walked into the sacred flame, where she danced as the fire surged and licked around her naked body, as all the colours paled away into a wispy smoke of white, and almost looked as if they were the feathered wings of a great white swan that folded all around her.

The scene was exciting, disturbing too. Such provocation in her face. Such sexuality conveyed as she smiled straight at the camera's lens, which slowly pulled away again to show the transformation as she aged from youth to middle years.

Soon she was bent and stumbling, black hair turned white, breasts sagging bags, the former plumpness of her thighs now shrunk to only skin and bone – until she finally collapsed, with nothing visible to see but a pile of ash, a human skull, and the scorpions, worms and beetles that crawled among the crown of snakes – the only thing to be unharmed, through which the wisping curls of smoke formed words that said:

'Forget me not. I shall return to thee again.'

The next scenes seemed much too hurried when compared with what had gone before. It was almost as if, without Leda Grey, the director lost all interest – though I wondered if that sense of speed was something done intentionally, to echo the victim's panic when escaping from the dreadful cave; running through dark tunnels, all but falling up some steep stone steps until, at last, he re-emerged through the door behind the golden thrones. From there, only his silhouette as he stumbled through the desert sands below the vast array of stars that glittered in the night-time sky.

After that, the very final scene, where the ancient queen's sarcophagus, last seen in the Historian's hotel room, was now being exhibited in the British Museum in London. It was there, or a representation of 'there', that provided the movie's climax, with the cursed coffin being viewed by a woman in a long white dress, a wide straw hat upon her head, with snow-white feathers coiled around, as if to echo all those flames seen burning in the sacred cave. And when this woman raised her head to glance towards the ceiling, at that point the camera's view was changed to look directly down on her, capturing the slightest twitch of a fleeting enigmatic smile, before panning back to the coffin lid, on which the painted face might be the very mirror of her own.

No final words were needed. The cursed queen had been reborn. Still searching for the man she loved.

*

I remained behind the projector, motionless for quite some time, long after my fingers had released their grip upon the handle. My eyes now fell on Leda Grey, surprised at the malice in her eyes while continuing to stare ahead at the blankness of the empty screen.

'What do you think about this film?' Her voice was sharp, devoid of warmth.

'What a world you all created! Even the most mundane of things were somehow extra-ordinary. The sacred fire. The dance of death. Those trails of mist that drifted round the cave after the queen had died, some even taking on her shape. And the desert scenes...' I carried on. 'They could have been location shots, as if you'd really travelled there.'

'That was one of Theo's models. Everything in miniature, and filmed before the water tank, while Amy and I climbed up some steps and sprinkled foil stars inside... where they swirled about and then sank down. A little like the snow globes that we used to have at Christmas time.'

'And some of the interiors.' My thoughts were quickly rushing on. 'They could have been paintings made by Klimt. The style of clothes. The way you posed.'

'Ah, yes! Beauvois did love his work. And I know you can't see it in the film, but most of the backdrops and the props, they shone with gold and silver leaf. Funnily enough...' she paused, 'I remember seeing a photograph of Klimt in a magazine one day. He and Beauvois might be brothers. Their physiques, and eyes... both so alike. Such a sensual intelligence. But the article, I didn't like. It claimed the artist's paintings were no more than pornographic works dressed up in allegory and myth, whereas I think that, like Beauvois, he transcended the merely sexual. Though, of course... there *was* that element.'

'Ivor Davies was a handsome man. He exuded sexuality.'

Leda inhaled deeply, sitting taller in her chair, tilting her chin to show the rigid smile frozen on her lips. 'Yes, Ivor was handsome, and Ivor was charming, and Beauvois was a jealous man... which caused us problems from the start.'

'What sort of problems?'

Leda shrugged. On her head the snakes were trembling. They made a hissing rattle, through which she carried on to say, 'Petty arguments over acting styles. I suppose you'd expect that sort of thing when you draw more people into it. And Beauvois was exhausted, not thinking rationally at all. He was working every day and night to have the final film complete and sent away to Edison before the contract could expire… and also so that we could have a private screening on the lawns, before Ivor had to leave us to take up other roles elsewhere. But that evening of our picnic… oh, such a lovely balmy night, and Beauvois and Theo tied a big white sheet up in the garden trees, and…'

She broke off, and when she spoke again her voice held such emotion. 'To have seen that film again tonight. To think of what it led to. Please, Ed… put it back inside the can. Take it away. Take them all away. I'll never look at them again.'

I did exactly as she asked, removing the film from the lantern's grips, then placing the can inside my bag, followed by the other films. All done with Leda's full consent, but still I was somewhat unnerved when frozen in her gimlet stare, when I feared she might have changed her mind. But she simply asked a question. 'Do you know the Scottish play?'

That drumming ache in my temples again, it was hard to keep thoughts focused. She'd mentioned the play in her *Mirrors*, and Ivor's strong connections too. Could there have been another film, despite what she had said before?

'Well?' she pressed, more urgently. 'What can you tell me about that play?'

I thought: *I could tell you all about the multitudinous seas incarnadine.* I said: 'I know it has witches.' *And now you're beginning to make me think that Lucy might have had a point. With that crown of snakes still on your head there might well be another witch sitting here in White Cliff House.*

'I looked like a witch in *The Cursed Queen*.' Leda's eyes were open wide, unblinking as they fixed on mine.

'Yes, you did.' I answered. 'But more of a glamorous sorceress than the usual ugly toothless hag.'

'Until my death . . . when I became the most hideous hag imaginable.' She offered me the saddest smile. 'Much as you can see me now.'

Death. Why speak of death so much? My mind saw visions of decay. The flies. The rotting apples. The flesh cremated in a cave, where the only things left living were the worms and insects crawling through the snakes that made up Leda's crown.

ALL HAIL, MACBETH

'What did it lead to, Leda? What happened when you made this film?'

'Not when we made it... afterwards. When I was blind to everything. If only I'd tried to make it stop, before it spun away from me. If only Theo hadn't brought Ivor here to White Cliff House.' She sighed. 'I can't talk about it now. I'm exhausted, Ed. I'm sorry. I did write about it... long ago. All there, inside my *Mirrors*.'

She closed her eyes and seemed to sleep. That was another moment when I could have gone back down the cliff, to meet with Lucy in the pub. But my curiosity was piqued. I took the *Mirrors* from my bag and then returned to sit again in the leather chair beside the desk.

I didn't need a candle's flame, not with the silver moonlight shining past the opened shutter, where some cooler draughts of air flowed through the broken wall and window panes. The sounds of distant thunder too, while nearer still the papers that I searched through crackled in my hands, until I settled on a page.

This memory is shining through the glaring of electric lights. But first, the growling motorbike, which I heard when coming down the stairs ~ rushing out of the door and to the porch to see my brother waving from the end of the lane of conifers, dragging his goggles from his eyes, and calling, 'Leda... Leda Grey! Look who's here to say hello!'

Through the drifting smoke of his bike's exhaust I could see the shape of someone else climbing out of the sidecar, along with Rex who must have ridden here upon the stranger's lap. When the old dog ran towards me, whimpering with squeals of joy, I lifted him up into my arms and looked between his greying ears to where the visitor was spending quite some time in patting out the creases from his rumpled clothes ~ and probably some dog hairs too. But then, he turned to look my way, and I took a step forward, and then one more, setting Rex down on the path while shouting, 'Ivor! Is that you? But you've changed. You're so . . .'

I couldn't find the words to say how much leaner and sleeker he seemed to me. But I didn't need to speak because then Ivor's hands were clasping mine, holding me back while laughing, 'Leda! Leda Grey! Theo told me how much you'd grown and bloomed . . . and now I see each word is true.'

It was true. I was no longer the same skinny chit of a silly girl with whom he'd shared the Brightland house, and more than happy to show off, twirling around upon the path while Ivor admired the dress I wore. A lovely gown from Liberty. An oriental silk design of muted blues and greys and greens, and totally unsuitable for the daylight hours at White Cliff House. But Beauvois liked me wearing it, being one of the gifts he'd sent for at the time when both my lovebirds died.

There were so many presents then. Sets of silver brushes. Embroidered linen bed sheets. A lovely painted cabinet that arrived at the house one afternoon. I don't know where he'd found that, but it really was the perfect thing in which to keep mementos from the films that we were making. And more to come with Theo back ~ my brother beaming happily as he made his way towards us, calling out, 'Where's Beauvois, Leda? Is he in the house, or at the shed?'

'Ah . . . the famous filming shed.' Ivor was glancing all around, searching for some sign of it.

'We'll show you.' I took his hand in mine, while Theo grasped my other one. 'Beauvois is testing out the lamps. Just wait until you see them! The electrician was here for days on end. A specialist, who came from Leeds. But I'm sure that Theo's told you . . . and I want to hear every single thing about what you've been up to. How was the play? Kismet?'

'Yes. Kismet. It ran for months. But you never came to see it!' He frowned mock disapproval.

'Did you notice? Did you care?' I was smiling, flirting shamelessly, but then more serious again when I said, 'I suppose you've heard by now, how everything changed after you'd gone. We had to sell the Brightland house . . . losing Mrs C as well. We never see her any more.'

His smile was sympathetic. '*Theo did tell me about all that. But, you know bad luck can turn to good.*' His hand was gently squeezing mine. '*Nothing lasts for ever. The thing is to keep looking forward. The future, that's the thing, old girl.*'

He changed the subject, tactfully. '*Now, what about these films of yours? Theo showed me some stills from The Mermaid when we met again at New Year's Eve... both knowing Tilly Davenport. What a small world we're living in!*'

'*And what about the big wide world? Did you make your trip to America? Did you manage to earn your weight in gold?*' I was so hungry for his news.

'*Ah, no. That is, not yet. The trip was doomed to failure before we'd even left the boat. Still on board in the New York docks when Marie Lloyd's new beau was then arrested on some trumped up charge of trying to sell the woman off as a whore for the white slave trade.*' Ivor laughed. '*What a fiasco! She must be twice his age, at least, and I doubt that any man could ever tell Our Marie what to do. But, the scandal didn't help me much... so, when my agent sent a wire with an offer back in London, it made more sense to jump on board the next ship sailing home again... to take a role at the Old Vic. Another go at the Scottish play. Can you believe it, Leda? I swear I'm cursed to act that part until my very dying day.*'

'*Tell her the rest,*' Theo urged. His voice becoming very tense as his hand squeezed mine yet harder.

Meanwhile, Ivor kept nattering. '*There were some scouts in the audience. Some film men from America. I'm meeting with D. W. Griffith. Have you heard of him, Leda? You must have done! He directs the most marvellous epic films, employing casts of thousands, with sets the size of villages. And I know I should probably make a stand and try to go for something new, but he's planning to film the Scottish play... though it does seem rather rum to me, when Shakespeare's all about the words. But they've promised sensational effects, and...*'

Ivor stopped walking, forcing me and Theo to stand quite still as well, both listening intently while he said, '*Why don't you come along? You should meet my agent, Leda. He has some splendid contacts when* it comes to all the moving films. And plenty of work for designers too . . . so Theo wouldn't be in need.'

I was flattered by Ivor's suggestion. Flattered, and excited too, though my voice was level when I said, 'But you've never even seen me act. Only that cremation trick.'

Theo sounded warier. 'Beauvois has American contacts too. A business agreement with Edison.'

The words had hardly left his mouth when Ivor interrupted, 'Then he's a fool! From what I've heard, Edison has just one thing in mind when it comes to any films made here . . . and that's to sink them in the mud. The man's a dictator. He's ruthless. He'll play your Beauvois for a fool. He'll sell him down the Swanee, and—'

'Beauvois's no fool. Far from it.' I came to his defence at once.

'Oh please, don't go and get upset.' Ivor was repentant. 'I'm only spreading gossip. You know I can't help myself at times. I promise . . . not another word.'

He pressed a finger to his lips, which was when Theo suggested, 'Well, Ivor, I doubt our efforts here can compare with your marvellous Griffith man, but if Beauvois agrees then how about you giving us a helping hand when we come to make The Cursed Queen? You said you'll be free for the next few months, and you know Tilly's involved as well . . . taking on a cameo? I dare say you could do the same.'

'Dear old Tilly. Such a brick.' Ivor was all smiles again. 'A lady after my own heart, with any excuse for a knees-up. It could be fun to hang around. Let's see what your lord and master says.'

Ivor's reply, those words he chose ~ those words of 'lord and master' ~ they somehow made me feel exposed, even more so when we reached the path with the statue from Delirium ~ which is where Ivor then stopped again to take a good long look at her, lifting a hand to stroke her arm, and reminding me so vividly of that time he'd tried to kiss me.

I simply had to turn away and carry on towards the shed. It looked magnificent that day, light shimmering across the glass ~ and to see the shock on Ivor's face when he saw the extent of our enterprise, which might not be the size of a village but was still a thing of beauty. And for which we now had electric lights.

The investment had been considerable, but there would be no more *delays should the weather prove too dull to film. We could work all day, and night as well if anyone was so inclined. Beauvois had even planned to run the wires up to White Cliff House. But then some things aren't meant to be. That's fate ~ and fate would also intervene in the making of our film.*

At first, there was only the engine's hum as we set across the meadow grass. And then the sudden flares of light and, 'Blimey O'Riley!' Ivor cried, and he wasn't the only one who stood there staring with a gaping mouth, when a crackling spark shot through the shed as if it was a thunderbolt. A sudden crashing bang rang out, and then nothing but silence, during which it seemed as if all time stood still ~ until Rex, who up until that point had been nosing around the hedgerows, went darting off to investigate.

A moment or two of dithering before I took off after him, grabbing my hems to lift them high and gasping for breath as I reached the doors and saw the ruin of the set. Three palm trees had been overturned. The pots in which they'd stood were shattered, soil spilling everywhere. One of the two stuffed peacocks that Theo sent up from the Brightland shop had fallen down beneath the weight of a collapsing backdrop. And there, in the midst of everything, Beauvois was lying on the ground, and next to him a rubber wire that buzzed with small blue sparks of light.

Beauvois had warned me many times of how dangerous the force could be, and I could see too clearly now that where his fingers brushed the end the shock was flowing into him causing his body to jerk and twitch, which Rex perhaps had seen as something dangerous and threatening. The dog's lips curled back from his mouth, exposing pointed yellow fangs. He was growling low inside his throat as he made a lunge for Beauvois's arm, after which he attacked the rubber wire, which I think he must have thought a snake. But this was a snake with a deadly bite that not even the fastest, bravest dog could ever hope to dominate. And Rex was old, his eyes half blind, and Rex was lying on his side, his legs convulsing horribly.

Such a horrible stench of burning hair, and then a cry from high above. Looking up I saw that Joe was trapped at the top of a scaffold tower, with an arc lamp just beside his head flashing on, then off, then on. I remember calling back to ask him how to shut the power down. But he didn't seem to understand. He was shouting, quite hysterically.

'We were almost done, Miss Leda... just the camera left to lift up here to use for all the higher shots. But one of the wires got tangled and wrapped round Mr Beauvois's feet, and now... No, Leda. Stop it! No!' He screamed when seeing me about to try and drag poor Rex away from the wire that was shocking him. 'Don't try and touch the dog or all those volts will pass from him to you. If you can, then kick the flex away... some part where the rubber's still intact.'

I did as Joe advised and saw the wire dislodge from Rex's mouth. But clearly it was much too late to have a hope of saving him. Too late the droning engine stopped ~ with Theo and Ivor having gone to shut the generator off ~ while I rushed to kneel at Beauvois's side, gripping his face between my hands, slapping his cheeks, thumping his chest, breathing my air into his lungs. All those medical things of which I'd read in *Three Hundred and One Things A Bright Girl Can Do*.

I prayed that just one thing would work. I prayed that the man I loved would live, still praying when he gave a groan and opened his eyes while asking, 'What the hell... what happened here? Where's Joe?'

I glanced up to see where Joe's two legs now dangled from the scaffold tower. 'He'll live,' I said, and looking back I saw my brother standing there, his face drained of all colour, the limp dog cradled in his arms.

Dragging my eyes back to Beauvois, I said, 'We'll get you to the house. We must call for the doctor and...'

'Stop fussing!' he snapped aggressively, pushing away the hand with which I tried to pull him to his feet. And that sudden rejection, so rough and unguarded, even though I knew its cause must be the pain that he was suffering, it hurt. It cut me like a knife.

No time for such self-pity. I simply did my best to help when Ivor appeared and then replaced the ladder against the scaffolding, allowing Joe to climb back down, after which all three of them helped carry Beauvois back to White Cliff House, where he lay on the sitting room sofa, clutching the arm that Rex attacked, and swearing oaths at anyone who dared to try and help him.

Ivor and Theo soon went off to fetch the dog and take him home. Joe went running to the farm where he said he'd use the telephone to call the doctor for Beauvois. Eventually that man arrived, assuring his patient of nothing more than a bruise to his right forearm, and a spraining of the ankle that would soon be healed if rested well.

When the doctor left you might have thought he'd given out a death sentence. The way Beauvois was sulking underneath a cloud of thick black bile, and that cloud only lifting up when Amy brought him cups of tea, to which he added several drops of his beloved St Peter's.

But even then, when he realised that I was crying over Rex, he raged, 'For Christ's sake, Leda! What a fuss to make about a dog. He was old. He stank. Pissed everywhere. A blessing for everyone he's gone. And as quickly and painlessly as that!'

I shouted back, 'Painless! You did not even see it! And no matter how old he might have been, Theo and I both loved that dog. Ever since the dreadful day, when...'

I couldn't go on. All I could see was my brother's face when he was twelve, when he'd stood at the side of the road on which our mother lay, quite motionless. And again today, inside the shed, when Theo stared at Rex and wept.

I stormed upstairs to sleep alone while Beauvois remained in the sitting room, until dawn, when I went back down again, shaking him awake to ask if we could drive to Brightland, to see if Theo was all right.

At once Beauvois was ranting back. 'How am I supposed to drive when I can't even stand on my own two feet? Go to the farm if you really must... ask Joe to take you in the trap. But I think you should get a sense of perspective. The most important thing right now is the fact that we'll have to delay the film. And that is a serious problem. Our investors expect to see at least three features by the summer's end. What chance of that if I can't walk?'

'You can still direct,' I answered. 'You can do that sitting in a chair.'
'But my acting part! Playing the lead. The Historian who...'
'Ivor can do it.' My voice was flat.
'Ivor?'
'Ivor Davies. He's played Macbeth at the Old Vic.'

What did I care if I said Macbeth, if the name was supposed to bring bad luck? I couldn't imagine any more... and Beauvois hadn't noticed. If he had, no doubt he'd think such superstitions idle tommyrot.

'How do you know this actor?' Ac-tor. The way he said the word. I don't know how I didn't scream to hear the depth of his contempt.

'He lodged with us in the Crescent, when he had a run at the Theatre Royal. Since then Theo's kept up with him, and he came to visit yesterday... which was really just as well for you, because Ivor turned the power off, and he helped Joe down from the scaffolding, and then he helped get you back here... for which he had no word of thanks.'

Beauvois appeared to be subdued. Was he shocked by the anger in my words? Was that why he apologised?

'I can see I've been a brute, Leda. I'm sorry about your dog. It's just... what this accident could mean, and happening at such a time.' He sighed, a hand pressed to his brow. 'There's no leeway with the contracts. We must start filming right away or else be bound to pay back loans for which there's not a penny left. So, if you think this friend of yours has the skill and the looks to play the part... and perhaps, of more importance, if you feel that you could work with him?'

'Don't you think it's more a case of whether he'll agree to work with me? Weren't you listening when I told you? He's an established actor!'

'Oh, Leda.' Beauvois took my hand, pressing his lips against it. 'There is no actor in this world who'd look at you and walk away. If he doubts, he'll only need to see the films that we've already made.'

His fingers raised to cup my chin, drawing my face so close to his that I smelled the pungent sweetness of the drops still fragrant on his breath. 'We'll visit Theo... of course we will. Joe can come and drive the car. He'll take us both to Brightland. We'll go this very morning.'

COURAGE TO MAKE'S
LOVE KNOWN

While reading about the accident that happened in the filming shed, I kept thinking about the stuffed black dog on the countertop in Theo's shop. How morbid and ghoulish that now seemed.

Looking up from Leda's papers I peered through all the shadows, back to the chair where she still slept, so deeply that she didn't give so much as a twitch when a bright white flash of lightning blazed inside the room. A monstrous thunderclap came next. The air vibrated to its boom and seemed almost too thick to breathe, until the silence had returned and I relaxed to search again through all of Leda's memories – skimming over the pages that described the making of *The Cursed Queen*, when Ivor Davies took the part that Charles Beauvois had hoped to play – before reading on more carefully to learn of what had happened here once all the acting work was done.

So often I'd go to bed alone, waking in the darkness to feel cold sheets beside me. And instead of Beauvois's sleeping breaths I'd hear the generator's thrum as it powered up the lights by which he worked all through the day and night.

But I didn't spend my days alone as I'd done in the long dull winter months, while he'd edited Delirium. I wandered down to Cuckham Sands, taking Amy with me to visit Tilly Davenport. Ivor and Theo came as well. We had a proper holiday. Picnics and deckchairs on the beach. The men rolling their trousers up. Our skirts held high above our knees while the sea came flowing round us. If it rained, we'd try to cajole dear Joe into driving us down to Brightland, where we'd visit the Queen Street bioscope where the colourised films were being shown. The Vicissitudes of a Top Hat. The Miracle. Gerald's Butterfly. The Cap of Invisibility.

I felt as if I wore that hat whenever I was with Beauvois, who barely seemed to notice if I stayed at White Cliff House or not. Not even on those mornings when I woke before Amy arrived for work and took his breakfasts to the shed, when I'd often bring those trays back to the kitchen, cold and still untouched. He said he had no appetite. Not even for a cup of tea. It was almost as if the work he did was enough to sustain his mortal flesh.

But it tired him terribly as well. Every day he looked older, drawn and pale, and he rarely thought to wash or shave, even to change his dirty clothes. Truly, it was a mercy when the work was finally complete, when the old Beauvois came back to me, and to the pleasures of our bed ~ where his new attentions helped to ease resentments that had festered since that dreadful day of Rex's death.

Forgiven, if not forgotten. But how could I have failed to smile, that morning when I woke to see him lying there beside me, when he kissed my lips and then announced, 'What do you think then, Leda? Shall we have a party on the lawns? A private show to celebrate completion of The Cursed Queen . . . before Ivor must leave us.'

I didn't say that Ivor had been celebrating every night since the acting work had ended. Why, even when it still went on, very often he and Theo would arrive and look exhausted, reeking of beer and still half drunk. It was all but miraculous, the way that Ivor only had to dress in costume to revive ~ though at times he got his scenes confused, with Beauvois forced to film those acts over and over and over again. Maddening, for everyone. But the thing about Ivor Davies was, he always seemed to pull it off. He had a real presence too ~ though Amy might have had a point, one day while we were carrying some costumes we'd been laundering back to the racks inside the shed, when she stopped at the edge of the meadow path, and said, 'I was thinking, Leda, Ivor is terribly handsome. A raw sort of masculinity. But his acting style, have you noticed . . . how it's all a bit old-fashioned? A bit too much of the pantomime.'

I tried to laugh it off and said, 'You'll be writing reviews for The

Stage next week. It's all the Shakespearian work he does. You did a bit yourself, you know, when you played the maid in *Delirium*.'

Still, she was right, and you'd have to be blind not to notice how often Ivor used all those flamboyant flourishes. All those poses struck with outstretched arms, and eyes as wide as saucers, though I thought Beauvois had done quite well in curbing most excesses, and what remained of them I knew he'd temper in the editing.

While thinking that, I was surprised to hear what Amy added next. 'Course, Beauvois tries to hide it, but he's not that fond of Ivor. That's obvious to anyone. Most likely because it's clear to see what a fancy Ivor has for you.'

'Ivor's all bluff and banter!' I said. 'He's the same with Tilly Davenport. And I've seen him cosying up to you.'

'Ah, but he's joking with Tilly and me. It's different when he's with you. I'd say he's got a big soft heart under that brassy front of his.' Amy grew more serious. 'Would you ever take your chance with him? I mean... if it wasn't for Beauvois?'

'Amy, don't be ridiculous! Ivor can be a dreadful flirt...' I was thinking yet again of that lurch he'd made, that afternoon back in the Brunswick Crescent house, when Ivor's lips had brushed my flesh, when he'd held my hands before he left.

'You do make a handsome couple.' She would keep on persisting. 'And you might well call it flirting, but I reckon he's been wooing you. All those days we spent on Cuckham Sands... and then, the acting in the shed. I thought the glass roof might explode from the heat you two gave off below.'

'But,' I insisted, 'that wasn't me. It wasn't Ivor either. We were only playing out our parts. Doing what Beauvois asked of us.'

With that I strode ahead of her, until she caught up at the shed's glass doors, her cheeks as red as beetroots when she summoned up the nerve to say, 'I know I'm a plain-bred country girl. No sophistication in my ways, but I see how Beauvois is with you... and then I see how Ivor is. And I know which seems the better fit.'

The thing is, I knew her words were true. Ivor and I got on so well. And when we'd acted in the shed, there had been something in the air. A buzz. Like electricity. A feeling that I can't explain, like...

Where can that breeze be coming from, rushing through the broken wall? The way the curtain flutters so. It distracts my thoughts. It makes me think too much of how the wind blew through the cloth tied in the trees that night when we had our party on the lawns.

At dusk, we brought out candles. They added such a dreamlike air to the illusions in the film. Effects that no one but Beauvois had so much as even glimpsed before. But by the time THE END flashed up we were all in a state of astonishment, and no one spoke a single word, not for several moments ~ until I couldn't bear it and rushed to where Beauvois still stood behind the lamp's projector wheel, embracing him, and calling out, 'Oh, Beauvois! The film was wonderful! And Theo ...' I reached for my brother's hands, 'all your sets were glorious.'

Tilly Davenport was next, struggling up from the blanket on which she'd been reclining, groaning, rubbing at one knee before flinging her feather boa back and puffing up her splendid breast to cry, 'Dear God, Beauvois! Are you in league with the devil? I've never seen a film like this!' She gave a throaty chuckle, while one of her scarlet-pencilled brows arched above an emerald lid. 'I'm glad to have had a gander too. Lord knows, I've prayed most every night that I wouldn't look like Malcolm Scott.'

'Who's Malcolm Scott when he's at home?' Amy asked, while Ivor laughed, and then explained to everyone, 'A man dressed up as a dame on stage. A lovely Salome, he always makes. What a figure with his corset on!'

Tilly gave another laugh, 'But still, with that witchy long black wig I like to think I wasn't too much in the shade of Leda Grey. I'm an old bird now at forty-three ...' She bumped one of her portly hips against poor Amy's skinny one, almost knocking the girl right off her feet. 'But I have the health and stamina of any woman half my age. And what do I put that down to? It's all about variety! Variety's the spice of life, both on the stage and off it. I'd like to see the man who has the nerve to try and pin me down! You girls'... she glanced at Amy, after which her gaze was fixed on me... 'should take good heed of my advice.'

'Have you never married, Tilly?' Amy was tipsy, giggling.

'No! Though not for the lack of asks, and I've had enough men inside my bed to warm me up till Judgement Day. But, I'm more your roaming gypsy type. That's why I love my railway car. I sit down there imagining I'm heading off most anywhere. A new companion every time.'

Amy gave a wistful sigh. 'I'd love to travel around by train, visiting all the theatres ... hearing all the latest songs. What could be more romantic?'

Tilly hooted raucously. 'Blooming hard work most of the time. Not that I'm ready to retire ... not now I'm a star in the moving films!' She winked salaciously at me. 'All the lovely trips I've had, travelling up from Cuckham Sands, bouncing on our Ivor's lap while Theo drives his motorbike. I do so like a firm young groin pressing hard into my own. That's my idea of living ... and I hope there's more of it to come. But, for now, it's cheers to all my friends ... and bravo to Le Directeur!'

She grabbed a bottle of champagne, refilling her glass while Ivor spoke, his words coming a little slurred while echoing, 'Bravo, Beauvois! And bravo to Theo and Leda too! What a shame the Egyptian Hall has gone. What a setting that venue would have made when this film is shown in London. I can almost hear the music now. The strings. The flutes. The beating drums. The dusky, swaying dancing girls ...'

And then, he simply stood there, grinning with his eyes half closed, swaying himself while champagne sloshed from his glass to bubble on the grass, over which he stepped towards me, his free hand reaching out for mine, then kneeling down to kiss the palm ~ from where he turned to face the guests.

Or was it Theo he addressed? I've often thought about that since, when Ivor started to recite,

> *'Who could refrain,*
> *That had a heart to love, and in that heart*
> *Courage to make's love known?'*

Back then, with myself and most everyone else assuming Ivor spoke to me, my foolish heart swelled up with pride to hear that pretty little speech. Yes, pretty, but how badly judged. How ill-interpreted as well.

I understand it better now. Since then I've spent so many nights, sitting alone in White Cliff House, reading the wretched Scottish play. I know that Macbeth said those lines when claiming that the vilest crime was but an outward show of love and loyalty towards his king.

But, he had not acted out of love. Macbeth had slain the innocent. And Lady Macbeth had aided him, after which her hands had dripped with blood. The stain of which would never leave her conscience, or her memory.

IN THUNDER, LIGHTNING,
OR IN RAIN?

What the hell could have happened at White Cliff House, for Leda to write of blood like that?

Setting the page down on the desk, my breaths were coming faster, inhaling the ozone static fizz, and gasping with the sudden shock when another strike of lightning flashed across the skies outside. A heavy pattering of rain, though it only lasted minutes. The crashing of a thunder roll. Rumbling vibrations running up through the floor and around the walls, as if the entire building might collapse on its foundations. Glass rattled in the window frames. The typewriter's bell was tinkling. The shell and the Egyptian props vibrated on the table top – and Leda Grey woke from her sleep, but seemed entirely serene.

She spoke in almost childish tones. 'This is really quite exciting. Like the time when the bomb dropped on the shed. And before, when we made *The Cursed Queen* ... when I danced in the cave with the sacred flame and Theo set off the smoke bombs. Potassium nitrate. Sugar. Flour. The same effects that we'd once used when performing our cremation trick: *Three Hundred And One Things A Bright Girl Can Do.*'

She all but chanted that title. And then, after a little pause, continued in a sadder voice. 'I was Beauvois's brightest girl ... until that party on the lawns.'

'But from what I've just been reading that evening was a great success.'

'You should read on, and then you'll see. Oh ... listen! It's that sound again.' She craned her neck and stared towards the window with the shutter gone, repeating a question that she'd asked when I'd first arrived at White Cliff House.

'Do you think that it could be a car... or Theo on his motor-bike? Someone driving up the cliff-side track?'

I said, 'It could be thunder.'

'No. They're here! They're back again.' Her fingers clutched at long black skirts, balling the fabric up so hard that her knuckle bones were gleaming white. I could see that she was trembling, and that motion swiftly taken up by the snakes that coiled above her head.

She drew a breath, then carried on. 'They haven't pestered me for years. Not since that night when I went down to play the last film in the shed again... when I stood there and projected it onto the whitewashed back stage wall. Running it forwards, then backwards. Speeding it up. Slowing it down. Trying to find some way to make time stop, or spin another way.

'That was when I heard the screaming jeers... all the people who'd been hiding in the trees from where they'd spied on me. What if they'd seen? The film? The proof?'

Her words were making little sense. She was on the verge of hysteria. 'And the lights... the lights now, in the trees. Do you think they could be headlamps? Or torches... people searching?'

I tried my best to calm her. 'There's nothing to be afraid of. Those lights you say that can you see, they could be some distant lightning strikes. Or the moon. It's very bright tonight... when the clouds don't blow across it.'

Those words seemed to appease her, with Leda's fears subsiding just as quickly as they'd risen up. She was smiling when she spoke again.

'There was a full moon shining down, on that night of our picnic on the lawns, when Ivor played the piano, after he and Theo dragged it out... even though it was as out of tune as the one in our Brightland house had been. But lovely to have the music. Dancing around in Beauvois's arms, with his injured ankle better then... though it tired him and he had to stop. And that's when Tilly Davenport decided to take a turn instead, strutting up and down the path while rattling out "*There Was I, Waiting At The Church*".

Leda's smile became a frown. 'Do you know the words, Ed?' Before I could think to answer, Leda was reciting them:

'I'm in a nice bit of trouble, I confess;
Somebody with me has had a game.
I should by now be a proud and happy bride,
But I've still got to keep my single name.'

She paused and then continued. 'All around me I heard laughter, but inside my heart was aching ... to think of my own single name. I felt relieved when Tilly stopped and followed her song with a belly dance. Her own particular homage to our latest film's Egyptian theme. And then, a grand finale, when she swished her skirts up high behind, panting and mopping at her brow while she all but collapsed into one of the deckchairs ... which was when Beauvois spoiled everything, practically exploding when he said he'd seen and heard enough of such a vulgar repertoire ... saying that Tilly Davenport was no better than a common whore, the way she always carried on. And he mumbled something after that, though I couldn't quite hear the whole of it. But I know he mentioned Malcolm Scott.'

Leda laughed. 'Oh, that was wicked. It really was too bad of him. But how foolish to offend our guest. The glare that Tilly gave him! The lizard green of her painted eyes narrowed to slits of disbelief as they followed him beneath the porch.

'Watching him storm away like that, I couldn't decide if I should go and try to calm him down again, or to stay outside with all the rest ... which was when Tilly turned her gaze on me, her temper scorching through her words.

' "Well, Leda, this needs saying, and this is the time to say it. Do you realise what a talent you have? What a future might await you? Charles Beauvois is a master of his art. But, the masses out there, the ones who pay to go and watch the moving films, they like a bit of fun, you know. A bit of ow's yer father, and a happy end when the curtain falls and they have to go off home again. The common man wants cheering up. But the sort of film we saw tonight... all those brooding supernatural themes... well, they might well be spectacular, but bloody depressing, don't you think?"

'She was drunk. That was clear to everyone, and when Theo suggested that Tilly leave and head on back to Cuckham Sands, she complained that if he'd wanted to take part in a Sunday School outing he should have joined the Methodists.'

Leda put on a cockney voice, as if to mimic Tilly then. 'I'm not at all "blottesque", dear boy. I'll drink every one of you under the table and still be up for more of it.'

But then she grew more serious. 'Oh Ed, if you could have heard her, ranting on about Beauvois. How she thought he was a man obsessed. How obsessions could be dangerous. How whenever she looked into his eyes she imagined a hawk when it's hunting a rabbit. "Remember that," she warned me. "You watch yourself with such a man. And I'm speaking more than professionally."

'I think it was Ivor who answered then, placing a hand on her shoulder when he also suggested Tilly leave. But she shook him off and grabbed my hand in a way that might be comical in any other circumstance, when she spoke in a whisper loud enough for everyone around to hear.

'"There are other directors making films. You should go on the ship with Ivor, ducks. Ivor will take good care of you. Treat you like a proper queen, not have you working like a slave, down in that shed from dawn till dusk. And under all those bloody lights! Christ, the stench of them. The dust. If you don't go blind, you'll choke to death."

'Even if I'd had an answer, I had no chance to offer it, not when we heard that sudden sound... like a gunshot going off it was, when one of the upstairs window frames slammed down with such a banging crash.

'My heart was thudding wildly, guessing that it must have come from the bedroom Beauvois shared with me, and he'd surely heard most every word that Tilly Davenport had said. Sounds carry far on clear dark nights.

'Ah well, she took the hint to leave, struggling up from her deckchair, and just as casual as you like, announcing that she'd best be off… that she fancied a nightcap on the beach.

'I watched her sashay down the path, with Amy and Joe Winstanley taking an arm on either side, leading her off in such a rush that Tilly quite forgot about the hat and feather boa left on one of the garden's picnic rugs.

'I didn't call out to tell her. I simply stood there on the grass, with my brother and Ivor on either side, feeling lost and miserable… until Ivor looked at me and winked and said that these things happened… that we'd laugh about it later… that Tilly was impossible when she'd been on the bottle for too long.

'"Darling," he said, "when she's in that mood, Beauvois could be the King himself at a royal command performance, and she'd still have torn him off a strip."

'Theo tried to calm me too. He said parties often went that way, and this was really nothing more than a storm inside a teacup. He said that I should leave Beauvois to simmer in his juices, that the man was clearly worn to shreds from the strain of filming for so long. And maybe, in the morning, when everyone had clearer heads, we could all go down to Cuckham Sands and try to make our peace again.

'He led me to a blanket lying underneath the conifers, where Ivor came to join us too, bringing glasses and champagne, and after he had poured the fizz he reached into his waistcoat and produced a little silver case. The very one that he'd once dropped when in our Brunswick Crescent house.'

Leda stopped, and made a humming sound, as if that thought had troubled her, before taking up where she'd left off. 'Theo must have given it back to him. Anyway…' she grew less pensive, 'Ivor flicked the lid right back to expose some black-wrapped cigarettes. The labels said "Cigarettes Saphir". I remember how elegant he looked when he struck a match to light his smoke, setting the tip between his lips while he closed his eyes and then inhaled, and gave a long contented sigh as streams of hazy smoke blew out.

'It had the sweetest perfume. I asked what it was. He said hashish, the very finest quality, at which Theo began to laugh and said that Ivor Davies was the greatest hedonist on earth . . . before Ivor passed the roll to him, and Theo blew more fragrant smoke, then offered it to me as well. I did feel somewhat nervous, not having a clue what I should do. But Ivor insisted I try it. And I did, and though I coughed at first, it was such fun to pass around. Almost a sacred ritual between our little trinity.

'I wish you could have been here, Ed. I wish you could have seen us. We fitted there so beautifully, lying back upon the grass and gazing at the skies above . . . and I really thought it such a shame when Ivor decided to leave us, announcing, "Music, don't you think! It's much too soon to go to sleep."

'I watched as he headed towards the piano where he started to play a melody. Something I'd never heard before, though later, much later on it was, when Theo visited one day, he said it was Debussy, that the music's name was "Clair De Lune". That both he and Ivor loved it.

'I loved it too. Those rippling notes. I thought of the aquarium, and the splashing of the waterfalls, and while I listened Theo asked, "Will Beauvois ever marry you, and stop all this pretending lark? Or is it a bit like Tilly's song? He already has another wife."

'I was shocked. What did my brother know? But I shrugged, and passed his question off as something of no consequence. I said that Beauvois thought of very little but the films those days. I didn't admit that we could not wed because, yes, he was married to someone else. I only repeated Beauvois's words if I should ever get upset . . . that we didn't need a marriage vow to know that we were blessed in love. That it really didn't bother us.

'"Maybe not him, but it bothers you." Theo was clearly unconvinced. "You're not as happy as you were. I see my sister's light has changed."

'I hadn't heard him talk about the lights since we'd been making films. I wondered what had brought that on. Ivor's exotic cigarette? But my brother seemed quite sober, and not at all distracted when I looked at him and asked, for the first, and for the final time, "Tell me what my light is like."

'I recall the moment perfectly. How Theo's pale blue gaze met mine. The long fair lashes round his eyes. How he all but whispered when he smiled, "You're golden, glowing like the sun. A halo all around your head."

'I thought of *Brightland Promenade*. It made me wonder yet again... had Theo seen my treasured things? But I didn't mention that to him, only said that now Beauvois had finished editing *The Cursed Queen* he'd soon be back to his old self.

'"What is this old self, Leda?" Theo wouldn't let it drop. "Do you think what we saw of him tonight was the real man beneath the mask? I never see his aura. He is too dark... sucks in the light. Is he kind to you? You must tell the truth. I mean, you smile. You seem all right. But..."

'"But my shining lights are fading." How bitterly I said those words, and how regretful Theo looked when asking how I'd feel if he was absent for the next few months. And perhaps it was the wine I'd drunk, making my mind too fuddled to understand what he could mean, but I simply thought he hoped to spend more time with all his Brightland friends. Or else to go to London, to brew more storms in teacups at those parties with the Cuckham gang.

'I said he must do just as he wished, that we both had separate lives to lead, whether in virtue or in vice – those last words spoken teasingly.

'But they only made my brother sigh, to answer yet more candidly. "Whenever I see you act, Leda, you look like a woman who's come to know every vice there is in this world of ours. But, underneath it all, you're still my little baby sister." He stroked one hand across my cheek. "I wish you'd always stay that way."

'I couldn't bear his gloomy mood. I tried to talk of things we shared. Brighter things. Exciting things... mentioning that Beauvois hoped to meet his sponsors very soon, to discuss some extra loans with which to build extensions to the shed. A larger space for editing. More sinks and drums in which to dip then dry all the exposure reels. Yet more exotic filming sets. These things all cost a fortune, but hopefully, by Christmas time our work would be distributed on screens in many English towns. Perhaps even America. There would be money coming in. We might be travelling abroad... following in Ivor's wake.

'"We might." My brother didn't seem as pleased as I'd supposed he would. "But remember what Ivor said before, about putting in a word for you with his agent... with other directors too?"

'I watched as he puffed on the cigarette. I said, "I promised Beauvois I would always stay at White Cliff House."

'I followed Theo's gaze and turned to look across the lawns again, to where Ivor still played that lovely tune ... and when he chanced to glance our way I sprang to my feet and began to dance, wanting to feel his eyes on me as I swayed through drifting palls of smoke ... until the music ended when I became quite still again, with Ivor standing at my side, crowning me in Tilly's hat, her feather boa round my neck. He was kneeling before me on the grass, just as he'd done much earlier, and I started to giggle and couldn't stop, trying to step away from him, when I fell and landed on my back in a hammock tied between the trees.

'It swung about alarmingly and made me feel very sick, so sick I had to close my eyes until the rocking motion stopped. And when I opened them again the other two had disappeared. But I really didn't mind. I was happy, drifting off to sleep, and now and then I raised my eyes to see the tips of trees above, and higher still the sea of stars all turning through a purple sky.

'I could have watched that sky for hours, seeing the trails of an ocean mist as it curled through all the branches, looking like the wisping curls of smoke in the cave in *The Cursed Queen*. Those last scenes had been disturbing. How hideous, frail and old I'd looked.' Leda gave a mocking laugh. 'How right I was to be afraid, reaching a hand to the grass below and grabbing the corner of a rug, pulling that across myself, then dragging the brim of Tilly's hat right down to cover up my face, ensuring not an inch of flesh was visible to any demons hovering around that night. And even though I fell asleep and didn't wake again till dawn, there was a part of me that still retained a glint of consciousness, to sense a presence lurking near, to hear the sounds of laboured breaths, of footsteps on the garden path. And then, the squabbling scream of gulls who circled round the trees at dawn, forcing me out of my sailor's bed to pick my way across the lawns and back towards the house front door... still open for me to walk on through, to climb the stairs and find the room where Beauvois sprawled in snoring dreams.

'I didn't think to get undressed. Only took the choker from my neck, then crawled to his side beneath the sheets, though I had to turn my face away to stop myself inhaling the heavy sweetness of his breath. His bottle of St Peter's was lying on the pillow. A dark and spreading stain where it had leaked... and for how many hours?

'When I woke again, a second time, the bottle and the man had gone. I was lying in the bed alone, hearing the twang of piano notes rising up from the floor below me, as the instrument was being dragged back from the lawns into the house. But eventually that "music" stopped and I went to look out of the window, seeing Theo, Ivor, then Beauvois making their way out from the porch and sitting down in deckchairs. All staring listlessly ahead at the big white sheet still in the trees.

'I went downstairs to join them, where Theo noticed me at first, exclaiming in a hoarse low voice, "My God, Leda. The state of you! Still wearing your party dress, I see... and all those grass stems in your hair!"

'"I could say the same about you!" I'd laughed, though I worried for my brother's health. The fevered colour in his cheeks. The shadows bruised beneath his eyes.

'"We're all a little worse for wear." Ivor smiled blearily, and offered me the cup he held, which he said was coffee, "still quite hot, and I've added a dash of whisky, to help blow all the cobwebs off."

'"A hair of the dog..."' I stopped at once, regretting that

mention of a dog. And, I really should have gone upstairs, to wash myself and change my clothes, because Theo was right – I must look a fright. But instead, I gulped the coffee down, then said as brightly as I could, "What shall we do today? I suppose we should tidy up the lawns, though I'm sure it can wait till Joe arrives. Amy shouldn't be too long... and it's such a lovely morning. What do you say we take a wander down the cliff to Cuckham Sands? Look in on Tilly Davenport?"

'I hoped Beauvois would understand the implication in my words, that the other two might back me up. But Ivor only sounded grim, saying he didn't have the time, that he needed to go to Brightland to collect his luggage from the shop; that he wanted to visit a barber too, before heading for Southampton docks.

'All the time, while we filmed *The Cursed Queen*, Ivor would shave three times a day, and even then you'd sometimes see a sort of blue metallic sheen. So it came as no surprise to me that a growth of stubble was already breaking through his morning skin.

'Passing the cup back to his hand, I asked, "What time must you be off?" At which he pulled a ticket from the pocket of his waistcoat, consulting that before he said, "At least by early afternoon. I'd like to get on board by six and settle in before we dine. We sail tomorrow at first light."

'I said, "I wish that I could come... to wave you off from the docks, I mean. If Tilly can squash in on your lap while Theo drives the motorbike, I'm sure that I could do the same. She must be twice as big as me and..."

'Theo shot a warning look while Beauvois glowered up at me. But I knew what I was doing, fully intending to punish him for the rudeness he had shown last night... wanting to make him jealous, to know he didn't own me... although Ivor, probably aware that there could be another row, insisted that it would be best if we left arrangements as they were. And then, with his usual grace and charm, he turned to face Beauvois and said, "Who'd want to leave this heaven? Whatever I've been told about the open Californian skies, when I look at the cloudless blue above I only wish that I could stay and make more films at White Cliff House."

'He didn't know, and nor did I, there would never be another film, although, when it came to *The Cursed Queen*, Beauvois was not quite done with us.

'He got up from his chair, his movements swift but also rather oddly stiff, and his voice unnaturally bright. "I had a sudden thought last night. I woke in bed and realised that I'd left the projector and film out here, so ..." He paused. Such a long long pause it was. "So I decided to get up and take them back down to the shed. And that's when it struck me: to be true, for the film to be authentic, *The Cursed Queen* must have another scene for me to edit in."

He smiled down at Ivor. "Could you manage to spare an hour or so? Only you and Leda. Theo can drive to Brightland and collect your luggage from the shop, if that would help to free you up. I promise we'll be done by noon."'

Leda sighed and looked towards the hearth. I couldn't see her face at all, when she said, 'Beauvois was lying, Ed. The film didn't need an extra scene. *The Cursed Queen* you saw tonight ... that version was the very one we viewed out on the lawns that night.

'Hard to think it was so long ago, when it seems like only yesterday that Theo headed off to town, when Ivor went upstairs to shave with Beauvois's razor, in his bowl. He never did get to a barber's shop, but that stubble would have shown on film, no matter how thick the greasepaint. And me, I did as Beauvois said. I went ahead, down to the shed, to find the costume ...'

Breaking off, she barely whispered, 'That sound, now that the rain has stopped? Surely you must hear it too? The turning of an engine?'

Still thinking she imagined it, deciding this might be my cue to say that I'd investigate, then take the chance to head away, I gathered up my pad and pen, and all of Leda's memories, placing them inside my bag before I went to stand beside the window with the shutter gone.

Peering through tangled ivy stems I could see the strips of rotting cloth still hanging in the conifers. Through them, some glints of light that might be shining from car headlamps. There *was* a mechanical thrumming sound. The tinkling crash of breaking glass – which was when I turned to Leda Grey, and said, 'Those lights, that noise you hear ... I think it's coming from the shed.'

SMEAR THE SLEEPY
GROOMS WITH BLOOD

Outside, the clouds were thickening, moving swiftly overhead. Dried ivy leaves were rattling while roses swayed and petals dropped. Their heady perfume mingled with the smells of dampened soil and grass – the grass on which my feet then slipped when coming to the garden's edge.

Taking a moment to steady myself, I peered along one darkened lane at the end of which the vintage car appeared to be quite undisturbed. But, the statue from *Delirium*, she had been knocked over, lying in broken pieces on the path that led to the filming shed – the place from which I heard some shouts and hoots of screaming laughter.

Again, that droning, thrumming sound. And now, I knew the source of it. The generator's engine had been started and was powering the arc lamps that remained intact, causing them to flash and spark above the crowd who milled below. The figures I could clearly see, drinking, dancing, clambering across the stage and scaffold towers.

I started to run through the meadow, screaming, screaming out my rage, thinking of things that Lucy said had happened there when she was young. About kids. Drunk kids. Kids partying. Kids who couldn't give a damn if they scared an old woman half to death.

Every one of them froze when they heard my cries, before fleeing through the broken door, and squealing like some frightened rats as they scattered out across the field to disappear between a hedge that marked its farthest barrier. Some shouts of mock bravado were shouted back as insults, but soon there was nothing left to hear but the engine's hum and my gasping breaths as I made my way into the shed to see the debris left behind.

Smashed bottles of cider. Cans of beer. The smouldering stubs of cigarettes. While my feet stamped down to crush those glowing tips to nothing more than ash, the lamps above me flared, then dimmed as the engine's power surged and ebbed. Lit that way, the shed took on a far more vivid atmosphere. Whereas before I'd seen a carcass made of rotting wood and glass, now, having viewed the magic of the films created in that space – whether the sweeter *Mermaid* scenes, or the darker films that followed on – I saw it as a temple to the skill and art of Charles Beauvois, for which the cracks of thunder and the streaks of lightning overhead formed the perfect gothic backdrop.

During each new flash of light, whether from inside or out, the stuffed dead animals appeared to spring to life before my eyes. A tiger poised as if to leap. The crocodiles with open jaws – until another lamp flared up and I was forced to shut my eyes against its sudden spitting white. But even then, through spider veins of red against my inner lids, I saw those creatures' solid shapes burned black against my retinas. And, something else among them. The elongated silhouette of a man some way ahead of me.

What a fool I felt when the shock had passed, when I realised that man was me, with my own shadow being cast against the boarding of the stage. When I lifted one arm to touch my head my mirror image did the same – which turned my thoughts to Mum again, comparing the shed's menagerie of morbidly weird exotica with all the creatures she once used to conjure into life for me. When she'd held her hands before a torch, and her fingers formed the shapes of dogs, and rabbits, mice, or little birds which flew and flapped their wings across the patterns of my bedroom walls, while my own small hands had gripped the bars of the cot that made my shadow cage.

Another sputtering of light and the memory was washed away, as was the silhouetted man. My thoughts were now distracted by the sight of props I recognised as seeing in *The Cursed Queen*.

The crumbling thrones where metal paint had all but peeled away from wood. Fine tapestries now full of holes. Pots of desiccated ferns with jagged fronds like rusted knives.

Where the trespassers had trampled on the lid of the sarcophagus, their weight had caused the painted papier mâché face to fracture. The white bird hands crossed at the breast now parted and a gaping split revealed the dark interior – where something red was glittering.

Intrigued to look more closely, I began to walk towards it. But I failed to notice what was lying on the floor in front of me. My shin slammed into something hard. I then spent several moments being almost blinded by the pain, until it dulled, my senses cleared, and I noticed what the culprit was. Another old projector, much like the one at White Cliff House, except that this machine was trashed and seemingly beyond repair. The lens of the lamp was splintered. The case was bent and fractured. A length of film spilled from its bowels.

Crouching down, using only the tips of my fingers, I lifted one edge of that ribbon up. How long was the reel? It was hard to tell, with most still wound inside the case. Twenty – thirty – sixty feet? At roughly a foot a second, that could be as much as a minute's worth when it was shown upon a screen. If anything remained to see.

The drone of humming faded. The arc lamps dimmed to nothing but the faintest yellow flickering. I froze and willed the power to surge, to give more light, to let me see the pictures on that celluloid.

As if in answer to my prayer a spear of lightning flashed above, and during those brief seconds I glimpsed the tearful features of a woman staring upwards, with the camera looking down on her, and seemingly from some great height. Foreshortened from that angle, her large dark eyes were magnified above pale cheeks smeared black with kohl. Below, her body had been sheathed in a clinging robe of sheer white cloth. A beaded collar at her breast, and on her head, the crown of snakes; the metal of it glistening, as was the object in her hands—

A voice called out my name. Surprised, I dropped the film, and then spun round to see that Leda Grey was standing very close behind me, and in her hands that surely was the glinting of a metal blade.

Was that the knife I'd seen inside her cabinet at White Cliff House? The knife I'd only just that moment witnessed on the celluloid?

'My God. Leda! I thought you were...'

'A ghost?' She gave a weary smile. The slightest shaking of her head, the vibration of which caused all the snakes coiled in the crown to hiss at me, through which she carried on to say, 'I see that you have found the film.'

I said, more calmly than I felt, 'I think it might be damaged. But I could try to wind it up. We could use the lantern at the house to—'

'No! I'd rather it was lost. Did you see my tears? Did you see my pain? None of that was make-believe.'

She might have been performing then, recapturing the stricken look on the face burned through the celluloid. She almost seemed to float across the debris scattered in the shed as she headed past me, on towards the racks of decomposing clothes, where she stopped and then turned back to say, 'This is where I came that day, looking for the costume that Beauvois wanted me to wear. But all the clothes were muddled up, and this particular garment, it had fallen from its hanger... lying on the floor beneath. Not that it really mattered. The silk was crinkled in the style of the Fortuny Delphos gowns, washed and twisted while it dried, then shimmering like skins of snakes while clinging to my body's curves.'

Her eyes left mine to cast around, fixing on a table and pointing with the dagger's tip. 'I'd left the beaded collar next to the serpent bracelets... though I felt quite sure they hadn't been in such a state of disarray. And the pots holding cosmetics... the way some lids had been removed. The powders spilling everywhere.

'But, I thought so little of all that while stripping off my clothes to stand before this very mirror, and' – again, she started miming – 'dipped a brush into the kohl, ready to paint around my eyes, to transform myself from Leda Grey into the cursed queen again. Upon my head, the fringed black wig. And this.' She raised her hands so that the dagger's blade was stroked across the snakes that framed her wasted face.

'While I gazed at my reflection, transformed within that looking glass, I couldn't help but cry out loud when I saw another figure there. But, it was only Charles Beauvois. And Beauvois was walking towards me, and all the while our gaze was held within the silver of the glass, where I felt myself quite mesmerised and forgot about the night before. I only saw the man's desire as his arms were circled round my waist, when I arched my back against his bulk and felt the stickiness of sweat already soaking through his shirt. How his body's heat scorched into mine. How strong the tincture on his breath, when he said my name … so earnestly, with such a longing in his voice.'

Her eyes were closed. Thin arms were raised. I could see those scars on her wrists again while she pressed her bony fingers to the sagging contours of her breasts. And during this disturbing scene, Leda's fragile body started bending back unnaturally, as if supported in mid-air by something – or perhaps someone – I simply couldn't see at all.

At that moment the generator failed. The lamps fizzed out and left an empty silent darkness in the shed. Only the thudding of my heart, and some other heavy breaths nearby – until the wires hummed to life and the bulbs around pulsated with a glaring incandescence, through which I saw not the Leda Grey who sat in the darkness of White Cliff House, but Leda as she'd been when young.

She was completely naked, except for the crown upon her head. She was standing so much closer too, though I hadn't heard the slightest tread of footsteps on the broken glass left scattered all across the floor. The only thing between us was the ruined old projector, over which she stretched her empty hands as if she wished to take my own.

I felt an exquisite sharp desire, just as I'd done the other night after reading of her meeting with Beauvois in the aquarium. And then, in Leda's bedroom when I'd looked into an oval glass and seen reflections from her past – and felt as if I'd been possessed.

In the shed, possession came again, when the hands I offered back to hers looked so much larger than my own, with the wrists extending from white cuffs showing a growth of thick black hair, and the voice that formed within my mouth much deeper, hoarser than my own, when it groaned, 'Leda... Oh, Leda.'

Although I said her name out loud, the words inside my aching heart were ... *Sorry... Sorry... Sorry*. How desperately I wanted her, moaning as I cupped her breasts, my fingers stroking downwards until I reached the hot damp cleft between the heat of parting thighs – which was when I flinched away again, cowering like an injured beast when I heard her cry, 'Beauvois, what's wrong? Are you in pain? Is it your leg?'

I was shouting back in anger, 'My leg? You think that pain could cause the misery I'm in right now!'

The blood was boiling in my veins. I felt enraged, too hot, too tired when I turned my face away from hers and headed back towards the doors that led across the meadow, where I stopped a while and then called back, my words still strained and thick with threat, 'I'll go and see where Ivor is. He must have finished shaving now. We need to have this filming done before Theo gets back from town again.'

'Beauvois,' Leda cried out to him, 'don't you think that would be better? If we waited for Theo to come back, to help you with the cameras?'

But Beauvois had no answer. His image simply vanished. I was back to my old self, standing exactly where I'd been before his mind had entered mine. And Leda, the ancient Leda Grey, with her lank grey hair, in her plain black dress, was still beside the costume racks.

Weary eyes in a wrinkled face stared back at me through the mirror's glass when she said, 'That's how he left me, Ed. And so, I began all over again... the process of making up my face, finding that transformation to be soothing and empowering. Seeing the eyes of the cursed queen and feeling the braveness of her soul. Knowing *she* would never be afraid of any man… or any fate.

'I remember my father telling me, "Be brave, darling Leda. Follow your dreams." But I never thought my dreams would lead to the nightmare Beauvois made of them.'

'What happened, Leda… with Beauvois?' I had to know the end of this, even though I feared what it might be, when I heard that talk of bravery and saw the gleaming dagger's blade extend from Leda's hand again. Her eyes too bright in a drawn skull face.

Had Leda murdered Charles Beauvois? Is that what made him disappear from White Cliff House so long ago?

Her voice broke through my own again when she walked towards the golden thrones, sounding totally deranged while she chanted a line from the play *Macbeth*. 'Is this a dagger I see before me?'

It was almost as if she'd been transformed into a ridiculous pantomime villain, until she said quite lucidly, 'That's what Ivor was reciting, doing his best to make me laugh when he posed there on his golden throne, wearing the costume of the king… and looking quite magnificent.

'I was doing my best to be serious, trying to listen to Beauvois who was shouting down from the scaffold tower. "You have to stab him in the heart, to show the moment when the cursed queen destroys the man she loved. I mean to splice this memory of hers into the current scene, where she takes the Historian to the cave to show him her dead lover's corpse."

'I looked at the dagger in my hand, where the jewels in the handle glinted. Beauvois had shown me how it worked, when he'd held the knife, then slammed the blade down hard against his empty palm… when I'd fully expected to see the tip plunge on through the other side. But that was before I'd realised the blade was made of rubber, retracting back into the hilt at the slightest hint of resistance. And he swore no risk of injury, and

Ivor only backed him up, saying he'd also used trick knives for his recent part in the Scottish play. I might happen to give him a bruise or two, but he promised that he'd suffered worse. "The things we thespians do for art!"

'Still, I wasn't entirely satisfied, trying to picture the scene on film, looking up to ask Beauvois, "But, will this look convincing if…"

'"If there's no blood?" Beauvois broke in, anticipating my own thoughts. "We'll do what we did before, when making *The Dreamer's Delirium*. One ampoule of the fake should do. We've plenty on the storage shelves. You plunge the knife, and Ivor breaks the vial between clenched fingers. He lifts that hand to clutch the wound and then… Hey presto! Blood will flow."

'But my nagging doubts would not abate. That sense of something not quite right. I found myself thinking of Rex again, with a horrible lurching in my heart when I glanced at the spot where he'd met his end, and those nerves were only made the worse by the generator's growling hum… and the heat and the stench of the spitting lamps. So many of them on the ground, and yet more hanging from above. As was the eye of the camera, like a monstrous cyclops looking down. The god who directed our every move… for whom nothing we did was right that day.

'It could have been my lack of sleep. The champagne I'd drunk the night before. Ivor's exotic cigarette? I was on the verge of fainting, struggling to stay alert when, at the third or fourth attempt to plunge the knife in Ivor's breast, the rubber blade did not retract but wobbled there above the flesh. More comedy than tragedy, and all made worse when Ivor laughed, when Beauvois's feet came clanging down the metal rungs of the scaffold ladder to scream his rage into my face. "Can't you try to look convincing? You're supposed to be a woman intent on murdering a man. You might as well be tickling him."

'If Ivor wasn't due to leave I would have suggested that we stop. Come back to the film another day. But Ivor was leaving, and so we simply had to carry on with it… to watch when

Beauvois grabbed my wrist and snatched the knife away again, muttering about the catch. Something about it having jammed.

'I looked at his hands as he held the knife, wet with sweat, and trembling. The way his eyes avoided mine. I could tell that Ivor was restless too, despite his play of bonhomie.

When he dabbed a towel at his breast to wipe away the sticky red, he was saying, "Darling Leda, won't you try and do it properly or we'll still be here at midnight, and I'll never reach the docks in time to board the ship before she sails."

'I took another cloth to help, knowing it was vital not to spoil our clean white costumes ... which would only lead to more delays if we had to go and change as well. And, while I was taken up with that I could hear the clicking of the blade, glancing back to see Beauvois still lost in concentration.

'I think of his expression now, as I've thought of it so often since. How he looked up and caught my eye, and the way his scowl became a smile, with all that dark cold energy turned into light and love again.

'Don't they say the best directors also make the finest actors ... that only through such empathy can they truly understand the craft? The psychology of the deceits?

'Oh, what a deceit he was to play. There wasn't a single doubt in my mind when he said that we could start again ... but before he went back to the camera, he'd show me one more time the surest way to strike the dagger down.

'Would you like to see it, Ed?' She held the weapon out to me, and as if I had been hypnotised by the knowing glitter in her eyes, I lifted my legs to step across over the wreck of the projector, walking on towards where she was standing by the golden thrones. But the closer I came, the dizzier, confused beneath the spitting lamps – through which I saw her change again. Not only her physical body, but the objects all around her too.

The whole of the decaying set now looked exactly as it had when *The Cursed Queen* was being filmed. The same lush palms and arching walls through which the pyramids were viewed. Two brightly gilded thrones, on one of which a man was lounging.

A long black wig upon his head. A leopard's pelt draped on one arm. A scarab beetle buckle on the belt below a hairless chest, from which the hems of long white skirts were puddled round his sandalled feet.

This was all so clear to me. So real that I was holding out my arms to circle Leda's waist, to place my hands on top of hers, the hands in which she held the knife. Four hands I then forced upwards. Four hands I held entirely still, as if all time had stopped until I seized the moment, and...

I remember the conscious part of me, the part that was not Charles Beauvois, thinking how strange for a rubber blade to look as hard as gleaming steel, and dazzling my eyes with light when it was driven down again – and then again, and then again – until my lips were forced apart, and I heard a short gruff gasping, 'Yes!' – and Beauvois's hold on me was gone.

He left me there, an empty shell, my heart an anguished thudding drum to echo the stamping of his feet as he ran towards the ladder, then climbed back to the very top, where the camera's handle whirred again as he stood and filmed the scene below, with those rattling vibrations somehow too loud inside my head, until I thought it would explode – which was when the vision disappeared. No Beauvois. No Ivor Davies. Only the aged Leda Grey. A look of horror on her face as she stared in distress at the empty thrones.

Her voice was choked. Her eyes were wet when she explained, so frantically, 'Ivor was gasping, much too pale. And that startled expression in his eyes. And the hot metallic smell of blood... Oh, much too much of it to have been stored in any little vial. It flowed across the leopard skin, through the zigzag hollows of his ribs, through the cloth that draped around his hips. That dripping sound. His awful groans... and then my own to realise that a blade supposed to do no harm had sliced its way through Ivor's flesh, as if that flesh was butter.'

Between her tortured rasping breaths, the words were barely audible. 'There'd been two blades in that trick knife: the dummy, and the real one, though I could hardly grasp that truth, looking up to see Beauvois still filming what was going on ... while I stood with the dagger in my hands and screamed at him, "What have you done! Ivor's bleeding. Ivor's hurt."

'When I looked back at Ivor there was only one thing I could think to do, letting the knife drop from my hands and pressing them against his wounds ... pressing down with all my might in the hope that way to staunch the flow. It was awful ... with the engine's thrum ... with the spitting glare of all the lights ... and then the sound of Beauvois's feet, descending the ladder yet again, standing there to watch us while he said, "I couldn't let you go. I couldn't let him take you. Not with everything invested here. In you ... in the films ... in White Cliff House."

'It was hard to comprehend those words. How could he speak so calmly? Straining to look back at him, I begged, "Please! Won't you do something? Go down to the farm ... the telephone. Get Joe to call someone for help."

'But he didn't move a single inch, not even when Ivor raised his head, his voice a thin and strangled laugh. "Well, Beauvois ... did you ever think this old man had so much blood in him?"

'Beauvois replied with sneered contempt. "I saw you both, in here last night, when I brought the projector and film back down."

'Despite the heat of Ivor's blood, I felt my body turn to ice, shivering with cold and shock, with everything around me then seen through a misty veil of white ... and Beauvois's voice too far away. But I still heard each word he said. 'I saw you, Leda ... fucking him.'

'"No!" I turned to face him, protesting, "You were dreaming. More of your elixir dreams. I didn't go near the shed last night. I slept in the garden hammock ... and then I came upstairs to you."

'He raged. "Don't lie! You know as well as I do. That was Tilly Davenport sleeping in the hammock. I saw her with my own two eyes."

'That was when I remembered. Tilly's hat upon my head. Her

feather boa round my neck. A blanket covering the rest. The sense of someone watching me.

I was weeping. "No, you're wrong, Beauvois."

Ivor tried to speak as well, but the effort proved too much for him. The lids of his eyes were closing while I stroked my hand against his cheek and held my mouth against his ear, saying, "Wait, Ivor... won't you wait for me? I'll go and find someone to help."

'But Ivor wouldn't let me go. His fingers clutched around my wrist, and a crooked smile upon his lips as they turned a ghastly bluish grey... those lips I'd once avoided when he'd asked me for a good luck kiss.

'Oh, I'd brought him nothing but bad luck.' Leda held a hand against her brow where a purple vein was pulsing fast. 'Since then, I've wished so many times that Charles Beauvois had died that day... when we helped to save him in the shed. His death would mean that Ivor lived. And I thought there might still be a chance, when Ivor opened up his eyes, and asked, "Is Theo back yet? Must leave... before we miss our ship."

'Our ship.' Her voice was small and shrill. 'That was the moment when I knew for sure what Beauvois must have seen, when a buried memory returned. My brother being drunk one night. My brother wearing women's clothes. My brother looking back to ask, "Can my little sister be that blind?"

'Beauvois had seen my brother dressed in the costume of the cursed queen. My brother had worn the fringed black wig. My powders painted on his face. And now, I wore the very same while kneeling in a sea of blood, while Ivor gave a long slow yawn before convulsing horribly, as if some electricity had jolted through his body. But it lasted no more than a second or two, and then he was quite still again, and I saw the "going" in his eyes, just like my mother's when she'd died.

'How heavy, old and tired I felt, as ancient as the sphinxes when I looked again at Charles Beauvois and somehow found the energy to struggle to my feet again... when above the generator's drone, I hissed, "You monster of a man! You used me. You deceived me."

'That's when I thought I saw a spark of the old Beauvois come back again, when he placed his hands on my shoulders and I saw the regret in bloodshot eyes, in the deep-etched lines and shadowed bags of a man who'd barely slept for more than an hour a night in several weeks; who'd become so immersed in imagined worlds he no longer seemed to understand where the fiction began and the fact might end.

'But then he started laughing. He looked like a man who'd gone insane ... and I do believe he had gone mad when he said, "What an actress, Leda Grey! What a Lady Macbeth you might have been. That's what he wanted, isn't it! For you to go and play *his* queen. To leave me for that Griffith man. If I hadn't seen you for myself, if I hadn't come down here last night, then even now you might still hope to persuade me of your loyalty."

'If only my brother had been there. He might have told Beauvois the truth regarding any loyalty. He might have seen my aura too. My rage, like tongues of burning fire through which I somehow found the words, "There's *nothing* I need persuade you of. I am innocent of any crime. But *you* ... I will never forgive you for the evil you have done today. You have ruined me ... my future life. Any future that *we'd* hoped to have. Why don't you murder me as well? Film two deaths instead of one!"

'Oh, Ed.' She looked exhausted, her face as grey as ashes. 'What a dreadful thought that was. It hit me like a hammer's blow. I wanted nothing more right then than to hide from the shed's accusing lights. For the film in Beauvois's camera to remain as always unexposed. For time to run back to another day, when I'd stood in a dark aquarium ... when I might never turn around or fall into a stranger's arms.'

She did turn then, to plead with me. 'You should go, Ed. Go away from here! This is my curse. I see it now. Everyone I've ever cared about is somehow broken in the end. Just as my brother's heart was doomed to be when he came back again ... when he saw me here, down on my knees. Not praying. Much too late for that. But I'd found a bucket and some cloths and started washing Ivor clean, dragging off the leopard skin, the blood-drenched skirts, the wig he wore. Somehow he'd looked too naked, except for those gashes on his breast where the red still spilled across the white.

'My hands weren't white. They were still red ... no matter how I scrubbed at them. So many nights I woke in tears, believing I was here again, smeared with blood, from head to foot, so much of it that Theo thought I must have been attacked as well.

He stood before the gilded thrones, staring up at Ivor's corpse, asking in a cold hard voice, "Leda ... tell me. Where's Beauvois?"

'But Beauvois was long gone by then. And he took that final film with him. I'd seen the flash of the metal where his hands had gripped the canister, and the gleam of that had screamed at me: *I am the proof that Leda Grey has murdered Ivor Davies.*

'I think it was Theo's quietness, unnatural though it seemed to be, that drove me to lose all self-control, when my brother dragged me to my feet, and I beat my fists against his chest, and sobbed, "He saw you here last night. He saw, and he thought that you were me. Now Ivor's dead, and Beauvois's gone. And he took the film. He took the film. He took ..."

'He took my soul away.'

FIRE BURN,
AND CAULDRON BUBBLE

Leda Grey appeared to be on the verge of a physical collapse. God knows how she'd ever managed to recount that day so vividly. I felt drained. I felt as if I'd seen each moment played before my eyes. And more than that. Much more than that. The sense that we'd not been alone, that somehow the spirit of Charles Beauvois had stirred within my flesh again. That, or I was going mad. As mad as he'd appeared to be.

But now he'd gone. I had no doubt. He'd left the shed, just as he'd run away some sixty years before, leaving Leda there to watch while Ivor died and...

And what had happened after that?

For some reason, my eye had been drawn back to the replica sarcophagus, where I saw a glimmering again, and nothing to do with the arc lamps, or the glare from any lightning strikes. This came from the interior, within the ruptured coffin lid where tongues of fire were darting up. Flames of orange, blue and green, like a vibrant magic lantern show.

I've thought about it often since. How the fire took hold so easily. But then, the shed was mostly wood, its timbers dry as tinder from the months of endless summer heat. I think about the burning cigarettes those kids had dropped there. One must have fallen through the broken lid of the sarcophagus. Perhaps another had been left to smoulder on electric wires that coiled across the floor below. But, whatever the sequence of events, a fire was quickly raging through the layers of paper and gelatin of which the casket had been made; glued to the galvanised metal base of the sort of trough you'd find in fields when used to feed farm animals. That trough had formed a cauldron from which small shreds of singed white cloth were floating up on rising air, hanging there like motes of dust caught in golden shafts of sun. What children think are fairies. But this was nothing so benign. Not with the noxious sulphur smell – and something more substantial in that casket than the little heap of ashes and the paper scroll I'd seen in the film, *The Cursed Queen*.

What I saw engulfed in raging flames was surely a decaying corpse. Some withered flesh still clung to bones, and the way the jaw was hanging, as if the body screamed in pain. And through its carapace of ribs, more shreds of cloth, all glowing red – until I realised that they were swarms of tiny beetles. Blood-red beetles scurrying away from where they'd made their nests.

Meanwhile, the generator buzzed, that searing high-pitched insect whine, and then another blaze of light. This time a power surge that caused most of the arc lamps to explode, with broken glass and battery acid showering down like molten rain.

Falling forward, wailing with the pain, one hand thrust out and grabbed onto the edge of the sarcophagus, which led to yet more agony – not only because of the scalding heat, but because I thought that I'd been struck by a sudden bolt of lightning. A shock of electricity must have passed through the metal of the trough from a damaged wire underneath, its circuit then completed when it flowed into my living flesh. Every muscle was jerking violently, and what happened to my vision I can only describe as resembling interference on a TV screen, when all that you can see are rows of black-and-white zigzagging lines.

The power died. I was released and must have fallen backwards. A horrible moment. I couldn't breathe, clutching a hand against my breast and fearing that my heart had stopped, until… 'Ugh,' I gasped. A rush of air filling up my lungs again. My heart renewed its pounding beat. My vision cleared when I first sat, then struggled to my feet to stand.

Casting around for Leda Grey, I called her name in panicked shouts as I strained to see through embers that were fizzing from the timber joists, with some of those small glowing sparks then dropping down onto the reel of film still spooled across the floor.

The film was melting, bubbling, releasing pungent chemicals that caused my eyes to blur and sting; my nose and throat to feel as if I'd swallowed a gallon of vinegar. And perhaps those fumes had also stripped my brain of any common sense, when I threw myself across the film and used my body as a shield, to try and smother any fire.

But celluloid nitrate does not need the breath of oxygen to live. Not even water can douse the flames. I know that now. I didn't then.

HAVE WE EATEN ON THE INSANE ROOT THAT TAKES THE REASON PRISONER?

Pain.

Needles.

Sleeping.

Dreams.

A fire.

A body in a box.

Lucy's voice – and then her smile, when I opened my eyes in the hospital.

It was Lucy who saved my life that night. She'd given up on the promise that I'd made to meet her at the pub. She was walking home along the beach when she heard a loud explosion, looking up to see the flames engulfing Beauvois studio.

The time? She said it was ten to twelve.

Later, she told me how it looked like fireworks exploding. The gleaming reds and oranges, fading to pinks, and then to white as splinters of glass came crashing down.

There can be a certain beauty, even in the most horrific things. Like the clouds rising up from atomic bombs. Like viruses, or cancer cells when observed through the lens of a microscope. Or the spider webs of ridging scars on flesh when it's been cut, or burned. It depends on your perspective. How close you are to the centre of things. And I had been too close that night.

It was more like a dream than a memory, when I thought of Leda standing there in the midst of all the blazing flames, how she'd called my name, and then reached down, and found some superhuman strength to drag me to my feet again and lead me through a stumbling daze of pain back up to White Cliff House.

And that's where Lucy found me, with Leda, in her sitting room, though I was barely sensible, unable to do much more than croak with all the smoke that I'd inhaled having scorched the lining of my throat.

I remember the desperate thirst I felt. Fighting against the arms of men who'd run up from the nearby farm to carry me across some fields, then down another cliff-side track to the doors of a waiting ambulance. I remember the bliss of the sedation, when my mind was dulled by opiates, when I lay on my back in an oxygen tent, fixed to rehydration drips, with antibiotics and sulphate creams applied beneath the bandages. The torture as the dead burned flesh was scraped away before the new was grafted on in place of it, when my every conscious thought had been eclipsed by such a searing pain – though there were some parts of my face and chest that would never feel pain again. And as for the nerves that did repair, the itching almost drove me mad. I imagined there were beetles. Tiny red beetles crawling underneath the surface of my skin.

For weeks, I was still unaware of the consequences of the fire, until the day when I woke up to see Lucy sitting by the bed. And there, in a chair on the other side, was Leda's brother Theo. But what about his sister?

'Is Leda all right? Is she here with you? I need to see her . . . to thank her.'

My head was fugged and heavy with the weight of the bandages wrapped around when I tried to sit up in the bed and said, 'You know she saved me, don't you. If she'd left me in the burning shed I might have ended up the same as . . . Oh God. I keep on seeing it. Every time I close my eyes. The body. The sarcophagus.'

Lucy attempted to soothe me. 'You're confused. Don't you remember? The police were here. They explained it all. I thought you'd heard . . . you'd understood.'

'What police?' I had no memory of any such encounter.

'The story made the national news. But your boss, the magazine editor, when he came here to visit you, he said he'd try to keep it down. Your name ... your involvement in it all. He sorted out this private room and—'

'He visited ... this hospital? For fuck's sake!' I was panicking. 'He came to steal the story. It's mine. Not anyone's, but—'

'Hey, stay cool. Calm down, Ed!' Lucy almost looked afraid, shrinking back into her chair before she took control again and said far more determinedly, 'I thought I was helping out, that's all. I found a business card in your wallet. In the rucksack you were clinging to when I found you that night at White Cliff House. I know the police would have wanted it. But I promised to keep it safe for you. And, somehow, in the panic, when all the people came to help and carried you down to the ambulance, I just pretended it was mine. I kept it till this morning, when I brought it to the hospital. It's in that cupboard by your bed, along with some clothes and other things collected from your hotel room. I found a receipt with the Brightland name. And I'd never normally go prying through your private things like that, but I thought, if there'd been family, or anyone you might have wanted here with you ... with things so bad. Still, I guess the police would have done all that. They had your car. The number plate. They could have tracked you down through ...'

'I don't have any family. And I don't remember having any visitors in here but you ... until ...' I glanced at the old man. 'Mr Williams today.'

While I spoke, Lucy was reaching down for a handbag placed beside her chair, sitting up again to say, 'I kept this cutting for you, Ed. It was in the local *Argus*. Can you manage to hold it?' she gently asked. 'Or shall I read it out instead?'

She read:

MYSTERY OF HUMAN REMAINS DISCOVERED AT WHITE CLIFF HOUSE

Unidentified human remains have been found at a house near Cuckham Sands. Formally used in Edwardian times as a base for creating silent films, a purpose-built studio in the grounds was completely destroyed when a fire broke out on the night of the discovery.

Initial pathology reports suggest that the remains are male, most probably in middle age. However, officials are yet to establish why and when his death ...

Before she could go any further, I protested, 'It was Ivor. Ivor Davies! He'd acted in one of the films. Leda told me everything. Leda said ...'

I turned to Theo, who looked even more fragile when removed from the setting of his shop. And his eyes, two pale blue wells of pain behind the grimy spectacles. I heard a rustling, crackling sound, reminding me of burning flames when he then leaned forwards in his chair and crushed the sheets of paper wrapped around some flowers in his lap. His tongue licked over bare cracked lips. He said, 'I'm very sorry, Ed. I should never have mentioned White Cliff House to you in the shop that after- noon ... not if I'd known what you would find. Mostly, I'd hoped that you'd come back and let me know how Leda was, and—'

'You're lying!' I was shouting. 'You wanted me to go and find the secrets that your sister kept. The skeletons in her closets. Those were the very words you said.'

'Yes, but I was warning you. A danger for myself as well. I knew that I was gambling, playing a game of Russian roulette, with no idea of what you'd find ... how much, if anything at all, my sister might confess to you. But secretly, I hoped she would. I hoped she'd let you find the films. These last few years I've fretted so, to think that work would all be lost. I knew she'd saved some prints of them ... even with the originals destroyed when that damn bomb was dropped. And if she showed you something more, if she took you down to see the shed ... well, I'd already decided to confess and take the blame for that. And really, there was little chance that Charles Beauvois would reappear, to carry out his wicked threats to testify against her name. Even if the monster's still alive, he'd be more than a hundred years by now.

'No.' He closed his eyes and sighed. 'I am quite sure he must be dead.'

'But I think he did come back again. I think he testified... to me.' My words caught Theo by surprise, eyes staring back in disbelief when I then carried on to say, 'I was down in the shed, with Leda. I saw things, heard things. Awful things! And...' I ruthlessly accused, 'I know the part *you* played there... dressing yourself as the cursed queen, which is how Beauvois discovered you. You and Ivor...'

'A mistake. A terrible mistake.'

The old man gave an anguished groan, before hiding his face in trembling hands – which was when Lucy got up to leave, turning back from the open door to say, 'I don't know what's been going on, but I think you two need privacy... some time to talk here on your own. I'll pop back in tomorrow, Ed.'

When she'd gone, as the door hushed shut again across the floor's linoleum, Theo raised his head and said, 'First of all, you need to know that I've been in talks with the police. I was going to tell them everything... and then as details were released I realised that I might have an alibi to use myself. I've told them that the burned remains were the bones of an old skeleton, used as a prop when we made the films. You see, we really had one. I've shown them the receipt I kept, from one of the London medical schools. But, I don't know if they've been convinced.'

'I need to tell them what I saw. That wasn't any skeleton.'

'Sometimes our eyes deceive us, Ed. Beauvois, he didn't witness what he thought he had in the shed that night. Even Leda made assumptions very far from the realities. I let her go on believing lies because of the need to protect her. If she'd known the truth. What Ivor felt. The future that she might have had...'

Theo struggled against his emotions, swallowing them down again as he gazed through damp grey lashes. 'When it comes to Monsieur Charles Beauvois, I understand we have a name for such controlling natures now. A sociopath, I think it is. Someone charming and attractive. But, oh, so vain and self-obsessed. A dangerous combination, particularly when all those traits are heightened by narcotic drugs. Delusions, Ed. Delusions.'

The old man gave a mournful smile. 'Beauvois possessed a genius when it came to making moving films, but those directing skills of his he tried to use in real life, and when he thought he'd lost control, then what new horrors he contrived. Taking Ivor's life away. Destroying Leda's future. And me, I've borne the shame and guilt for every living moment since.'

I felt a rush of sympathy. 'I'm sorry. I know that you've both paid the price for Beauvois's jealousy. I know that you did nothing wrong. You weren't even there, at White Cliff House, when...'

I couldn't go on. I only said, 'Leda told me everything.'

'She told you?' He looked more surprised, taking off his spectacles while he rubbed a hand across his eyes, sighing when he carried on, 'Then, I think it's only fair for me to explain what really happened. The truth weighs much too heavily.'

He touched a hand against his heart, just as I'd once seen Leda do, when I first arrived at White Cliff House, when she feared I'd come to bring distressing news about her brother.

He said, 'I should have told her... I should have told her years ago. You see, Ivor never wanted me. It was Leda. Always Leda. And she, entirely blind to that. Always devoted to Beauvois.

'That night of the garden party, when Leda collapsed in a hammock... when we thought Beauvois was sleeping soundly in a bedroom at the house... Ivor and I went to the shed. We took some bottles of champagne. We lay on the chaises that we'd used as part of the set for *The Cursed Queen*. We talked of Ivor's future hopes, which included him professing, for what must have been the hundredth time since he'd come into our lives again, the desire he felt for Leda... of his wish to some day marry her. He really didn't mind the fact that she'd been living with Beauvois. But then, he was used to the theatre life, where moral codes have never been as strict as those in other worlds, even all those years ago.

'We talked about my future too. I was going to leave Beauvois's employ and travel to America, where Ivor said he'd try to use his influence to find me work in some of the studios over there. I'd had enough experience to offer new directors and if, as Ivor really hoped, my presence might lure Leda too ... well, we both knew *she* couldn't fail. She wasn't the flibbertigibbet type who'd be pretty and pout for a year or two. She was a star. She shone, Ed. She embodied every part she played. You simply couldn't drag your eyes away when she was on the screen. Ivor Davies was the same. If you could have seen *The Cursed Queen*. The chemistry between them.'

I didn't say I'd seen it, or that inside my rucksack, and only inches from us then, that film was in its canister. *Delirium*, and *The Mermaid* too. No, I didn't tell him that, only held my tongue while he went on.

'That night we'd smoked some cigarettes that Ivor brought along with him ... what you might call wacky baccy. I told you once before, I think, we were anything but dull back then.' He shrugged. His lips were twisted to give the semblance of a smile. 'Ivor drank and smoked so much eventually he passed out cold. I did my best to wake him. Called him, tried to drag him up from the couch where he was snoring, but when I saw his sleeping face ...

'He really was quite beautiful. And I was drunk. Much much too drunk to contemplate what risks might be involved when I walked off towards the room with all the costumes, where I dressed myself as Leda. Leda, as the cursed queen. I even painted up my face by the light of the moon that shone above, and then pulled on the long black wig ... and what a transformation!'

The old man gave a dreamy smile. 'I made a lovely girl, Ed. I was young, and I was slender. I was full of lust and madness too when I pleasured the man who I'd adored since he'd walked into our Brightland shop for me to take his photograph. To hear him gasp and moan with joy, even if he'd called another name, when ...

'These are the things I can't forget, even though Ivor said we must. In the morning – I don't know what woke us – but

I know how shocked he seemed to be to see me dressed in Leda's clothes ... to find some of his own removed. He must have guessed what had happened. Well, who could fail to realise? But he showed such cold indifference that ... well, I knew that what I felt could never be requited. But, the thing about Ivor Davies was, he was never one to hold a grudge. I treasure the fact that he waited there while I went to change and wash my face. And then, before we'd left the shed, how he offered me that charming smile, and said, 'We'll still be friends, old chap. But I'm simply not that way inclined. Let's put it all behind us. Forget it ever happened.'

But it couldn't be forgotten. Not by me, and not by Charles Beauvois, who'd spied on what I'd done that night. And, he *was* one to hold a grudge.'

'Where did Beauvois go?' I asked. 'Did you ever hear from him again?'

'Oh yes, we heard from him again. A few weeks after Ivor's death. A package arrived at White Cliff House which held a copy of the film that Beauvois made that morning, and ...'

Theo broke off when a nurse came in, pushing the trolley which contained more of my medications, ushering the old man out with, 'Visiting hour's over, sir. You can come again tomorrow. By then, our Mr Peters will have had those bandages removed. But we don't want you to wear him out. Not when he's on the mend at last.'

Theo dragged himself up from the chair, looking as if he was the one who needed to be in hospital. But before he shuffled from the room he reached out with one swollen hand and placed it gently on my arm. As light as the wings of a butterfly.

I didn't realise until he'd gone that he had left a gift. A photo card beside my hand, from which Bette Davis offered me that wry and knowing smile she had. And those flowers he'd held, some roses – he'd left them lying on his chair, where the nurse as quickly snatched them up, saying she'd go and find a vase, though I think she must have thrown them out. They had been wilting, turning brown. But still, the sweetest fragrance.

It lingered in the room a while, reminding me of Leda Grey, and her face so strongly in my mind when Theo made his last goodbye. 'Please, Ed, if you could find it in your heart to try and forgive me … and if you ever want to talk, you know exactly where I am. Always there, in my shop, in the Brightland Lanes.'

Later that day, while waiting for my bandages to be removed, I reached down to the bedside cabinet and dragged my rucksack out of it, hauling it up onto the bed and rummaging around inside until I found the papers containing Leda's *Mirrors*. And, how swiftly I was reimmersed, reliving the horror of the shed, still sensing Theo's misery when I came to Leda's final lines.

I saw my brother's dumbstruck face and thought, this is it. This is the end. Beauvois is gone. Ivor is dead. Theo will hate me for evermore.

But, eventually, I calmed myself. I told Theo what Beauvois had done, and Theo held me in his arms as if he'd never let me go, just as he'd done on that first day when we rode the bike to White Cliff House, very almost flying to our deaths.

After that, my brother also wept, then railed at the name of Charles Beauvois. He said he'd like to destroy the man, that he wouldn't let him ruin me, the only person in the world who Theo loved … and who still lived.

When Theo suggested that we hide Ivor's corpse in the sarcophagus, I simply did what he told me, never thinking of the consequence, though how heavy Ivor's body was. I hardly know how we lifted him. But we did. Somehow we managed it, and when the lid was on the box, when Theo sealed it up again, it was easier to make believe he wasn't even there at all.

Theo fetched Ivor's suitcase. The one he'd collected from the shop. And then the clothes that Ivor wore before he'd donned the costume for that final scene in Beauvois's film. He took the cigarette case out of Ivor's waistcoat pocket, but apart from that small silver box and a crumpled roll of banknotes there was nothing else to find there. No passport, or ticket for the ship. Or had we somehow missed that, when we took his clothes away to burn, along with everything that might have shown the slightest trace of blood?

We doused the lot in paraffin and made a night-time bonfire, standing to watch as thick black smoke came blowing back into our eyes, our vision blurred while all those little scraps of cloth went floating up. They glowed like tiny rubies. They sparkled there among the stars. Though, in truth, they'd never go so high. It was only an illusion.

Theo stayed at the house with me for weeks. By day, he watched me like a hawk. By night, when Amy wasn't there, I often followed when he'd go down to the shed to sit beside the tomb in which his lover lay. He could not bear to let him go. And, of course, everybody else assumed that Ivor had gone to board his ship, that he'd sailed to America and, once there, if he'd failed to meet his friends, or appear for meetings he'd arranged ~ well, these things happened, didn't they? People sometimes disappeared.

Ivor was not the only one. When Amy or any others asked, we said that Charles Beauvois had also made a trip abroad that year, meeting with European promoters in the hope of distributing films in France, and also Germany. The Germans were mad for the vampires, so it really wasn't all that strange. But harder to make excuses when the mail arrived from creditors demanding that their debts be paid. All the money borrowed for the sets. The building of the studio. All the legal suits from Edison when the deadline for the films was breached. I suppose we could have sent those films. We still had copies at the house. But no. We'd rather sink into obscurity than help promote the name of a man like Charles Beauvois.

When the bailiffs knocked upon the door we did not take them to the shed. We looked for things in White Cliff House with which they might be satisfied. Paintings. Carpets. Furniture. Some jewels. My mother's furs and clothes. Anything of value that Beauvois had found in auction sales.

This was also around the time when Theo returned to the Bright-land shop, though rather than taking photographs he started up his soothsaying ~ a trade that proved most lucrative, with plenty of clients at the door when men were being killed like flies in the battles *of the First World War, when those at home who'd been bereaved sought solace in what forms they could. So many local men were lost upon those European shores. And Charles Beauvois was just one more.*

Theo said they made films of the trenches. They showed reels in the Brightland cinemas. He sometimes used to go along and sit through every news report, until the day when someone dropped a large white feather in his lap. But my brother was not a coward, not like some who trembled here at home. He did try to enlist, to go and fight, but was rejected on account of all those fits he used to have. The attacks that started up again, after... well, it must have been the shock of seeing Ivor dead like that, and knowing that his sister's hand had held the knife that killed him.

The memory also made me ill. For years I thought of little else. Before the German bomb went off, when nothing remained but empty air, each day I'd walk across the grass that used to slope behind the shed, stopping on the cliff-side path where we had burned all Ivor's things. And there, while staring out at sea, looking over the gleam of tide-wet sands, I'd sense Charles Beauvois's eyes on me. I'd hear his voice inside the wind, sometimes so loud I thought my head would burst while he 'directed' me to spread my arms as wide as wings, to fling myself into the air and plunge down to the rocks below. To join the mermaids in the sea.

So often, when I woke at night, I'd think that he was back again, his dark eyes boring into mine as he lay beside me in the bed, his whispers hot inside my ear: 'Drink the St Peter's, Leda. Drink the drops to make you sleep ... to stop the torment of your dreams.' There were times when his whispers turned to screams. 'Go and find the knife we used. Use the blade to slash your wrists.'

My brother found me in the shed. He washed and cleaned the cuts I'd made and bound them all in torn up sheets. Later, when I asked him about what I had worn that night ~ our mother's silk kimono ~ he said that it had been so stained he'd given it to Amy in the hope that she could get it clean. She said she'd had to throw it out.

I grieved for the loss of that garment. How silly, to miss a bit of cloth. But I also found my mind again, because that knife, I'm sure it cut the demon's spirit out of me. As I lay in the bed recovering, I decided to go to the police and confess to everything I'd done. I believed that, if I told the truth, then somehow it would be all right. Ivor could have a funeral. His people and friends could be informed, allowed to grieve and see him off.

But then Theo told me about the film that had arrived one day during my recovery. No writing on the packaging. No label on the canister in which the reel was safely stored. But Beauvois sent a warning that I had no option but to heed, because, when I was watching it (thank God, with Theo at my side), I saw what other eyes would see. They say the camera does not lie. But it can, and very often does, and who better at the lying art than the master of deceit, Beauvois?

In this new sequence of events he'd spliced in fragments from those takes when I'd plunged the blade with no success, and all reinvented in such a way that the crime of Ivor's murder appeared to be entirely mine. What better proof than in my face, in those moments when I'd held the knife and gazed up at the camera's eye, when Charles Beauvois had captured every ounce of guilt and fury there. And how he'd magnified that look, using a prism on the lens so that when the final scene was played my face appeared a hundred times, as if in shards of shattered glass. So many broken Leda Greys. No way to make her whole again.

I think about the Scottish play . . .

> *Out, out brief candle!*
> *Life's but a walking shadow, a poor player,*
> *That struts and frets his hour upon the stage,*
> *And then is heard no more. It is a tale*
> *Told by an idiot, full of sound and fury,*
> *Signifying nothing.*

WHAT'S DONE
CANNOT BE UNDONE

I didn't go back to the Brightland shop. Not then, though I would eventually. I didn't visit Lucy in her railway carriage by the sea, or try to find the car I'd left abandoned by the Cuckham pub. More likely than not the Mini would have been towed away by then. To be honest, I didn't really care.

When my bandages had been removed, when I looked into the mirror that one of the nurses held for me, the shock was such that I could only think of trying to hide away from everything and everyone who I had ever known before. Before the old Ed disappeared.

It wasn't the easiest of tasks, not with one of my hands so badly burned, the tendons frozen in a claw. But when the nursing staff had gone and the night-time hospital was still, I replaced my striped pyjamas with a T-shirt and a pair of jeans I'd found with all the other things that Lucy had fetched from the hotel. No spare trainers to put on. But that was good to aid escape. Bare feet made hardly any sound when I slung the rucksack on my back and left the side room I'd been in, walking the aisle of the general ward and ignoring the nurse on a telephone, who chatted away not noticing the patient turned to fugitive.

Eventually I found my way through a maze of stairs and corridors to see the big glass doors that showed the real world on the other side. Standing on the pavement edge, I shivered, cold without a coat. I was anxious, disorientated, like an alien from outer space who'd suddenly been dropped to earth – whereas I'd been lost in some inner space, trapped by my wounds, my memories; all too rapidly coming to depend on others for my every need.

Now, my main concern was in pretending not to notice when a group of drunks had gathered round to mock the freak show of my face, though their shrieking laughter was soon lost in the blare of horns, the screech of brakes, when I stepped straight out into the road and was almost crushed beneath a cab.

I felt too vulnerable, too small, and also too conspicuous when the driver got out and took my bag, then helped me climb into the back. When he'd settled at the wheel again, when his eyes met mine through the rear-view mirror, he'd said, 'Ignore the ghouls, mate! Comes with the territory round here. Just tell me where we're heading for.'

We arrived as dawn was breaking. I paid the driver with some money from the wallet in my bag, then slowly trudged four flights of stairs to reach my flat on the attic floor, panting for breath while fumbling with the keys to open up the door, which was almost jammed by all the mail piled on the other side of it.

The air inside seemed much too close. Last summer's endless heat had been replaced by cooler temperatures, but I'd left no windows open. The atmosphere was rank with food that festered in the kitchen bin. There were maggots. Dead flies everywhere. On the worktops, floors and windowsills, though one or two still buzzed about as I dropped my bags and thought again of Beauvois's film, *Delirium*.

It was all too vivid in my mind when I opened the window above the sink, then lifted the bin and threw it out; just as I'd done with the bread and fruit in the kitchen back at White Cliff House – though when I heard it crashing on the garden lawns so far below I was grateful for the early hour, with none of the other residents likely to be outside just then.

After dumping the post on a countertop, I spooned some coffee in a mug and filled the kettle up to boil, but changed my mind on opening the fridge to find the milk I'd left had turned to a solid sludge of green. But there was a bottle of champagne, and even if there didn't seem to be that much to celebrate, I popped the cork – eventually. Nothing was easy with my hand.

I sat at the kitchen table, drinking cold fizz from a chipped white mug while going through my stack of mail. Some bills. Some party invites. One envelope was trickier. I'd had to use my teeth to tear the thick brown envelope apart.

Inside, a letter from my boss, and dated several weeks before. After he'd been to visit me? He said how sorry everyone at *City* magazine had been to hear about my accident, but I was not to worry about hurrying back to work again. The magazine had been reviewed. The 'Hip and Happening' page was gone. But, whenever I felt up to it, we could meet for lunch at his London club and talk about the way ahead. He'd always had great faith in me. He knew that I could offer more.

I didn't see the positives. I only thought, *The way ahead! He's sacked me. The bastard's sacked me.* In a rage of sheer self-pity I threw the letter to the floor, but then began to laugh out loud when I snatched it up again to read the terms of my redundancy. Wasn't this what I had wanted? He was giving me my freedom, and bought at very little risk. The money to pay my mortgage off, and plenty spare for living on, which meant that I could take my time recovering my health again – though, even then, who would employ the monster that I had become? The skin of my upper arms and chest melted to a wax-like sheen. Two holes in one side of my head to mark the place where an ear had been before. The upper lid of my left eye dragging down and mottled red, so permanently swollen it would never really close again. And that ridge of scars across one cheek – for some reason that reminded me of the organic spread of stems that swathed the walls of White Cliff House.

That was it! White Cliff House. With the films, the voice recordings, the photographs and scrapbook – thank God Lucy had kept them safe – I had more than enough to write a book. A book that Leda Grey could hold. Something tangible to show for all those years of her obscurity. To make her proud, and proud of me.

I'd start the project straight away, as soon as I'd gone around the flat removing mirrors from the walls, and closing every curtain up to block reflections shining back through any darkened panes of glass. I'd start to write the minute after making a call to a dealer friend. I'd need some heavy-duty stuff to mute the pain, just nagging then, but soon to be more serious when the morphine in my blood had gone.

Morphine. Codeine. Heroin. Etorphine. Methyldesorphine. I got it whichever way I could over the next ten years or so, starting with that bottle of elixir brought from White Cliff House. My local doctor offered me legitimate prescriptions, but medical students could be found who, for sufficient recompense, would sell me almost anything. Not hard to avoid suspicion, having soon worked out a circuit with a different pharmacist each week. But, apart from all those tours I made around the city's suburbs, I rarely left the flat by day. I bought my food in corner shops where doors were open late at night. I no longer went to music gigs, or parties after theatre shows. Not even a drink in the local pub.

Hadn't Theo Williams once said that Leda only felt alive whenever people looked at her? For me, every stare was a living death, though that reluctance to be seen, ironically, went on to give my name professional allure. The elusive Ed Peters. The Hermit, only reached through letters in the post, or as a disembodied voice on the other end of a telephone – which was all I really needed, although there were occasions when I set the receiver on its stand and thought of calling Lucy.

I'd dialled directory enquiries once. But something always stopped me. Why would she want to hear the voice of the wreck of the man that I'd become, both physically and mentally, never really escaping White Cliff House, never really free of Leda Grey, who still haunted my every waking hour? Even at night, in morphine dreams, I saw her face continually. Leda, the pubescent girl with the crown of snakes upon her head. Leda the mermaid with silver curls. Leda the vampire with jet-black lips. Leda Grey, the aged queen, by whom I'd been both cursed and charmed.

Charm, from the Middle English. An incantation, bond, or spell.

The second day in my London flat, I carried my rucksack down the hall and into the little box room converted as an office. I cleared the clutter on the desk, emptied the contents of my bag, then stared at all the cans of films. One by one I picked them up, unscrewed the lids and looked inside. One by one, my spirits fell when I realised what they contained.

The Mermaid had all but melted into an oozing noxious slime, giving off such acid fumes my eyes were streaming with the sting. *Delirium* was a frothing red, with every blistered bubbling coil of film fused in a solid lump. Most of the reel of *The Cursed Queen* resembled crumbling flakes of rust, with any frames that did remain so blighted by the chemicals it looked as if some fungus has been blooming on the celluloid.

How could such damage have occurred, when I'd seen those films in White Cliff House with barely a scratch upon the screen?

In a state of confusion, with trembling hands, I picked up the pad on which I'd written notes while Leda spoke to me. But I couldn't decipher a single word. Every shorthand symbol looked more like Egyptian hieroglyphics. Pictures of birds, and small stick men. Circles, squares and triangles. Curling waves, or zigzag lines. None of them meant anything.

I plugged the cassette recorder's lead into a socket on the wall, pressed the button to play the tape inside, then heard my introduction with the words I'd said to Leda Grey all being clear and sensible. But a prickling fear crept through my veins when no answering voice was ever heard. There was me, then there was silence, just the faintest squeaking as the tape continued spinning on its spools. The distant cry of a gull perhaps. A rustle of cloth. Some footsteps. A buzzing noise, like wasps or flies.

By the time the recording reached its end I really thought I'd gone insane, lost in some waking nightmare state while tripping to whatever drugs the dealer gave me yesterday – then almost weeping with relief when I realised that I still had the scrapbook bought in Theo's shop. And, somewhere inside that book, a photograph of Leda Grey.

That picture still existed. So did the undeveloped roll of film inside my camera. I could take that to a chemist's shop. But then, how long would I have wait while they sent it off to a photo lab? And what if they lost it, or damaged the pictures? No, I couldn't take the risk. I'd go to the magazine's picture department. I'd ask them to develop it. Even if the column had been axed, surely the other staff I knew would be prepared to help me.

With a hat worn low on my forehead, a scarf wrapped high around my face, I walked the short distance from the flat to the doors of *City* magazine. The concierge gave a cursory glance before waving me through the turnstile gate. Upstairs, the floor receptionist had a glacial smile fixed on her face as she stared above my shoulder to some point in the middle distance. But at least she was professional. No questions asked when I walked past the doors marked 'Editorial', and then continued in the lift to the Picture department just upstairs.

The girl there didn't do so well. Not when I handed her the film and the scarf slipped down to show my face. Before I'd gone off on my Brightland trip she'd blushed every time I'd smiled at her, as if I'd given her the world. Now, she only looked appalled, turning white and lost for words, until she said, 'Oh, Ed… it's great to see you here. But, are you sure you're well enough? Why don't you go back home again? We've got your address. I'll call a bike and get these pictures couriered round as soon as I've developed them.'

'No. I'll wait, if that's all right.' I settled in an empty chair, crossing both my arms and legs as she gave a nod, then disappeared with the precious film clutched in her hands.

God knows what thoughts were in her mind when she brought the pictures back again. Not that I stopped to look at them, only grabbed the large brown envelope and all but ran back to the flat, where I poured myself a whisky and took a long deep slug of that while I made the fervent, silent prayer: *Please let these photographs exist.*

They did. But not in any form that I might have imagined them.

Where Leda had been standing in the meadow in front of the filming shed, there was no woman to be seen. Only some gulls in the sky above. Only the wrecked glass house behind, and the glisten of the blazing sun as it dazzled on the camera's lens to form an oil-like residue. Shimmering. Slick with yellow light.

There were more, where she was visible. That first shot taken secretly, when I'd climbed onto the window ledge and looked in through the damaged wall. Some others when I'd been inside, when she'd worn the crown of snakes and leaves. But, in all those pictures it was clear that Leda Grey was not alive. She'd been dead when I'd thought her sleeping. She'd been dead when I'd set the crown of snakes upon her head of long grey hair. And she must have been dead for quite some time, her body clearly mummified beneath the heavy woollen throw, with her bitten fingertips splayed wide as they gripped the arms of the fireside chair, where the bones of her hands could well be claws. Or the skeletal wings of two white birds.

It was all I could do not to vomit.

I thought of Leda's *Mirrors*, when she wrote of the damned Egyptian queen, and how a journalist who'd gone along to the British Museum once to investigate that story became tormented in his mind when a photograph he'd taken of the casket's painted human face – a face normally quite serene – had looked entirely different when the picture was developed. When he saw such a Hellish countenance he'd lost his wits and killed himself.

An hour or so later I found the wit to dial a number on my phone, to speak to the girl from the lab again, mumbling excuses about those pictures being made on the set of a recent horror film. I said that all the images were embargoed until the film's release; that I knew that I could trust her not to talk about the ones she'd seen. But, I couldn't think of what to say when she took me at my word, and gushed, 'Incredible … that make-up, Ed! The flies all swarming round her head. The actress must have hated that. What some people will do for the sake of art!'

LET ME ENFOLD THEE AND
HOLD THEE TO MY HEART

With every year that followed on, I felt as if I lived a dream, a chimera of the man I'd been. But eventually I found a way to exist in the land of the living again, when applying for a post I'd seen advertised in a Sunday newspaper.

Curator of Edwardian films, based at the London Film Archives. A place where I could work alone inside a fireproofed basement room, surrounded by the piles of cans containing films all waiting to be catalogued and safely stored upon the Archive's warehouse shelves. The cans in which I always hoped to find some trace of Leda Grey.

It was something of an irony when, after almost forty years, I'd agreed to meet a journalist from the staff of *City* magazine. A cocksure young reporter, not unlike myself in younger days, who'd come to talk about the latest film that we had digitised, ensuring that it might then be preserved for many years to come.

The film was *Brightland Promenade*, directed by a Charles Beauvois, with its Edison label on the front, and only found the year before, dumped in a New York building skip when one of the old Nickelodeons was being demolished for something new. If you happened to be that way inclined, I guess you'd call it kismet, with the restoration coming only weeks before the publication of my book on Leda Grey.

The Mirror Of A Mystery had been a long time in the making, and this actual of *Brightland Promenade* might well provide some stunning stills to add to those inside the book – though, in the end, there'd been no lack of images to print there.

All the eerie pictures in the shed. The beautiful, but ghoulish scenes of Leda sitting in her chair. The portraits that her father made. Theo's postcards from the shop, along with the stills of film sets that he'd designed for White Cliff House. What's more, an archive specialist had managed to salvage several frames from the remnants of *The Cursed Queen*. Not forgetting those items I had found in the canisters devoid of film. All the magazine cuttings and scribbled notes, and the photographs of Leda Grey that Charles Beauvois had taken to inspire some of his future films. The films that never would be made.

There she was, on her hands and knees, posing naked in front of a large white swan with its wings stretched out on either side, where the swan might be making love to the woman, or the woman might have grown those wings, about to escape and fly away. Such a clever ambiguity.

Here was a spider in its web, a close-up shot Beauvois enlarged, with the spider's head being replaced by that of Leda Grey instead.

Here was Leda lying down by the bones of a human skeleton. Her dark eyes gazing back into the empty sockets of its skull.

And here, she lay upon a bed, the sheets covered in rose petals, her hair spread out behind her. White rosebuds wound through all those curls, and in her pubic hair as well. The most sensual vision of a bride who awaits her groom on their wedding night, and long before Lady Chatterley was ever adorned in such a way.

A comprehensive record of a life condemned to darkness when it should have been so different, with a mystery at its very core that had never truly been resolved – which is why it sparked such interest now, with a prominent US studio producing a major feature film, though I wasn't so sure what I thought of that. Who could play the heroine? Who could even begin to compare with her? And, of course, it all came much too late for Leda to appreciate.

Nearly too late for me as well.

The book was only written when I'd finally felt brave enough to face the truths of White Cliff House, never really sure if what I'd seen was real, or visions born of grief. But, eventually, I'd reached a point when I couldn't care less what people thought, but rather believed the sentiment that more things exist in heaven and earth than we can ever understand. Even so, when the *City* journalist asked if I believed in ghosts, I'd slanted my answer in such a way as to speak of people from the past who continued to live through celluloid, who haunted the flickering black and white through which they danced – or walked – or smiled. Just as Leda Grey had done.

On the day of my book's publication I travelled down to Brightland to spend it with my dearest friend. I didn't want a party, only to be with Lucy – who still lived in her carriage by the sea, just as she had so long ago when she'd seen the fire in the shed, then visited the hospital on almost every single day of the weeks that I had spent there.

When I'd disappeared without a word she'd traced me through the magazine, turning up at my London flat one night, and bringing along some objects that she'd managed to save from White Cliff House when all the contents had been cleared. Since Leda's death the ownership had reverted to Winstanley's farm, with the ground on which the building stood only ever being leased before. Not that any rent had been paid in years. Not since Beauvois had disappeared.

Any good furniture was sold. What remained had been burned on a bonfire, including Leda's crown of snakes. Lucy said she'd heard the serpents hiss while flames were licking round them. She said those creatures seemed to writhe, as if they were in agony, before they melted into ash. But she'd managed to save a cabinet, now in her carriage by the sea. The one with the nymphs and swans on front. The one with broken mirrors.

For me, she'd brought the shell, the large brass beetle, and the ankh sign. She said her relative had called them, 'Wicked, evil, pagan things that brought that Leda Grey no luck. That sad old maid, alone for years, hiding away from the outside world.'

Lucy was an old maid too. She'd never married. Nor had I. But over the years we'd often met, whenever I came to Brightland, when I stayed in the rooms above the shop that Theo Williams left to me, having died of a stroke about a year after the death of Leda Grey. Not that anyone really knew the date when she had come to meet her end. Only that it must have been in that summer of 1976.

Hard to know why Theo Williams had left his whole estate to me, someone he'd only briefly met. But he had no living relatives, and then there was the guilt he felt. And, well, perhaps the old man hoped that I'd preserve *his* memories. That collection in his Brightland shop.

I did. I didn't sell a thing, keeping every item safe behind the shop's locked shutters, except for a cigarette case that made a handsome paperweight in the office of my London flat. It still held some black-wrapped cigarettes, but I would never smoke them. That cough I had. My wheezing lungs. The result of inhaling nitrate fumes released by burning celluloid. I kept putting off the X-rays to prove what the doctors suspected.

What do you think then, Leda? I'd say there's life in the old boy yet. I often addressed the picture frames that cluttered up the shop's dark walls, most of which showed Leda Grey – and now with Ivor at her side, his handsome features half-obscured in trails of white tobacco smoke. I felt that they watched over me whenever I was visiting, when I sorted through the treasure troves that cluttered all the shelves around: all the things that Theo hoarded from the worlds of film and theatre, as well as the glamorous studio shots of the later stars of Hollywood. Even some musty magazines once published in America. The ones containing articles about an Ivor Davies.

How could that be, when Ivor's corpse had lain at White Cliff House for years, before being stored in boxes on the shelves of some pathology lab? The police hadn't let the matter drop. They'd come to see me in my flat. They'd interviewed me there for hours. But, with the burns, and my mental state, still then refusing to believe that I'd spent three days conversing with the mummified corpse of Leda Grey, I was hardly a credible witness.

And Theo's explanation had provided elements of truth. He *had* purchased a skeleton from one of the London medical schools. The proof was there in his receipt, and the photographs that I had found in the empty canisters of film. The file on the case was duly closed.

For me, the mystery endured, intrigued by any mention of the name of Ivor Davies – the man who, so the articles in all those magazines had said, travelled from England in the months leading up to the start of the First World War, where he found some work in Hollywood, directing lesser feature films made in the silent era. But it seemed he hadn't fitted in with the studio system over there, eventually withdrawing and devoting himself to photography, with many of his images then reproduced in magazines during the 1950s. All with an esoteric bent and dubious underground followings. But then, his pictures did possess a certain grotesque quality. A brutal sexism as well. Not explicit but, nevertheless, intrinsically disturbing scenes.

A woman dressed in shreds of rags was bound in heavy metal chains attached to an enormous wheel. Another, naked on the ground, appeared to be quite terrified, holding her hands up in defence of the looming threat of the man above who was dressed in the costume of a bear. Or could that be a living bear? Or was that creature the result of a skilful taxidermist's art? Hard to tell with the dark noir quality of the black-and-white exposures, with Davies' artistic tastes apparently so influenced by the work he'd done with Charles Beauvois – with some pictures in the canisters that I had saved from White Cliff House being so similar in style.

Had Theo Williams always meant to set this lure for me to trace? To investigate the enigma of this so-called Ivor Davies – the name Beauvois had stolen. But, Beauvois *had* to be dead by then. If not, he'd surely bathed each day in the flames of everlasting life. Just like his cursed queen before.

Could there be another book in it? Some justice gained for Leda Grey?

I stood behind the counter, searching for answers in the eyes of the child with roses in her hair, stroking a hand along the back of the dog with a crown upon its head, and a plaque below engraved to say,

Rex. Beloved Friend.
Who Bravely Fought The Serpent.

This afternoon, I left the shop with a carrier bag in my one good hand. I walked to the Brightland Cemetery, though I'd never been inside before. I waited for Lucy at the gates. She was late. She's nearly always late.

She made breathless apologies. 'I'm sorry, Ed... a dealer rang. He wants to see more paintings. More for my New York Christmas Show.'

'What a star you are these days!' I smiled. 'Soon we'll all be trailing on the tail of Lucy's comet.'

'Won't you come along with me this time? You know I'd really love that.'

'Oh... let's wait and see, shall we?'

'Hmm. I know what that means! But, Ed, we could stay for a month or two. You've had invitations from festivals, to go and speak about your book... and what about the film? The chance to visit all the sets. To meet the actors taking part? Don't you think Leda would like that... to see it all on her behalf?'

I shrugged, but made no answer while Lucy insisted on giving me that penetrating clear blue gaze, staring up intently from beneath the thick grey fringe she wears – that Cleopatra style of hers. *To hide the wrinkles*, so she says. But to me she looks as radiant as she did that night on Cuckham beach, hardly a blemish on her face, and still a smile to light the world. I'd follow that light most anywhere. Even through the graveyard's gates.

It wasn't remotely depressing, more like a park where people strolled or picnicked on the sloping lawns, though, 'We need to be careful,' Lucy warned when we turned onto a narrow path, so darkly overgrown I thought about the lane of conifers that led the way to White Cliff House. The names on graves set either side were obscured by moss or ivy leaves. Branches of yew trees softly groaned as a breeze was rushing through them. Through that, the squawking cries of gulls, and over them a sweeter sound. A lovely piercing melody.

'Blackbird?' I asked, not being sure. But Lucy didn't seem to hear, too busy walking on ahead, then turning back to wave at me. My heart responded with a lurch, but I soon moved on to join her, to stand before the grave that I had never wished to see before.

A marble angel had been raised to pose upon a granite plinth. Two feathered wings folded behind. The palms of both hands were lifted to cover up its face and eyes.

'This is it then. The Williams' family grave.' Lucy was the first to speak.

'It looks like her,' I murmured. 'That statue in *Delirium*.'

'Yes,' Lucy said. She gave a sigh. 'I think Theo had that in mind when he commissioned this design. Strange though, the inscription ...' She recited from the stone. '"The Egyptians Say To Speak Of The Dead Makes Them Live Again."'

She paused and then turned back to ask, 'What's that stain ... that rust colour, covering the angel's hands? It must be a kind of fungus. I imagine we could rub it off.'

'Leave it,' I said, as my fingers dipped inside the plastic bag I held, extracting the garland of rose petals that, for more than a hundred years, had hung on the corner of a frame on the wall of Theo's Brightland shop.

I set it on the angel's head.

'Perfect!' Lucy stated. 'I'll take a picture, shall I?' But no sooner had she opened up the pocket of her shoulder bag, about to fetch her camera out, than the wind got up and the fragile wreath was lifted from the angel's brow. Brown petals swirled, then blew apart, carried away and up the path as if they were confetti.

We didn't stay much longer, but wandered into town again. A meal at our favourite restaurant. A walk along the promenade to the spot where Lucy's car was parked. While we stood there looking out across the pier and to the sea below, she lifted a hand to trace the patterns of the scars upon my face. All faded now. A silver grey, and nowhere near so obvious.

She made herself taller, on tiptoes, and kissed that cheek, and then my lips. Just briefly, but her mouth on mine was the most exquisite, blissful thing that I'd experienced in years. The shock of the sudden rush of desire – it took me completely by surprise, mind spinning back to a long-lost night when Lucy made pink cocktails. To this day, I still have no idea as to what the two of us had done, or hadn't done at Cuckham Sands. It's not something we ever speak about. But perhaps we should, while there's still time, while I still have a chance to swim to shore and to grab at the hand of the girl who called: *'Hey! Hey you, out there in the water... don't you know how fast the tide comes in?'*

I watched her drive away from me, still staring after, up the road, long after she'd been lost from view in a flowing sea of traffic. Had the town always been this busy, with the thrumming vibrations and palls of grime pumped out from all the car exhausts? Even the Lanes were rowdy. A crowd spilling out of the Bath Arms pub when I wandered back to the shop's front door, where, just for a moment, I paused and thought of heading back to buy a pint.

Turning the key inside the lock, I re-entered the world of shadows, trudging up the narrow stairs to the room where Leda Grey once slept. The room in which I also sleep whenever I am staying here, surrounded by so many things that Leda might have left as clues. I like to think of it that way, whenever I open the wardrobe doors to touch the clothes still hanging there, still giving off the scent of rose. When I lift the books down from a shelf and the pages scatter glitter dust. And, on the wall, though most were lost before I had a chance to get the leaking gutters fixed again, the remnants of cuttings and postcards that Leda Grey once pasted there. All those lovely young women who'd played their parts in Edwardian theatre and silent film.

I don't want to change a single thing. I sense her here so

strongly, particularly when I strike a match and use its flame to light the wick of the single candle on a stand.

So many times over the years I've knelt on these bare wooden boards as if I am about to pray – instead, to perform the ritual that Leda Grey had written of, when my hands reach underneath the bed to find a leather canister, inside of which there is a film.

Holding the reel before the flame, I see a different version to the one in the London Archives. This is something quite unique, even when compared with all the digital wonders of our age, when, with only the swipe of a fingertip we can create small miracles. But you still need the eye and the inner perspective to reveal the art within the frame. And the eye is what Charles Beauvois had. That flawed but unsung genius from the infancy of silent film. And then, there was his unsung muse. The girl whose face still has the power to stir my heart when she appears at the end of *Brightland Promenade*.

Such anticipation at the start – with the sun glinting sharp on the grey iron railings, through which we can see the grey sweep of the sea, and the grey-hazed struts of the Brightland Pier with all the people walking by.

I doubt we'll ever know *their* names, but it really doesn't matter. What matters is what's coming next. The entrance arch, and the flags above as they flutter in a gentle breeze. The towering domes and spires behind as they rise to the white of a cloudless sky, when you'd almost think it deliberate to have this shimmering palace of dreams create the perfect backdrop, when the very last person walks into view, as if making her entrance on a stage. As if she's been there all along, just waiting for her time to shine.

And how she shines, this lovely girl, even though her white dress with its shabby lace appears to be too big for her, even though if you look below her knees you'll see black stockings, slack and torn. And there, beside her scuffed black boots, a little black-haired terrier. It really is quite comical, the way it sits there begging, and how, when she scoops it in her arms, its tail is a fury of wagging delight. And the string that's been tied to its collar, how it winds like a snake about her feet.

The girl and the dog seem to be well acquainted. The way she allows it to lick her cheek, and to sniff through the hair falling loose at her shoulders, with those curls so frizzed and knotted they might not have seen a comb in days. But, somehow, that wildness, it only enhances the spectral paleness of a face that is damp with the glisten of dog spit, where wide black eyes are raised to meet the lens of the camera held above.

During these last few moments the camera zooms in very close. Close enough to realise that this girl is not a conventional beauty. Not for the times in which she lived. Her features are strong, not delicate. There are dark circles round her eyes. Unusual in one so young – unless, of course, you realise that only moments earlier those eyes had been smudged with the black of kohl. Her mouth is wide. Her lips are full. Not for her any simpering Cupid's bow, but something much bolder, more sensual, something more of the twenty-first century when they part to reveal her perfect teeth, with a smile that seems to speak, to say, '*I know you. Yes! I know you . . .*'

It's when I reach that point tonight that I seem to hear the creak of feet as they pace the boards behind me – and then the whimper of a dog – and something ticking rhythmically.

Could it be the time for me to hold the film against the candle's flame, to lose myself in dreams containing mermaids, vampires, cursed queens, to ignite the fire that shines so brightly round the head of Leda Grey; that gilding spreading out each side to look like wings of red and gold? The wings on which we'll fly away.

From the cobbled lane outside the shop I hear the echo of a laugh. A small brown petal flutters through the gap in the open window frame. In my ear, the faintest whispering of *Out, out, brief candle!* as the flame begins to sputter, until nothing remains but a haze of grey that dissolves in coils around my head, while the spool of celluloid is dropped to puddle on the wooden boards.

But I don't try to pick it up. I reach instead for the mobile phone that's buzzing loudly on the bed. I flick the cover open and see the number flashing up. Below that number, Lucy's face, smiling, glowing out at me through the glassy blackness of the screen.

The End

Acknowledgements

This novel, a story based on words, has been enormously inspired by the visual world of moving films made at the dawn of the century, sometimes only fragments of which survive. For what remains I give my thanks to the true magicians of celluloid; all those pioneering directors, designers and stars who brought the screen to life.

In the present day I'd like to thank Isobel Dixon, my agent and Kate Mills, my editor at Orion Books, who have been so instrumental in bringing *Leda Grey* to life for me.

For invaluable friendship and support, I would again like to thank Wendy Wallace. Also, Linda Buckley Archer, Susannah Rickards, Margot Steadman, Denise Meredith and Kit Berry. All wise and generous women.

To those who share 'The Lounge' with me. Online haven of talent and daily wit.

And last, but never least, to my husband. For patience, love, and sanity.

BIBLIOGRAPHY

Many books inspired the writing of this novel. Here is a small selection:

Life in Edwardian England by Robert Cecil
The Edwardians by Vita Sackville West
Lost Voices of the Edwardians by Max Arthur
Edwardian Summer, 1900s, Reader's Digest
Seventies by Howard Sounes

100 Silent Films by Bryony Dixon, BFI Screen Guides
Gothic – The Dark Heart of Film, A BFI Compendium
The Haunted Gallery: Painting, Photography, Film Around 1900
   by Lynda Nead
Disappearing Tricks by Matthew Solomon
The Story of Film by Mark Cousins
Silent Movies by Peter Kobel, and the Library of Congress
Legitimate Cinema: Theatre Stars in Silent British Films
   1908–1918 by John Burrows
Bungalow Town: Theatre and Film Colony by Neb Wolters
Cinema-by-Sea by David Fisher
Alfred Hitchcock by Peter Ackroyd
A Life in Movies by Michael Powell
American Grotesque: The Life and Art of William Mortensen by
   Larry Lytle and Michael Moynihan
Magic. Taschen. Eds Noel Daniel, Mike Caveney, Ricky Jay
   and Jim Steinmeyer

Macbeth by William Shakespeare
She by H. Rider Haggard

FILMOGRAPHY

Some of the films that inspired *The Last Days of Leda Grey*:

Electric Edwardians: The Films of Mitchell and Kenyon, BFI
Silent Britain, BBC/BFI
R. W. Paul, Collected Films 1895–1908, BFI
Fairy Tales: Early Colour Stencil films from Pathé, BFI
Inferno directed by Giuseppe de Liguoro
Cabiria directed by Giovanni Pastrone
Das Cabinet Des Dr Caligari directed by Robert Weine
The Lodger directed by Alfred Hitchcock
The Magic Box directed by John Boulting
The Haunting directed by Robert Wise
Dead of Night directed by Alberto Cavalcanti, Robert Hamer,
    Basil Dearden, Charles Crichton
Many of the glorious, magical films of Georges Méliès, found
    online

Shown on UK Children's Television of the 1960s and 1970s,
and available on DVD under the general heading of *Tales
from Europe*:

The Singing Ringing Tree
The Adventures of Robinson Crusoe